# Survivors
# of
# Origin

PAUL SWAFFIELD

The Book Guild Ltd

First published in Great Britain in 2021 by
The Book Guild Ltd
9 Priory Business Park
Wistow Road, Kibworth
Leicestershire, LE8 0RX
Freephone: 0800 999 2982
www.bookguild.co.uk
Email: info@bookguild.co.uk
Twitter: @bookguild

Typeset in 11pt Adobe Garamond Pro

Printed on FSC accredited paper
Printed and bound in Great Britain by 4edge Limited


ISBN 978 1913913 434


British Library Cataloguing in Publication Data.
A catalogue record for this book is available from the British Library.

*For my Mum*

# Prologue

Edward Buckingham rode into the confines of his fine home. He brought the horse to a standstill, leapt from the saddle and handed the reins to a waiting groom. Without speaking, he turned and marched to the house. As he entered, he threw off his jacket, letting it fall to the floor. He walked into his study and poured a large glass of brandy. He never took the few seconds required to savour the subtle flavour of the expensive drink. He had no interest in the taste, only the effect. This had been his routine since the death of his wife.

It had been the happiest day of his life. And the saddest. His wife Rebecca had given birth to their daughter whilst Edward had paced the floor of the grand entrance. The first sounds he heard from their bedroom were the healthy squeals of a newborn child. He didn't wait for an invitation. He had waited long enough. It took him four great strides to reach the landing, where he took a moment to compose himself. He walked calmly to the door, knocked once and walked in.

Rebecca's physical beauty had drawn Edward to her, but after ten years of marriage, during which time they had endured the loss of three unborn children, it was his wife's resilience, her fortitude, that had intensified his love for her. Rebecca's family had been against their union. They believed their daughter would be marrying beneath her, and they had done everything in their power to dissuade her. The rows had been ferocious, but Rebecca was in love and she knew – as did her parents – that nothing would stop her from being with Edward. The couple were eventually married with the begrudging blessing of Rebecca's parents.

Cecil Buckingham had taught his son well. He had been the proud owner of *Felicity-Ann*, an old and creaky schooner, which he sailed regularly across perilous oceans, exporting goods from England and returning with an array of exotic materials that he would sell at the port on his return. As a young boy, all Edward ever wanted to do was to set sail with his father. At the age of fourteen, his mother had relented and the boy's ambition was realised. He left the safety of his home and began his seafaring adventures with the man he revered more than any other. At the age of twenty-four, he commanded *Felicity-Ann* for the first time, taking her through the Bay of Biscay to Portugal. Fifteen years later, he owned six ships and had amassed a fortune by importing goods from around the world. It had been many years since he had set sail, and the ocean had yet to lure him back. He had found contentment with Rebecca. Having a child would be the fulfilment of their happy life together.

*

The room was poorly lit; a fire crackling in the grate, however, created a warm glow. Candles flickered on the bedside tables, with the flames casting mysterious shadows up the walls. Edward didn't recognise the room. Everything looked different; there were too many people. He couldn't see Rebecca because the physician who had been at the house for several days, at great expense, and old Ma Fish (who had been commandeered for the duration, on account of her having seen more babies born than the whole town put together) were fussing around her.

Lucy, one of the servants, held the baby, who was tightly wrapped in a muslin cloth. "Beggin' your pardon, sir, but you can't come in 'ere."

Edward approached the girl, ignoring her protestations. "Is the baby okay?" He eased the cloth back a fraction and he felt his finger brush the child's soft skin.

"It's a beautiful daughter you 'ave, sir, and she's fine. A sweetheart, sir, if ever there were one."

The doctor turned away from Rebecca and addressed Edward. "Mister Buckingham; please, sir, it really would be better if you left the room."

Edward took a few steps towards the bed and saw his wife's face. Her eyes were unblinking and her hands were gripping the bed sheet; her complexion was eerily translucent. He forced himself to stay calm. He knew how Rebecca dealt with pain. There would be no screaming and no crying.

"Mister Buckingham... Edward." The doctor turned and looked fleetingly at the beleaguered husband. "There is another child."

"It's bein' born, Doc." Ma Fish interrupted the two men.

The second baby arrived in the world and although distressed, fought gamely for its first breaths; its right to survive.

Edward Buckingham knew in those few moments that he had lost Rebecca. The birth of the second child had killed her. In his mind, the baby trapped behind his perfect daughter had taken his beautiful wife, and there would be no reconciliation. The events he had just witnessed shocked him to his core. The great Edward Buckingham, helpless, inadequate, unable to bring his influence to bear.

*

One year on, the pain of Rebecca's last moments and his reaction to the second child – a boy, who was crumpled, purple and half the size of his beautiful daughter – still haunted him. The doctor had said the boy wouldn't live, but old Ma Fish had wrapped him up, and although he had yet to utter a sound, she could feel his faint breaths as she held him close. Edward had ordered Ma to get rid of the child. He didn't care whether it lived or died, he just wanted it out of his house. Forever.

# Chapter One

Five miles along the coast from Edward Buckingham's estate, the boy had enjoyed a good life, albeit a tough one, with Fred and Mary Quicklock.

The day he was born, Ma Fish had walked the mile and a half to her home, clutching the frail child. She knew if she caught Pa Fish before he started drinking his home-made cider, she would be able to persuade him to help. She pushed her way through the front door slightly breathless. "C'mon, Pa, get off yer bony arse."

"Christ al-bloody-mighty, woman. Can't a man have a quiet drink in 'is own bloody 'ome? What ya got there and where ya bin all bloody day?"

"I've warned you about blasphemin' under this roof. I won't 'ave it, Pa. This 'ere is a baby, an' we got some work in front of us if we're gonna save it." Before her bewildered husband could respond, Ma spat out her orders, "Go get that flea-bitten mule of yours, hitch it to that pile of junk you call a cart and let's get on, afore it's too late."

It was an unlikely trio that pulled up outside the small,

stone dwelling on the edge of Old Milford a short while later. The creaking tumbril rumbled to a halt, and as she dismounted, Ma began to wonder if she was about to deliver a dead child to her only daughter. She offered up a silent prayer, knowing his chances were slim.

Ma stayed with her daughter for two weeks, and between them they watched as the child gained weight gradually. "A bloody miracle" is what Pa Fish had called it. And, in truth, it was. The baby had fought for every breath, and with the dedication of Ma Fish and Mary the boy survived.

Ezra Quicklock responded well to the dedicated attentions of the two women. His poor introduction to the world proved to be a temporary setback, and as the years passed, he grew into a strong, healthy lad. Fred and Mary had been given something special – someone special – and they loved the boy more than either of them could express.

They had found it a little difficult at first to explain the arrival of a newborn child, and Mary had even been chided over "the immaculate conception". Ma Fish, though, had concocted a feasible explanation by saying that the boy's parents had been killed in a terrible fire, but the baby had somehow survived. Nobody knew how, as it was all a terrible tragedy.

So, as the years slipped by, Ezra became the son of Fred and Mary, without question.

*

The five-mile distance between Ezra's new home and his birth home could have been five hundred miles. Edward

Buckingham and Ezra Quicklock had no inclination of each other's existence.

"C'mon, Ezra, I'll not tell ya a third time." As Mary passed the bed she gave her son a playful kick with the bottom of her foot.

Ezra rolled over and pulled the prickly blanket over his head.

Mary continued, "'Iding neath the blanket won't 'elp. Yer father'll be back in a minute or two, and then we'll see 'ow fast ya can move."

Ezra heard the clunk of the door, and before it closed, he was out of his bed and pulling on his clothes.

"'Ow d'ya do that, Fred Quicklock?" Mary shook her head as she asked the question.

"Do what, me dear?" he replied.

"That." Mary pointed to their dishevelled son.

"Sorry, woman, you'll 'afta be a bit clearer. I ain't got much of a clue what yer on about." Fred stared across the one room of their cottage and wrinkled his face at Ezra, who had just finished dressing.

Ezra returned the expression. Apparently, neither of them had any clue what Mary was talking about.

Mary muttered an unintelligible response, all the while smiling to herself.

Ezra had been helping his father every working day for as long as he could remember. They had a good walk to Fred's ramshackle workshop where he had been repairing and making all things wooden. This included cartwheels, furniture, doors and the thing Ezra enjoyed most of all: bows and arrows. As yet, he hadn't mastered the art of creating the perfect piece of furniture, but he had mastered the art of creating the perfect bow. His marksmanship astonished Fred. Every spare moment, Ezra would disappear into the back yard, where Fred had set up a target, and practise the art of releasing arrows.

Ezra was a happy boy. He was content, to a point. When he wasn't working or firing his arrows, his instinct took him to the sea. The cliff tops were a ten-minute walk from their home. Ezra had found a pathway down to a ledge where a natural pool had developed, and when the tide receded, he had his very own lagoon. Ezra spent hours swimming and diving to the bottom, watching the strange creatures that shared his secret location. At one end there was a prominent rock that overhung the water, and after many attempts at hitting the water without hurting himself, Ezra had developed a passion for diving. Initially, he would jump feet first, but the urge for more excitement led him to plunge headfirst, refusing to let the pain of his mistimed entries into the water deter his efforts.

However, as he grew older and stronger, the urge to test himself began to manifest, and from his lagoon, he would look up to the cliff top, which formed a jagged promontory jutting over the sea. He had examined the climb and spent many hours staring at the intended point of entry where the force of nature crashed relentlessly into stubborn resistance. He also knew that, once in the water, if all went well, he would have to swim a good half-mile to the beach. There was no other way out of the sea. Ezra knew that, one of these days, he would have to confront the irrepressible desire that was mounting inside him. He spent long periods contemplating the facets of the task he had set himself: the climb, the dive, the explosion as he hit the water and not least the swim to safety. Why? He had no answer to the question that prodded his good sense constantly.

Ezra's apprenticeship with Fred continued to go well, although both parents had noticed their son's momentary lapses into a sombre mood. These silent abstractions, however, didn't appear to affect the boy in a detrimental way, and his parents tried their best to accept that his lineage was somewhat different to their own, and that there was something inherent in common folk that alienated them from the upper classes.

Fred had experienced the odd skirmish with the owner of all a person could see for miles around. Notwithstanding these incidents, he had found Baron Milford to be a reasonable-enough person, providing you could supply him with his requirements, as and when ordered. And, of course, pay your rent on time. His son, however, was proving to be more than a little worrying.

"Quicklock." There was a pause. "*Quicklock!*" The sound carried into Fred's workshop where Ezra was working. "Get yourself out here, you lazy dobbin."

Ezra came out and saw Persius Milford sitting atop his fine horse, flanked by two burly-looking guards dressed in full regalia, with their tabards displaying the Milford ensign. Persius, now twenty years old, was the eldest son and he was determined to exact his authority, as he saw it, over the inhabitants of Old Milford and the surrounding district.

"How may I help, sir?" Ezra managed the enquiry in the most subservient manner he could muster. *Perhaps an arrow through the eye?* He kept that thought to himself.

"You – you little bastard – can't help me at all. I want to speak to Quicklock."

"Beggin' you pardon, sir, but I am the only Quicklock available right at this moment. My father—"

"Did you hear that, men? The boy thinks his father is Quicklock himself. The son of a so-called master tradesman he thinks himself, indeed he does. Look at him! He's nothing more than a miserable little bastard." Persius Milford was in his element; he had a victim, and his vicious tongue was only equalled by his propensity for violence. "Now run along, Pissquick, and fetch Quicklock."

The three men all chuckled at the boy's new name.

"Ezra, get in 'ere." Fred beckoned his son just in time to prevent a reaction from him.

Ezra could feel anger and confusion welling inside himself, and at the sound of his father's voice, he turned and left the smirking Milford to deal with Fred.

"Arrows, Quicklock. My father requires two hundred for next weekend. See to it, Quicklock. You know his terms." Persius pulled sharply on his horse's left rein and applied his heels to its flanks, and with a snort and a grind of an iron-clad hoof on the dusty ground, his horse turned and lumbered away, its rider puffed up with self-gratification.

Ezra watched from the doorway as the men disappeared. Their gold-coloured tabards were emblazoned with the Milford ensign: the halberd with its scrolled decoration and the tip split into two points. Ezra didn't know what it meant, but he would never forget it.

"What's he mean, Pa? I ain't a bastard. He's a bastard."

"Aye, lad, 'e's a bastard all right, but we need to stay on 'is right side, Ezra. 'E's a wrong 'un." Fred could feel the anguish inside him as he searched for the words to reassure his son. "Take no 'eed of 'is words, Ezra; 'e 'as a cruel mouth and 'e'll goad a person into confrontation. That's what 'e wants, lad – a fight – an' 'e'll pick on anyone who's beneath 'im. 'E's a bully, Ezra, but 'e's a dangerous young man, so when 'e comes callin', promise me you'll not vex 'im. C'mon, let's get on with 'is order, else we'll all be in the muck." Fred wrapped a comforting arm around his son's shoulders and walked him into the workshop. "Why don't ya go out the back for a while an' shoot a few arrows, to take yer mind off that dollop o' donkey shit."

Ezra smiled at his father; he had never heard him speak in that way before. "Okay, Pa."

Ezra took his bow, put on the leather sleeve that Fred had made for him to protect his wrist and disappeared into the yard. All he could see as he took aim was the pasty, slimy features of Persius Milford. The centre of the target stared back at him as he released his arrow. It passed, dead centre, through the eye of his tormentor.

*

During the next ten days, the Quicklocks – all three of them – concentrated on meeting Baron Milford's order. Mercifully, they'd had no more contact with Persius, and a small cart arrived to collect the arrows on the due day. Fred watched as the output from their last ten days of relentless toil disappeared from sight, and he wondered how long he would have to wait to be paid. The one positive he could draw from his pondering was that at least Persius wasn't in control. Not yet anyway.

Ma and Pa Fish arrived at their daughter's house with the same "flea-bitten mule" and creaky, old cart with which they'd delivered Ezra exactly seventeen years ago. They were ageing and so they found the journey a touch arduous, but they were very fond of their grandson, and with an overnight stop (albeit a slightly chaotic affair), they managed the experience without too much fuss.

Mary had told Ma about Ezra's meeting with Persius Milford and how he referred to Ezra as a bastard. "The thing is, Ma, should we tell 'im, 'bout us not bein' 'is real parents?" Mary went on to explain how Ezra sometimes lapsed into his own world, which was a place where no one could reach him.

"Mary, my dear child, you an' Fred Quicklock are as real to that boy as it's possible to be. I've seen first 'and where 'e comes from. 'E's gonna be different; it stands to reason. Without yours an' Fred's attentions, that beau'iful boy would not 'ave lived one night on God's earth. You remember that, Mary Quicklock; you remember what you an' Fred 'ave given 'im."

Mary turned to her mother and put her arms around her. "Ma, without you, 'e wouldna survived for more than a few moments, an' fer that I thank you from the bottom of me 'eart."

The two women held each other, and Ma whispered in her daughter's ear, "Mary, I reckon that boy'll always find a way to survive, no matter what."

*

Ezra's compulsion to conquer the dive from the clifftop gnawed steadily within him, stirred up by the stinging words of Persius Milford, or so he thought. The confused youth believed that his angst would disappear once he had summoned the courage to defy the unease that threatened to prevent his mission. The plunge into the swirling waters that crashed relentlessly against the ancient rock face would surely alleviate the intense foreboding that rebounded inside his young head. His birthday would be as good a day as any. That day had passed, and his resolve had waned, but he could wait no longer.

Ezra stood by his lagoon and stared up at the cliff face. He removed his boots and jerkin and then placed them on a ledge to prevent the incoming tide washing them away. In bare feet, he began the climb. Part way up, Ezra began to wonder if discarding his boots had been wise; however, he found that if he could withstand the discomfort, he could use his toes for extra grip. It was an arduous task, and with the summit tantalisingly near, he made himself as comfortable as possible and rested his burning muscles. The few minutes rest helped his tired body, but he found himself losing his concentration and doubting his ability to reach the top.

Refusing the temptation to look down, he reached for the next handhold, which was a thin branch protruding from the rock. As Ezra pulled himself upwards, the branch – long since without any roots to bind itself to its harsh surroundings – became suddenly entirely superfluous to his cause. With his grip severed, Ezra's body twisted around, and he found himself hanging by one hand, having lost his footing in the same moment. He floundered against the jagged rock, trying desperately to get a foot hold. The effort to support himself with one hand was immense, and he knew his next move would be vital. Willing himself to hang on, he began to assess his options. He looked down. Letting go was not an option he relished. If he let go, he would have to push himself away from the cliff face somehow to stand any chance of survival. Ezra's instincts kicked in. He swung his free arm across his body and secured the edge of his foot on a narrow ledge. His fingers gripped the rock face, and he felt suddenly secure.

He composed himself for a brief moment and then continued the ascent. A few minutes later, he pulled himself over the precipice and lay face down on the hard ground. His legs were grazed, and blood was seeping from a jagged cut on his forearm, but he was safe – for now.

Ezra pulled himself to his feet and began to survey his surroundings. Where he stood was only accessible by an arduous climb – unless you happened to have wings. The gap between the rock and the grassy clifftop must have been a minimum of ten feet, and as he peered over the other side, he could see the water swirling and foaming as it was forced into a V-shaped ravine. There was one way up and two ways down. He knew he wouldn't be climbing down. He walked to the spot where, for many months, he had imagined himself standing and gazed across the sea. The view reached the horizon, and it frightened and excited him in equal measure. He wondered what lay beyond the thin line that separated ocean from sky.

Ezra composed himself, concentrating on the thin line, not the sixty-foot drop into the sea. He remembered the first time he had dived into the lagoon and what a mess he had made of it; he had hit the water too flat, and the stinging sensation so nearly dissuaded him from making another attempt.

*Perhaps I should jump,* he thought. *After all, it is the first time, so no one would know. I could dive next time. But only Ezra Pissquick would jump in having taken the effort to climb up here.*

With his mind set and his toes curled round the edge of the rock, he allowed his knees to bend, and with his arms outstretched, he hurled himself into the great open space before him. It took him a split second to align himself, and within a few adrenalin-filled moments, his body pierced the iron-grey sea. The sea gobbled him up, and instantaneously repaired the hole that had allowed Ezra into its mysterious depths.

Beneath the waves, Ezra was exhilarated beyond his imagination. He swam to the surface and stared up at the pinnacle that had, without doing anything other than endure, coerced him into risking his life. He savoured the moment, laying on his back, his arms out wide and his hands swaying gently to aid buoyancy. It took Ezra a second or two to realise that the great rock was slowly diminishing; the sea was now in control of his destiny. He rolled on to his front and began to swim towards the shoreline. After five minutes of rigorous effort, Ezra realised that something was wrong. Instead of moving parallel with the coast he was being dragged in the opposite direction. He tried again to swim against it, but it proved impossible. He was expending his energy without reward. Helpless, Ezra rolled onto his back and stared in dismay as the great rock became smaller and smaller.

# Chapter Two

Rebecca Buckingham swept down the main staircase, at the bottom of which her father stood, anticipating her arrival. It was her seventeenth birthday, and she looked stunning in her new dress, which was woven from the finest cotton. Her hair, the colour ineffable, (perhaps the mysterious shades of autumn leaves just before they flutter to the earth), tumbled to her shoulders in natural waves. Her eyes were the deepest green, their viridescence emitting a mesmeric glint from beneath her arched brows. Her complexion, subtly dappled with tiny freckles and free of any artificial enhancements, had a silken quality. Around her slender neck hung a beautiful necklace. Attached to the bodice of her dress with a long, diamond-studded pin lay a heart-shaped brooch embedded with sapphires, creating a stunning contrast to her eyes. Both pieces of jewellery had been favourite items of her mother. Edward Buckingham could only stare, totally entranced by the young woman who stood before him.

It had taken many painful years for Edward to accept that he had lost his beautiful wife. She had been everything to him, and all the wealth and importance – of which he possessed plenty – could not replace the huge void that Rebecca's death had left. Gradually, his daughter began to fill that void, and as he witnessed this young lady descend the staircase, his emotions finally swamped him. He fell to his knees and covered his face with his palms. Tears seeped through his fingers, coursing their way through the greying hairs on the back of his ageing hands. Those tears were the first to escape since he had knelt beside his wife's grave and begged her forgiveness for his ill-considered actions, and as then, he felt powerless to check their progress.

"Papa." Rebecca knelt down in front of her father and took his hands away. "What is it, Papa? What's wrong?"

"Sorry, my darling. When I saw you… I saw your mother. You have that beauty of which you are blissfully unaware… and it makes… I can't explain… but your mother had it, and you have it. It's an extraordinary quality, one that makes you the daughter of a woman I loved more than I can tell you." Composing himself, Edward got to his feet and wiped his face with a silk handkerchief. "Come along, young lady, we've a party to host."

\*

Rebecca had reached the age of seven before her father began to take notice of his daughter's existence. All her needs had been met through carefully appointed assistants. Edward was discharging his role as a parent with the utmost diligence, using the method he applied to all things that required a solution: money. And in his experience, it seldom failed. His daughter, however, had other ideas. Rebecca began seeking out her father, asking questions, wanting to know things about her mother and refusing to be deflected with meaningless answers. Edward found himself enjoying her company, and Rebecca would listen attentively as he regaled her with stories of his seafaring exploits, demanding as much detail as her father's memory would allow.

A few days before Rebecca's tenth birthday, Edward travelled to Old Milford, where he selected and purchased a dapple grey horse from Baron Milford's personal stock. Rebecca's sense of joy and elation when he presented the animal to her gave him a sense of complete satisfaction, the like of which he believed had been lost forever. Edward took immense pleasure in teaching his daughter to ride; as the years passed, and Rebecca grew stronger and more confident, together they would hack through the countryside, testing their ability to the full.

*

The guests began filtering into the main hall, where they were received graciously by Edward and Rebecca. It was a proud moment for a man who, through the companionship of his own daughter, had relearnt the fundamental things that inevitably made him happy. She had made him function again.

Over fifty people had been invited, several of whom would be staying overnight. One family whom Rebecca particularly looked forward to seeing were the Dunsmoores: Henry; his wife, Emily; and, if he wasn't away at sea, Rebecca's favourite person, their son Isaac.

The atmosphere in the house was convivial, with groups of people chatting freely, their senses relaxed under the influence of the fine punch being served by the conscientious staff. Edward and Henry had found a quiet corner, and as always when the two men met, the subject of their conversations was predominantly business.

"So, Edward, *Rebecca-Ann* is afloat. I was aboard her yesterday with Isaac, and she looks a fine ship, Edward; a fine ship indeed." Under most circumstances, Henry kept any hint of excitement he may have been feeling fully restrained, but the opportunity to trial a new ship with his son – a ship that Isaac had helped design – was edging his deportment to euphoric proportions.

"My dear Henry, do I detect the merest hint of excitement?" Edward smiled at his oldest and most trusted friend.

"Indeed, Edward. Not since the day my girders began to creak have I felt so passionate... about anything." Henry rubbed his long, grey whiskers in a playful gesture.

"I'm not altogether sure I believe that, old friend, because as far back as I can recall, all I could ever hear was the creak of your girders, and if you'll forgive me for saying..." He gave Henry's belly a playful tap. "This won't be helping."

"Ah, indeed it won't, but I do feel that, if through some strange happenstance it should disappear, I would become totally unbalanced – out of kilter if you will – and for a seafaring man, that would never do; it would never do indeed." Henry, having finished rubbing his whiskers, rested his hands on his protruding stomach, as if he needed to add some extra gravitas to his hurriedly contrived thesis.

Realising that Henry would always have a rational and compelling argument, Edward returned the conversation to business. "What of *Felicity-Ann*, Henry? Do you think her days are done?"

"I believe she could serve our coastal operations well enough for the next few years. It would be gratifying to see her finish her long service closer to home."

Both men had a soft spot for the old schooner, and Edward was delighted with Henry's opinion regarding the future of the trusty old vessel. "Excellent news, Henry; excellent news. If *Rebecca-Ann* serves half as well, she will be a resounding success, and if your son commands her as you have commanded my fleet, Henry, we will both be proud and happy men." Edward raised his glass. "To Isaac and *Rebecca-Ann*, a fruitful and compelling combination."

Henry echoed the sentiment and was about to discuss loading and departure dates for the ship's maiden voyage when a gruff voice interrupted.

"Buckingham, my good man, how's the old nag that I practically gave you coming along?" It was the unmistakeable tones of Baron Milford. "Henry, old chap, girders still creaking, I presume?" The baron's questions were rhetorical, and he moved the conversation along quickly. "When do you anticipate this monstrous pile of timbers and pitch to be leaving Milford Port?"

"Well, Rufus, if all goes to plan, *Rebecca-Ann* will set sail two weeks tomorrow, wind and tide permitting. And as for my girders, they are in fine fettle and creaking more than ever. As for the nag, I wouldn't presume to answer, but if the rumours in the trade are to be believed, the beast will probably drop dead any day." Henry could always be relied upon for a swift retort.

"Touché, Henry old chap. Touché." Under most circumstances, Rufus Milford was not a man to retire so early from badinage, but he had what he knew would be a contentious issue to discuss. "Gentlemen, I have a thorny issue to raise with you, but before I do, please be aware that I have not undertaken to ask this kindness of you without heed, and knowing your thoughts on such a matter, I trust you will give the request due consideration."

Instinctively, Edward and Henry realised this would not be a request but a command.

Rufus continued, "As you know, I have a brother, Lionel, who lives at the arse-end of our isle – a godforsaken hole if the truth be known. Anyway, his daughter and son-in-law and their daughter are seeking passage to South America, and he has solicited me to arrange the aforementioned. I have assured him that, as I am indebted to him for one or two kindnesses, I would endeavour to secure the best possible transportation as is in my power to do so. The family are travelling already and are due to arrive in Milford within the week." Rufus raised his hand to prevent any response from his audience. "Now is not the time to mither over such things, so why don't we agree to meet in a few days to give yourselves some time to consider the request. The one consolation, if you will, is that Lionel has more money than sheep dung, and although he's ordinarily a touch careful, on this occasion he's willing to pay a premium to augment their comfort and safety."

Baroness Milford and Emily Dunsmoore arrived to interrupt the three men's conversation, and soon all thoughts of ships and passengers and cargo and faraway countries receded as the party's ambience engulfed the room.

*

Rebecca had been enjoying herself immensely. She couldn't remember a time when she had felt so happy. Against her father's advice, she had drunk a glass of punch, and on feeling the need for some air, she slipped unnoticed into the garden. Savouring the cool evening breeze, she wandered along the pathway beneath the pergola. The scent of the honeysuckle trailing over the wooden construction was intoxicating, and she took a moment to lean against the stone wall that separated the landscaped gardens from the stables. Rebecca tilted her head to one side. She could hear voices. With a degree of apprehension, she pushed open the gate set in the archway of the high wall and walked towards the stables. Above the occasional whinnying of the horses, the voices became louder. Adjacent to the stables was a feed store, and amongst the hay, Rebecca could make out the shape of a man kneeling. As she approached, she saw the young girl pinned to the ground.

"Stop wriggling, you little whore," declared the man.

Rebecca recognised the voice instantly. She moved silently into the store, grabbed a pitchfork and walked calmly up behind the distraught girl's attacker. Steadying herself, she pressed the cold, iron prongs against the bare skin of his neck. "Get off her."

Persius Milford released his grip and eased himself off the girl tentatively. The dishevelled creature jumped to her feet and ran from the store into the darkness without a word. Rebecca kept the pressure constant and Persius held his hands away from his body in mock submission.

"You are a disgrace to the Milford family, forcing yourself on young innocent girls. You should—"

Before she could finish the sentence, Persius swung

round, and in one fluid motion, he grabbed the pitchfork and wrenched it from her grasp. He threw it to one side and took a step towards the startled girl. "Disgrace, am I? I'm going to show you who's a disgrace, and when I'm finished with you, you prim-arsed bitch, we'll see who's a disgrace."

Before Rebecca could respond, Persius shoved her hard against the wooden slats of the building and forced himself hard against her. She felt trapped.

"Well, this is my lucky night; a slutty servant girl for starters and some posh bitch for the main course. Couldn't have worked out better," he crowed.

Persius Milford's foul breath drifted towards Rebecca's face, and she threw her head sideways as he tried to force his mouth on hers. Persius grabbed her chin and wrenched her head upright. Her mind began to race. He was physically too strong for her.

"That's it; relax, girl. I'm well practised with the ladies. I promise you won't be disappointed."

She waited, focusing on his movements. Persius took a small step away from Rebecca and, staring directly into her eyes, he began to unbutton his breeches. His crooked smile sent a shudder down her spine. Forcing herself to stay calm, she met his gaze, gave him a sweet smile, and then reached up to the bodice of her dress as if to release the strap from her shoulder. Unbeknown to him, Persius Milford was about to become a victim of his own vanity. Rebecca took a breath, and in a swift movement, she snatched the pin from her brooch and rammed it firmly into the side of her abuser's face.

Persius fell to his knees, grunting in agony as he wrenched the pin free. The diamonds had left a jagged tear, and his blood was running freely. From his prone position, he looked up and saw the girl disappear through the gate. He needed to get away. In a desperate attempt to staunch the flow of blood, he ripped the pocket from his waistcoat and held it against the wound. Still kneeling, he crawled towards the opening of the feed store to check there was nobody heading his way. He was unsure if the girl would be hysterical and subsequently bring all manner of shit to his door.

*The bitch will pay dearly for this one day,* he thought.

As he eased himself through the dusty hay, his knee landed on something hard. He cursed. Fumbling in the dark, he picked up the object and examined it in the poor light. Rebecca's brooch sat in the palm of his hand. A sneer came across Persius Milford's face. He stuffed the brooch and the blood-smeared pin into his remaining pocket, and stooping low, he ran into the dark shadows of the night.

# Chapter Three

Ezra had been treading water for nearly two hours when he spotted the plank of driftwood. Summoning his last reserves of energy, he swam towards the life-preserving detritus. The plank was actually two planks, roughly five feet long, two feet wide and held together with cross bearers at both top and bottom, with one end having been cut square and the other jagged where it had been ripped from its original fixture. He flung his arms across the slimy wood and hauled his weary body out of the water. Ezra lay face down on his precarious raft and let his arms dangle, one on each side, to gain a modicum of stability. He felt the afternoon sun warming his body and relaxed momentarily, relishing his change in fortune. Ezra lifted his head and looked around; there was no sign of land in any direction.

The sea remained calm, and the weather clement. As darkness fell, Ezra felt the warmth ebbing from his body. He began to wonder how he would survive the hours of darkness that lay before him. The pangs of hunger he could deal with, but he felt desperate for a drink – anything, even a slurp of his grandad's home-made cider would do.

In a natural progression, his thoughts delivered him to his parents: *They'll be searching for me. If they go to the lagoon maybe they'll see my boots and jerkin. Oh shit... shit... shit.*

Ezra thumped his head against the wood that was keeping him afloat and regretted his action immediately. "Ow." It felt strange hearing his voice. "*Ow... oww... owww... owwww,*" he shouted, his words getting longer and louder. It seemed to help for a few minutes; he had forgotten his dismal predicament momentarily. It was this lapse that encouraged him to rearrange his thoughts: *Stay afloat, stay calm and stay alive. You lured me to you, and here I am, but you can't have me... You can't have me... You can't have me...*

*

*Rebecca-Ann* swayed gently against her moorings, serene against the chaos of Milford Port. Her cargo and provisions were stowed already and her crew were making final preparations for her imminent departure.

"She looks well, Captain." The man standing next to Isaac Dunsmoore was tall and elegantly dressed. "I believe you had influence over her design."

"Unfortunately, I cannot claim any credit for her stunning appearance; I merely made a few design tweaks, in collaboration with the shipyard," Isaac responded.

In fact, Isaac had fundamentally changed the ship's design. Her length had been increased, her beam width reduced and her forecastle height reduced – all changes that the young captain was certain would improve her speed and finesse. He was anxious to see how she performed. The trials had been promising, but he knew the real tests would come soon enough amidst the great oceans. The ship's payload had increased marginally, which was a satisfying side effect of the changes, especially so for the ship's owner.

"I'm afraid, sir, that the changes did not include a suite of cabins for passengers, and I fear the journey could prove arduous for your family," explained Isaac.

"Please, Captain, call me Wesley," the man offered. "I know our being aboard is difficult for you, but we are all tougher than we appear, and I promise I will do my utmost to ensure our encroachment is minimal."

Isaac immediately regretted the slightly barbed comment. His initial reaction to the inclusion of passengers had been one of annoyance, and he had argued his point as far as he reasonably dared. Ultimately, although the captain, he was subject to the owners demands, and the passengers would be aboard when the ship left Milford Port. Isaac had warmed to Wesley Marrick's easy disposition, and he was even anticipating the congeniality of his company during the long voyage.

Isaac inclined his head towards the taller man and thanked him for the invitation to use his Christian name. "Perhaps, Wesley, it would be prudent to address me as Captain in front of the men, but please, at all other times, call me Isaac."

The two men shook hands, as if to seal the arrangement, and any lingering awkwardness there may have been dissipated in those few moments.

Isaac then went ashore to greet the Marrick family, but not before standing off *Rebecca-Ann* to inspect her trim.

Satisfied her cargo and provisions had been loaded as per his instructions, he bid the two crew members to make for the harbour steps and wait for the passengers.

Edward Buckingham's carriage arrived dockside, its iron rims clattering on the cobbled road. The party included Cordelia and Joanna, the wife and daughter of Wesley Marrick, respectively; Edward Buckingham; Rebecca Buckingham; and Henry, Isaac's father. The group gathered on the quay, looking at the ship, where the crew were busying themselves with the final arrangements; the whole scene was creating an air of nervous excitement.

Isaac knew he had to get the guests aboard ship and weigh anchor with the minimum of fuss. The tide waits for no man, especially at this time of year. The strong current would carry the ship from the harbour to the open sea, no matter her size or weight. He felt the responsibility creeping through his system, antagonising his calm nature. He required all his good sense to pilot the vessel through the deep but narrow channel that would carry them to the ocean and to the beginning of a new adventure.

The sight of Rebecca – her excitement infectious and her beauty enchanting – inwardly challenged his dependability as captain of the ship bearing her name. It was a constant reminder of the young lady who had captivated him and who, he had to keep telling himself, could never be any more than a friend; she must remain merely a companion with whom to share stories of his seafaring adventures.

Unsure if any of his feelings had been outwardly visible, Isaac reinstated his temperament, and quickly enough, had everyone where they needed to be with the minimum of fuss. Edward and Henry stood on the quayside whilst

Rebecca made her way down the steps. The Marrick family were all guided into the gig without incident.

Before Isaac could board, Rebecca reached out and took his cuff.

"Stay safe Captain Dunsmoore, I insist."

Slightly abashed, Isaac nodded his assent, bade farewell to the young lady, and feeling more than a little awkward, stepped into the small craft (a task he ordinarily accomplished without any pernickety movements) and promptly lost his footing. A huge hand belonging to the first mate, Horace Clunk, saved him from eternal embarrassment.

"Thank you, Mister Clunk; I'm most grateful," Isaac declared.

"'Tis a mite slippy, sir, and no mistake." There was a twinkle in the dark eyes of Horace Clunk.

"Indeed, Mister Clunk." Composing himself, Isaac made his way to the helm. "Away now, lads."

The young captain tilted his head towards Rebecca and raised his eyebrows. Unconsciously, he twisted the gold band on his little finger, which had been a present from his mother. A smile flickered across Rebecca's face and she raised her hand to wave. The movement was stilted, reserved and not for everybody, although none of the events during the last few minutes went unnoticed by Cordelia Marrick. She decided to spare the captain any further embarrassment.

The gig lay at the port quarter of the ship, where a chair was lowered. Isaac excused himself and was first aboard. Horace Clunk hoisted Cordelia into the chair as if she were an errant feather shed from a circling gull, begging her pardon as he did so. Before she had time to protest or agonise as to her fate, she was on deck, slightly flustered but nonetheless safe. Her family followed in short order, and with the gig safely stowed, Captain Dunsmoore – now in full control – gave the order to weigh anchor.

Within the hour the ship was in full sail, cleaving effortlessly through the light chop and leaving a white-tipped foam in her wake.

"How's she feel, Mister Potts?" queried the captain.

Taylor Potts was at the helm; he was a spindly specimen as hard as the English oak used to construct the ship he was piloting. "I can feel her through my feet, sir. Built for this, sir, so she is."

"Indeed she is, Mister Potts; indeed she is."

Isaac spent the next few hours patrolling, talking to crew members, checking for problems constantly and generally ensuring the ship's smooth running. It would be a while before he was satisfied that there were no major issues. He was standing at the bowsprit when Wesley Marrick joined him.

"How are the ladies, Wesley?" Isaac enquired, as Cordelia and Joanna were both suffering from the malady of seasickness.

"Thankfully, they have ceased vomiting, but both are colourless, feverish and unable to raise themselves from their cots." Wesley had been tending them and had escaped momentarily for some air.

"It will pass, but I fear it could be a few days before they are able to get about the ship. Have you any symptoms yourself?" Isaac knew how debilitating it was. He remembered his first voyage. "Some people are sick the moment they step aboard; it's something to do with their balance, so they say."

"A strange occurrence—" Wesley never finished his discourse on seasickness.

A shout from above, just audible through the rushing sound of the westerly wind, interrupted their discussion.

From the masthead top, able seaman Will Nye yelled through cupped hands. "*In the water, starboard bow. Looks like a person, sir.*"

Isaac and Wesley gripped the handrail and stared across the low foamy peaks.

"There," stated Isaac, pointing, as both men spotted the hapless creature.

"Wesley, if you will, fix your sight on him and nothing else." Isaac turned, and whilst making his way to the helm, he shouted orders for all hands to go to their stations, "*Reef the top sails. Upon my order, Mister Potts, put her into the wind.*"

The ship had come to life. Men scrambled up rat lines without hesitation. There were no questions.

"Hard a' port, Mister Potts," commanded Isaac.

*Rebecca-Ann* heeled to the command with a certain amount of vehemence, and any remaining sail drooped in response to the lack of wind. Isaac made his way to the bow where Wesley Marrick had not taken his eyes off the forlorn castaway.

"There he is, Captain," stated Wesley.

"Mister Clunk, let's have the gig in the water, quick as you like. Take two men with you and recover the poor wretch," the captain directed.

These orders were duly followed, and soon the two oarsmen manoeuvred the stern of the gig skilfully towards the lifeless figure. Horace ordered the men to the bow to compensate for his huge bulk. For a big man, he was surprisingly agile, and leaning over the transom, he plucked the sodden creature from the makeshift life preserver into the boat. The slimy planks that had kept the boy alive bobbed in the water. Perhaps they would serve again, or perhaps they would simply wash ashore and provide firewood for an hour or two, warming the bones of a weary traveller. Whatever their fate, they had kept a young boy alive and delivered him into a life he could never have contemplated.

# Chapter Four

Horace Clunk stood on deck with the limp body draped in his arms. The crew busied themselves, following their captain's orders; the boat was stowed and the sails rigged – all was as it should be.

Now the captain would attend to the needs of the youth plucked from the Channel. "Mister Clunk, take the boy to my quarters for now, and we'll assess his condition. Mister Nye, have Seddon report to my quarters."

Seddon passed for the ship's doctor. Just. He qualified through years of being asked to patch up crew members, not through any training he may have had. His skill set was more surgical than medical; he would always do a fair job of stitching a person back together, and although there was only his word for it, he had once amputated a leg. There was no evidence to support his actions, confirm whether the patient had survived or, indeed, if the leg needed to be amputated in the first place. He was only ever known as Seddon – not Doctor, not Doc and not Mister Seddon, just Seddon – and he had been the nearest thing to a ship's doctor that Isaac had been able to find.

Isaac went swiftly to his cabin, and Horace ducked into the captain's quarters after him, wary of the unrelenting lintel above the entrance. His hairless head was garnished with wounds, some healed and some fresh, which had been acquired through involuntary confrontations with the ship's structure below deck. He placed the limp body in the cot and returned to his duties.

Before Isaac went to the boy, there was a tap on the door. He shouted, "*Enter!*" expecting Seddon, but it was Wesley Marrick who entered.

The two men crossed to the cot. Isaac stared at the boy, gasping in disbelief. He grabbed the cot's side to steady himself.

"Isaac… Captain." Wesley tried to get his attention. "Is everything okay? Is it the boy?"

Isaac regained his wits and asked Wesley to chase up Seddon. He needed a moment to compose himself because – unless his eyes deceived him – he was staring at a clone of Edward Buckingham, and although the boy's eyes were closed and sunken from his ordeal, the likeness was unmistakeable. The young captain's thoughts drifted back to the rumours all those years ago. He was only a boy himself. The gossip had meant little to him. Any mention of what happened the day Rebecca Buckingham lost her life in childbirth was quashed swiftly; nonetheless, the rumours existed, and they were spread idly and carelessly. Like most gossip, however, the story reached its crescendo, at which point the perpetrator of these evil actions had behaved like the devil himself by casting his unwanted child from the bedroom window in an uncontrollable fit of rage. Gradually, the rumours evaporated, leaving half-truths and accusations to fester in the dark shadows of the tale-teller's imaginations.

Seddon barged into the cabin, neither waiting for an invitation nor asking for one. Isaac overlooked the discourtesy and stood aside allowing Seddon access to his patient.

"The boys alive," Seddon declared in his raspy voice, "and that's a good start in any bugger's language, I should say. 'Is pulse is steady, but a bit weak, enough t' keep this young scoundrel alive, I shouldn't wonder. 'E needs some water, Cap'n, and some rest. I'll be back t'morrow t' sew up that arm. No point doin' it now, just in case 'e don't make it through the night-time." Before Isaac could respond, Seddon dismissed himself with the same air of familiarity with which he had arrived.

"Strange fellow. Perhaps a little work is required to perfect his bedside manner," declared Wesley, who had returned with the "doctor", being anxious to see if the lad was okay and curious to ask his new friend if all was as it should be. "The last time I saw you, Isaac, you looked as though you had seen a ghost."

"Wesley, take a close look at the boy. Tell me what you see," Isaac requested.

Wesley bent over the cot and studied the boy's countenance. It took a while for him to register the likeness, not being so familiar with the family. "My God. It can't be, surely... How can... It's not possible, Isaac... The son of Edward Buckingham floating aimlessly in the sea. How is that possible? I never knew he had a son."

Isaac went on to explain the rumours from all those years ago. Wesley Marrick listened in what appeared to be stunned silence.

They rigged a hammock in the cabin, and Isaac spent a fitful night, checking the boy firstly and then skipping onto the deck to satisfy himself all was well.

As the sun appeared on the port quarter, he heard the first sound from the castaway. Isaac almost fell from the hammock in his haste to ensure the boy's welfare.

Ezra opened his eyes and saw a blurred face staring down at him. He tried to ask for water. His voice was a croak.

Isaac held a cup of water to Ezra's lips, and putting his arm under Ezra's shoulders, he eased him into a sitting position. "Sip it gently now, lad, don't gulp it down."

The water hit Ezra's empty stomach, causing him to grimace. He sipped some more and lay back on the captain's pillow, and before Isaac could elicit a scrap of information, the boy fell sound asleep. Isaac smiled to himself; the boy would be okay.

Seddon arrived mid-morning, carrying a small, canvas bag. He entered the cabin with his usual impertinence. "I'm 'ere t' stitch the boy up, Cap'n. I take it 'e's still with us and not bin transported t' 'eaven above or the other place, come to it; you know, Cap'n, the other place." He glanced at the floor as he spoke.

"Seddon, if you please, I realise I am merely the captain of this ship, but if you could take a moment to tap on the door on your arrival, I should be most grateful." Isaac kept his voice light and the hint of sarcasm drifted aimlessly past the makeshift surgeon.

"Beggin' yer pardon, Cap'n. No offence, but 'tis in my nature t' get on; I 'as a lot to get through in the course o' me workin' day, Cap'n, as I'm sure ya knows."

Isaac sighed inwardly. "Get the lad repaired, Seddon."

The last thing he needed was a lengthy discourse with the slightly deranged Seddon, regarding the merits of his working day.

Ezra did not flinch as Seddon drew the jagged edges of the wound together with a deftness that surprised the watchful captain. Seddon then excused himself, obviously being keen to resume his busy schedule, and Isaac, desperate to discover as much as possible about the boy's life, began his gentle enquiries.

An hour passed. Ezra fell back to sleep after eating a bowl of broth and some biscuit, and Isaac sat at his desk in his new cabin, sharing the company of a young lad who was undoubtedly the son of a man whose belief in his abilities had given him, Isaac Dunsmoore, the command of a new ship and with it all the opportunity a young seafarer could wish for. The decisions he made as captain of the ship now paled into insignificance as he pondered the bizarre situation in which he now found himself.

A tap at the door disturbed his reverie. Not wishing to call out, he walked to the door, half expecting to see Seddon demonstrating his fledgling ability to be courteous when the occasion demanded. However, it was Wesley Marrick. The two men adjourned to the desk, which they sat around, and in hushed tones, Isaac began imparting the information he had gleaned thus far.

The boy's name was Ezra Quicklock, and he lived on the outskirts of Old Milford. His parents were Fred and Mary, and Ezra worked with his father, learning carpentry. He was clearly very proud of his father's craftmanship, but he had become very agitated about the fact that his parents would be missing him and he had no way to let them know he was still alive. Ezra had decided to keep the fact that he had dived from the cliff to himself, instead telling the captain how he had gone for a swim from the beach and the tide had swept him away. There had been nothing he could do to stop it. He had been adrift for three nights. He went into the sea on the 27th June, 11 days after his seventeenth birthday. Isaac had shuddered as Ezra imparted that crucial piece of information. Whilst his sister had been celebrating her seventeenth birthday in the opulent surroundings of her beautiful home, her brother had been contemplating risking his life for a reason that made no sense and had been rescued after floating aimlessly in the ocean, desperate to survive.

The two men talked at length about Ezra's future. On the ship's return to its home port, should they get the lad back to his adopted parents and say nothing? Should they tell him who he was? One of a twin. Would Edward Buckingham want to see the boy, his son? He was the living proof of prolific rumours. There were too many questions and no answers as yet. The consensus was that they would do nothing for the moment. They would look after the boy, teach him what they could in the time available, and a plan would hopefully manifest over the coming months. Isaac had been grateful for the opportunity to confide in someone like-minded who was sympathetic to the predicament.

In any event, he resolved to write a letter to Fred and Mary Quicklock to inform them of their son's ordeal and his subsequent rescue. Heaven only knew if any correspondence would arrive home before them, but he would try anyway. He also decided to compose a draft setting out the details that, without a doubt, he believed to be true. Wesley excused himself to check on his wife and daughter, and

Isaac composed the communications. These he sealed and addressed each to its respective recipient: Edward Buckingham and the Quicklock family at Old Milford. He put the letters together and locked them away in a drawer of his bureau. There was nothing more to be done. Secrets had been kept. Promises were broken. Mysteries were unravelled. Life was a cauldron of anomalies. The boy's lowly existence was shrouded in shadowy circumstances.

*

Three days passed, and Ezra was back to his old self. Isaac had spoken with Horace Clunk, not to ask for special treatment for the boy but just to keep an eye out for him, help him settle and show him the ropes. Horace had cocked his head at the captain, his gesture a silent question. Why? The answer was not forthcoming, so Horace accepted the order without further enquiry. Ezra was soon gadding around the ship, asking questions, climbing the rigging and learning to sail. The crew took to him, but if anyone should have a problem there would be Horace Clunk to deal with. Ezra was totally unaware of his status. Had he been dragged from the streets of Milford Port as a fledgeling sailor, his life on board ship would bear little resemblance to what he was experiencing now. Not that he wasn't worked hard. Every man had to put in his fair share. It was a large ship, with minimal crew, that had been designed to carry cargo not personnel, and they all sweated to keep her orderly and close-hauled.

" *'Tis not a place for a loaf,*" Will Nye shouted to make himself heard over the rushing wind. *"Ya must keep an eye out and keep yer wits about yerself. Take care, young Quicklock;*

*sometimes you'll see what ain't there, 'specially if ya've bin up 'ere awhile."*

They were in the crow's nest and Ezra was preparing himself for his first stint as watchman. He loved being up in the rigging, eighty feet above the water, with the ship heeling and the sails billowing, propelling them relentlessly through the steely ocean.

"Ya spot anythin' other than water, 'oller fer all yer worth," instructed Nye.

Ezra's reply was lost to the wind, and Mister Nye disappeared down the rigging in a blur of movement. He wanted to know what Mister Nye had meant about seeing things that weren't there.

*

Isaac watched Ezra from the quarter deck. He stood beside Potts at the helm, his feet apart and his hands clasped tightly at the base of his straight back. "Tell me, Mister Potts, what do you think of the boy?" His eyes remained fixed on the crow's nest. "Please speak freely."

"I like the lad, sir," Potts answered. The only thing the crew knew of Ezra's life was what he had told them himself, none of which had any connection to Edward Buckingham. "It strikes me, Captain, that he was made for seafarin'. I might be wrong, of course, as I ain't seen any of his carpentry as yet."

Taylor Potts was one of the few crew members who were able to read and write. Isaac knew little of him. He knew he was intelligent, capable and that you would want him on your side in a scrap.

Isaac smiled. "I've spoken with Mister Clunk, as you may be aware, and he is ensuring young Quicklock's well-being, at my behest. I don't want and I will not tolerate tittle-tattle regarding my motives. I would, however, ask a kindness from you, Mister Potts. You may decline if you wish." Isaac turned to face the helmsman. "I would like you to teach the boy how to defend himself."

"Defend himself, sir?"

"That's what I said, Mister Potts. Defend himself." Isaac replied irritably, as if to remind Mister Potts repeating himself should be unnecessary.

"I'll teach him to fight, sir. Don't know anythin' about defendin' myself."

"Very well, Mister Potts. That'll do nicely. I'll make sure your duties coincide. I'll leave you to initiate the proceedings."

With that, Isaac left a slightly bemused and curious Potts at the helm. He looked to the crow's nest and wondered to himself how a miserable wretch found adrift in the ocean could warrant such treatment from the captain.

\*

Ezra's watch was nearing its end when the two ladies appeared on deck. The man was guiding them, walking between them with their arms linked. They made their way to the port quarter, where they clung to the rail and stared across the Atlantic Ocean. Directly above them, the sun's rays glimmered intensely as they rebounded off the surface of the water back into their vista, forcing them to squint. A few wispy clouds hung in the sky, with the light breeze unable to stir them.

Cordelia Marrick gulped the sea air. "I was beginning to think we'd be imprisoned below deck forever." She felt lightheaded as her lungs expanded, and the rush of air accentuated her breathing.

"I'm sure you'll both be fine now." Wesley tried to keep his voice sympathetic.

"A week cooped up in a dingy hole, puking until there's nothing left to puke, and all you can say is, 'You'll be fine.' Great," scoffed Joanna.

"Joanna, please, there's no need for such language. It's a beautiful day, so let us make the most of being outside. A few days more and I'm sure we'll have forgotten all about our poor start." Cordelia said the words, but she had not convinced herself that she meant them.

Wesley managed to disregard his daughter's retort.

"A few years more like." Joanna was struggling to evaluate her parents' decision to sail across a great ocean to a place she had never heard of. The disgruntled girl unlinked arms with her mother, took a step sideways and turned to survey the ship. She admitted to herself it was a sight to behold. She glanced to the crow's nest and momentarily locked eyes with the watchman. He averted his gaze immediately. She did not. The wind flicked his long, dark hair around his tanned face, occasionally forcing him to tame it with a free hand. His shirt, virtually threadbare and open to the waist, revealed his muscular torso.

Ezra could not resist the temptation. He looked again. *Was she staring at him?* He couldn't be sure. He looked away, unable to process his emotions. Being eighty feet above deck and the girl being towards the bow of the ship, the distance between them was enough. In those brief glimpses, Ezra had discerned her pale complexion and her blonde hair, which fell almost to her waist and was tied back with a pale-blue ribbon to match her dress. *Where has she come from? Why have I not seen her before now? Who is the other woman? I've seen the man before, talking with the captain.* All these thoughts served to distract him from his duties.

A calloused hand cuffed the back of his head, jerking him back to reality. Shocked, Ezra swung round to confront his assailant.

"Steady, lad." Will Nye had climbed into the crow's nest unheard. "Take a look to starboard."

Still flustered Ezra scoured the horizon. Then he saw it.

"What d'ya see, lad?" asked Nye.

"A boat," Ezra confirmed.

"No, ya don't, lad." Nye shook his head as he spoke.

"Yeah, it's a boat, Mister Nye. I can see it." Confused, Ezra pointed to starboard where the outline of a tall ship almost blended into the mist of the horizon. "It's definitely a boat."

"Well, let me see if I can't put ya straight about this 'ere boat yer lookin' at."

Ezra looked perplexed. He was positive he wasn't seeing something that wasn't there. He knew he'd let himself down by not spotting the ship and alerting the crew.

"See, lad, this 'ere is a ship, an' that o'er yonder's a ship." Nye then pointed to the gig lashed to the deck. "That there's a boat. D'ya know 'ow I knows that?" Before the bewildered Ezra could reply, Nye continued, "I knows that, young Quicklock, cos ya can fit a boat on a ship, but as 'ard as ya try, ya can't fit a ship on a boat."

Ezra took a moment to decipher the information.

"And whilst I'm at it," Nye continued, "nobody never 'eard no shout o', *'Boat ahoy!'* P'raps it's just as well we never 'eard no shout – boat, my arse!"

"Sorry, Mister Nye, I was lookin' elsewhere."

"I knows that, lad, dun I? An' the cap'n knows, an' 'alf the bloody crew, I shouldn't wonder. Git yerself down t' the deck, lad, an' report t' the cap'n. Quick as ya like."

Ezra shimmied down the rigging, and as he hit the deck, he shot a quick glance in the direction of the girl. He whispered to himself, "What a cock." He made his way to the quarter deck where Captain Dunsmoore stood, looking an imposing figure.

"Ah, Mister Quicklock." Isaac beckoned Ezra and led him to the starboard rail. "Tell me, lad, what do you see?"

Ezra stared across the ocean, scanning the horizon.

"Well, lad, anything to report?" the captain asked.

"I can't see no bo— ship, sir." Ezra was completely bewildered. How could it have disappeared in those few moments? It was impossible.

"There's the thing, Mister Quicklock; you can see it from the crow's nest, but from here it's invisible. So, perhaps you now realise the importance of the watch duty. The ship has many dangers to confront, especially on a voyage such as this, not least from marauding privateers and pirates who would think nothing of stealing our cargo and killing anyone who dares to defy them. It takes but one person to neglect their duty, and the whole ship could be lost." Isaac spoke sternly, but kept his voice level. "Now perhaps you're wondering how I saw the ship from here? Would that be a fair assumption?"

Ezra looked askance at the captain. "I dunno what

an ass-ump-shun is – beggin' yer pardon, sir – but I was wondrin' 'ow you seen the ship, sir, yes."

Isaac felt a mixture of emotions at the youngster's poor grammar. He promised himself to address the problem, so far as possible, during the time they had together. "See the wooden box there, lad?" Isaac pointed to an object approximately three feet long by ten inches wide. "Lift the lid off and pass me the tube."

Ezra obeyed his instructions diligently and watched as the captain held the unwieldy object to his eye. He had never seen anything like it before. Ezra studied the wooden cylinder. He noticed a bronze plaque with some writing etched into the alloy. It was no help. The object was a mystery.

*

During the autumn of 1609, Captain Henry Dunsmoore had sailed into the port of Amsterdam. The cargo of sheep skins had been discharged and silk now filled the holds. Henry sat in the office of the agent, a Dutchman by the name of Jan Holsboer. After a few sips of genever, Jan handed Henry a long, wooden cylinder and instructed him to hold it to his preferred eye and look through the window to where *Rosetta-Ann* was moored.

After a moment or two of wrestling, Henry held the device steady and stared through the tube. His reaction brought a guffaw from the Dutchman. Henry had jumped back in amazement. His ship was outside the window, no longer five hundred yards away. The bewildered captain lowered the magical contraption to check the real whereabouts of his ship. Once again, he peered through the tube. There she was, just as before, right outside the window. Henry could do little but shake his head in wonder.

Holsboer took the "looker" and showed Henry the inscriptions. There were two small, bronze plaques. One simply said "Hans Lippershey – Holland" and the other "Henry Dunsmoore, be the first to see, Jan".

Henry had never been sure if the message to him was a play on words. Jan Holsboer spoke good English, but Henry had learnt over the years that when speaking with his overseas colleagues, the finer details could sometimes be misinterpreted. He did, however, treasure the gift. And without doubt it had given him the advantage in certain situations. Henry proudly passed the looker to his son in the knowledge it would help him to "be the first to see".

*

Ezra held the looker to his eye, as per the captain's instructions. Everything looked strange. A bank of white cloud seemed to separate the ocean from the sky, filling the lens. And then he saw the ship. He reacted how everyone does the first time they experience the magic of the looker: he jumped back in amazement, and having lowered the device to check with his own trustworthy vision, he raised it up to his eye and looked again. And there it was.

Isaac had to pry the telescope from Ezra's grasp. "The ship is a merchant vessel and holds no threat, but we'll monitor her course for as long as we have sight of her. Sometimes, the privateers disguise themselves, hoisting an ensign to deceive their intended prey. In any event, we shall leave her in our wake, so no harm done."

Ezra felt thoroughly dejected, but gave a sigh of relief at the captain's words. "I'm sorry, Captain, sir, I was distracted. It all 'appened so quick. Do you want me t' get back up there, sir? I promise I won't let you down next time, girl or no…" Ezra realised suddenly that he had admitted to his mistake.

"It's all right, lad; I know what distracted you. No, no, your shift is at an end, and I want you to find Mister Potts. Just tell him I sent you. One more thing before you go, just tell me what it says on the plaque." Isaac handed the looker to Ezra.

The words meant nothing to him. He shook his head and remained silent.

"Okay, lad, go and find Mister Potts."

As Ezra disappeared to seek out Potts, Isaac understood there would be another obstacle to overcome if he were to *do right* by the son of Edward Buckingham.

*

Cordelia Marrick had celebrated her fortieth birthday shortly before agreeing to venture across the globe to begin a new life. Her father was deeply fond of his eldest daughter, but he knew she needed something to quench her disquietude. Lionel had pondered long and hard because he knew that, once the proposition had been made, there was a chance he would never see his daughter again. He also knew that dealing with the underlying problem in his own way would also damage his relationship with Cordelia irrevocably. So, on the recommendation of his London-based agent, he invested in a *slightly run-down* sugar plantation approximately ten miles inland from the port of Belém, in the country of Brazil. There were fortunes to be made. What Lionel Hartshorne needed was someone he could rely on to deliver his agent's promises. What pricked at his conscience, though, was his daughter's happiness combined with the promise of a fortune. Had he got the two things muddled? It was no matter. He had made the proposal and, notwithstanding the relentless discussion and intense deliberation, the decision was made. Lionel knew that if the plantation were to be successful, his daughter would be the driving force.

The only thing belying Cordelia's age was the silver threaded through her blonde hair. Her complexion had lines that enhanced her elegant looks, though they appeared only when she chose to express an emotion. Her eyes were intensely green; her gaze ardent and compelling.

Being a head shorter than her willowy daughter, Cordelia tilted her head upwards to meet Joanna's piercing blue eyes, inherited from her father. "Did something distract you, my dear?"

Joanna felt herself blush. "No, no, I was just looking around and checking things out. I must say, Mother, the ship is quite beautiful. There's so much to look at, it's difficult to take it all in. I shall look forward to exploring further."

Cordelia allowed herself a brief smile before responding, amazed at her daughter's new-found interest in the ship that was transporting her to a foreign land. "Well, I'm glad you're feeling a little more positive."

"Yes, Mother, I believe I am. It must be the fresh air."

"I shouldn't wonder, my dear; the Atlantic air, so it would appear, is a certain remedy for a dose of the horrors."

Wesley gawped at his wife and daughter, totally bemused.

*

Ezra found Taylor Potts eventually, who – in an effort to find a private space – had been forced to reveal his intentions to the ship's cook. Pott's request to use the storeroom raised little more than an eyebrow with the surly cook. Elwyn Sakkit was a man of few words; he had a mop of red hair and the pasty complexion of someone who spent too much time cooped up in a ship's galley. When a red hair was found in the food, any doubts as to its origin were immediately annulled. Elwyn had no defence, except to say, *"Don't eat it if ya don' wan' it!"* Such was his attitude. He was not pursuing his *calling*.

Ezra entered the room. An oil lamp swung idly from a convenient hook, it's flame struggling to fend off the dingy atmosphere.

"About time, shit for brains," Potts snarled angrily.

Ezra was utterly dumbfounded.

"Well, you snot-nosed bastard, don't just stand there; say somethin'," demanded Potts.

Potts's attitude caused the memory of Persius Milford to flood his senses. He lunged at Taylor Potts. His tormentor was totally prepared for the flailing attack, and in a deft move, he blocked Ezra's wild swing and delivered a straight jab into his sternum. The punch was restrained, but it winded Ezra, and he bent double momentarily, letting out an involuntary grunt. Potts stepped in, put his leg behind Ezra's knees, and with an arm across his chest, he sent the startled youth to the floor. In a flash, he had a bare foot pressed hard against Ezra's temple, pinning him to the hard floor. The whole episode had taken seconds. The blur of movement had totally caught the young man off guard and he now lay on the wooden floor with a gnarly foot squashing his head. Ezra tried to fathom his options.

Then he heard Potts speaking in a soothing voice. "It's okay, Ezra. I'm gonna take my foot away, an' I want you to stay calm." He lifted his foot and quickly took a couple of paces back, as if he'd just let a snake out of a sack.

Ezra rolled on to his side, and with a clumsy movement, he tried to stand.

Potts spoke again. "Take your time, lad." He could sense Ezra was not yet ready to give in. "I know what just happened was a shock, and I'm not gonna apologise because I'm tryin' to help you."

Ezra got to his feet and stood with his arms by his side, his hands balled into fists. He couldn't work out what was going on.

"Listen to me, Ezra; I'm gonna explain what just happened. I made you attack me. I made you lose your temper. You made it easy for me, lad. Me an' you are gonna meet down here every day 'til we see land, an' I'm gonna teach you the rules. My rules."

*

Isaac Dunsmoore sat with his elbows on the desk, his thumbs under his chin, and his fingers steepled across the bridge of his nose. The charts were spread before him. He had spent the last hour pondering their destination. The information was patchy at best, and he felt sure he would need a pilot to guide the ship through the mouth of the Guama River. The prospect imbued him with a nervous excitement. A tap at the door interrupted his thoughts.

Wesley Marrick poked his head around the door. "Isaac, you wanted to see me?"

"Yes, yes, Wesley; come in and sit down. I wanted to go over a few details if you're agreeable," Isaac explained.

The two men exchanged pleasantries for a few moments before getting down to business.

"What's this fellow's name again?" enquired Isaac.

"Garcia Paz." Wesley spelt the surname, and Isaac jotted it down.

"And you've never met the man, I'm assuming?"

"No, I encountered his agent in White Bay a month or so ago. Bit of a surly type. He assures me, though, that Paz will make contact with us at Belém and ensure us a secure passage through the delta."

"Excellent. What's the agent's name? The fellow in White Bay."

Wesley looked a little flustered. "Strangely, I can't recall his name. I'm sure it'll come back to me at some point, and I'll let you know."

Isaac accepted Wesley's disclosure without censure and set down his quill. All he could do now was navigate his way to Belém and then put his trust in Garcia Paz.

"Wesley, I fear I'm forever seeking favours, but where young Quicklock is concerned I feel a deep sense of responsibility and a genuine need to do all I can to improve his situation." Isaac felt he was continually repeating himself. "The boy can't read and his speech is terrible. Do you think it would be too much of an imposition to ask Cordelia—"

Wesley interrupted, sensing Isaac's uneasiness. "I shall speak with her, and I'm sure she'll be more than happy to help."

Cordelia had educated their daughter and had thoroughly enjoyed the experience.

They made arrangements for the lessons to take place in Isaac's cabin, where there would be access to his compact library and a good degree of privacy, which would be essential if Cordelia were to make an impact in the time available. Isaac knew that the attentions his influence was bringing to bear on the castaway would arouse suspicions and gossip. However, he felt confident that Clunk and Potts would quench any unnecessary prattle, wherever possible.

*

Ezra had been instructed to report at four bells in the forenoon to the captain's quarters. He tapped gingerly on the door, distracted momentarily by its fine workmanship, particularly the filigree around the frame. With his index finger, he followed the carved woodwork, admiring the smooth finish.

Isaac had gone to escort Cordelia to his cabin, and the two of them had approached the cabin in silence. He noticed Ezra admiring the craftmanship. "Ah, I suppose you have an eye for such work, given your background."

"Oh, sorry, Captain, sir. My pa would do work like that. 'E was busy teachin' me, but I don't reck'n I'll ever be any use at it. P'raps when I git 'ome, he'll start learnin' me again." Ezra felt a pang of sadness as he thought of his father.

Isaac could see the melancholy supressing the boy's demeanour. He wished he'd kept silent. Reminding Ezra of his past had been a mistake. Doing his best to lighten the mood, Isaac shuffled his guests into the cabin and introduced teacher and pupil. "Ezra, I'd like you to meet Cordelia Marrick. Cordelia this is Ezra Quicklock."

Instinctively, Ezra stuck out a hand, as his father had taught him, and without hesitation Cordelia responded. The young man shook her delicate hand with some vigour. "Very pleased t' meet ya, missis."

Cordelia was momentarily taken aback, but regained her composure immediately, allowing herself a wry smile. "Likewise, Ezra." In those few moments, Cordelia Marrick knew she would enjoy spending time with the young man standing before her, albeit that he was uneducated, unkempt, unrefined and slightly awkward. Fortuitously, she enjoyed a challenge.

# Chapter Five

The lives of Fred and Mary Quicklock had been torn apart. The loss of their son had left them bereft; their existence was virtually meaningless.

Fred and Mary had made their way to the lagoon, guided by the last dregs of daylight. They spotted Ezra's boots and jerkin on the rocky ledge, and they immediately feared the worst. They called out his name whilst staring into the limpid waters of the lagoon. Nothing. Their son had been swept away, taken by the sea, and yet Mary could not reconcile herself to accept the overwhelming evidence confronting her. She felt his heart beating. Wherever he was, irrespective if she ever saw him again, she knew it: he was still alive.

As the weeks passed, their lives became more difficult. Fred could not get Mary to accept the facts. Ezra had been swept out to sea and drowned. There was no other logical explanation, and Fred, above all, dealt in logic. So gradually, as the tears relented, they began to argue. When they finished bickering, they ignored each other. Fred stayed longer and longer at his workshop, whilst Mary would spend hours at the lagoon, her eyes fixed on the horizon, asking herself what could have happened but never relinquishing her belief that Ezra was still alive.

Fred trod the beaten track from the small, stone cottage, the only home their son had ever known, heading for the lonely workshop. He was thoroughly miserable. The boy had arrived under strange circumstances, bringing with him something that he and Mary had never thought possible. The circumstances under which he had disappeared were even stranger, and the impact on their lives even greater. As Fred continued his journey, his steps were heavy and his shoulders slumped under the unremitting consequence of misery. He began to think of his own father. Sid Quicklock had been a stoical man, and Fred had inherited many of his characteristics, instilling in him the necessary fortitude to endure whatever his Creator chose to hurl at him. Fred was ten years old when his two elder brothers contracted scrofula and died within weeks of each other. He remembered little of it and now found it difficult to conjure an image of his lost siblings. As he wandered aimlessly along a familiar road, he began to remember how his own father had changed after the death of the boys. The spark of emotion that occasionally shone through his stern demeanour – the spark that made them all coexist in relative harmony and that bound the family together – had been extinguished.

Fred realised suddenly what he was doing. He stopped abruptly, turned on his heels, and with a renewed vigour, he began the walk back to their small cottage. His mind was full of the things he needed to say to Mary. Together, whatever the fate of their beloved son, they would get through this. The alternative was unbearable.

Engrossed in his own thoughts, Fred was oblivious to the sound of horses behind him. He turned slightly sideways at the last moment and stepped off the track. The three horses pulled up, and Fred looked up to see a surly young man with a patch over his left eye. It was Persius Milford.

*

The night of Rebecca's party, after the incident in the stables, Persius had no option but to make his way home, knowing he needed some sort of feasible explanation for his injury. Clutching the wound with the torn off pocket, he stumbled along the dark road to Old Milford cursing his misfortune. The journey took him the best part of two hours, and the big house was firmly shuttered by the time he arrived. Still cursing he made his way to the stables and settled himself down amongst some loose hay and fell soundly to sleep. He awoke at dawn to the sound of horses nickering and the grooms beginning their days work. Feeling wretched, he rolled himself from the hay, dusted himself down, grimaced at the pain in his face and made his way to the servants' entrance. Always wary of his vile temper, the staff ignored him, trying desperately not to look at his face. He demanded they bring him breakfast to his room as he marched through the kitchen. Once there he took the piece of material away from his eye and examined the damage in a mirror. With a piece of clean cloth soaked in water, he dabbed the wound, cleaning away the congealed blood.

*It doesn't look too bad*, he thought, *Christ Almighty, why does it hurt so much?*

Persius had tried to eat something, but despite the pangs of hunger the very thought of food made him retch. He told Monica, the servant who had lost the argument about who should take breakfast to his room, that he didn't want to be disturbed under any circumstances, and then put himself to bed.

Later that afternoon, Baron and Lady Milford arrived home more than a little curious as to the whereabouts of their son. They found him in his bed, half-delirious and groaning in agony. Rufus immediately sent a member of his staff on horseback to fetch the physician.

Through the fog of pain and sweat Persius struggled to explain how he'd decided to walk home because he had drunk too much punch. He told his parents how the three vagabonds had jumped on him in the darkness and tried to rob him. Persius described how he managed to fight them off, but not before one of them had stabbed him in the face with *some kind of weapon*. It had all happened so quick. They ran off empty-handed, and Persius somehow managed to get himself home, though he couldn't remember how he had done so. Nor could he give any indication as to the identity of his attackers or indeed any sort of description that could possibly help with their apprehension, which was totally understandable given his condition.

The physician arrived and quickly ascertained the young man's predicament. He ordered a large table to be brought to the room. He needed hot water, clean cloths (preferably cotton), some more candles, some long lengths of bedsheets cut into strips, two strong lads and a bottle of best brandy. When all his instructions had been met, the doctor ordered the two lads to lift Persius onto the table. They were then told to hold him down whilst he placed the strips of bedsheet over the patient's forehead, chest and ankles, tying them tightly so as to secure him to the table. Everyone was ordered from the room except the two lads whose job it would now be to ensure Persius was kept as still as possible. When he was satisfied the patient would be unable to move, the doctor poured brandy over the wound and then took a healthy swig himself.

Persius had little strength left, but when the physician removed his left eye, the scream resonated through the walls of the great house, and it took a determined effort from the assistants to keep him still. At this point, Persius Milford fell unconscious. The doctor sloshed more best brandy over the wound and then sewed the eye socket together declaring that if the patient were still alive in forty-eight hours, he could reasonably expect to die of some other ailment.

Whilst Rufus escorted the physician to his carriage, Baroness Milford went to her son. He lay in his bed, his head swathed in bandages of cotton sheets. She was acutely aware of his shortcomings, but she loved him. She couldn't help herself. His actions sometimes infuriated her, but she always searched for a reason to forgive him and to find a reasonable excuse. Mostly, she blamed herself. Whilst sitting on the edge of his bed, she noticed his clothes strewn across the floor. She gathered them up and was surprised by a clatter of something hitting the floor. The baroness gasped in horror at the sapphire brooch and diamond-studded pin.

*

"Quicklock." It had been five weeks since the doctor had removed his eye, and Persius was keen to reinstate his authority over the hapless community. "Why are you walking in the wrong direction? Don't you have orders to fulfil?"

"Yeah, I do, but I forgot somethin'. I'm just poppin' 'ome an' I'll be back at it soon enough." As he said the words, Fred touched his forelock with all the sincerity he could muster. In the last few moments, his mood had lifted.

"You make sure those barrels are ready on time. Oh, by the way," Persius continued, his tone lighter, "I hear that bastard son of yours went for a paddle and never came home. Still, look on the bright side, Quicklock – it's one less mouth to feed."

Fred launched himself at the sneering, one-eyed youth, and with all the strength his reckless anger had provided, he hauled Persius from the saddle. Both men hit the ground hard. The two guards, momentarily surprised by Fred's action, were slow to respond, and by the time they reached the tangle of bodies Fred's powerful hands were crushing Persius's windpipe, gradually strangling the life out of him. The first guard kicked Fred hard in the ribs, followed by a knee in the face, and as Fred's grip slackened, the other pulled him off, and together they began driving vicious kicks into Fred's body.

"Enough." Persius's voice was little more than a croak.

The guards relented.

"Get him up on his feet," Persius ordered.

The guards hoisted up Fred's limp figure and held him upright. Persius pulled on the heavy leather gloves that had hung through his belt, and after making a show of pulling them on, began punching Fred in the face – blow after blow after sickening blow.

*

Fred lay in the long grass at the edge of the track, his breathing was raspy and the pain was excruciating. The afternoon had brought with it dark clouds that lingered in the sky, and Fred could feel the dampness of the grass beginning to suck the warmth from his aching body. He knew he must try to get back to Mary. With all his remaining strength, he staggered to his feet, the pain searing through his rib cage causing him to wince with every movement.

Mary had spent the day immersed in meaningless tasks. When the door crashed open and her battered husband lurched into the cottage, she cried out loud. Seeing Fred's horrific injuries snapped Mary from her ambivalence, and the deep affection she had always felt for him immediately overwhelmed her, followed by a practical desire to do everything in her power to make him comfortable and tend his wounds as best she could. Fred was in no condition to explain what had happened, so Mary bathed his bloody face and settled him on the bed. She whispered in his ear that she was going for help and would be back with him as soon as she could.

Mary was a practical woman. She'd had little choice over the years. Her natural disposition, however, would adhere to impulsiveness when the opportunity arose, which – given her circumstances – rarely happened. Her features were an open book, which Fred and Ezra had learnt to recognise; unlike her rather stern-faced mother, Mary's face was an invitation into her unreserved sanctum. Mostly, she scraped her lightly greying hair onto the top of her head where she held it place with a wooden pin that Fred had fashioned for her many years ago. Fred loved to see her with her hair down and often threatened to burn the wretched pin. "Burn that pin, Fred Quicklock, an' I'll cut up yer best breeches for cloth," had always been Mary's response.

Now, as she stared in utter disbelief at her battered husband, she fought desperately to fend off any vulnerability that threatened to interfere with her decision-making. The only person she knew who was qualified to assist, the person who could give Fred the best chance, was her mother.

Having composed herself, Mary hitched up her skirts and began running the quarter of a mile to her neighbours' property. She couldn't remember the last time she had run. She felt a tremor through her legs and her breathing became ragged; her predicament, though, abetted her endeavours. A dogged determination enabled her to continue. A pair of squealing buzzards circling above a giant elm, their space invaded temporarily by a handful of crows, distracted her momentarily, but her pace never slackened.

Si and Martha Crust owned around four acres of land – although the boundaries became blurred as fallow met the great forest – on which they kept goats, a few pigs, a dozen or so chickens, and a shire horse called Boris. They grew enough wheat to supply themselves and their seven children with bread, and enough vegetables to keep the family well fed and healthy. Mary never saw much of her neighbours, but over the years, she had been there for Martha, mostly at the birth of one of the children. When Ezra came into her life, Mary wondered how Martha coped with having seven children in ten years, and a home to keep; Mary felt sure it was beyond her own capabilities.

Gulping the early evening air as if it were in short supply, Mary arrived at the Crusts' place, unlatched the gate and made her way to the house.

A voice stopped her. "Aunt Mary." It was Peter, the eldest son. The children had always referred to Fred and Mary as Uncle Fred and Aunt Mary.

"Oh, Pie," replied Mary. (Peter's name had been changed to "Pie" as far back as Mary could remember). Suddenly, as if speaking to another person was a key that had unlocked a chest full of emotion, the tears began.

Pie shouted for his mother and Martha emerged from the house to find her eldest son awkwardly trying to soothe their neighbour's sobs. Mary composed herself and explained why she was there. Pie skipped off and returned quickly, leading Boris by a halter. Pie leapt effortlessly onto the bare back of the huge animal, whilst Mary had to be hoisted onto Boris's great rump by the unforgiving hands of Si Crust. Then the unlikely trio set off – firstly, going to the Quicklocks' home to set Mary down and then on to collect Ma Fish.

*

The big shire stood patiently outside Ma and Pa's. The light had all but disappeared. Inside, Ma had tried in vain to stir her husband, who had succumbed to the effects of his home-made cider. From where he stood outside, Pie caught a waft of stale cider and understood immediately why the old man was unresponsive. Ma came out of the front door only to be confronted by Boris, the proposed mode of transport to her daughter's house.

Ma's eyes widened in horror. "You can't be serious, young 'un. 'Ow d'ya expeck me t' git on that brute? An' more to the point, 'ow d'ya expeck me t' stay on 'im?"

Right on cue, Boris lifted his tail and deposited a huge pile of steaming dung onto the cobbles. Ma turned up her nose in disgust. Pie led the horse away from the mess and made him stand alongside a low stone wall, whilst trying to reassure Ma that she had nothing to fear. She, however, remained unconvinced. Pie stepped onto the wall, and extending his hand, he eased her up with him. That was the easy part. He made a cup with his hands and instructed Ma to place her left foot there and to place her hands on Boris's withers. Pie realised he only had one chance to get Ma onto the horse, so taking a deep breath, he hoisted the plucky lady onto Boris's bare back. Ma's legs hung at a strange angle; her frame had not been designed for such escapades. Pie shuffled Ma towards Boris's hind quarters, and with an unnatural yet dextrous move, he launched himself in front of Ma. The bewildered lady hugged the young man and Boris set off at a gentle pace. Ma clung to the youth with a tenacity only Pie could describe, and as her confidence grew, she felt the presence of the great shire beneath her and the comfort of Pie's warm body gradually easing the tension she had initially felt. *Whatever next?* she wondered.

# Chapter Six

Ezra took to his lessons. He enjoyed Cordelia Marrick's company, how she spoke and how she showed him things – things he knew nothing of. Books were full of stuff he wanted to read about, not necessarily because he had any particular interest in the subject but because the words had been written and he wanted to read them. She taught him about aitches, how it had eluded him all these years, and how just by introducing it into the spoken word, it would transform his speech. She gave him a sentence to practise: "Hard-headed Hector hardly has hysterics, honest." Cordelia smiled at his first effort: "'Ard-eaded 'Ector 'ardly 'as 'isstairicks, 'onest." He'd followed the words with his index finger, as a young child would have.

Gradually, the aitches arrived. They were initially overemphasised, his enunciation unnatural. The last word – honest – gave him the most trouble. *Why,* he wondered, *would the inventor of the English language, whoever he was, start a word with a letter he didn't want anyone to use?*

After a conversation with the captain, it was agreed that

Ezra would have a two-hour lesson every morning and every afternoon. All his other duties and commitments would revolve around these.

*

By the time they had been at sea for thirty-seven days, the confident young man bore little resemblance to the bedraggled youth plucked from the sea, except for his clothes, which consisted of a threadbare shirt without a single button and a pair of breeches that ended at his calves – the latter, when wet, were becoming more transparent by the day. Without any drawers, this would be yet another problem for the captain to address. After all, the boy was no longer a boy!

Taylor Potts reported Ezra's progress to his captain regularly, saying, "He's a handful, sir."

Horace Clunk assured Isaac that the boy had been readily accepted by the crew, and there had been very little gossip regarding his treatment.

*

Joanna decided she needed a closer look at the ragged specimen she had first spotted hanging out of a basket high above the ship's deck. She knocked once and entered the cabin. Ezra had his head in a book, studying a map of the world whilst trying desperately to fathom how it could possibly be round, and either ignored the intrusion or was totally oblivious.

"Joanna," questioned Cordelia, her tone a little sharp, "what is it?"

Ezra tilted his head and peered over his book. Joanna walked to the desk; she stared at Cordelia, her gaze unflinching. The ragamuffin with the book completely invisible to her.

"Ah, Mother, I was just curious—" Joanna began.

"Yes," Cordelia interrupted, "I'm sure you were my dear; I'm sure you were."

"You misunderstand me, Mother, I am simply looking for my embroidery. I have searched our quarters and it is not to be found anywhere, so I wondered if you had picked it up in error and put it in your sack with the books?" Joanna had incorporated a loftiness to her tenor, endeavouring to maintain the moral high ground. "That is all. I can assure you I am not here under any other pretence, which if I am not mistaken, was the inference. In fact, if—"

*Rebecca-Ann* pitched violently to port. A rogue wave hit her starboard quarter. The helm was snatched from Taylor Potts's grasp; Horace Clunk bashed his head; Captain Dunsmoore took ten or more pigeon steps, faster than he would have liked and only stopping when he reached the rail; Will Nye fell from his hammock; Elwyn Sakkit's dinner preparations were flung across the galley, as was he; and, amongst an array of other minor occurrences, Joanna Marrick hurtled herself (involuntarily, perhaps) at Ezra Quicklock.

Whilst the other victims of nature's sudden disturbance began to rearrange themselves, Ezra and Joanna lay in a tangled heap on the floor, unable to disentangle themselves, or so it would seem. Cordelia had managed to grab the desk, thus preventing herself from joining her daughter and pupil in an indivisible liaison and sparing herself from any further embarrassment, other than the charade she was presently witnessing.

Sprawled across a half-naked stranger in the presence of her mother didn't appear overly to bother Joanna. Her hair was loose. She lifted her head, causing it to flop over Ezra's face. It felt soft. She put the palm of her hand on his bare chest and pushed herself into a sitting position, with a leg each side of his thighs.

"Hi." She smiled sweetly. "I'm Joanna."

"Ezra," he muttered whilst clearing his throat.

"Joanna, get up at once." Cordelia tried her best to install severity into her tone, but instead she found herself biting her lip. This was no time to laugh. She walked around the desk and held out her hand. With (it seemed to Cordelia) an air of reluctance, Joanna took the proffered help and eased herself from Ezra's lap. She stepped to one side and flattened her dress with long, sensual movements. Ezra never moved.

"Well, Mother, if you don't have my embroidery, I shall resume my search elsewhere. Nice to meet you, Ezra." And with that, she flounced from the cabin as she had entered, less than five minutes ago.

Ezra eased himself into a sitting position, trying desperately to make sense of the last two minutes. Embarrassed by his thoughts – which were primal, yet natural enough – he felt his cheeks begin to burn. Cordelia surveyed the scene. A bewildered youth, one of the captain's chairs with a broken leg, volumes strewn everywhere and an undercurrent of indecorous insinuation hanging, unobserved, over the innocent player.

*My God,* she thought, *vulnerability has never looked so becoming.*

Ezra gathered the books, placed them on the desk and began inspecting the broken chair. "Perhaps, missis, I should take it to the carpenter's shop." Giving the damage a closer inspection, he announced to Cordelia that he would, if the carpenter were agreeable, repair the damage himself.

"Good idea, Ezra. I think the disruption has more than interrupted our learning this morning, and I have some work that requires my immediate attention. So, notwithstanding any further dramatics, we'll continue this afternoon."

Ezra gathered up the battered chair and headed off to the carpenter's shop. He was in desperate need of something to distract his brain from replaying those few moments of indescribable elation. The broken chair proved woefully inadequate.

His body began to react. *Oh shit,* he thought. He felt himself trembling. He had never in his life been that close to a girl. *She smelt wonderful… Her hair was so soft; it tickled my face… Her body felt firm, warm and enticing… Her hands were on my bare skin…* He had to sit. He plonked himself down on a coil of rope, discarded the useless chair, and sat with his hands clasped between his knees, his elbows on his thighs. Leaning forwards, he began taking deep breaths in an attempt to halt the rush of blood, which – given the right incentive – had found a natural path to its inevitable destination, the consequences of which were most unwelcome at that particular moment. *It could have been worse,* he thought, *it could have happened five minutes ago.*

"Young Quicklock." The deep voice shocked Ezra. It belonged to Horace Clunk. "You 'urt, lad?"

"No, sir, Mister Clunk. Just on me way to the carpenter's shop with the cap'n's broke chair," Ezra explained.

"Well, lad, call me what ya will, but it strikes me that – like as not – yer sittin' on a coil o' rope lookin' like ya could do wi' a visit to the docs, ne'er mind the carpenter's shop." Horace brushed a finger over his latest wound. "'Appen I'll see ya there."

"No, no, I'm fine."

"Be off with ya then."

Ezra grabbed the remains of the chair, held it surreptitiously "amidships" in an attempt to cover his "overabundance", and shuffled off in a bid to complete his mission.

Horace watched him go. He shook his damaged head. "Young 'uns; I dunno."

By the time Ezra had clambered down the steep, narrow steps that led to the dingy space inhabited by Aubrey Darricot, his ardour had subsided. Grateful that nature or physics or chemistry (Ezra's knowledge of those subjects had yet to be awakened) had reduced the mistimed enlargement, he bundled into Darricot's realm, wrestling with the chair.

"Ah, young Quicklock. The chosen one if I'm not mistaken." Although pleasant enough, the carpenter's tone had more than a hint of sarcasm. "I wondered when you'd turn up."

Still a little flustered, Ezra felt unsure of himself. "Sorry, sir, I dunno what ya mean." His recent elocution lessons had deserted him. "I just come to—"

"You don't have to call me 'sir'. Mister Darricot'll do for a start, and I can see very well why you're here. If I'm not very much mistaken, that's one of the captain's chairs."

Darricot had a waspish disposition that made him difficult to like. His countenance would not endear a stranger to engage him in any voluntary way. His head was large and peculiarly round. He was in possession of several strands of grey and black hair, which travelled from east to west across his dome. His eyes were bulbous and difficult to ignore. One was the deepest green and the other a torpid brown; both ominous in their own way. On his left cheek, he had a patch of raised skin, dark brown in colour, out of which grew three hairs, stiff and black. His lips were puffy, and he habitually put his bottom lip over the top one as if impersonating a great North Sea cod.

"I thought I might fix it myself, Mister Darricot, with your permission, of course." Ezra had rediscovered his composure, but found it difficult not to stare at the three hairs growing contentedly in their little patch.

"Fix it yourself, eh?" Aubrey sounded most indignant. "Well, I can only imagine the kerfuffle when the captain sits on his chair expecting to be supported in comfort only to be flung to the floor amongst a heap of fine English ash. No, Quicklock, I'll mend the captain's chair."

"But Mister Dar—" Ezra's protests were in vain.

"I'll fix the chair. Come back tomorrow and fetch it. If I don't have any major interruptions, it'll be ready."

Ezra nodded his assent and turned to leave. It was then he spotted the bow hung on the wall. All thoughts of the disagreeable carpenter dissolved and happy memories of helping his father overwhelmed him. Ezra reached up and lifted the bow from its hook. He felt its tension and let his hand caress the smooth grain of the yew. Aubrey Darricot's immediate reaction was to ask the boy what he thought he was doing, but he watched as Ezra handled the bow, mesmerised by its simple lines, so he held his tongue and allowed him to continue.

"Beggin' yer pardon, Mister Darricot, but 'ow... how long 'as it bin 'ang... hanging like this?" Ezra was desperately trying to remember his aitches.

"Ever since I came aboard, its bin there. It's never bin moved, so far as I know." Aubrey passed a rough finger over the three hairs, their familiarity providing solace. "You have an interest in such things, I can see."

"My pa makes 'em. I 'elped 'im." Ezra didn't bother to correct his speech. "It shouldn't be left strung like that Mister Darricot. You need to let the tension out of it... beggin yer pardon, sir... when yer not usin' it."

"Well, I can tell you that it won't be me usin' the ham-fangled contraption, I promise. Dangerous bloody things they are. Anyway, lad, unstring it if it pleases you."

Aubrey watched as Ezra positioned one end of the bow against the bench leg and pushed hard. With the hemp string slackened, Ezra released it from the notch and felt the yew gradually seek out its natural tendency. He thought of the simple rack his father had made specifically for storing the relaxed long bows.

"Would you have a short length of string or yarn of some description, Mister Darricot?" Ezra enquired.

"Certainly, lad." Intrigued, Aubrey cut a length of twine from a coil and handed it to Ezra. "That enough?"

"Perfect, Mister Darricot, thank you."

Ezra whipped the twine around the end of the bow and tied it off. He then made a simple figure of eight knot in the other end and hung the bow on the hook.

"Are there any arrows, Mister Darricot?" As Ezra's confidence grew, his speech improved.

"Have a look in the chest over there." Aubrey had

warmed to the chosen one. He pointed to a narrow crate by the far wall.

Ezra lifted the lid and, to his delight, discovered at least three score of finely made arrows. "Perfect," he muttered.

*

For a short moment, Cordelia thought to seek her husband's permission. Having made the decision to bypass that particular obstacle, she rummaged through his large sea chest, which was packed with fine clothes. Selecting a pair of grey cotton breeches and a white linen shirt, she tidied the contents hurriedly and closed the lid.

*Rebecca-Ann* had made excellent progress since her departure from Milford Port. On the fortieth day at sea, however, she came to a virtual standstill. Her movement was almost imperceptible. The sun beat down from a cloudless sky, the lank sails that were untouched by the merest breath of wind were reefed, and the ship floated aimlessly in the still water of the Atlantic Ocean.

It never ceased to surprise Isaac how quickly the mood aboard ship could change. He had experienced how a couple of days in the doldrums affected the crew of a ship, with their normally busy and arduous routine replaced with inactivity and mundane chores. Boredom could be a tiresome and vexatious adversary.

Ezra approached the captain, resplendent in his new outfit. Cordelia had altered Wesley's clothes expertly, and when she presented her pupil with his new livery, he struggled to overcome his emotions and extended his hand awkwardly in a gesture of thanks. Cordelia brushed the hand aside gently, and stepping close, she gave him a hug and told him she had enjoyed the task immensely and how fine he looked.

"Well, now, young Mister Quicklock, don't you look a sight in your new slops, although I could hardly call them slops. Very smart, indeed," the captain declared.

"Thank you, sir. Missis Marrick made them for me." Ezra brushed a hand along the sleeve of his new shirt as he spoke.

Isaac eyed the handsome clothes and could only wonder how Cordelia had managed to find such fine material.

Ezra continued, "Sorry to bother you, Captain; I just wondered if I may ask you something?"

"Bother me, lad?" Captain Dunsmoore was standing at the taffrail, staring across the limpid ocean, with the sun slowly crisping his pale skin, "I could stand here for another week, judging by the weather, and you still wouldn't bother me. So, ask away, lad; ask away."

"Well, sir, there are a couple of things. I found a bow in Mister Darricot's workshop, and I was wondering if, perhaps, you know, as there's not much going on…"

"Spit it out, lad; c'mon now." Their becalmed circumstance had begun to erode even the captain's forbearance.

"May I arrange an archery competition… for the men, sir?"

Without removing his hands from the rail, Isaac scrutinised Ezra whilst contemplating the request. He knew the men were restless and that Horace Clunk had intervened on more than one occasion to quell unrest between certain crew members. Isaac returned his gaze to the placid ocean.

Ezra felt unsettled at the enduring silence.

"Hmm, very well, but if I find so much as one hole in my new ship, I'll be after you, Mister Quicklock. I shall hold you responsible. And make sure nobody gets shot. I can't afford for any of the men to be out of action when the weather turns." Before Ezra could respond, Isaac continued, "What was the other thing?"

"Would it be okay to go for a swim, sir?"

"A swim. A swim! Are you mad? Should I call for Seddon? Has the sun affected your senses?" The captain was clearly shocked at the request; in his experience, no sailor put themselves in the water voluntarily. Sailors do not like the water. If they found themselves in the ocean, it was because there was no ship or boat or indeed anything that floated and had the capacity to keep a person from drowning. "Forgive me, lad, but didn't we pluck you from the sea? And not a moment too soon if I remember correctly. And now you wish, without any good reason, to plunge back into the very place from whence you were rescued. What nonsense!"

Ezra's request had clearly taken the captain aback. "But, sir, if I had not learnt to swim, I would not have survived long enough to be rescued."

The young man's speech and growing confidence impressed Isaac immensely. But then, his father was an impressive man, so there should be no surprise in the boy's progress – although without the efforts of Cordelia Marrick and certain crew members, this would have been somewhat limited.

"Get along and organise your archery competition, lad, and let's hear no more nonsense about swimming," Isaac commanded.

Ezra turned to leave.

"And remember – no holes in the ship," the captain reiterated.

*

The following day, after his lesson with Cordelia and a particularly brutal session with Taylor Potts, Ezra finished setting up the target. He had fashioned a series of planks, which he had scrounged from Aubrey Darricot, into a rectangle six feet wide and eight feet tall. With some white paint, also courtesy of Aubrey, Ezra carefully painted a series of circles, ending with a bullseye no more than three inches in diameter. He then bored two holes, through which he passed a length of rope and knotted each end. It was a cumbersome affair but Ezra knew most of the crew would need something fairly large to aim at. With the help of Horace Clunk and Taylor Potts, who was brandishing a split bottom lip, they carried the target to the starboard bow and secured the unwieldly construction to the rail.

With some gentle enticement, Clunk and Potts rounded up six other men to participate in the Atlantic Archery Competition, which had been thus somewhat grandly entitled by its founder. Wesley Marrick also wished to participate, so Ezra decided there would be two teams of five, with each team having five shots per man. Using his newly acquired skills, Ezra marked the target with numbers indicating the score for each ring. He then placed a length of rope on the deck fifteen paces from the target. He didn't want any arguments, so they would all fire from the same spot. With nothing readily available to write the scores on,

Aubrey Darricot provided a heap of offcuts that could be placed in relevant piles to denote the result of each shot. Clunk and Potts were the team captains, and they took it in turn to select their team members. Ezra was in Team Clunk, along with Will Nye, Ed Monk (a fresh-faced young man in his early twenties) and a weather-beaten sailor by the name of George Burdock, who was commonly known as Prickle. Team Potts consisted of Wesley Marrick, Elwyn Sakkit, Noel Finn (a quiet, methodical man with a shock of blond hair) and Tod Harris (a rangy young man who gave the impression of complete disinterest, but who performed his duties with an efficiency that belied his demeanour).

Horace Clunk had the first shot. Ezra had restrung the bow and gave Horace a cursory lesson by demonstrating the method. Horace held the bow in his giant mitt and fumbled with the arrow. Once he had arranged both objects to his satisfaction, he pulled the string back, flexing the bow to its limit, and released the arrow. It proved beneficial for the onlookers that they were watching from behind as the arrow flew wildly to the left and embedded itself in the handrail.

"Oh shit," Ezra muttered, and he buried his head in his hands.

"Whoops!" Horace said. "It's 'arder 'n it looks."

Whilst the crew fell about laughing, Ezra dashed off to find Aubrey who had declined the offer to take part. Half an hour later, Ezra could scarcely see any evidence of a repair. The arrow had a metal tip with no barbs, so Aubrey had simply cut the arrow flush with rail and applied a dab of varnish over the exposed end. Breathing a sigh of relief Ezra continued with the competition.

Horace decided that his first shot didn't count. He would have another try. Nobody argued although there was a low rumbling of discontent amongst Team Potts. Ezra tried once again to coach Horace, but he could see the bow was too small, it made the big man look cumbersome. Ezra held his breath as Horace released the arrow and watched gratefully as it continued unencumbered on its journey over the ocean, eventually plopping into the still water. Lost it may have been, but there were no more holes in the captain's ship.

Once they managed to retrieve the bow from Horace, the competition got under way. There was a great deal of cheering and cajoling, and some fine shooting. It began to emerge that Ezra and Wesley Marrick were the best marksmen. On his turn, Ezra had focused on a small knot slightly north-west of the bullseye, satisfying himself that he had not lost his ability to hit what he was aiming at. Wesley's arrows, Ezra noted, were constantly hitting the edge of the bullseye. He wondered if Wesley had adopted the same tactic of not wishing to expose his real capabilities.

They counted the two piles of sticks, and despite Horace Clunk's contribution, the scores were even. It was decided that the two best marksmen would have a shoot out to decide the overall winner. They would have three shots each, with the winner being the one with the most arrows nearest the centre of the target. By now, some more of the crew had assembled, along with Captain Dunsmoore, Cordelia and Joanna Marrick.

Wesley had the first shot. He stepped up and shot his arrow calmly into the bullseye, less than half an inch off dead centre. There was a big cheer. Wesley stepped away and bowed slightly to his audience. Ezra, meanwhile, had been undecided if he should reveal his true ability. He now knew his opponent had been disguising his own marksmanship. In response, Ezra's arrow thudded into the bullseye, leaving enough space to pass a feather between the tips. There was a gasp from the onlookers. Clunk and Potts went to the target and removed the arrows. There was nothing, they decided, to choose between them. The following round produced the same result.

Wesley Marrick stepped up to the rope and, with a sideways glance at his opponent, took three paces backwards. There was a low rumble from the expectant crowd. Wesley's arrow hit dead centre. Once again, the self-assured Marrick bowed to the audience, unable to resist raising a smile.

Ezra took a breath. He stepped up to the rope, and without ceremony, he turned and took ten paces away from the target. There was rumbling from the crowd. He looked at the arrow embedded in the centre of the target and then took half a step to his right. The crowd were now silent. Ezra raised the bow, pulled the string and released the arrow in a fluid movement. The metal point smashed into Wesley's arrow just above the tip, splitting it apart before embedding itself in the bullseye. There was a brief moment of silence and then a huge cheer as the skill of the shot became evident.

Acutely aware of the audience, Wesley Marrick went to Ezra and with all the good grace he could muster shook his hand. "Fine shooting, lad. Well done."

Ezra felt a moment of unease as his hand was constricted in Marrick's forceful grip, his truculent gaze at odds with his congratulatory remarks.

*

The ship remained becalmed for a further three days, during which time the archery competition became more and more popular. Horace Clunk, however, could not master the technique and was becoming increasingly frustrated.

\*

Horusni Anwar had been born into slavery. His grandparents originated from Africa, but were removed forcibly from their humble village, along with any able-bodied person – male or female, young or old – by bloodthirsty pirates who masqueraded as privateers acting with their country's permission. His father was an overseer on a sugar plantation in Jamaica, a white man whose physique and rugged appearance were generally enough to instil discipline. That did not stop him from brandishing the whip. The man was a vicious bully, employed by wealthy white people to ensure that the enslaved black people harvested the precious sugar. When he wasn't forcing himself on the vulnerable young ladies, he was happy to let them feel the sting of the lash. Horusni's mother died shortly after giving birth, and the boy grew up lonely and unloved, and although he wasn't the only mixed race child, he survived in a strange world where the colour of his skin defined his boundaries. Neither black nor white, he existed in a passage of indifference and cruelty, working twelve hours a day cutting sugar cane – until he could take no more.

At the end of another arduous shift, Horusni laid down his machete and walked away from the plantation. A few watched him go, but said nothing. It was an hour or so before the overseer, his father, realised he was missing. On horseback, he soon caught up with the weary slave. From the saddle, he lashed Horusni, leaving a livid welt across his neck and chest. The second one never landed. Horusni grabbed the whip and hauled the unsuspecting overseer from the horse. He crashed to the hard ground. Horusni knelt calmly on his chest, clasped his huge hands around his father's head, glared unblinkingly into his tormentor's black eyes, and then twisted with all his strength. There was a sickening crunch of bone and sinew. Death had been quick for Horusni's father. Without emotion, he picked up the huge corpse and dumped it in the brush by the side of the track. It landed in a heap, with the head at a grotesque angle, and on its face was a bewildered expression – the eyes wide open, seeing nothing. Horusni took the whip, smashed the ebony handle across his knee and tossed the remains into the undergrowth; it would not mark another slave.

The horse wandered to the side of the track and began munching the scorched grass. Flies ignored the grazing animal and swarmed around the corpse.

Horusni carried on walking. He walked through the moonlit night, expecting to be captured at any moment. He was now prepared to fight for his freedom; just walking alone along the lonely track, he felt free, and it felt good. It was the first time in nineteen years, and he would not surrender the feeling easily.

He walked under the cover of darkness for twenty days, sleeping during the day, eating berries and fruit, and finding water where he could until he came upon Port Antonio. It was the first human contact he'd had, and much to his surprise, nobody took any real notice of him. He wandered to the wharf, where a Portuguese schooner was being loaded with sugar for her return trip to Lisbon. Exhausted, Horusni sat himself on an upturned crate and watched the chaos around him. The first mate was shouting orders, trying desperately to meet his deadline. He spotted the dishevelled giant scrutinising the activity, seemingly entranced by the commotion. Gambling that he didn't speak Portuguese, the first mate spoke in broken English, offering Horusni the chance to join the crew. They were in desperate need of crew members. Horusni agreed.

It had been an arduous crossing. The crew had not been particularly welcoming, but Horusni worked hard and stayed out of trouble. The ship arrived in Lisbon and was due to return to Jamaica as soon as her holds were full. Horusni watched it sail into the distance; he now had to survive on the streets of Lisbon. His meagre wages diminished rapidly, and he began a life living rough on the dockside, grabbing jobs where he could and doing his best to avoid trouble. It was mostly the drunks staggering from the bawdy taverns who, in their stupor, overlooked his vast bulk and allowed their sodden brains to dictate their foolish actions. These interruptions had proved no more than irritating diversions for the big man, and although tired and hungry, he managed to stay safe.

Henry Dunsmoore had been walking along the wharf, having visited his agent, when he noticed a large mound partly covered with an old piece of sail cloth. Discerning a person, he leant over and shook the mound gently. In a flash, Horusni was bolt upright ready for action. Henry, at first shocked by the speed of his movements, showed no sign of fear; he could see a giant youth, his body undernourished, his clothes mere rags, and his dark, sunken eyes a melange of misery and determination. Seeing the youth's potential, Henry offered him a job.

During the subsequent voyage back to England, Horusni became Horace, and because he continually bashed his head on the ship's structure someone called him Clunk, and the name stuck.

Horusni Anwar, now Horace Clunk, would walk to hell and back for Henry Dunsmoore. And now he would do the same for his son.

*

Ezra decided he would make a bow especially for Horace.

Aubrey Darricot observed the young man as he went about the task of creating an oversized bow. Ezra unearthed a length of ash, which he selected from a bundle of oddments that Aubrey considered vital to have about the workshop – *because you never knew when such a noggin may come in handy* – and after a few minutes of examination, he began removing the bark with a knife. The slightly curved blade was eight inches long, very sharp and had a shaped handle made from hickory. The branch of ash was three inches in diameter, almost twice the thickness he would have used for a standard longbow. It was also a foot longer. Ezra guessed that Horace must have stood six feet ten inches tall, so he settled on six feet six inches for the bow's length.

Working on the bow rekindled memories of his father. Every stroke of the knife evoked a memory.

"You need to concentrate, young 'un, or you'll 'ave a finger off." Aubrey's remark refocused Ezra's efforts.

Over the next couple of days, between his duties, his lessons and the brutal sessions with Taylor Potts, Ezra finished the bow. The standard size arrows were useless, so he had managed to make half a dozen oversized missiles, which – Ezra couldn't help thinking – a person would do well to avoid in a confrontation.

When Ezra presented him with the bow, Horace took it and held it with a reverence that belied his huge frame. He saw the two letters engraved on its underside: "HC". He recognised their meaning. "Is it mine to keep?"

Ezra stared up into the dark eyes of Horace and saw the glint of moisture, enough to betray the big man's feelings momentarily. "I made it for you, Mister Clunk. I thought it would be easier for you... you know, being a bit more to your size... You know how Mistress Marrick made my clothes to fit..." Ezra made a motion with his hands, demonstrating his new clothes. "Well, I made the bow to fit you, Mister Clunk."

"Can't recall ever 'avin' a present afore this day." Horace fell silent for a moment. "Nope." He'd obviously been trying to remember such a moment in his life. "An' very touched I am, young Ezra Quicklock; very touched." He drew a giant forearm across his eyes.

"Perhaps we should put it to the test." Ezra was keen to see how the bow would react in its new owner's powerful grip.

"What is this?" The captain's voice sounded unusually harsh. "If I knew no better I'd swear this ship is being manned by roustabouts and tricksters. What of your duties? Perhaps you feel they are someone else's responsibility. Well, I can assure you that whilst you stand here discussing the merits of novelties and knick-knacks, there is a ship to sail. I expect to make landfall in a few days, and I'll have the crew prepared accordingly, Mister Clunk, if it's not too much trouble."

"Aye aye, sir." Horace knew it was a good moment to keep quiet.

Ezra, however, thought it best to explain the situation. "Beggin' your pardon, sir, I—"

Isaac knew he'd overreacted to the situation, but he was still in no mood to retreat. "I find it irksome in the extreme having to repeat myself, young Quicklock. When I issue an order, I expect an 'Aye aye, sir,' and then I expect the said order to be executed to the best of that person's ability. So, notwithstanding your recently acquired knowledge of the English language, I trust I have made myself understood."

"Aye aye, Captain… sir."

The test launch would have to wait.

# Chapter Seven

Prickle's voice, directed through cupped hands, wafted through the ship. "Land ahoy. Two points off the starboard bow."

When a man has been at sea for so many weeks, living together with others, sharing limited space, repeating tasks day after day, and deprived of the habitual deeds normally provided by towns and cities, it is no surprise that the sight of land will affect his good sense. A buzz of excitement reverberated around the ship.

"Aha, Mister Potts, if my calculations prove correct, this should be the entrance to the great river," Captain Dunsmoore said as he peered through the unwieldly looker. "The Amazon Basin, Mister Potts, doubtless a place of unsolved mystery and adventure."

Taylor Potts was at the helm. "Aye, sir, and I'll wager a place of skulduggery."

"If I were to wager against you, Mister Potts, I fear t'would be me who was minus a stipend." Isaac lowered the looker, narrowing his eyes at their destination. "We need to be about our business, Mister Potts." And as the words were spoken, he felt the weight of them.

Wesley Marrick approached the captain, interrupting his ruminations. "Isaac... Captain Dunsmoore, may I congratulate you on a fine piece of navigation? Absolutely first class, if I may say."

"Well, we need to be certain we're at the entrance to the basin, Wesley, but I must say that it looks promising. I confess that a few days in the doldrums can have an adverse effect on one's calculations, but it would appear I have been fortunate with my estimations," replied Isaac, trying to diminish the compliment. "This fellow Paz, does he wield much influence hereabouts? And this other fellow whom you say recommended Paz's services, what of him?"

Wesley Marrick realised it was now time to give Isaac a name. There was little to be done today if the captain had heard of him. "Spurt... Rothwell Spurt, that's the fellow." Wesley met Isaac's gaze to gauge his reaction.

"Can't say I've heard the name, although I'm a little surprised you managed to forget such a moniker... Rothwell Spurt." Isaac said the name again.

Wesley shifted his weight, but kept eye contact with the captain. "I'll be damned if I didn't remember it during the voyage and before I'd a chance to tell you; well, the blasted name went right from my head."

"I'm sure the name Rothwell Spurt will no longer elude you, Wesley, as you now have Mister Potts memory to rely on, as well as my own." There was more than a little irony in Isaac's tone.

Taylor Potts stared implacably at his destination. "Aye aye, sir. That you will."

\*

Rothwell Spurt was commonly known as Roth, and sometimes Spurty, but never within earshot. He was not particularly tall, but what he lacked in height he made up for in brawn. His shoulders were broad, and his arms, on which a gallery of images was tattooed indelibly, were heavily muscled. He was, as Wesley Marrick had observed, a surly-looking fellow. His features revealed years of turmoil and hard living, with scars and pockmarks etched into leathery flesh. Above all else, he was a vicious tyrant. He took what he wanted, trusted nobody and thought very little of killing anyone who interfered with his plans. He saw himself as a businessman, a man of the sea, and a man who could negotiate a deal with any man, regardless of rank or stature. Captain of his own ship, *Angerona*, he was – simply put – a pirate.

For many years, he had been a scourge along the east coast of England, raiding vulnerable merchant ships, and causing mayhem and misery when ashore. Three months before *Rebecca-Ann's* maiden voyage, Roth and half a dozen of his men were drinking in a bawdy tavern in the port of White Bay. Roth was playing cards with a tall, well-dressed stranger – a dandy in his eyes. For him, the rules were simple. He would never lose. If the dandy walked out of the tavern with his purse bulging, courtesy of Rothwell Spurt, he would follow the man out, slit his throat and take his money back, plus anything else worth taking.

That night, Wesley Marrick (the stranger in question) felt the sweat cooling as it trickled gently down the back of his neck. He didn't usually find himself on the losing end of a hand of cards, especially when playing ignorant braggarts such as the one sitting before him. Wesley had drunk too much, mistaking his opponent for a dim-witted sailor, recently paid after months of hard toil. Feeling confident that he could yet get the upper hand, Wesley offered his opponent his marker, which promised to pay should he suffer the misfortune of further losses. With his purse empty, Wesley continued his losing streak and finally admitted defeat. He was in debt to the man opposite for twenty pounds, which was nearly a year's wages for a local tradesman.

"Well, Mister…" Rothwell paused for effect as he searched his memory for the man's name. "Marrick, what say you to this predicament?"

"My marker is good, sir. I can assure you as a gentleman that you have my word the debt will be paid at my earliest convenience." Wesley regretted the words the moment they were delivered.

"Gentleman, you say. You dress as such and you talk as such, but here you are – all up shit creek without an oar – hoping I'll wait until your earliest convenience for my recompense. What say you to that, my dandy friend?"

"Sir, I must protest." Wesley bitterly regretted his string of mistakes that evening. He'd given his real name, he had drunk too much and he had totally underestimated the man sitting before him, but he pressed on. "Surely, in your hand you have a perfectly sound arrangement between two gentlemen, and if it's all the same to you, sir, I'll bid you goodnight." Wesley began to raise himself from the chair, and as he did, so he felt the unmistakeable caress of cold steel on his jugular. Two of Rothwell's men stood behind him.

"Oh, so we're both gentlemen now. I feel honoured. Touched I am." Rothwell patted his heart as he spoke. "Allow me to enlighten you on one or two issues that appear to have somehow evaded whatever good sense you may have had when you swanked into this fine establishment tonight. See, I can make the pretence of a gentleman, but, Mister Marrick, let us both be honest." Rothwell hesitated. "Do I look like a gentleman? Ah, no need to answer; the question was… Damn and blast, what's the word? It's lost to me. Damn and blast!"

Unsure if Spurt's momentary memory lapse was intentional, Wesley answered, despite his misgivings. "Rhetorical."

"There we are, you see, men. A fine, educated fellow who seems to have got himself into a pretty pickle. Anyway, where was I…? Ah yes, yes. Tomorrow, you see, Mister Marrick, we sail for Belém, which – as I'm sure you know – is well appointed in the Americas, so your offer of payment at your earliest convenience is totally irrelevant. So, let me sum up your situation as succinctly as possible, Mister Muck." Rothwell paused for effect. "You, sir, are fucked!"

Wesley knew his immediate future lay in his ability to stay calm and talk his way out of what he now knew to be a serious threat to his well-being. When Rothwell said the word "Belém", Wesley immediately began formulating a plan to save himself. "Belém, you say, Mister Rothwell? Well, by the strangest of circumstances, I too am heading for the very same destination."

"Do not play games with me, Marrick, or I'll have you filleted where you sit and feed your guts to the gulls."

Wesley felt the pressure of the blade intensify, but he pressed on. "Three months from now, I set sail on a new-built vessel from Milford in the south of England. I sail with my wife, she being the daughter of the duke. We are to take over a sugar plantation ten miles overland from Belém. Perhaps, on this account, there is something I could do to… as it were… un-fuck myself."

Until this point, Rothwell Spurt had been toying with his victim. He knew well enough that Marrick had no intention of settling his debt. This, however, could be an opportunity to make some serious profit, so his personal greed overcame the pleasure he'd have taken as he watched the dandy squirming and moaning whilst bleeding to death on the cold, hard cobbles of White Bay.

"It would seem that, my dapper friend, your arrangements could yet prove a fortuitous coincidence. All you need do to reinstate your un-fucked existence is to recommend to whomever oversees the operation that, on arrival in Belém, they contact a man by the name of Garcia Paz. This person will provide your captain with a pilot to negotiate a channel into the port, and to facilitate the offloading and reloading of cargo. He will almost certainly know of the plantation and will offer any assistance you may require in that regard. It sounds simple enough, so I daresay even a stuck-up prick such as you should be able to manage. Have I been explicit enough for you, Mister Marrick? Has my discourse penetrated your fuggy mind? Because let me assure you, you'll be the first person to walk away from me still owing twenty pounds, so know this: your debt will increase by twenty pounds every month it remains unpaid."

Wesley gasped, but he wasn't afforded the opportunity to respond. Rothwell struck him with the back of his hand with such force and speed that Wesley crashed to the ale-sodden floor. Blood oozed from his nose and mouth.

"Are the arrangements to your satisfaction, Mister Marrick?" enquired Rothwell.

Wesley staggered to his feet and managed to position himself back on the chair. "Absolutely, Mister Rothwell. I see no complications." He let the blood run freely as he spoke. He was now fully focused. "Just one question. How do we make contact with Mister Paz?

"Send a couple of men ashore to make enquiries. He's not a difficult man to find." Rothwell could see that, although Marrick's demeanour was everything he detested in a man, he'd taken the blow well, and when the alcohol dissipated, he would be plotting a way to secure an advantage. "So, Mister Marrick, I eagerly await our next meeting. Let us imagine ourselves business partners, shall we not? Eh, what say you?" Before Wesley could respond, Rothwell continued, "Although I must say 'tis a lopsided affair that, when this fine partnership resumes beneath the warm sun in a foreign land, one should be in debt to the other for what..." He broke off, making a show of calculating with his fingers "A hundred and twenty pounds or so. We can round up the shillings nearer the time, eh. Splendid!"

Wesley had not expected the second blow; indeed, he had not seen the first one coming. It struck the same spot as before, with enormous force. The chair followed him to the floor, and before he could react, he felt the sole of Rothwell Spurt's fine leather boot pressing down on his temple, forcing the side of his face to contort against the filthy floor.

"Remember this, Mister Muck. Your status of un-fuckedness is dependent on carrying out these simple orders, and whilst you may not think so at this present moment, you have been most fortunate." Rothwell released the pressure.

Wesley rolled over and watched as his tormentor left the tavern, followed by a horde of pitiless men all dedicated to serving their captain, Rothwell Spurt.

*

Wesley Marrick had been ill at ease for many days after his confrontation with Rothwell Spurt. As the months passed, however, he began to realise there was little he could do to avoid another confrontation with the *vile pig* who had treated him so badly, apart from telling Cordelia that he wasn't going to sail. The thought had occurred to him to leave his wife. But where would he go? How would he live? He pondered the questions he'd posed to himself. The answers were disagreeable.

He was damned if he would walk away penniless from a loveless marriage. He had invested too many years with Cordelia to allow this opportunity to slip through his fingers. Thousands of miles from home, and without the influence of her father, she would bend to his will, one way or another. All he had to do was stay away from the demon drink and hold his nerve.

Wesley did not love his wife. He thought less of his only daughter. He had charmed Cordelia and had spent the whole of their married life trying to extract money from the family purse, with limited success. There had been a few occasions when Cordelia had asked her father for money to assist her husband. Lionel Hartshorne never pushed for a reason. He knew his daughter would not ask without good cause. Between them, they set a monthly allowance for Wesley of five pounds, which Wesley had said was derisory and mean. Cordelia had argued that any amount of money would instantly burn a hole in the pocket of his best tunic. The ensuing arguments were fierce, but the stint was set.

Cordelia and her father had endured intense discussions regarding the new venture. Finally, they decided that a new challenge – the responsibility of managing a business – could be the making of him. Lionel, though, had insisted that if she were unhappy and couldn't see a way to make the venture work, she should seek the soonest passage to England and leave the plantation to her feckless husband. Cordelia loved her father, and she knew he had been more than tolerant of Wesley's truculent behaviour. This was their chance, she believed, to salvage something from her ill-conceived marriage.

*

Isaac had considered dropping anchor off the western tip of Mosqueiro Island, but he decided to venture further into the basin. Under short sail, *Rebecca-Ann* eased through the calm water around her bow, creating a curl of foam. Will Nye shouted depth readings. George Burdock would once again holler through cupped hands if the water changed colour, signifying variations in depth. There were no indications on his own charts of shallow water in the basin, but Isaac would take no unnecessary risks. Running the ship aground would be a disaster.

Potts and the captain were alone at the helm. Everyone without an immediate duty gathered at the handrails, enthralled with the landscape. A harpy eagle drifted on the invisible thermal currents, with her black-and-white plumage a stark contrast against the ardent sky.

"Captain, if I may, sir?" Potts had waited for Wesley Marrick to leave before he spoke.

Isaac inclined his head, silently inviting Potts to continue.

"Rothwell Spurt, sir, is a murdering bastard," declared Potts.

"Say it how it is, Mister Potts; don't mince your words on my account," replied the captain.

"Beggin' your pardon, sir."

"No, no, Mister Potts. Out with it. Tell me what you know of the man."

Taylor Potts went on to describe how, at the end of their last voyage, he made his way back to Lowestoft to visit family. On the captain's advice, he would have a month or so before *Rebecca-Ann* was due to launch, which was more than enough time to catch up with his ageing parents and, hopefully, meet with his younger sister and her children.

Potts enjoyed a drink along with the next man, but he rarely got drunk and never squandered his money. Consequently, whenever he was able to visit, he would always top up the family's coffers before departing for his next voyage.

During his stay, the talk was of a pirate ship – *Angerona* – captained by a vicious tyrant called Rothwell Spurt. According to local gossip, the Royal Navy had commissioned a frigate to patrol the east coast in a bid to put an end to his marauding. The merchantmen were up in arms and had, apparently, petitioned the Admiralty. Nobody could verify the account, although it mattered little. There was a frigate. And there was Rothwell Spurt.

\*

*Angerona*, having had her cargo holds filled with stolen merchandise, would slip across the channel, where Rothwell would exchange what he could for gold or silver; that was his preference, though he would sometimes accept currency, and sometimes he simply needed supplies to restock the ship. Along the stretch of European coast encompassing the Netherlands, Belgium and France, he had particular contacts. This also had the effect of reducing his profile along the east coast of England. The Royal Navy had little intelligence on his behaviour, but Rothwell Spurt knew you could only rob the same people for so long. Eventually, they would react.

His last visit to White Bay had been a risk. It was time for new exploits. He'd concluded his business with an agent who had given him all the details required to fulfil his next mission. He had heard that the transportation of black Africans stolen from their homes and sold in South America, could make a man huge sums, paid in silver. After a profitable night at the card table (where he had meted out a lesson to some pompous dandy and let him walk free, owing a sum of twenty pounds), he slipped out of White Bay with an armful of charts – his destination being the west coast of Africa, where he could ransack any number of villages and imprison the inhabitants – and a contact in the port of Belém: Garcia Paz.

As *Angerona* slipped through the cold, grey waters of the North Sea, her dull-grey hull barely visible against the murky dawn, Rothwell Spurt wondered if perhaps he had been lenient with Marrick and so had shown weakness in front of his men. No, it was a business decision. If Marrick introduced the captain to Garcia Paz, all well and good. If not, well, nothing lost. Except twenty pounds. Plus interest. He put the thought from his head. He never really expected the *slimy shit* to uphold his side of the bargain. Chances were he'd never clap eyes on him again. Still, if he did…

\*

"So, they've not come close to capturing him?" Before Potts could reply, the captain continued, "I'm surprised we hadn't any warnings of his exploits."

"I suppose if, like they say, he has concentrated his pillagin' along the east coast, it would be a while afore the news filtered along the south coast. People – it strikes me – tend to worry about their own problems; they won't be giving much of a flying fart – beggin' your pardon, sir – about anybody else."

"Flying fart or no flying fart, Mister Potts, it would seem we have a problem." Isaac felt a knot tighten in his gut. They were vulnerable. He instructed Potts to steer a point to port and yelled for Horace Clunk. Isaac decided to drop anchor at the next island. Marajó was marked on his chart. He needed a strategy. The problem was that he had no idea what it should be. What he now knew was that Rothwell Spurt was no agent.

"*Stay sharp, Prickle,*" Horace Clunk yelled.

"Aye aye, Mister Clunk," Prickle concurred.

"Depth please, Mister Nye," requested Clunk.

"Twenty-two fathoms, sir," Nye confirmed.

"Keep me posted, Mister Nye."

"Aye aye, sir."

"See that outcrop of rock at the tip of the island, Mister Potts?" Isaac pointed to a rugged cliff that towered a hundred feet above the rest of the island. "If there's enough water, I want you to put her two hundred paces offshore in the lee of that rock."

Potts could see exactly where the ship needed to be. The cliff jutting out would afford cover from the port of Belém, and the bay looked negotiable enough. They would be vulnerable to the rear, but Potts recognised the advantage, all things considered.

The crew did their job and *Rebecca-Ann* soon came to rest with twelve fathoms of clear water beneath her. She adjusted herself to the anchorage, and her tether relaxed.

Happy with her position, Isaac had Mister Clunk gather the men. He needed to alert them to the situation. As he stood before them, he noticed Wesley Marrick was absent. He would be the captain's next problem.

"Men, it appears we may have sailed into a nest of vipers." Isaac waited for the hubbub to calm down before he continued, "Through information gleaned from our passenger, Mister Marrick, there is a strong possibility that a pirate ship, captained by a certain Rothwell Spurt, is active in and around the port of Belém. He leads a gang of cut-throat mercenaries who think little of killing to meet their own ends. We need to be vigilant, men. Perform your duties. Our survival may well depend upon it." Isaac silenced the crew's mutterings.

"I have decided to lie at anchor to see if we can't gather some intelligence as to the whereabouts of these ruffians. Let us not allow the idyllic surroundings to dull our senses. Should the moment arise, we need to be ready."

Isaac knew that if it came to a head-on battle, they would be severely outnumbered, many of them would be slaughtered and the ship lost. Nevertheless, he had Horace Clunk break out the weapons. Each man now had a cutlass hanging from his waist, except for Horace, who carried a massive forester's axe. Isaac generally discouraged the carrying of weapons, because he knew that if a fight erupted, he was more likely to lose a crew member if weapons were involved; however, most of the men carried knives because they were an essential tool in their everyday duties. There were a dozen muskets in the armoury, which were made available to any crew member, but the sailors found them unwieldly and cumbersome, albeit they were fully aware of the weapon's lethal capabilities.

Isaac carried a fine sword that had been passed down to him by his father, and a pair of flintlock pistols that had been a gift from Edward Buckingham. Buckled to his left leg, just above his ankle, a tooled leather sheath held a knife with a long, slender blade, its handle hewn from an unfamiliar, exotic wood.

*Rebecca-Ann* was equipped with four twelve-pound cannons, which were cast in bronze. This had been a contentious issue during the design and build. Edward Buckingham had originally commissioned half a dozen six-pounders in traditional (and much less expensive) cast iron. Isaac had finally won the argument, convincing the owner that the saving in weight and space would eventually pay dividends. The young captain wanted the ship to be nimble, responsive and fast. He wanted it to be sailed with the minimum of crew whilst maintaining a healthy payload. He wanted a ship that he and his crew would be proud to serve aboard. With Edward Buckingham fully invested in his ideas, Isaac – having sailed her across the great ocean – was convinced *Rebecca-Ann* was one of the finest merchant ships afloat. All he had to do now was to make sure he didn't lose her to a gang of ruthless thugs.

Isaac dispatched Clunk, Finn, Potts, Nye and Monk to the island. They were to make a rudimentary search for a freshwater supply and check if there were any signs of human habitation. The predominant reason for the mission, however, was to see if there was a way to climb the rock. This, Isaac reasoned, should give them a clear sight to the port of Belém. Perhaps *Angerona* was at anchor less than a few miles away.

Empty hogsheads were stowed aboard the gig, which bobbed gently in the glimmering water.

"Mister Clunk," Isaac called to Horace, "perhaps now would be a good moment to assess the merits of your latest acquisition."

Horace cocked his head to one side, a quizzical expression his only response.

"Your bow, Mister Clunk; take your bow and a handful of those monstrous arrows and see if you can't hit something by design," commanded the captain.

"Ah, aye aye, sir."

Captain Dunsmoore watched his men beach the small craft, and a sense of trepidation crept up his spine. Now he needed to find Marrick.

Isaac could see Cordelia and Joanna at the port quarter, their demeanour signifying their fascination with the surroundings. He made his way to their cabin and tapped on the door. Knowing that the ladies were on deck, he opened the door and stepped in. Marrick was perched on the edge of his cot, swilling ruby port from the bottle.

"Ah, Isaac, my friend, come, come; join me in a swallow of this fine port." Wesley attempted to stand without success. He fell back on the cot, spilling the last dregs of the port.

The young captain contained his anger. "What is your connection with Rothwell Spurt?"

"Ha, dirty, squirty Spurty. The ruffian. The next time I clap eyes on him, I shall take one of my fine pistols and shh-hoot the man right in his fat, ugly head. How would that be, my fine captain friend?"

"Twice since I stepped into your cabin, you have made reference to me as your friend. Yet there you loll, a treacherous, deceitful drunk who is incapable of understanding the true meaning of friendship – a bond between us that has meant nothing to you. You have duped me – to what ends I cannot fathom – but as God is my witness, I will have the truth, Marrick. If you have endangered this ship for your own ends, I am empowered to dispense suitable punishment." Isaac felt his anger rising. "And be under no illusion, I have the wherewithal, the inclination and – should there be any ambiguity – a stout length of rope that's ideal for the purpose."

Wesley tried desperately to make a defence.

Isaac silenced his wittering. "As the world and his dog are abundantly aware, to enter a meaningful discourse with a drunk is a fool's errand. I will have you sober and then we will continue until I am satisfied I have discovered the truth behind your guile." He turned to leave.

Cordelia stood in the doorway.

"Cord— madam," Isaac corrected himself, "my apologies for any offence given, but we find ourselves in a difficult situation that, in all probability, has arisen from your husband's indiscretions. I would beseech you, madam, if you have information – anything – that would help unravel this disagreeable situation, please tell me now." Isaac thought he had kept his tone formal.

Cordelia baulked at the captain's menacing voice. She raised her hands covering the look of horror on her face. She had seen her husband slumped on his cot, dribbling at the mouth, with ruby port staining his fine blouse and breeches. "My God," she muttered under her breath.

Isaac ushered her from the cabin, closed the door and locked it from the outside. Cordelia was shaking, and tears stung her eyes. She knew this would be the end of their fateful marriage. Their fresh start was a shattered dream. What a fool she had been.

*

A scant few minutes later, alone in the captain's cabin, Cordelia gave Isaac a candid narrative of their turbulent marriage. She left little untold. However, after some gentle questioning from Isaac, it was clear she knew nothing of this Rothwell Spurt or of her husband's motives for his now obvious pretence. Cordelia had convinced herself that, having survived all these weeks at sea without overindulging in alcohol, Wesley would go on to be the husband she had longed for.

*Damn him to hell,* she thought.

As that foreboding implication permeated her mind, a muffled blast stunned her momentarily. Isaac jumped to his feet, and after bidding Cordelia to remain in his cabin, he hurried to the Marrick's quarters. A sense of dread engulfed him.

\*

Wesley Marrick had somehow managed to load one of his pistols. He sat on the edge of his cot, steadying himself with his free hand. He tipped his head back and wedged the barrel into the roof of his mouth.

*Fuck 'em all,* he thought, *I shall un-fuck myself.*

He squeezed the trigger.

\*

A cloud of grey smoke helped to disguise the horror that confronted Isaac Dunsmoore. A plume of red covered the wood panelling, with particles of human tissue clinging to the warm blood. Wesley Marrick's disfigured head slumped forwards. His arms flopped by his side, with one hand still gripping a pistol. All his misgivings had now transferred to the living.

Isaac slammed the door and put his back to it. "God's breath," he cursed.

Two crew members came rushing down, having heard the shot. Cordelia, ignoring the captain's order, tried to enter the cabin.

Isaac physically restrained her. "Cordelia, please." He then ushered her back to his cabin.

He ordered one man to guard the door and sent the other to fetch Seddon and Elwyn Sakkit, who soon arrived on the scene.

Isaac returned to his cabin.

"Tell me, Isaac, has he...?" Cordelia stopped short of asking the question in full.

Isaac assented with a nod and a blink. At that moment, he had no words. He was angry with himself. He'd meant to search for the pistols and remove them.

Unanswered questions, sedition, culpability, resentment, sorrow and bitterness swirled around his head; Isaac couldn't arrange his thoughts. They were bombarding him. He wanted to yell at Cordelia. Instead, he embraced her. Somehow it felt right. He asked her to be strong, for her own sake and for her daughter's. It was a tender moment amongst the chaos.

Joanna joined her mother in the captain's quarters. They wept in each other's arms. They were badly shaken, but they were not broken. Even the death of an uncaring, selfish husband and an indifferent father was – under the circumstances – horrific. Cordelia had felt comfortable with Isaac Dunsmoore's arms holding her close. He would keep her safe. He would care for them both, of that she felt sure.

*

Seddon had witnessed many a grizzly scene during his thirty or so years at sea. Nonetheless, when he entered the cabin, the iron scent of fresh blood mingled with cordite turned his gut.

Elwyn Sakkit, by contrast, remained unperturbed. "Ne'er 'ad 'im pegged for a muzzle muncher," Sakkit declared without remorse. "Should we 'ave them boots off 'im? Don't seem right to sew a man up in 'is best boots."

"Remove 'em if you must, Sakkit; do I look like I care?" asked Seddon.

With the boots removed, they wrapped Marrick's corpse in the blood-soaked bed clothes. They sent for sail cloth and yarn, and then sewed him into his shroud once they had received it.

"Well, wherever 'e's goin' 'e's gonna arrive wrapped in best sail cloth," Sakkit declared.

"Aye, an' minus 'is best boots."

\*

Isaac stepped onto the deck and – without contemplation – took deep breaths, devouring the fresh air. He stared at the beach and could only see one man. *Monk,* he thought, *guarding the boat.* He needed them back here to transport the corpse to the island. They could not dispose of Marrick's body in the sea whilst at anchor, as it would attract all sorts of carnivorous *sea monsters* to the ship. He was reluctant to dispatch another launch with a burial party; it would leave *Rebecca-Ann* shorthanded if they were forced into action. Isaac needed to attract their attention without unduly alerting the continent to their presence. He recalled a request that had been made to him whilst they were becalmed.

He was about to yell for him when Ezra appeared, carrying two buckets of sea water. He was headed for the cabin.

"Young Quicklock." The captain beckoned him over to the rail where he pointed to the island. "Two hundred yards or so to the beach; what say you, Master Quicklock?"

"I reckon, sir. Give or take," Ezra confirmed.

"Still in the mood for a paddle, lad? Because I need you to fetch the men back off the island with the minimum of fuss. I'll have you lowered over the—"

Before Isaac could finish, Ezra had shed his newly issued cutlass, relinquished the buckets and, placing his palms flat on the rail, he sprang atop it. "No need for that, sir." Ezra balanced on the narrow handrail, slightly bent his knees and was about to launch himself into the cool, blue waters of the Amazon Basin when a thought struck him. He had his best shirt on. His only shirt. Balancing on his narrow perch, he slipped the precious garment over his head, folded it twice and with a half turn he passed it to the speechless captain.

Dumbfounded, Isaac watched as the young man pierced the surface with scarcely a splash. Then he watched. And waited.

Ezra swam deeper and deeper, and then struck out towards the island. Multi-coloured fish darted this way and that, seemingly unperturbed by his presence. He swam beneath the surface until he thought his lungs would burst.

Isaac watched in earnest as, fifty yards from the hull, a mop of dark hair broke the surface. He breathed a sigh of relief. The young man continued his mission, powering his way towards the beach. The bemused captain wondered if there had ever been an order expedited in such short order and with such enthusiasm. He doubted it. Isaac folded the shirt once more and slid it inside his own tunic, safe and sound.

# Chapter Eight

Rothwell Spurt sat opposite a man who made him feel slightly uncomfortable. There was, he supposed, a first time for everything.

Garcia Paz stood the better part of six feet tall. He was lean and immaculately attired. Approaching his fortieth year, his charcoal hair had a hint of silver at the temples. The mirror that hung above his terracotta basin was of high quality and ripple free. It reflected the truth: a visage difficult to consider unattractive. Eyebrows that arched over dark eyes; a long, slender nose that could have dominated, but didn't; a mouth perfectly framed with a charcoal goatee; and a robust jawline that was accentuated when in profile.

The sumptuous environment wasn't necessarily to Rothwell's taste. Conceivably, he could live with it. Or even get to like it. The Portuguese man who was now replenishing his weighty crystal glass with the finest white port, however, would undoubtedly be a man to heed.

"A toast, Senor Spurt." Garcia Paz held up his glass. "To the fine haul of negroes."

Rothwell raised his glass, and the chinking sound of fine crystal diffused into the cavernous space.

*

Five years ago, where they now sat sipping their fine white port there stood a wooden fort guarding the entrance to the port of Belém. The governor general of the state of Para, Raphael Mendoza, had commissioned the building of a somewhat palatial fortress to replace the old wooden structure. He never got to live in it. His instructions were to move south to Sao Luis, where he would oversee Portugal's commercial interests. Garcia Paz became the resident of the splendid fortress, along with gaining the task of providing funds for the expanding empire, which would be transferred to Mendoza, who would redistribute it in turn as he saw fit. At least three times a year, a flotilla of ships would set sail for Lisbon, transporting vast amounts of silver. One ship would carry the precious cargo, and the rest were to make sure it reached its destination.

Raphael Mendoza issued Garcia Paz a letter of authority that enabled him to act on behalf of the country of Portugal. There were no boundaries. There was only one rule: two-thirds of all he plundered would come to Mendoza. And that rule was set in stone. A commandment.

With his piratical activities legalised, Garcia Paz had set about his task with great exuberance – and great success.

*

Paz continued, speaking impeccable English, "You see, Senor Roth, if I may call you so?"

Rothwell nodded his assent.

"The problem I have is that I have established a precedent with the governor general, and he is not a man to disappoint, as I'm sure you can imagine. So, I find myself constantly having to… What's the term?" Paz paused for a moment as if deep in thought.

Rothwell thought, *Having to be more and more greedy,* but he said, "Raise the bar."

"Exactly. Thank you. To alleviate these pressures, we need to mine more silver, and to do that we need more negroes. Fit, strong black men and women whom we can put to work. We also need them for the plantations and to trade. They are a commodity, Senor Roth. They are the basis of our success, and the core of our operation. This is why I have paid you so handsomely for your services, and why I am willing to do so again and again."

"I am a man who is not averse to a handsome payment, Senor Paz, but if I had to acquire these savages through the normal methods, the payment would not be so handsome. It's difficult work, as I'm sure you can imagine."

Garcia Paz was taken aback by the man's response. His demeanour, however, revealed nothing. He began to realise that the ignorant ruffian before him should not be underestimated. "Indeed, Senor Roth, I must agree. If you find yourself having to barter at a slave castle, then I see no reason why our negotiations may not be adjusted to suit the situation. Although I think the present arrangement would be of superior benefit to us both."

"To be clear then, if I were to return with a cargo of negroes that I have paid for, the basis of our negotiations will revolve around that figure. I have no wish to become the captain of a merchant ship being paid to transport merchandise across the Atlantic. A share of the profits, Senor Paz, is my incentive." Rothwell placed his empty glass on the table and, using his index finger, gave it the merest of nudges towards his host.

There followed a moment of silence.

Paz picked up the decanter of port and replenished both glasses. "We are of one mind, Senor Roth. A toast to the share of the profits."

"The profits." Rothwell took a sip. It was indeed a fine port. "I wanted to mention to you, Senor Paz, an incident that occurred back in England that may be of some mutual benefit."

"Please, Senor Roth, enlighten me."

Rothwell went on to describe the incident in the White Bay tavern, omitting certain irrelevant details. "So you see, I have already instructed the feckless dandy to persuade the captain to report to your good self on arrival, whereupon you would facilitate the smooth running of their business here in Belém."

"Ah, I'm afraid I am a little ahead of you, Senor Roth. You must understand that there is very little that goes on here of which I am unaware. I am in charge here, senor, and it is my business to know the comings and goings. I have eyes and ears to support me, Senor Roth; not only here but also in the place you speak of."

It was now Rothwell's demeanour that remained inscrutable. He thought he'd stumbled on a scheme to earn some easy money. The man sitting opposite, despite living thousands of miles from White Bay, was more than one step ahead. The stuck-up shit who owed him money would not be walking away from their next encounter.

Paz continued, "I am expecting *Rebecca-Ann* any day now; in fact, I'm surprised she hasn't arrived already. Still I'm sure she'll be along shortly. I will tell you, Senor Roth, that she is commanded by a young and apparently very competent captain by the name of Isaac Dunsmoore. On board are the Marricks, who believe they are the new owners of a sugar plantation, which is probably no more than ten of your English miles from where we sit. Before I continue, I would remind you that what I tell you in this room is confidential. I am not a great admirer of tittle-tattle; I believe that is the expression."

Rothwell said nothing. He acquiesced with the merest tilt of his head.

Paz pressed on, "Ernest Blink, the agent in London who acts on occasion for both Edward Buckingham – who commissioned the construction of *Rebecca-Ann*, and as I understand it, sought no shareholders or investors with whom to share the risk – and Lionel Hartshorne (a wealthy land owner), facilitated the sale of the sugar plantation. He also furnished both men with the details of a reliable contact who would ensure the smooth running of their business here in Belém. You see, Senor Roth, this is the third time I have sold the plantation."

Rothwell said nothing.

Paz could see he had his full attention. "Things became a little more complicated when Blink informed me that Hartshorne was sending his son-in-law – the stuck-up shit, I think you called him – and his wife and daughter to take over the plantation. However, Senor Roth, the presence of the wife and daughter should prove advantageous."

Rothwell interjected. "I think my men, as depraved

as they are, would relish taking turns with the wife and daughter whilst the popinjay looks on."

"No, no, Senor Roth. I'm afraid I can't allow that. Perhaps at some point in the future. Be my guest with the… What is he now? A popinjay? Do with him as you see fit."

"You would deny me the pleasure of watching him squirm as my men took—"

"Senor Roth, if I may say, your eye is wandering from the prize. Allow me to explain."

Rothwell Spurt, with his glass once again replenished, leant back in his chair and, with the utmost effort, allowed himself to be managed. It was one of those days. There was a first time for everything.

Paz continued once more, "The ship is on its maiden voyage, and if the information received from Ernest Blink is to be believed, and I see no reason why the intelligence should be in any way…" Paz took a moment, apparently searching for a word.

Rothwell thought, *Perhaps "bullshit" would fit.* He said nothing.

"Compromised. He has proved himself a very worthwhile informant, if somewhat expensive. Still, Senor Roth, what price good information, eh? Anyway, where was I? Ah yes, the ship. *Rebecca-Ann* is newly built, and the young captain has – in association with the shipbuilder – incorporated some new ideas. She has an excellent payload, she is nimble, she is quick and she can be managed by a crew of twenty, providing the majority are worthy seamen, of course.

"This, Senor Roth, is my proposal."

# Chapter Nine

The original landing party found themselves back on dry land, accompanied by Captain Dunsmoore, the two ladies, Ezra Quicklock and a corpse.

Joanna Marrick sat huddled close to her mother, and her gaze disengaged from her dead father's shroud, which was slumped in the gunwales of the small gig, and instead moved to the shirtless young lad whose damp hair clung to his neck and shoulders.

Ezra and Taylor Potts hopped into the shallow water and hauled the boat onto the wet sand. Unsure of the etiquette, Ezra stuck out a hand to assist Joanna from the boat.

She dismissed his hand with a contemptuous motion. "I'm sure I am more than capable of disembarking such a diminutive vessel."

"Beggin' your pardon, miss." Feeling a little awkward, Ezra withdrew his hand.

Joanna placed one foot on the prow, promptly slipped, and in the most ungainly fashion, fell onto the damp seashore.

Suppressing a smirk, Ezra kept his hands by his side.

"Well, don't just stand there looking gormless; help me up," ordered Joanna.

"You're the one sprawled on the beach all skew-whiff and you're calling me gormless." He made no effort to help.

Foamy, white water washed over the sand, soaking the forlorn girl's dress.

Joanna tried to stand. Her foot sunk in the wet sand. She twisted sideways and collapsed onto the shore once more. She heard her mother's voice saying, "Joanna, this is no time for your nonsense. Get up at once, you silly girl."

Before she could respond, Ezra scooped her up and trudged through the soft sand, finally setting her down on the remains of a fallen tree. She tried desperately to protest, but the words wouldn't come.

After a quick recce, they found a suitable burial site that was perhaps a hundred yards from the beach. It was a small clearing amongst the thick vegetation. A suitable grave was swiftly dug in the soft ground. Horace Clunk and Ezra lowered the shrouded corpse into the hole as carefully as possible. Cordelia took a handful of loose sand and tossed it onto the body. She linked arms with her damp and bedraggled daughter, and they turned their backs on the scene before them and walked slowly towards the beach. There were no prayers, no eulogy and no marker – merely a hole in the cool ground.

Nye and Monk continued filling the grave.

Ezra walked with the captain. "Captain," Ezra said with his head bowed, "if that was my pa in the hole…"

"I know, lad. I know." Isaac paused for a moment. "Some relationships are not what they seem; it's difficult to understand, I know, but there it is, lad. Here, take this." He slipped the shirt from inside his own tunic and passed it to Ezra. "Mister Clunk."

"Aye, sir," Horace replied.

"Take Mister Potts and young Quicklock, and see if you can't get yourselves to the top of that rock. I'll send the gig back for you. Keep your wits about you, Mister Clunk."

"Aye aye, sir."

The three men disappeared into the vegetation, hacking their way towards the summit. It proved an arduous task; although they were partially shaded by the leafy canopy, the sun sapped their energy and the mosquitos perpetually besieged the space around them before attacking their chosen patch of skin. Nonetheless, they made good progress, and a couple of hours later, they found themselves on a plateau high above the ocean.

The vegetation now consisted of rock-hugging plants and a handful of wizened trees that were stunted and bowed by the persistent breeze. Free from the bombarding mosquitos and refreshed by the cooling wind, they took a moment to survey their surroundings. *Rebecca-Ann* – reduced to the size of the captain's gig and swaying gently at her mooring, with the afternoon sun rebounding off her royal-blue livery – lay to the north. To the south lay the port of Belém: a stone fortress imposing itself on the scenery, even at a distance. There were other ships lolling at anchor. None of this told them very much.

They made their way across the plateau, maybe sixty to seventy paces, moving silently. Below them a ship, very much in the same way as *Rebecca-Ann*, was swaying gently at her mooring, her dull-grey livery, however, seemingly absorbed the sun's rays. There were men scattered around on the beach, sprawled on the sand, sitting in small groups and not performing any particular tasks. One small boat had been hauled on to the sand and now sat tilted to port in an ungainly fashion.

Ezra remembered when he first began to meet the crew of *Rebecca-Ann*. They put him on edge and made him wary. As he scanned the scene below him, he began to realise the seriousness of their situation. A nest of vipers, the captain had said. The description didn't come close.

"Come away, lad." Potts whispered.

Ezra never moved.

At the far end of the beach, a figure lay spread-eagled on the sand. It was a lady with black skin. He could make out the stakes, driven deep into the ground, at her wrists and ankles. He couldn't discern her features; she was too far away. She was naked, and the sun beat mercilessly down on her.

Taylor Potts watched Horace Clunk's huge frame shudder. If the big man decided to go crashing down there, Potts knew nothing would stop him. All three watched in absolute horror as a sailor approached her. They could only see the back of him. His black hair was tied at his neck with a short length of hemp, and then it fell down his back in a tail. He stood over the piteous creature, planted a foot in the sand each side of her and urinated.

Ezra turned away his gut churning. Horace began to unsling the huge bow from his shoulder.

Potts put a hand on his arm, gently. "You'll give away our position, Mister Clunk. Horace."

The big man waited.

"Let's get back to the ship," Potts continued in a whisper, "as quickly as we can."

*

When they returned to the beach, they were relieved to see Ed Monk and the gig waiting for them. The three of them had not spoken during their descent and they remained silent even under a barrage of questions from Monk.

Once back aboard ship, they found the captain in his quarters, and the explanations were left to Mister Potts.

Isaac absorbed the information and let out a long breath as if to rid himself of the atrocities and to allow his brain to function tactically, which it did.

"Were there any sentries posted?" Isaac spoke to no one in particular.

"None on the beach, as far as I could see. Nor in the boat." It was Potts who answered. "Common sense would say there must be at least two men aboard the ship. Mind you, if they're in a similar state to their shipmates, they won't be payin' much attention to anythin'."

Horace said, "I reckon they've all bin at the grog, Cap'n. Bin hittin' it 'ard, they 'ave."

"Okay." Isaac paused for a moment. "The tide, Mister Potts. What hour would you estimate the turn to be?"

"Sunup, sir, give or take," Potts confirmed.

"My conclusion also, Mister Potts. Ezra lad, if you were put in the water at the tip of the island, do you foresee any difficulties making it to their ship? Bearing in mind that you'll need to achieve this without being spotted."

Ezra dwelt on this fleetingly before responding. "I

reckon it's maybe five hundred yards, so I'd have to break the surface four or five times; yes, sir, I can do that okay."

"Mister Clunk, one hour before sunrise you will row to the end of the rock, where you should see their ship. Put young Quicklock into the water and then make your way onto the beach, keeping in the lee of the rock. Your objective is to steal the boat undetected. Take Mister Potts and a couple of hands of your own choosing. Once you have the boat, make your way towards the port of Belém, where if all goes to plan, we shall all rendezvous. We need to keep these vagabonds stranded on the island.

"Young Ezra, I need you to swim up to their ship." As Isaac spoke, he leant over, unbuckled the sheath at his ankle and passed it to Ezra. "Climb the anchor cable until you reach the hemp. Make yourself as comfortable as you can and then cut through the rope. It's no easy task, lad, as it's as thick as a man's leg. The ship'll start tugging, so the last moments may well be more difficult. Hold your nerve, lad; stay calm and quiet, and you'll succeed. Once the ship starts to drift, swim away under the water as far you can, and if all goes well, Mister Clunk will pick you up."

"We've plucked 'im out the sea once. Don't see why we can't do it again, Cap'n," Horace stated.

"Indeed, Mister Clunk," Isaac continued, "I shall sail *Rebecca-Ann* back around the northern tip of the island and intercept the drifting ship. Once we have it under our control, we'll make our way to the port, where I shall contact the appropriate authority. I'm sure this Garcia Paz will be of assistance. These men need to be incarcerated and justice duly served. Remember, lads, these men are vicious killers. Our plan depends on stealth and cunning, not confrontation."

Isaac once again felt the weight of responsibility on his young shoulders. The plan had been hastily put together. He had deliberately not mentioned the poor girl's plight. An attempt to rescue her would jeopardise the whole operation. It would increase the risks dramatically. There were maybe thirty or forty men, and he wondered what the chances were of one of them raising the alarm. He would have the answer by sunrise tomorrow.

# Chapter Ten

Two of Rothwell Spurt's men had rowed him from the island where *Angerona* lay at anchor and the rest of his men were enjoying the freedom of loafing around on a tropical beach with a plentiful supply of alcohol. Their captain had allowed them one black girl from the one hundred and ninety slaves they had captured and transported to Belém. Rothwell knew only too well how his crew functioned. When they were at sea, planning raids, they behaved professionally; Rothwell had drilled them well and punished them hard when necessary. When they were at rest, they thrived on hard liquor and whores. When there were no whores, a black slave would do. The gift to his men came directly out of his profits, so as the small craft left the island, he shouted back to his men, telling them to do as they wished with the girl, but not to kill her. She would still be worth a few shillings.

"You're a filthy bastard, Rudd. Pissin' on that girl," declared one of Spurt's crew.

"Watch ya mouth, Fuck-face. I gotta piss somewhere, so it might as well be on that black bitch." Having sailed with Rothwell Spurt for the past five years, Rudd had honed his vicious temperament. The only man he'd ever feared was Rothwell Spurt himself.

Fuck-face had been raised in the poorhouse, where he had been given the name Lance Tucker. Rudd was the one who had started calling him Fuck-face. Tucker hated it and he hated Rudd. He knew there was little to be done. The only sure way to get the better of Rudd would be to kill him. One day, maybe the opportunity would arise.

Tucker decided to abandon his confrontation with Rudd. He filled a bucket with sea water and walked to where the girl lay, staked to the ground. He sloshed the cool water over her. She emitted a soft groan, and her eyelids flickered, but remained closed. The stench of Rudd's urine began to dissipate.

Lance Tucker made his way back to the water and refilled the bucket. He trudged back to the girl. He couldn't help but admire her naked body. Despite her wretched condition and her helpless circumstances, he felt an unmistakeable urge, swiftly followed by guilt, as he noticed the dried blood clinging to the inside of her thighs. Again came the same groan as he trickled the water gently onto her abdomen, allowing it to eddy through the cluster of becurled hair. He hoped it would help. Her ordeal had been unremitting, and the men's appetite for her voracious.

The words of his captain as he left the island – *"Do what you want with her, but don't kill her"* – resonated through Tucker's mind. If anyone challenged his actions, he would remind them of those words, because they carried an ominous threat. He drew his knife, cut the girl free, eased her into a sitting position, dragged her to the shade of a broad-leafed palm and leant her against the gnarly trunk. He gathered an armful of fallen fronds and covered her legs, providing extra protection from the fierce rays of the equatorial sun. With some reluctance, he refastened her wrists behind the trunk. Tucker knew that if she were to regain her senses and disappear into the depths of the island, his life would be over. Mitigating circumstances meant little to Rothwell Spurt.

Satisfied that she was secure and as comfortable as he could make her, he went and fetched some drinking water. The girl's head was slumped to one side, but he managed to hold it upright and coax a dribble of water into her mouth. He persevered for a few minutes, and then vowed to return at regular intervals and make her take the water. There was no more he could do for her. She would live or she wouldn't.

*

Rothwell accepted Garcia Paz's invitation to stay overnight. The promise of a roast pig and a comfortable bed overwhelmed any desire he may have had to return to his crew and *Angerona*. Paz arranged for his two men to be looked after, with orders that they should return fit for duty mid-morning the next day.

Garcia Paz explained his strategy to Rothwell. It wasn't necessarily a proposal or a plan, but more of a summary of the events that were about to unfold, according to his prophecy.

*Rebecca-Ann* would sail into the port of Belém, where the captain would contact a man recommended to him by the ship owners' agent. There would be no reason for him not to. A warm welcome would be extended to the newcomers. Initially, they'd be put at ease. All the necessary arrangements would be made and executed through him, Garcia Paz. The family expecting to take over the plantation would be incarcerated in the fortress; well, the two women at least, as the man had been promised to Spurt. The previous two buyers of the plantation had been held for a year under ransom. Paz had found it a tedious affair, and he'd eventually dispatched the disillusioned speculators with a lead ball through the forehead. It appeared to be an obsession with the English gentry: sending family members abroad to enhance their lives and their fortunes. The paperwork, Paz had realised, was as easy to destroy as it was to create, and no one had come in search of their relatives as yet. If they came, he would be ready.

The only wrinkle in the preparations now would be if the *popinjay* had aroused any suspicions. Rothwell, in his eagerness to earn some easy money, may have triggered a needless conversation, possibly bringing Paz's intentions into question. If *Rebecca-Ann* sailed into port and the captain sought out Garcia Paz, then in all probability – Paz reasoned – everything would be as he'd anticipated. He would keep the situation fluid and allow events to unfold, with a tweak here and there. Perhaps, if needed, he would make an example to remind people around him of his rapacious zeal. An act of extreme violence usually sufficed.

Paz had thought carefully about the relationship between the family and Captain Dunsmoore. He would invite them to dine at the fortress, enabling him to assess the dynamics. Paz was a man who relied heavily on his instincts. Dunsmoore, he surmised, would be a smart, young man –

he had to be, no question. Was he an English gent? Would he put the welfare of the ladies first? Perhaps he would consider them as collateral damage or perhaps he would sacrifice them to save his ship and his crew. His gut told him that if they were threatened with ill-treatment, death even, the young captain would comply. The answers to these questions would become apparent as he got to know his unsuspecting dinner guests.

Notwithstanding the outcome, he would enjoy the manipulation, the utter astonishment when someone realised they have been deceived, their vulnerability and their sheer helplessness. These reactions invigorated Paz and emboldened him to pursue even more power and wealth; destroying people's lives gave him a feeling he couldn't replicate. A sordid romp with two or three beautiful women; chewing on the leaf of the coca plant, a habit introduced to him by a local merchant; and drowning himself in his favourite tipple, the finest white port, were all pursuits that were his for the taking. Easy. Luring the quarry into his web, witnessing them issuing threats, telling him that he *won't get away with it.* And then they wriggle. And then they beg. And then they give in. Like signing their own death warrant. Trapped firmly in the web. He was the beneficiary.

"So, you see, Senor Roth, I shall take their nice, shiny, new ship and I shall put her under your command. It will take perhaps a couple of weeks to repaint her and reconfigure the cargo hold," declared Paz.

Rothwell interjected, "You fully expect the captain to comply. Maybe he won't give two fucks, pardon my Spanish, about the ladies. Maybe he'll be happy to betray his boss. He may even look to encroach on my profits, in which case he'll have another problem that he doesn't want."

"No, no, Senor Roth. He is the captain of a merchant ship. His crew are merchant seamen. I do not expect anything. Expecting something, Senor Roth, is being optimistic but uncertain at the same time. No, Senor Roth, *Angerona* and *Rebecca-Ann*, although we must change the name of the latter, will be sailing for the coast of Africa with or without the young captain and his crew. Of this, Senor Roth, you may be certain."

Rothwell Spurt took another sip of port, relaxed into the back of the ornate chair and began to think of his stipend when he returned with two shiploads of black flesh. In a couple of years, perhaps, he would buy his own plantation. Then he could take life a bit easier. He looked around. He could definitely get used to this.

# Chapter Eleven

The crescent moon, suspended in the macrocosm, lay on its back; an array of stars in the background created a boundless, glimmering meadow of exotic mystery. The occasional cluster of black cloud drifted serenely across the night sky, blocking any white light generated by the depleted orb. Not the best of conditions, but by no means the worst.

Isaac gave the order to weigh anchor at dusk. Under short sail, *Rebecca-Ann*'s progress through the still water appeared effortless. She was retracing her obsolete wake, at least until the opposite tip of the island. Isaac had allowed himself adequate time to traverse a broad sweep, ensuring the presence of deep water. Navigating alien territory at night could be challenging. He needed to judge his position with a good degree of accuracy. If they were sighted from the beach or the pirate ship, the plan would almost certainly fail. Without the services of Taylor Potts, Isaac took the helm. The crew were at their stations, sailing the ship.

Cordelia approached the captain. They had not spoken since her husband's burial. That had been an uncommon hour or so. For all those years, she had reassured herself that Wesley would one day be a man she could truly love, a man she could respect and a man she could trust. He had been none of those things. Thousands of miles from home, she now knew she had meant nothing to him. To him, she had been a seam of precious metal, which he had tried desperately to mine during their marriage. If only he had just loved her, those rewards would have followed, absolutely, instinctively, without administration and without prejudice. They would have been happy.

Composing herself, she decided to keep her address formal. "Captain, would now be a convenient moment?" She understood the pressure he was under.

"Cordelia, please, come." He beckoned her to stand beside him. "You have my sincere apologies." His gaze remained fixed on the dark horizon. "My insinuation that you may have somehow known your husband's intentions…" Isaac's voice trailed off.

Cordelia released an involuntary sigh. "I refute your apology, Captain Dunsmoore." She paused for a second.

Isaac turned his gaze on her for a moment.

"You owe me no apology, Isaac." She rested her hand on his forearm. "It is I who should apologise, and I do, unreservedly."

"Here." Isaac stepped aside keeping one hand on the wheel. He ushered Cordelia to the helm and released his hand. She clung to the polished spokes as if her very existence depended upon it.

"I can't. What are you doing?"

"Just relax, Cordelia. Relax. You're just holding her steady."

Gradually, her grip loosened and her stance became comfortable, natural; all thoughts of apologies and recriminations were dispelled. She felt the cool night air pushing gently against her face, Isaac's warm breath on her neck, and the inextricable power of the ocean moving through the ship's fabric and into her hands and feet – her whole body, in fact.

"You should take the helm when she's making eighteen knots in a swell, with her bow rearing up towards the sky, like an angry bear, and her stern bucking into the air, like an unridden horse. The connection with the ocean is there in your hands, as something inexplicable but nonetheless tangible." Isaac leant forwards. "I'd best take her, Cordelia."

They stood side by side, untroubled momentarily. The breeze colliding with sail and water making way for the ship's bow were the only sounds to punctuate the silence.

"How is Joanna coping?" enquired the captain.

"She has a resilience, which helps immensely. And, Isaac, I don't know if you've noticed, but she has… How shall I put it? A preoccupation with a certain crew member." Cordelia tilted her head towards Isaac and raised an eyebrow. She thought but never said, *Not that I blame her.*

"I suppose, under more pleasant circumstances, the incident on the shore would have been picked over, and their actions analysed and discussed, if indeed this needed to be the case," Isaac continued, "Alas, my experience in these matters is somewhat limited, though I must say, from my perspective, I see no reason to analyse their situation. Although, on a more sombre note, I fear our current predicament could dictate all our futures. I have given the young man a dangerous mission, Cordelia, and the only way I can reconcile it is by reassuring myself that he's the only man on board capable of succeeding. If I were to throw any one of the crew overboard, they would last but a few moments before sinking to the seabed, of that I am certain. When we make it through this, I shall instigate swimming lessons for all, including me."

Cordelia smiled at the thought. "I have grown extremely fond of Ezra, as I know you have. I don't think I've ever encountered a more determined, straightforward and, quite frankly, likeable person." *Present company excluded*, she thought.

"Indeed, I have warmed to him greatly. There would appear to be no injurious aspect affecting his disposition, and I am convinced his adopted parents have raised him well, notwithstanding his lack of education." Isaac hesitated. "I believe the owner of this fine ship would be more than proud of his estranged son."

Cordelia acquiesced with a nod.

Isaac's voice once more adopted a sombre tone. "You understand, Cordelia, that we are all in great danger. I want you to know that I will do everything in my power to keep you and Joanna safe. I shan't, however, make you false promises or give you any guarantees."

Cordelia felt the weight of his words. She desperately wanted to ease his burden. "Well, sir," she began in a mocking tone, "I would expect nothing less from a perfect gentleman and an excellent captain to boot."

Isaac hesitated before interpreting her response. "Indeed, madam, you should not. And thank you for your most gracious elucidation."

The mood lifted and the moment passed, engulfing them in a comfortable silence.

Three men stood at intervals at the starboard rail. Prickle was the first to notice the end of the island, which was silhouetted in the distance, abutting the dark sky.

Isaac asked Cordelia to lock herself and Joanna in his cabin, and if all went well, he would tap the door himself when the threat was over. He bid her goodnight and thanked her for her pleasant company.

"It has," she said, "been my pleasure," and after wishing him luck and telling him to stay safe, she made her way to his quarters, where Joanna would be waiting, probably with a million questions.

*

Horace Clunk rowed the gig. He was sitting on a square of sail cloth that had been scrounged from Aubrey Darricot's storeroom. His huge bow, half a dozen oversized arrows and his axe lay in the gunwales. The sun would be up within the hour, and the tide would begin to ebb.

They rounded the tip of the rock, keeping as close as they dared to the jagged stone waiting to obliterate the small craft.

Horace stowed the oars and whispered to Ezra. "It's time, lad."

Potts winked at him and wished him luck, mouthing the words.

Horace moved his huge frame to the opposite side of the boat, and without further ceremony, Ezra slipped silently into the cool water and disappeared out of sight.

Tod Harris and Ed Monk were in the gig with Potts and Clunk. Harris took over the oars and eased them steadily into the shallow water in the lee of the towering rock. Horace slid belly down over the transom into the water, followed swiftly by Potts. Harris and Monk had instructions to wait for a few minutes and then make their way into the bay, far enough away so as not to be seen.

Clunk and Potts waded quietly through the water and came out onto the beach beneath the cliff.

Potts pointed to the sail cloth tucked inside the big man's shirt and said, "I suppose your gonna tell me what that's for," his voice a muted whisper.

Horace stooped to whisper in Potts's ear, "I'm gonna go get the girl."

"Shit, Horace," Potts hissed. He should have known. "Shit."

"Listen to me, Taylor; we're not leavin' without her."

"You've got some sort of plan?"

"We're gonna wade through the water, as deep as we can, to where the boat is. We're gonna drag it into the water and make our way to the far end of the beach where she's staked out. You stay with the boat; I'll go get her. Then we're out of here."

\*

Ten feet beneath the surface, Ezra felt the water temperature drop; it was now a dark, foreboding world. His need for air forced him to break the surface. Noiselessly treading water, he surveyed his progress before filling his lungs and descending once more. He could feel the current coaxing him away from the shore. His thoughts returned to his previous encounter with the ocean's tides. He ploughed on, his strokes invigorated by distant memories and an overwhelming urge to complete his mission.

After two more ascents for air, he reached the ship. Her stern was facing out to sea, and the dawn light was beginning to impose itself, giving the atmosphere an ethereal flush. It was neither dark nor light. He clung to the slimy chain, assessing his next move.

*

Potts and Clunk crept on their bellies out of the water and up to the rear of the boat. Using clumsy hand signals, Horace told Potts to wait. He crawled on his front, easing himself through the sticky sand until he reached the bow. From his position, he surveyed the beach. There were prone men scattered randomly, some in isolation, some in clusters and all, it seemed, in alcohol-induced comas. Several fire pits had been reduced to grey ash, emitting the occasional whiff of smoke as a light dawn breeze disturbed the embers. Horace grabbed the rope that lay coiled on the sand and began the awkward task of crawling backwards. Potts could only watch in awe as Horace heaved on the rope from his prone position. The boat swivelled in its own length and, gradually, inch by inch, slid towards the water. It was a task two men standing would struggle with.

Once afloat, they pulled the now weightless craft to the far end of the bay, watching constantly for movement on the beach. Potts stared at the ship and could just decern a figure clinging to the anchor rode. There was no movement on deck, so far as he could tell. He then watched as Horace crept silently through the sand towards the girl.

She had been moved. Horace paused. She was sitting up, leaning against a tree, with her head flopped to one side. Not five yards from her, a man was lying on the sand asleep, as far as he could see. Horace crept into the vegetation, and with uncanny stealth for a huge man, crept up behind the palm. He drew his knife and was about to cut her bonds when he noticed the man stirring. Horace sunk down onto his belly and waited. The sailor sat up, rubbing his eyes, and began rotating his head, doing his best to relieve the cricks lodged in his neck. He had no idea that it was a pointless exercise. He got to his feet, involuntarily rubbed his hands over his head, walked to the start of the vegetation, and with his back to Horace Clunk, he began to piss.

Horace lay motionless. *Christ Almighty*, he thought. *I've seen donkeys piss less.* He made the decision, as he couldn't afford to wait. Horace crept up behind the unsuspecting man. He slipped one giant arm around his neck, and with the other, he snapped the man's neck. The only noise was the sickening crunch of bone and tendon and sinew. Death was instant. He dragged the limp figure into the vegetation and quickly covered his body with the fallen fronds.

Horace returned to where the girl was sitting; he couldn't be sure she was still alive. After he had freed her, he held her in his massive arms, wrapped her in the sail cloth, and walked upright along the sand and into the water. When he reached the boat, he laid her gently in it and hoisted Potts in behind her before slithering over the transom himself.

*

Ezra tilted his head and looked up. He could see where the warp had been spliced to the iron link of the chain. It was common practice on merchant ships to have the ship's anchor attached to chain. The principal reason for this was to reduce the risk of possible chafing or severing, usually on rock, whilst resting on the seabed. Generally, the chain would be roughly the length of the ship and thereafter heavy-duty rope was employed to save weight.

There was roughly a foot of warp protruding through the hawser. Ezra realised that he would have to somehow hang from that short length of rope with one hand and cut with the other. To help him climb the slippery chain, he managed to get his fingers partway through the links helping him to grip. He was now completely exposed. He kept going, inching his way upwards, and ignoring the slime and the smell of rotten seaweed as best he could. Ezra reached the point where iron met hemp, and accepted quickly that he would never be able to grip the rope with one hand. It was too thick. The angle at which the rode lay meant he could wrap his feet around the chain, locking them together, whilst he reached down for the knife. The iron links gnawed at his skin as he clung on with his feet and the fingers of one hand.

He drew the knife across the rope. He watched as the strands parted and frayed. He repeated the action until he was halfway through. He could feel the tension through the cable. She was ready to be taken by the tide. Ezra put the blade of the knife sideways in his mouth and pulled himself up until his head was touching the ship's planking. He reached up with his left hand and gripped the edge of the ship's deck. Unlocking his feet, he let his legs dangle. His grip was tenuous. He twisted his body and sliced at the rope. Once. Twice.

A face appeared over the rail. It gazed in astonishment at a youth hacking his way through the ship's umbilical cord. Their eyes locked for the briefest of moments and then the culprit fell into the water.

"What the fuck?" The bewildered sailor peered over the rail, staring in disbelief at the glassy water. There was nothing but silent ripples. And then he saw the rope. And then he heard it. A groan, a creak, another groan and then a twang. His eyes grew larger. The chain fell into the water and disappeared out of sight forever. *Angerona* began to drift.

*

Beneath the water, Ezra repositioned himself, slipped the knife into the sheath and began to swim. His mind was racing. He had failed. He'd been discovered before completing his mission. He'd let down the captain and all his shipmates. He swam deeper. He would lie on the seabed and let his lungs fill with the strange fluid, which was neither salty nor fresh, but would inevitably drown him just the same. He swam deeper. He felt the pressure multiplying. Any second he would have to let it in and allow it to destroy him. Images of all the people he would never see again flashed like bolts of lightning through his mind: Fred and Mary, his beloved parents; Captain Dunsmoore; Mister Clunk; Taylor Potts; Cordelia Marrick; and there in the forefront was a beautiful girl, he couldn't be sure who she was, pleading with him to seek air.

He pushed away from the seabed with all his might. His coordination had deserted him. His arms were flailing. He could sense his legs doing something. A yard before he broke the surface, he tried to breathe. Instinct told him that if he opened his mouth his lungs would fill with air. They filled with brackish water. He spat, he coughed and he vomited a plume of ruinous effluent. And then he gulped the dawn air. Fresh, invigorating, life enhancing and critical.

He felt his body readjusting to its natural environment. The pressure inside his head began to normalise. His heart was quick to adopt its metronomic rhythm once more, enabling him to take regular breaths. Treading water and fully composed, he began to assess the situation. To his indescribable relief, he saw the grey hulk of the pirate ship drifting awkwardly away from the island. He could hear muffled voices. He tilted his head to one side and smacked his ear with palm of his hand. Then he did the same with the other ear. The sound of his name became clear, and spotting two small boats in the distance, he began to swim.

*

The crack of a musket shot echoed around the bay. Rudd was awake in an instant. He leapt to his feet, ignoring the thump inside his skull. As his eyes adjusted to the dawn, he saw *Angerona* crabbing her way towards the horizon. "Holy shit."

He kicked the man nearest to him, who had not stirred. Then he began to yell. "*Up, you lazy fuckers. Up!*" He ran around kicking and shouting. He ran to the shore searching for the gig, shaking his head in disbelief. "Fuck me, no." And then he felt the crushing pain in his head. And then he puked.

He turned to the tree where the girl was tied. He couldn't see her. He trudged through the sand looking, as she had to be there somewhere. He saw the discarded rope, a few loose fronds, an indent in the sand and some footprints.

"*Tucker,*" he yelled. "*Tucker, are you there, you lazy bastard? Where are you? Tucker.*" Nothing. "Shit."

Rudd began to piece the riddle together. Fuck-face had stolen the gig and made off with the girl. But what about the ship? It didn't make sense. All he knew for sure was that they were stranded on the island, and if they ever saw their captain again…

His brain wouldn't allow him to process that information.

*

Will Nye had spent the last three hours in the crow's nest, focusing on the vast expanse of water before him. *Rebecca-Ann* lay at anchor, her sails furled. The captain stood at the bow with the unwieldly looker at his eye. The sun was easing itself into view, chasing away the last remnants of darkness.

"C'mon, c'mon, where are you?" Isaac muttered under his breath. Then the doubts crept over him, like a contagious rash. All the misgivings he'd harboured about each facet of his plan were now threatening to overwhelm him. He'd put the overriding safety of the ship before anything, asking his men to endanger their lives on what now appeared to be an ill-fated mission. He made the decision to weigh anchor. Now was the time to show themselves, regardless.

Whilst he busied himself giving orders, he heard the shout from above. He instinctively inclined his head towards the crow's nest.

"*Two points to port, Captain,*" declared Nye.

Isaac snatched up the looker. There she was – a spooky, grey hulk, drifting aimlessly.

\*

There were only two men on board *Angerona*. They had complained, but only to each other, after being left on the ship. When Rothwell Spurt gave you an order, the sensible reaction was to obey without question, however disagreeable that order may be.

Roly Smith had, he believed, drawn the shitty end of the stick, as not only had he been left on board ship but he'd also been saddled with one of the most disgusting men he had ever encountered: Burt Treadwell.

When he realised he had been posted with Treadwell, Smith immediately set about rigging his hammock on deck. Amongst his array of vile habits, Treadwell farted continuously, and they stank. Mind, the whole ship stank since the enslaved Africans had come aboard. However, they were cooped up in the hold, twenty-three hours a day, for weeks at a time, so they couldn't help it, he reasoned. They were held in irons and given a handful of buckets in which to do their business. Treadwell, in comparison, was just a dirty bastard.

Swinging in his hammock and staring up at the night sky suited Roly Smith well enough. As dawn broke, he felt himself stirring. Perhaps it had been the light breeze causing a scant drop in temperature, possibly it had been the half-light or maybe he sensed something sinister. He rolled out of his hammock and made his way to the bow.

On peering over the rail, he was stunned to see a black-haired vagabond sawing through the anchor cable whilst dangling by one hand from the edge of the ship's deck. They had locked eyes for a second, and then he was gone. Smith soon felt the ship tugging at the tenuous strands of rope, desperate to snap her leash and drift, freed to roam the great ocean unfettered, and to go wherever the wind and current may take her. And then, to Roly Smith's utter dismay, there was a groan, a creak, another groan and then a twang. They were adrift.

Roly went and grabbed a loaded musket, then fired a shot into the air. Next, he scrambled below deck to wake Treadwell, whose prolific snoring echoed through the empty space. The foetid air made Roly gasp as he yelled at Treadwell. There was no response. He prodded Treadwell with the barrel of the musket. This time he was rewarded with a stifled groan, followed by an elongated fart – which reminded Roly of a duff note produced by a novice on a battered, old cornet – being the only retort.

"Fuck you, Treadwell, you useless bag of shit." Smith smacked the musket down as hard as he dared on Treadwell's head.

The bag of shit came to life. It screamed, it flung its arms in the air, and then it rolled over, farted and fell from its hammock, landing with a dull thump.

Roly ran from the mess and waited on deck for Treadwell to appear. He stood aiming the unloaded musket at the space Burt Treadwell was about to fill.

"You little prick. You bastard. You fuckin' moron. What the…?" Treadwell burst into the dawn only to be confronted by the unwavering, dangerous end of the musket.

"Calm down, Burt. We've got trouble," stated Roly.

"God's fuckin' breath, we're on the fuckin' move," Treadwell spluttered.

"I bin tryin' to tell ya ferever an' a fuckin' day. We gotta do summat."

"The kedgin' anchor – we need t' get that overboard. It mayn't halt us, but it'll slow the ol' gal down." Burt Treadwell may have been the world's biggest slob, but he knew a thing or two about sailing a ship.

The kedging anchor was used to stop the ship swinging on the sheet anchor. It was employed in crowded harbours or narrow waterways. It could also be used to turn a ship or pull her along, which was an arduous task that required plenty of hands. Although not as bulky or heavy as the sheet anchor, it was still a cumbersome item, and too heavy for the likes of Treadwell and Smith to manhandle.

Working in close proximity with Treadwell was not high on Roly Smith's list of priorities. As they wrestled with the block and tackle that was needed to hoist the kedging anchor overboard, Treadwell's reaction to the sudden exertion was to open his mouth and let out a grunt. Smith jerked his head to one side and retched, instinctively releasing his portion of the weight at the same time. The stench of Treadwell's breath was indescribable. It wafted over Smith like a cloud of sulphur siphoned from the depths of the earth's crust. The handful of discoloured teeth, scattered randomly in the foetid cavern, reminded Smith of a sketch he had once seen. It had been framed and hung on the wall of a scruffy tavern somewhere in the south of England, though he couldn't remember where exactly. He couldn't read the inscription, but as far as he could make out, it was an ancient monument, built years ago, before modern techniques became available. That much he knew. It was made of big, old stones sticking out the ground in a circle. He hadn't seen the point of it, but it had intrigued him, nonetheless.

Now, saddled with the full weight, Treadwell felt his back give, and the block landed on his foot. He yelled in agony and cursed Smith for letting go.

Whilst the two men argued, hurling insults bitterly at each other, an elegant, blue ship glided to their port side. A dull thump, the scraping of timber on timber and a sudden jolt brought them to their senses. Before they could react, the hapless pair were confronted by six men, all wielding assorted weapons.

# Chapter Twelve

Garcia Paz rose from his bed and attended his toilet. His regime was repetitious. He followed the same fastidious routine that he followed every morning, unless he decided a plunge was in order. Conny – a supple, dusky-skinned girl – supplied the necessary accoutrements for a successful bathe. She was also on call for any of Paz's other personal requirements. Therefore, a rap on the bedroom door by someone other than Conny would likely bring some form of important news.

Standing in the hallway, Captain Tiago Marinho tugged anxiously at his collar. He heard Paz shout for the girl. She never responded so, highly irritated at being interrupted, Paz marched to the door and flung it open.

Marinho snapped to attention. "Senor Paz, my apologies for the intrusion. The ship you have been waiting for has arrived."

"Ah, excellent news, Capt—" began Paz.

"My apologies again, senor, but the ship has another ship attached to it. A dull-grey monstrosity, senor, which, unless my eyes are playing tricks, must belong to Senor Rothwell."

Garcia Paz processed the information and dispatched Marinho to wake Senor Rothwell. He quickly finished dressing and made his way to the rampart, from which he had an excellent view across the harbour. A wry smile interrupted his stern visage momentarily. *A most unusual combination*, he thought. *I wonder who's in charge of this peculiar convoy? A bunch of ragged-arsed pirates or Captain Dunsmoore?*

Paz ordered his men to the quayside. After a moment's pause, he altered the command. "Captain, on second thoughts, go down to the dock yourself and take just one man with you. Leave your weapons behind and extend a warm welcome to whomever disembarks. Have your men ready for action, but keep them out of sight. I suspect, Captain Marinho, that you will be extending a warm welcome to one Captain Dunsmoore. If not, it will be Spurt's crew. Invite the captain to the fortress and extend the invitation to the Marrick family. If it's Spurt's crew, just bring one of them here, whoever's in charge. I shall keep an eye on proceedings from the rampart."

Soon after issuing these orders, Spurt himself arrived on the rampart beside Paz. It took a few minutes for Paz to calm Rothwell Spurt. The sight of his ship tethered to another larger and altogether more elegant vessel irked Rothwell beyond his sensibilities. Paz used his charm and guile to stop the enraged captain from storming down to the quay. Together, they admired the sleek ship, the command of which Spurt had been promised.

"Huh," grunted Spurt, "it'll look better in grey."

Paz chose to disguise his feelings regarding the future colour scheme. Grey would suit the purpose well enough; although he admired *Rebecca-Ann's* livery (albeit from a distance) and he considered it a pity to interfere with her present appearance, the ship's outward façade had to be altered.

*

*Rebecca-Ann* eased into the harbour. The captain gave the order to drop anchor further away from the quay than he would normally expect to berth. The two small boats had been strung together and were hauled alongside. Isaac had been mightily relieved to find his men rowing towards the port.

He had been shocked to see the girl, but not totally surprised. He made no mention of her. "I see everything went to plan, Mister Clunk."

"Aye aye, Captain. No dramas," Clunk confirmed.

Potts raised his eyebrows, but said nothing.

"Young Ezra," the captain asked, stealing Horace Clunk's word, "any dramas?"

"No, sir." Ezra went to unbuckle the sheath at his ankle.

"You hang on to that, lad; you never know, it might come in handy another time." Isaac added, "Mister Clunk, let's get that poor creature to my quarters. *Seddon.*" He yelled again, "*Seddon!*"

Isaac went to his cabin and rapped on its door. "Cordelia, it's me, Isa—Captain Dunsmoore."

Cordelia had been waiting for this moment throughout the long hours of darkness; her sleep had been snatched in perfunctory segments. Her relief when she opened the door and saw Isaac was palpable, albeit her demeanour outwardly displayed an air of equanimity. *Thank God,* she thought.

The sight of a dark-skinned wretch wrapped in sail cloth, looking diminutive in the arms of Horace Clunk, left Cordelia and Joanna aghast. In a hushed and slightly awkward tone, Isaac quickly outlined the girl's plight.

"Lay her on the cot." Cordelia's calm demeanour regained control. "Thank you, Horace. Captain, perhaps it would be appropriate for yourself and Mist—"

Isaac interrupted. "Away now, Mister Clunk; let us leave the ladies to their work."

As they left, Seddon appeared, marching purposefully towards the cabin.

"Ah, Seddon." Once again Isaac found himself with the disagreeable task of explaining the girl's plight.

On hearing a soothing female voice, the girl opened her eyes. She saw two white-skinned ladies. One stood slightly to one side, pouring water onto a square of white material. The other stood at the end of the cot, her hands covering her face. Then came a man's voice. She closed her eyes. Her hands gripped the side of the cot.

As he entered the cabin, Seddon gave a perfunctory nod to Cordelia and Joanna. He held the girl's arm and felt her pulse. He then pulled one of her eyes open with a gnarly thumb.

"I understand she bin badly got at." He addressed the comment to no one in particular. "Still don't you worry, 'er pulse is pumpin' like a set o' bellows. Strong as mules, they are. You get 'er cleaned up, an' if you need me to, you know... check out the mechanicals, give me an 'oller.

She'll be all right in a few days. Big boned, they are, and tough as 'ell." And touching his forelock, with the diagnosis complete, Seddon left the room.

"Promise me, Mother, that if I should fall ill, do not let that man anywhere near me." Joanna shuddered at the thought.

"I promise," Cordelia declared.

Little by little, they cleaned her gently, washing away the physical evidence. The mental scars would never be washed away. Joanna clutched her hand and talked in soothing tones, telling her she was safe. Cordelia smiled inwardly at her daughter's compassion; although thoroughly shocked by the girl's condition, Joanna had demonstrated unwavering benevolence.

The girl opened her eyes. These large, deep-brown pools of sadness stared at a female whose skin was as white as the moon, her eyes the colour of the sky on the clearest summer day, and her hair the colour of the burning sun. A strange but beautiful creature.

Cordelia was searching for a suitable dress. Joanna's would be a better fit. She was holding a thin, pale-blue, cotton dress in front of herself, turning her head from side to side, as if that would somehow help her to decide, when she heard Joanna speak.

"Hello, my name is Joanna."

The girl moved her gaze to her hand, which was held firmly by the white lady.

"You're safe now. This is my mother. Her name is Cordelia." Joanna spoke slowly, in short sentences. "Do you understand? What is your name?"

Cordelia came to the cot, clutching the dress to her

bosom. She smiled at the girl and unfurled the dress, holding it in front of herself. "I found this for you. Would you like to put it on? It may make you feel more comfortable."

A silence pervaded, but then the girl spoke. "Dey call me Tomilola. My mammy call me Tomi. Dey take her. Dey take all dem. My famlee."

Joanna stared at Tomilola, trying to imagine the pain she must be feeling. Her own life was in disarray. She thought of her father putting a pistol in his mouth and pulling the trigger, and how she'd struggle to grieve for him. Somehow, she couldn't summon up the feelings she thought she should have. There was something missing; there always had been. Perhaps, in time, she'd interpret how she felt about her dead father, who was now lying in an unmarked grave, on a deserted island, on another continent, in another world.

Tomilola eased herself into a sitting position. The sail cloth fell away, and Joanna could not thwart the inclination to admire her. Her muscles rippled gently beneath her smooth, deep-brown skin; her breasts were generous yet firm. Her face was beautiful. Her large, round eyes – now watery with sadness – were shadowed with long, upturned lashes; her nose dipped at the bridge and broadened subtly at the nostrils; and her lips were pink against her tawny complexion. Her hair was the darkest black and hung in long, twisted tresses to her bare shoulders, exquisitely framing the portrait.

Joanna felt her stomach tighten; a tremor ran through to her core. She'd felt the same when she'd found herself sitting astride Ezra in this very cabin. She thought she knew what the feeling meant, but what she didn't understand was why she felt the same way now. She suddenly felt embarrassed and a little awkward. She knew her face was flushed.

Cordelia stepped in and dropped the dress over Tomilola's head. The two of them helped her to stand, and with a slight wiggle, the dress dropped into place. They watched as Tomilola puckered the material between her fingers. It felt soft and cool against her skin.

A tap at the door evoked a fretful reaction from Tomilola. Her head jerked towards the door and her eyes widened. Cordelia reassured her that she was safe and opened the door.

Horace Clunk filled the space.

Tomilola's expression changed. She turned to face Horace. "Dis big man carry me away." After placing her right palm on her heart, she extended it to Horace. And then her legs refused to support her, and she sank involuntary on to the cot.

Horace thought she looked beautiful in the pale-blue dress. He thought she'd looked beautiful when ravaged half to death. His manner gave no clue as to his thoughts. "Good t' see ya up an' about, young miss."

"Her name is Tomilola," Joanna said.

Horace tilted his chin in acknowledgement.

"And this, Tomilola, is Mister Horace Clunk," Joanna added.

"De big man carry me away." Tomilola closed her eyes and fell asleep.

Joanna stepped towards the big man and rested her hand on his massive forearm. "You are a brave man, Mister Clunk; thank you for saving Tomilola."

Horace tilted his chin once again. He turned to Cordelia. "Regards from the captain, missis, 'e's bin ashore an' sent a message back. Would you an' Miss Joanna join him."

Joanna spoke first. "You go, Mother. One of us needs to stay with Tomilola."

Horace Clunk allayed any concerns Cordelia may have felt at leaving her daughter. "Don't fear, missis, I'm gonna be 'ere."

*

Cordelia felt excitement and trepidation in equal measure as she perched in the bow of the gig, admiring the fortress that was imposing itself on the vista. Ezra was at the oars, powering the craft towards the quay. Potts sat at the stern, his arm drooped idly over the helm.

Already on the quay, Captain Dunsmoore had received a cordial welcome from Captain Marinho. His relaxed nature and the absence of any weapons put Isaac at ease. After a stressful and sleepless night, he felt the tension drain from his body. Whilst he waited for the gig to return, he outlined the events preceding his arrival.

After the gig had returned to the quay once more, Cordelia also disembarked and walked up the quay steps. At the top, she stopped, smoothed the front of her dress and ran her fingers through her tousled hair, aware suddenly of not having checked her appearance before leaving the ship.

Isaac made the introduction. "Captain Marinho, may I present Mistress Cordelia Marrick."

Marinho removed his hat and swept it through the air before him whilst performing an elaborate bow, which was executed from the waist with great aplomb and sincerity.

"At your service, madam. Come now, Senor Paz is waiting. Captain Dunsmoore, your men may find themselves a suitable tavern if they wish. Perhaps they should return in a couple of hours or so."

"Well, lad, it looks like we've got a little free time. C'mon, let's go have a poke round and see what's what," said Potts.

For someone who had never ventured further than Old Milford until the last few months, the surroundings were fascinating. The quayside was bustling with activity. There were carts loaded with goods, pulled by short-legged horses – sturdy-looking beasts that were capable of withstanding the midday sun. The noise, the clatter and the smells – Ezra absorbed it all. Potts, who had witnessed scenes like these many times, couldn't help wondering what mayhem would occur when darkness fell, and ale, rum and cheap wine had been consumed. They turned down a street leading off the quay, paying little heed to their surroundings.

Two men stepped out of the brothel onto the street. One put his hands over his eyes and winced at the bright light. The other fiddled at his crotch, trying to rearrange his privates into an acceptable position.

"That bitch done summat to the end of my dick." He fiddled again. "Real tender 'e is."

"You lucky bastard. Stop whinin'," ordered his companion.

"I might go back to see if she's got some potion or other she could rub in; you know, make 'im soothed a bit."

"You go back in an' it'll be 'er askin' you fer a potion t' stop 'er itchin'. Any'ow, none of it makes no diff'rence, cos if we're late back, Spurty'll cut our bollocks off."

Mister Tender-dick gave his mate a playful shove, and he – caught off balance – staggered across the narrow street and clattered into a man who had deliberately moved over to one side when he saw the two men coming.

Taylor Potts raised his hands in a submissive gesture. "Steady, fella," he said in a neutral tone.

"Don't fuckin' 'Steady, fella' me, you scrawny—"

All Potts's instincts told him there would be no other way out of the situation. So before the man could finish his diatribe, Taylor Potts delivered a vicious punch that was straight, lightning quick, accurate and packed with momentum. It connected with the man's Adam's apple, and down he went.

Tender-dick went for a knife at his waist. Ezra drove the heel of his right foot into the man's groin, waited for one second as the man leant over clutching his privates, then punched him on the temple and watched as he staggered sideways across the street, tripped over his prone companion, smacked his head against the stone wall of a building and fell to the ground.

All the bruising hours spent in the storeroom manifested into a few moments: no pointless banter and no hesitation; deal with it and leave if you are able. They were able.

Walking back along the quay, Potts was the first to speak. "Good work, Ezra; well done."

"I had a good teacher," Ezra concluded.

*

Isaac felt relaxed for the first time in many days. Marinho had done his job. They walked towards the sombre-looking fortress. Constructed of grey stone, it had castellated walls and a square tower, with no frills other than narrow slits interrupting the functional stone; it was maybe a hundred and fifty feet tall and its foundations dipped into the water. It dominated the harbour. Isaac noticed cannons on the ramparts, their barrels directed ominously across the bay.

A pair of stout doors – which were made from a dark, exotic hardwood – lay open, secured against the inner wall of the entrance. A short, dark passage took them to another set of identical doors, which were hung on the same iron hinges but opening in opposite directions. *It's about as secure as you could make it,* Isaac thought as they passed through and into an open courtyard.

The exterior was sombre, functional and, for an enemy, foreboding. Inside, Paz's quarters were sumptuous. It had been designed for a man who enjoyed the fine items that wealth and power could provide. Cordelia's family home was a grand affair. Its walls were adorned with serious, dull portraits of ancestors long gone and mostly forgotten; these dominated the interior along with huge open fireplaces, chunky oak furniture and silver candle holders. Now, as she surveyed her surroundings, she couldn't help but admire the contents. An enormous painting took over the back wall, presenting a tangle of bare flesh, with arms and legs entwined, and beautiful bodies curved, voluptuous and alive. The furniture was formed from exquisitely grained timber, which was hard, durable wood and yet was soft and easy on the beholder. The deep-blue fabric overtly invited a person to repose.

Also present in the room was Paz, who allowed his guests a few moments to absorb the ambience. He was also puzzled at the absence of a husband and a daughter. "Welcome to Belém, to my home. I am Senor Garcia Paz."

Marinho stepped forwards and introduced Captain Isaac Dunsmoore and Mistress Cordelia Marrick. He then stepped back and stood sentinel at the door.

"Forgive me, madam, but I was expecting Senor Marrick and your daughter to join us," stated Paz.

Isaac intervened and explained the events of the last few days, concluding, "Hence, Senor Paz, I have sailed into Belém tethered to a pirate ship, and only Mistress Marrick has accompanied me."

"My condolences, madam, for your loss. Captain, I congratulate you on a tactical triumph over such a band of cut-throat mercenaries. A daring and courageous exploit with, one would imagine, a most satisfactory outcome."

Paz had now collated all the insight into Dunsmoore's character he required. He was a man of honour who would put the lives of Cordelia Marrick and her daughter before his own. A highly capable and shrewd captain, unafraid to issue orders and unafraid to ensure they were followed. Notwithstanding these attributes, Paz was unable to ascertain a ruthless streak in the young captain. Regard for human life, he knew only too well, hampered one's ambition for wealth and power. And, ultimately, survival. The trap was set. He offered Marinho a subtle nod, and the captain exited the room.

Isaac felt a moment of anxiety at the almost imperceptible nod; *Marinho has been well briefed,* he thought.

Paz interrupted his musing to ask him questions about *Rebecca-Ann*, how she handled, how many knots she could achieve and how he had influenced her design. Any disquiet Isaac had felt dissipated as he responded to Paz's enquiries.

There wasn't a knock, but the door bumped open. A surly-looking man burst into the space, his pockmarked face flushed with anger. Marinho and two of his men ushered themselves into the room after him, eager to prevent a premature affray.

"Ah, Captain Dunsmoore, allow me to introduce Captain Rothwell Spurt, the owner of *Angerona*, which is the ship currently tethered to your own splendid vessel."

These were the very moments Garcia Paz thrived on.

The desolation, the shock, the total bewilderment and the palpable fear of his victim.

# Chapter Thirteen

Ezra and Potts retraced their steps along the quay. They stopped to check the gig, and Ezra collected his bow and a set of arrows, which he had previously laid in the gunwales. They carried on walking, following the cobbled road along the southern wall of the fortress. The rear wall was lower than the main front wall, but it was still probably twenty feet high. The street was shaded between the fort and tall trees that abutted the cobbles. The road became narrower as they progressed, and the trees and vegetation became denser. Looking up, they could see the back of the great square tower, its height appearing reduced due to its proximity to the ground. It was as if the forest had never existed beyond where they stood, and as if the earth had always been bare, waiting for a band of intrepid explorers to come along and build a great fortification specifically to protect the forest and everything that lived and thrived in it.

Eventually, they were walking along a track that was wide enough for a cart, but little else. There was a comfortable silence between them, which enabled both men to become attuned to their surroundings. The canopy of trees supported all kinds of birds and mammals, each one emitting its own personal announcement.

The track began to rise. They could feel the tension building in their thighs and their calves. Although protected from the direct sun, the heat was intense. After forty minutes of walking, the trail led them into bright sunlight, high above what they now realised was a massive river, which was unlike any they had ever seen. They both stopped intuitively to survey the vista.

Looking back, they caught glimpses of the tower, which was partly shrouded by the forest canopy. The edge of the track nearest to the river had stunted trees clinging stubbornly to the rock, and plants and vegetation poked through narrow fissures.

They walked some more.

Ezra put his hand on Pott's arm to stop him. "Listen," he said.

"Voices," Potts observed.

They made their way to the edge and peered cautiously over the escarpment. They saw no one, but were convinced the sounds were emanating from below them. They walked on cautiously, listening. They came to a narrow path leading down towards the river. Slowly, they made their way to the voices, which were now mingled with laughter and the splashing of water. They crept on using the vegetation for cover. They saw two boys, maybe fourteen or fifteen years old, standing on a rocky ledge and peering into the water. Their skin was brown (*Not as dark as the skin of the girl Horace Clunk had rescued,* Ezra thought), and they were each naked apart from what looked like a pouch made from animal hide that was hanging from a length of yarn tied about each of their waists.

The two youths suddenly cheered with excitement. A few minutes later, a third boy clambered up onto the ledge. He had a crude-looking knife, and after emptying the pouch onto the rocky ground, he began prying open the dark-blue (almost black), elongated shell he had carried with him. After a few minutes, the halves of the shell finally parted, and muffled groans filtered through to the hidden men. A slimy, yellowy-brown substance was scraped out of the shell and swallowed instantly by the excitable youth. The ritual was continued until half a dozen shells lay empty on the ground.

Before Potts could stop him, Ezra broke cover and clambered down to the ledge, making no attempt at disguising his arrival. The three youths reacted as if a monster had been sent to devour them. They brandished their crude knives and went into a semi-crouched stance with their arms out in front, bent at the elbows, and poised for conflict. Ezra raised his hands in a submissive gesture. No one spoke. The boys rocked from side to side on the balls of their feet. Very slowly, Ezra eased the bow from his shoulder, and along with the arrows, he laid them on the ground. He picked up a discarded shell and – still using slow, deliberate movements – he held it in his open palm and pointed, a quizzical look on his face. They began to speak, chattering excitedly to each other. Ezra couldn't understand, but he could tell they were having a conference. The words were a jumbled bundle of sounds that Ezra could not decipher; however, their interaction told him the story. Cautious acceptance appeared to be the verdict. The white-coloured monster was not going to eat them!

Potts decided to stay hidden; he didn't want to spook them any more. He was fascinated with the proceedings, but was ready to intervene if necessary.

Ezra told them his name. They looked bewildered. He pointed to himself and said his name repeatedly. The nearest they could get to it was Ra-Ra. They continued the ritual. After ten minutes of shouting and pointing, Ezra thought he had their names or at least an acceptable abbreviation of them.

Potts decided to join them. Again, there was another period of tension and confusion, and then another round of charades as he was introduced. Struggling to pronounce the P they settled on "Rots" for his name.

The boy whom Ezra was calling Agu began pointing at the river and then at Ezra; words tumbled from his mouth in a tangle of syllables. They wanted him to dive with them. It took Taylor Potts all his persuasive skills to resist their demands. Ezra pulled off his shirt to a cacophony of jabbering and finger pointing, compelling Ezra to stare at his own body to check for glaring abnormalities.

Potts smiled at the scene before him.

Agu and Ezra walked to the edge; the other boys – Idogbe and Ilamyo – stood back. Ezra and Agu glanced at each other, gave each other a cursory nod (as if acknowledging an international signal for "ready") and then, in unison, dived into the great river. Potts and the two boys walked to the edge and watched the pair disappear beneath the water.

Ezra followed Agu, deeper and deeper, turning in the water to face the rock. Agu pulled out his knife and began prying the black shells from the rock and placing them in his pouch. Ezra pulled his knife from its sheath and began collecting his own shells, although he had to put them in Agu's pouch.

Potts continued to stare into the water. "God's blood," he muttered, "no one can stay underwater that long." He turned to the boys who weren't perturbed in the least. "Get in. Go find them. Don't just stand there like a couple of half-baked donkey turds."

Idogbe and Ilamyo ignored Potts's behaviour. After a short discussion, they reached the conclusion that Rots had been in the direct sun for too long. It was not good for white-skinned men. They were delicate creatures.

Ezra broke the surface first. Potts – in a combination of excitement and relief, which together overwhelmed him momentarily – lost his footing and tumbled into the river.

Ezra retrieved a spluttering Potts and manhandled him onto the bank. They climbed up to the ledge to find the two boys laughing uncontrollably. Whilst pulling off his shirt, Potts muttered some unintelligible comment. He threw the dripping garment at a bush, where it hooked itself. Droplets of water plopped onto the rocky surface.

"How the devil can you stay underwater for so long? And that other lad… Strike me dead, but he's still down there. Christ Almighty, they must be half fish." Potts hesitated for a moment before correcting himself. "Part fish. Check behind their ears to see if they've got gills or somethin'."

Ezra said nothing; he was staring at a livid scar that coursed from Potts's breast to his navel – a diagonal lesion that had clumsily been repaired, either by a novice or someone who thought they were wasting their time.

Agu erupted into the daylight, distracting them. They watched as he floated calmly on the surface, his head slightly tilted, his arms outstretched, his legs hardly moving, and his body gradually returning to normal as his heart rate increased steadily. Ezra watched Agu's ritual, intrigued. Every time he had surfaced, he took great gulps of air in an agitated manner, desperate for air. Ezra counted in his head whilst he was underwater, something he had started doing when swimming in his lagoon. This time, he had reached two hundred and eighty-seven. Ezra reckoned Agu must have been down there for around four hundred. *Unbelievable*, he thought.

Agu clambered up to the ledge, his lissom manoeuvres making light work of the task. He tipped out the contents of the pouch, and they all began opening the mussels. Potts had tasted such things growing up in Lowestoft. Ezra had to close his eyes before dropping the slimy mollusc into his mouth. The taste, once he'd mastered the peculiar texture, was good.

Suddenly, Agu jumped in the air, up and down, up and down, shouting excitedly. Idogbe and Ilamyo joined in the boisterous behaviour. They had found something. Agu approached Ezra, his hand open. In his palm sat a spherical stone, which was quite small, the size of Ezra's thumbnail perhaps. It shone in the sunlight, creating subtle changes of colour: pinks, greys and whites. Agu placed it in Ezra's hand. Ezra held it up between his thumb and index finger, admiring the exquisite gem.

"It's a pearl," Potts said. "The ladies wear them round their necks. Well, leastways, the ones who've got plenty of money do."

Ezra admired it some more and then tried to give it back. He was met with a very stern look. Agu pushed Ezra's hand away.

"I reckon you'll upset the boy if you don't take it," suggested Potts.

Ezra thanked the boys in turn, and they continued opening the shells.

Potts rescued his damp shirt from the bush, gave it a shake and drew it on, pulling and tugging as the material stuck to his skin. "We'd best be gettin' back," he declared. He saw Ezra leaning against the trunk of wizened tree. His palms were against the trunk and his head was bowed. "Ezra, c'mon lad."

Ezra couldn't move. He began to vomit. His legs liquefied, and he fell to his knees. Sweat poured from his brow into his eyes, down his face, through his stubble and off his chin. His gut churned, forcing pain up to his throat and around his jaw. The sun beating down on the back of his neck was unbearable. And then he collapsed.

# Chapter Fourteen

Isaac felt his world crumble. All the deceit. The lies. The capricious fondling of the truth by Wesley Marrick. How had he not sussed out Marrick from the beginning? He had allowed this moment to happen through his vacuous conduct. He'd had time during the voyage to question Marrick thoroughly, yet he had chosen to take the man into his confidence, having considered him a person of propriety. What he chastised himself for the most was that Marrick had actually been a warning, because it was clear that he was destined to sail into the clutches of Garcia Paz whatever happened.

Cordelia was physically stunned. She felt her legs give way. Isaac supported her as she wobbled, keeping her upright.

"You're the wife of that pompous bastard Marrick?" Spurt ignored Dunsmoore for the moment.

Paz intervened. "Really, Senor Roth. Let us maintain civility. This is indeed Cordelia Marrick, but I'm afraid there's been a slight mishap regarding Wesley Marrick."

"'E'll 'ave more than a slight fuckin' mishap if 'e don't turn up 'ere with the money he owes me." Spurt's language had a habit of deteriorating the angrier he became.

"Now, now, Senor Roth. It seems you must have frightened the hapless Marrick more than you realised. It appears he shot himself, not a day or two since."

"Shot 'imself?"

"Apparently so."

"Then the debt falls to you, madam. Let me see." Spurt, his composure resumed, made a show of calculating, muttering numbers and counting days. "A hundred and fifty of your fine English pounds should cover it, and I'll overlook the spineless shit not turning up in person. And you, madam, may take comfort from knowing he would have died a gruesome death at my hand."

Cordelia gasped. Isaac gripped her tightly, supporting her weight.

"I'm sure the good lady and your good self can reach an amicable agreement, one way or another, but for now, we have more pressing business," Paz continued, "Your men are stuck on the island, a problem that needs your urgent attention, Senor Roth. We need to secure Captain Dunsmoore's ship, or should I say *our* ship, and we need to get work underway immediately to get her repainted and the hold reconfigured. Oh, and I understand you will be needing a new anchor for *Angerona*." Paz smiled to himself as he said the last words.

Cordelia regained her composure. "In the unlikely event you can show me satisfactory evidence that such a preposterous debt ever existed, I shall give the matter my fullest consideration."

Rothwell Spurt felt Wesley Marrick taunting him from his hole in the ground. He wanted, more than anything, to subject his widow to some inexplicably horrible torture; however, he managed to control the rage welling inside him. Instead, he offered Cordelia a crooked smile, which sent a shiver up her spine.

Isaac fixed his gaze on Paz. "What are your intentions?"

Garcia Paz had been disappointed at Dunsmoore's stoic reaction. The woman had shown early signs of hysteria, but had now rallied. "I need the cooperation of you and your crew. To achieve this, Cordelia Marrick and her daughter, when we catch up with her, will be incarcerated here in the fortress. If I receive your full cooperation, they will remain unharmed and will be treated with respect. Once the ships have been prepared, they will sail to the west coast of Africa and return to Belém with negroes. Senor Spurt, here, would just as soon slaughter all of you, but we are short of good hands to sail the ships. These blacks are a vital part of our thriving economy, Captain Dunsmoore, and Senor Roth is very good at... How shall I put it? Relocating them. If I have satisfied myself that you pose no threat to the operation, I will allow you to accompany Senor Roth on the expedition, but you will be stripped of your rank and put to work with the rest of the crew." Paz paused for a reaction. There was none. "Your choice, Captain; your choice."

Paz nodded to Marinho. Two of his men stepped forwards and led Cordelia from the room. Her eyes locked fleetingly with Isaac's and then she was gone.

"Senor Roth, I suggest you organise a flotilla of boats to fetch your men from the island," Paz went on. "Captain Marinho will provide men to power the oars. Captain

Dunsmoore, you will return to the ship with Tiago – Captain Marinho – and you will explain the situation to your men. Any resistance, Captain, will be met with the utmost force. In case you are thinking of jeopardising the operation in any way, you may look to the gibbet overhanging the north wall. There you will see a naked Cordelia Marrick hanging from her ankles. Your fate for any disruption would be similar."

Isaac had little doubt that Paz would carry out his threat. He also had little doubt he would have to capitulate to Paz's terms. For now.

*

A group of Paz's men left the fortress with Spurt. Outside the doors, slumped against the wall, were two men. When they saw their captain, they staggered to their feet. When questioned by Spurt, one could only respond with muted grunts, and the other – who had congealed blood stuck to his face and neck – struggled to stand upright and spoke in short bursts whilst clutching his groin. They had, it seemed, been attacked by a gang of drunken foreigners just looking for trouble. They had managed to deal with at least four of them, but, eventually, there had been too many of them and they were overpowered.

Rothwell Spurt had just grunted and told them to shift their arses.

There was work to be done.

# Chapter Fifteen

Ezra opened his eyes. The surroundings were unfamiliar. He felt like he was reliving a previous experience. A picture of his parents – Fred and Mary – hung in front of his vision like a faded portrait. He tried to touch them. They disappeared. Then there was nothing.

*

The limp body of Ezra Quicklock swamped the slighter frame of Taylor Potts. When your limbs appear to be made of iron, the size-to-weight ratio becomes defunct. Nevertheless, it had been a difficult descent to the riverbank.

Potts was totally confused. He thought Ezra would die. He knew there was stuff growing in places like this that would kill you, and animals that would eat you or inject you with deadly venom. He also knew Ezra's best chance of survival would be with the people who lived and thrived upon the forest's bountiful ingredients.

Habitually, the boys had hauled their slender canoe

from the river and hidden it amongst the vegetation. After loading the men aboard, Idogbe and Ilamyo now paddled furiously upriver, with the sick white man slumped in the arms of his companion. Agu scooped water gently onto the swollen face of his new friend, chanting unintelligible words, then berating the two boys. *Faster. Faster.*

That had been two days ago.

\*

Jonas Carp had emerged into the world destined to achieve God's work. His father, Reverend Bartholomew Carp, had been the very symbol of piety and Jonas had proved an excellent study. The urge to spread the Word of God to those less fortunate and the opportunity to explore new worlds in this modern era overcame Jonas. He set sail from England clutching a small valise, a copy of the Holy Bible, a crucifix, and a heart and soul full of righteous goodwill.

Now he sat cross-legged on the ground, praying for the life of a white youth, speaking out loud in his native tongue – it was the first time for years that anyone had understood him. It had been Jonas Carp's good fortune that a white missionary had arrived before him and had promptly been eaten. Ironically, his bones – in no particular order – hung from a makeshift cross for all to admire. Despite his protestations, Jonas could not persuade them to bury the remains. The whole tribe had disliked the white flesh immensely. Apparently, it had been stringy and tasteless. Jonas's good fortune now extended to a couple of strangers.

He had lived with the tribe for nearly three years, and he had learnt to understand their language and their rituals.

They were offering up prayers, not to God Almighty as Jonas had wished, but to the sun, the moon, the stars, the forest and the great river that sustained them. Jonas took solace in knowing that God had created all those things.

Jonas heard a muffled groan. The young man was awake.

Ezra eased himself up and rested on his elbows, a bewildered look on his face.

"Fear not, Ezra the good Lord has spared you. He has seen fit to place you in the hands of these unenlightened but worthy savages. Let us pray together, Ezra, for our eternal souls, to ask God our Saviour to keep us safe, and in turn to show our friends the path to forgiveness and righteousness."

Ezra stared in disbelief. *Shit,* he thought, *I'm dead.*

Potts burst into the small, triangular-shaped hut. "Thank Christ."

Agu followed him in, dancing on the spot and chattering excitedly. His friend was saved.

Jonas could only hope that his perseverance would one day overcome the need for blasphemous remarks and ritualistic prancing, although as time slipped slowly by, he had begun to realise that an ingrained belief had gradually turned to hope. Nevertheless, it gave him something to cling to.

*

On the fourth day after their arrival in the village, Ezra and Potts were ready to leave. Ezra had suffered an allergic reaction to the freshwater mussel. The tribesmen had seen it before. The fever, the swelling and the red blotches were the body's rejection of an alien substance infiltrating its works. Sometimes you were taken. Sometimes you weren't.

They were keen to get back to the ship. Potts knew the captain would be searching for them, but he would have to leave eventually, with or without them. Jonas Carp had refused their invitation to join them. He still had hope.

Agu had given Ezra his pearl. He had threaded a thin line of animal gut through a minute hole he had somehow made in it and hung it around Ezra's neck. Jonas explained to Ezra that it was a great honour and a symbol of their friendship.

Ezra and Potts were taken by canoe to the same spot where they had first met the boys, and they were soon on the track making their way towards the fortress.

They mulled over the events of the previous days whilst they walked. The tower came into view, and they fell silent. They could hear voices mixed with the chinking of iron and the rattle of carts and hooves on cobbled ground. They made the decision to duck into the vegetation for cover. It had been more of an instinctive action than one based on physical evidence. It proved to be the right one.

The convoy came into view. A pair of mules in harness dragged a wooden cart. A wizened man, his shoulders hunched, stood in the load bed with his thighs against the headboard; he held the reins loosely, encouraging the animals to adopt a steady pace. Another man sat on the tailgate, his legs dangling and a bull whip laid casually over his knee. Tethered to the rear of the cart was a black man. Behind him was another and another, forming a long line of maybe thirty souls – mostly men, but a few women. They were all shackled, at their hands and their legs, with the iron pressing and chafing with every movement. A loop of rope connected them. At the end of the shackled line was a giant. He stood head and shoulders above everyone and was neither black nor white. Behind him came another pair of mules, pulling another cart; another man stood at the front, and yet another sat on the tailgate, swinging his legs and holding another whip. Tethered to the cart was a string of six mules, all laden with cargo. Another two men on foot cajoled the sturdy creatures and any of the slaves who slackened the pace. These men all carried muskets and cutlasses hung at their waists.

Ezra and Potts watched the last swishing tail disappear beneath the canopy. The two men stayed crouched in their hiding place, stunned at the sight of Horace Clunk hobbled to a string of black men and women. Something had gone horribly wrong. They spat theories to each other, hissing the words. There were more questions than answers. Their conclusion was that Rothwell Spurt had somehow escaped the island and, working with Garcia Paz, had captured *Rebecca-Ann*. These were reasonable assumptions given the circumstances.

They had a terrible dilemma. Horace Clunk was being led away; the iron shackles, they knew, would be a bitter reminder of his distant past.

"They would have done better to put a ball through his head than put him in chains." Potts thought he had said the words to himself, so wasn't necessarily expecting an answer.

"We've got to do something, Taylor. We can't let them just take him. We can't," Ezra declared.

"You're right, lad, we can't. We know this track goes one way, at least for an hour or so at the pace they're movin' at. That'll give us a little time to see if we can see the ship, and try to get an idea of what's happened."

They crept out of hiding and into plain sight. There were no men on the ramparts; the track was deserted. They were vulnerable; although only a handful of Paz's men had seen them when they brought the captain and Cordelia Marrick ashore, an air of menace percolated through the atmosphere, clinging to their skin like a heavy mist.

They ducked back into the vegetation.

Ezra shrugged off his bow and arrows. He pointed to a Brazilian logwood tree and told Potts to give him a leg up. Once amongst the branches, he climbed steadily until he found himself peering through the top of the canopy. Behind him lay a carpet of green, in front of him lay the port of Belém, and to his left lay the fortress.

He could not see *Rebecca-Ann* or the stinking, grey pirate ship.

He could see people milling around in the vast courtyard of the fortress. His gaze locked on to a pair of black girls carrying large, earthenware pots. One was dressed in a fawn skirt and a reddish shirt, with the sleeves rolled back to her elbows. The other wore a pale-blue dress. Something else caught his eye: a corpse hanging by the ankles from a stout, wooden pole jutting from the north wall. The flesh had been torn to shreds; the carcass all but putrefied.

He was about to make his way down when a thought occurred to him. Ezra looked down, but he couldn't see Potts through the thicket of branches and rich foliage. He climbed stealthily along the branch he had been perched on until he reached a branch of an adjacent tree. He crept along until he reached the trunk and then he did the same again. He was able to select stout enough branches without too much difficulty, and in a few minutes, he was four trees along from the original. Then he climbed down. Silently.

Potts stood at the base of the tree, staring up into the branches, catching only glimpses of blue sky and the odd disgruntled bird, squawking at the intrusion. He rubbed the back of his neck in a vain attempt to relieve the knot.

Ezra dropped the last ten feet to the forest floor. He landed with scarcely a sound. Briefly, he considered sneaking up on Potts, but thought better of it. It would be like poking a wild animal with a stick, whilst it was eating its dinner. Too dangerous.

"Hssst. Hssst."

Taylor Potts swung round ready for action. He saw Ezra smirking from behind a tree. Not the one he watched him climb with his own eyes, but a tree twenty paces away. "Christ, Ezra. Bloody hell. What're ya tryin' to do to me, lad? Bloody hell. How d'ya manage that?"

Ezra explained how the branches intermingled with each other to form the canopy. He then told Potts there was no sign of either ship.

# Chapter Sixteen

Both ships had been moved to the far end of the quay. *Rebecca-Ann*'s transformation was nearing completion. Isaac Dunsmoore could not believe he had taken part in her decomposition. He watched in horror as the pallid grey engulfed her; *Rebecca-Ann* was erased, with a new name crudely embossed on her bows: *Gemini*.

Isaac shook his head in ironic disbelief. *What next?* he thought.

*Gemini*'s cargo holds were unrecognisable. There were rows and rows of shelves, no more than two feet wide with maybe eighteen inches of headroom between each one. There were heaps of iron shackles and chain lying on the shelves. There were stacks of wooden buckets in readiness: human cargo produced a lot of waste. Iron bars were placed strategically for ballast. They would be rearranged when the ship was fully loaded with black slaves. Stocks of food and water were replenished. *Gemini* was ready.

Rothwell Spurt was in a foul mood. He had sourced a used anchor to replace the one nestled into the seabed barely a mile from where he now stood on the poop deck of his newly named ship, and it had cost him dear. He had no choice but to pay, as the supplier had been recommended by Garcia Paz. *I bet that bastard'll be 'avin' his cut,* he thought. *When I find the little fucker who cut through the warp, I'll 'ave the skin off 'is back.*

The boarding and securing of *Rebecca-Ann* had been straightforward. Isaac had come aboard with Captain Marinho and four of his men, who were armed but relaxed and seemingly good natured. Isaac had Horace Clunk assemble the men on deck. As he explained the situation, unrest grew amongst the men. Captain Marinho had his men raise their muskets, and he took his pistol and held it to Captain Dunsmoore's head. Isaac knew the threat to Cordelia Marrick would mean little to most of his crew. He also knew they were unlikely to rush a handful of soldiers who were pointing muskets at them when they had been told their lives would be spared if they cooperated.

Marinho went with Dunsmoore to escort Joanna on deck. He was shocked to see the black girl. He looked to Isaac for an explanation.

"We rescued her from the island," was all he said on the matter. "Joanna, you need to gather your things and your mother's. You and Tomilola will be going to the fortress. Cordelia is already settled there. I'm afraid, Joanna, things have not worked out as we'd hoped."

Captain Marinho had silenced Joanna's protestations.

The party arrived at the quayside and were ushered up the stone steps where Paz was waiting.

Garcia Paz could not help himself. The sight of Joanna and Tomilola together – one fair, one dark and both beautiful – caused a leering smile to cut across his face. *My, my,* he thought, *it just gets better and better.*

The crew were lined up on the dock. "Captain Marinho, have the ladies escorted to the fortress. Put the daughter with her mother, for now. Take the black to Conny and tell her to show the girl her duties. If she proves useful, she can stay at the fortress. And get that great brute shackled up; he'll be better off at the mine."

Isaac had protested, or at least he had tried to. He knew it had been a mistake.

"Captain, when you give an order on board ship – which is not something you need concern yourself with now, I might add – do you expect that order to be obeyed or do you expect to have a five-minute debate and then issue a different order? Perhaps a show of hands, Captain, or a vote to make sure the majority are satisfied." Paz's tone was dripping with sarcasm. "Personally, I find democracies tedious. Allow me to demonstrate."

Garcia Paz drew his sword. His gaze settled on Tod Harris. To his credit the young man never flinched until the tip of the sword touched the skin, under his chin. Harris allowed his eyes to look down; the steel blade glistened in the sunlight. Paz increased the pressure forcing the young man to tip his head back. It could move no further. His neck was completely exposed. Harris thought, as did Isaac, that he was about to die. There would be no such luck.

Paz pierced the skin, enough to watch a dribble of blood form on the steel, and then he drew the blade down, very slowly and gently, until he reached Tod's breastbone. Paz took a step back to admire his work. Harris gawped at his wound. Before he could react two of Marinho's men stepped forwards, knocked him to the ground, stripped him naked, and bound his wrists and ankles. The length of rope was thrown over the yard arm. The wriggling Tod Harris was hauled up in jerky movements, dangling helplessly, with the blood from his wound now running in the opposite direction – over his chin and jaw, up his face, and into his eyes. He began to shake his head, attempting to remove the blood from his face. It was hopeless.

Isaac Dunsmoore stared impassively at Paz, knowing he had been responsible for young Harris's torture. "You have made your point, Paz. You'll hear no more complaints from me."

"Well, Captain, you may think I've made my point. Another few minutes should do it, I think." Paz looked to the sky. "The harpy eagle, Captain, which is normally extremely wary of us mortals. The sight of blood, however, emboldens them. Maybe they remember their last tasty meal, served from this very spot? Who knows, eh?"

Isaac shuddered. The men gasped in horror. The raptor plummeted from the sky. It was an amazing spectacle, according to Paz. Adjusting its angle of descent and stretching its wings to their full extent, the harpy landed on Tod Harris's face using its vicious talons for grip. Harris tried to scream, but a claw had wedged in his mouth and protruded through his cheek. The mighty bird swivelled its head, its black eyes checking for danger. The eagle's instinct was to capture its prey – a sloth or perhaps a monkey – with its powerful talons, and then return to its nest to eat or feed its young. The mighty raptor spread its wings and took to the air. Ribbons of sinew and bloody flesh hung from its talons – ripped from Tod Harris's face.

"Fear not, Captain, the eagle will return shortly. Perhaps a few more will join in the feast as well; all the better to speed up the young man's demise, don't you think?"

"You are a sick bastard, Paz." Isaac was struggling to control his guts, and he felt sure he would puke. Some of the other men had.

"I've been called worse, Captain, as you may imagine. I think we understand each other, no? You will sail with Rothwell Spurt, Captain… I forget myself – plain old Dunsmoore you are now. And you and your men will obey his orders. Do we understand each other, senor? Because the next person to dangle from the bird feeder will be one of the Marricks if my orders are disobeyed." Paz waited for a reply. "Do we understand each other?"

"We do." Isaac nearly choked on the words.

*

Sometime later, the two ships sailed from the harbour, a grey swan and a grey duck; their destination was Cacheu on the west coast of Africa.

Isaac Dunsmoore stood at the helm of *Gemini*, responding to instructions from his captain, Rothwell Spurt. His only conciliatory aspiration was Potts and Quicklock. They were out there somewhere.

Endure today, embark upon tomorrow afresh. That was all the succour he could allow himself.

# Chapter Seventeen

Ezra and Potts could hear the faint noises created by the ragged line of men and beasts: the chink of iron on iron; a cart, subjected to uneven terrain, groaning; its payload challenging the fabric to remain intact. They had tracked the convoy for three days. These noises were as familiar to them now as the noises created by the inhabitants of the mighty rainforest. For two nights, they had hoisted themselves into the crook of a tree and snatched sleep in blissful segments. The forest was an eerie bedfellow.

They had a plan, such as it was. The three days, by their reckoning, had taken them far enough away from the fortress, although they had no sense of how far they were from their destination. Now was the time. They had observed the men's habits and had got a feel for their routines, some of which had been sickening to witness.

The sun had begun its ascent. So had Ezra. He was climbing up into the canopy, with his bow slung over his back. It took him forty minutes to get where he needed to be, which was ahead of the convoy. The climb, however, had been arduous. It was harder than he'd thought. Sometimes, he found himself changing direction to find a branch that would support him. He couldn't see, but he sensed he had gone far enough. He began his descent, moving stealthily, branch by branch, until he settled in a fork, in which he was able to stand by pressing his back against the trunk, his feet pushed firmly on the opposing branch. This gave him a clear view of the track.

He had to be comfortable and stable; the accuracy of his shots would depend on it. He could not afford to miss.

There were six men. He had four arrows, one of which he held loosely in the bow. The other three he had forced into the hard wood of an adjacent branch, enabling him to reload quickly. All he could do now was wait.

The only weapon Potts had was his knife, so in the interests of self-preservation, he had cut himself a stout length of wood, as tall as himself and a couple of inches in diameter. He then whittled the end to form a lethal point. Hefting it in his hand he thought, *This should do the job.*

Ezra had waited for what felt like an age. His muscles were beginning to tighten. He eased himself into a standing position, stretching his limbs the best he could.

The green anaconda slithered down the tree, winding its huge body around the branches, its awesome power disguised by its effortless movements. Ezra heard the braying of a bad-tempered mule. The leading cart came into view. Ezra moved to position himself and then he saw the snake. Its mottled head hung motionless in the air, and a black eye reflected Ezra's own face. He froze, staring into the eye of the snake. The convoy was getting closer. Moments passed. Ezra stayed focused on the black sphere, suspended in time. The magnificent creature was staring into Ezra's soul – or that's what it felt like – assessing and probing for clues; was he friend or foe? Unexpectedly, the snake seemed to sense danger from another source and slithered past Ezra, brushing his arm with its body and dropping to the forest floor. He watched in awe as fifteen feet of greyish-green skin, overlaid with elliptical black patches, oscillated past him.

The man standing in the first cart looked up instinctively. As the message from his eyes registered in his brain, the arrow pierced his heart. His body flopped over the headboard. The mules kept walking, with the reins dragging along the ground behind them. There was another whoosh and a dull thud. The man sitting in the back, his legs dangling, toppled to one side; the tip of the arrow, having passed through his back and into his heart, jutted through the fabric of his shirt. Blood dripped onto the wooden boards.

The man in irons directly behind the cart stayed perfectly calm and kept walking; he had spotted the man with a bow, who was balanced in a tree.

The next guard was walking alongside the string of prisoners, about halfway back. The good news was that he hadn't seen or heard anything untoward. The bad news – for Ezra, at least – was that he was on the far side of the line. It would be a difficult shot, maybe impossible. The man stopped walking abruptly and began whipping a slave who had stumbled, causing a temporary disruption to progress. Ezra could just see his head; for a moment, he had a clear shot. The arrow pierced the man's left eye. Blood spurted from the wound, covering the poor slave who had been whipped savagely. The man's scream resonated through the forest as he collapsed into the vegetation.

Ezra had loaded his fourth and final arrow.

Taylor Potts chose the same moment to spring from the vegetation, shouting at the top of his voice. Of the remaining men, two were at the rear and the other one was walking alongside Horace Clunk, goading Horace in his broken English, telling him how he would only survive for a couple of years working in the silver mine, even a giant like him. Horace swung his shackled arms, smashing the man on the side of his face, and pulling the prisoner in front of him to the ground at the same time. He had started a chain reaction. Up the line, men and women stumbled until they all came to a halt. The iron brace of Horace's shackles cut deep into the man's cheek, and he fell into the vegetation, where in a few minutes, he would take his last breath.

The two men at the rear grabbed for their muskets, which were a mere yard away, lying in the cart. They both turned to see a white man brandishing a crude spear thirty feet away. There was enough time for one of them to take careful aim and shoot the madman with the spear and enough time for the other to shoot the giant.

Ezra let his breath out slowly. It had taken him a few precious seconds to figure out the order. The man pointing the musket at Potts fell to his knees. The arrow on a downward trajectory had pierced the back of his neck, and it now protruded just above the breastbone. His face hit the ground with a thud.

Potts had the whole of the other man's back as a target. He threw the spear whilst running at full tilt. It somewhat fortuitously hit the man between two ribs and went far enough through to stick out of his chest by several inches. The musket went off as he fell; the spent shot crashed harmlessly through the thick vegetation. The pointed end of Taylor Potts's spear snapped as it hit the ground.

Ezra dropped to the forest floor. He walked over to the mules; they were scuffing the ground with their hooves. One at a time, he took the bridle of each and scratched behind its ears, talking in a soothing tone. He stared at the man folded in half over the headboard. A few minutes ago, he had never killed a man, now he had killed four.

The slave tethered to the cart seemed to read the young man's thoughts. "Dem wicked, dey are. Dey anmals preshuss. Dem men wicked; dey deservin' dem arras ya put innem. Dat good shootin', tanks."

Ezra nodded; he'd grasped the general drift.

Potts had freed Horace Clunk from his shackles. They had chafed the scar tissue of his old wounds.

"You two took yer sweet time. Three days I've bin wearin' these things. I never thought I'd let the bastards put 'em on me agen. Muss be goin' soft."

Potts looked over his shoulder at the man with his face smashed. "Tell that to him, Horace."

They set to and freed the line of prisoners. They dragged the corpses into the undergrowth. Ezra removed the arrows. It proved a gruesome task. He put his foot on the man's face and pulled the arrow from his eye, then he turned his head away and retched. The others had been slightly less harrowing. *Either that,* he thought, *or I'm getting used to it.*

The scene in the midst of the Amazon Rainforest was a little chaotic. There were thirty-three would-be slaves, half a dozen mules and three merchant seamen, all of whom had nowhere to go except a silver mine in one direction and the fortress in the other.

Horace had explained the events on the dockside. He told them that the ladies – including the black girl they had rescued from the island, who was called Tomilola – were being held hostage in the fortress, and the captain would now be part of the crew that was sailing with Rothwell Spurt to the west coast of Africa to capture more slaves. Garcia Paz had told the captain that any mutinous behaviour would result in one of the ladies being strung up like poor Tod Harris.

"God's blood," muttered Potts, "what a shit state. *Rebecca-Ann* won't be back for what…" He paused. "Ten, maybe twelve weeks? What d'ya reckon, Horace?"

"That's about the way of it, given some good fortune an' a fair wind," Clunk confirmed.

Ezra looked at Potts. "We can't go forwards and we can't go backwards; I reckon we'll have to go sideways, down to the river."

"What's at the river?" Horace asked.

"The Tupi tribe." Potts explained to Horace the events that, although nearly fatal for Ezra, had put them out of harm's way.

They decided to retrace their steps for a day, rest overnight and then cut their way through the jungle towards the river. They loaded as many people into the carts as they could and began the ponderous journey.

Ezra sat on the tailgate, with his legs dangling, just as the man he had shot through the heart had done a couple of hours earlier. A man sat next to him. His clothes were filthy, his wrists and ankles were badly chafed, and down the side of his face and neck there were livid tracks where he'd been whipped. Unprompted, he began to talk. He spoke in the pidgin English that had spread into the African villages since the arrival of European traders. Ezra was becoming attuned to the subverted language.

The man told Ezra of the night his village was invaded by men – white men who looked like Ezra – and how they killed anyone who tried to fight back. He was separated from his wife, and their youngest children, aged just five and seven, who were left behind. He had not seen his twelve-year-old son or his wife since they docked in Belém. The voyage was the worst thirty-five days (he had counted them) of his life. They were all shackled together in the hold, lying on narrow, wooden shelves on which there was not enough room to sit. They only had buckets for a toilet, which overflowed constantly. The stink was unbearable. They were dragged onto the deck for an hour once a day. The foul stench from the hold would follow them up, he said. And then when they thought it was impossible for it to get any worse, they were sold off to the highest bidder – enslaved. He must be one of the lucky ones, he told Ezra, because he was sitting on the back of a cart, talking to a white man who had removed his shackles and who meant him no harm.

Ezra asked his name.

"Oluwafunmilayo. Dey calls me Olu," the man replied.

"Hi Olu. My name is Ezra."

*

His knots and ricks and aches were enough to bestir Ezra from his slumber, though the cacophony of sounds from the forest dwellers were there to wake him otherwise. Sleeping had become a strange experience, not a continuous, uninterrupted event, leaving him refreshed and ready to begin a new day.

Ezra found Potts, who had just endured a similar night, and the two of them headed out to search for a suitable spot to start their journey towards the river. Ezra was pulling at a piece of corn bread. It was dry, chewy and tasted like it should have been eaten a week ago, but he persevered.

Potts wasn't exactly sure what a suitable spot would look like, but he knew he would recognise it when he saw it. However, he was sure that he was the only one looking for it. "What's on your mind, lad?"

"Roasted pig." Ezra threw the remains of the corn bread in the air, waited a second, then kicked it into the undergrowth.

"Yeah, now you mention it, I think I can smell it."

Ezra took a deep breath. "Smells good, doesn't it?"

"Sure does."

"I killed four men, Taylor. They never had chance to fight back. I killed 'em, Taylor; I shot 'em like they were sick dogs."

"D'ya remember that, just before you took ill, you were starin' at this?" Potts lifted his shirt, revealing the scar.

Ezra nodded, a little embarrassed. "I wanted to ask you about it."

"I call it my sympathy scar, Ezra. See, what you did was that you killed four men who needed killin'. Four men who'd've killed you, me, Horace an' all them slaves without a second thought. And you killed 'em without flinchin', Ezra. If you'd've shot the one who was gonna shoot Horace, I wouldn't be here now. This is why you needed all them hours in the storeroom, Ezra. There's no explainin' to someone what your gonna do to 'em before you do it, an' no second thoughts, cos you'll end up with one of these…" Potts lifted his shirt again. "Or worse. You can bash yourself about, lad, but you saved all of us an' gave them black folk another chance, such as it is. I gave someone a second chance, long time ago, got me best mate killed and got this for me troubles."

"Thanks Taylor."

Together, they carried on searching.

# Chapter Eighteen

The grey ships dropped anchor in a secluded harbour a mile or so along the coast from the port of Cacheu. They had been at sea for thirty-four days.

Spurt had put Rudd in command of *Angerona* and split Isaac's crew between the two ships. The crossing had been tedious and mostly uneventful, but not quite. The new captain was desperate to have *Gemini* under full sail, but he decided to remain in convoy – for now, at least. He would test her out on the return journey.

Dunsmoore's crew had settled well; the sight of their mate being pecked and ripped to death by the harpy eagle had subdued them nicely. He had to admit that it would be a while before he erased the image from his own warped mind. However, he desperately wanted to find the wretch who had cut *Angerona* free. He needed to be taught a lesson. He questioned Roly Smith and smacked him full in the face with the back of his hand when Smith told him the culprit wasn't amongst the crew. He'd questioned Isaac and told him not to lie. Isaac told him the truth and then added that if he knew anything, those two would be long gone by now, especially if they had seen poor Tod Harris strung up. He didn't ever expect to clap eyes on them again.

"It's just as well for the fucker who left my anchor to rot on the seabed. Mind, you'd've given the order, so I suppose I should hold you responsible, Dunsmoore," Spurt declared.

"Aye, Captain, you should," concurred Isaac.

Rothwell Spurt held his temper. He desperately wanted to hurt the smug bastard – to physically injure him. He knew, however, that Dunsmoore had not been given the captaincy through some act of favouritism or misguided nepotism. His skills coursed through his veins like blood itself. Perhaps, one day, he would get to spill some. For now, his services were invaluable.

None of this had put Spurt in good humour.

Mister Tender-dick and his mate were on board *Gemini*. The one Potts had punched was still unable to speak. He communicated in grunts and croaks. He couldn't eat properly and choked when he tried to drink. He'd lost weight, felt weak and spent most of his time in hiding, trying to make himself invisible to his captain. His luck had just run out. Spurt had him brought to the helm where he stood next to Dunsmoore.

The man had black rings under his eyes, which were gradually disappearing into their sockets, and his pallor was a sickly yellow. He knuckled his forehead in a pathetic attempt at subordination.

"Ah, Jakes. How're ya feeling?" Rothwell said in a mocking tone.

A faint croak was the pathetic response.

Rothwell put his hand to his ear. "Speak up, man."

There was another faint croak.

"Dunsmoore, here, wants a break. 'E's bin at the 'elm for a good while now; ain't that right, Dunsmoore?"

Isaac felt helpless, but he attempted to help the poor wretch. "I reckon I could carry on a bit longer yet."

"Stand aside, Dunsmoore, and allow Jakes to do his duty," Rothwell growled.

Isaac stood aside, and Jakes tried to take the helm. He clung to the spokes in desperation.

Spurt bellowed, "*Two points to starboard.*"

Jake tried. His body would not respond. He knew it was the end. Briefly, a mawkish sense of relief overwhelmed him.

Rothwell grabbed a handful of Jakes's hair and smashed his face into the ship's wheel. He yanked it back and examined the result. Jakes opened his mouth and feebly spat his two front teeth onto the deck; a pathetic groan escaped from somewhere inside him. He felt himself being propelled along, though his legs were struggling to keep up. He was raised over the rail, cartwheeled through the air and then his weak and battered frame, hit the cool water of the Atlantic Ocean. It was soothing for a moment, but then burning as it filtered past his crushed trachea before filling his lungs. Then came the blessed relief.

Rothwell came back to the helm, brushing his hands together as if removing unwanted remnants of something. "Just in case you were wonderin', that's what happens to the rubbish." The derision in his tone was evident. "Hold your course, Dunsmoore. Keep *Angerona* in sight; I'm going to my quarters for a lie down."

Isaac looked to the coast, wiping the sweat from his eyes. The intense heat created distorted images. Thermal eddies blurred his outlook. His thoughts took him to Cordelia. He had promised to care for her and Joanna. He had let them down. He had failed them on every count. It should have been him hanging from the yard arm with the eagles ripping his face to shreds. He asked himself if it was a forlorn hope he clung to. Were Potts and Quicklock out there somewhere, plotting? Most likely they had been captured. The lad would never know his lineage. For now, though, he told himself, he had to get through this godforsaken voyage, get back to Belém and take any opportunity, should it arise.

Before retiring to his cabin, Rothwell barked his orders. They would make camp onshore and be ready to leave before dawn the next morning. He decided to leave Isaac aboard ship with four of his men. They could guard both ships. He reckoned that he would struggle to get Dunsmoore to drag defenceless creatures from their villages, or maybe even have to kill the odd one or two if they met resistance. He didn't want any unnecessary distractions. He would have Dunsmoore clapped in irons whilst he was gone – just to be sure he couldn't get up to any mischief.

# Chapter Nineteen

The cluster of bewildered children, all holding hands, walked into the neighbouring village. For three days they had followed the Cacheu River, walking in silence, living off berries and drinking the brackish river water. They huddled together to try to sleep. The nightmares came when darkness fell: their families torn away, shackled and beaten; and their village wasted.

Ekundayo sat cross-legged on the ground next to the fire. A pyramid of sticks supported a small mammal that was being roasted steadily over the hot embers. She had berated her husband (Bukar) and her eldest son (Issouf) for bringing her such paltry fare. That would never feed seven. It would not be a meal, she had complained, but a squabble over scraps. Bukar and Issouf disappeared back into the tropical forest, determined to fulfil the new order.

Ekundayo took the roasted mammal and wrapped it in a thick, broad leaf. She set it on the ground and went to fetch a pot to boil some rice. She saw the children huddled together, too frightened to come any closer. Ekundayo put the pot down and went to the children. She didn't recognise them; they were not from her village.

The eldest boy stepped forwards. "Dey take 'im, miz. Dey white man. Dey leave uz."

Ekundayo ushered the children into her hut. She rounded up her other five offspring and made them sit by the fire, giving them strict instruction not to move. She ran through the village until she came to the elevated hut. An old man sat on the veranda, clutching a wooden stick with an animal's head carved into a nub at the top. A necklace composed of ancient molars hung at his wrinkled neck. The spotted skin of a leopard hung over one of his shoulders and across his midriff, and was joined at his bony hip. A bark-cloth skirt, tied at his waist, hung to his calves.

It was unusual for a woman to approach the tribal leader. Ekundayo raised her arms above her head, palms out. She bowed in deference to the great man. "Chief Abioye, *wahala*[1] comin'. Dey comin', Chief. Dey white man comin'."

Chief Abioye stared at Ekundayo; his dark eyes, although retracted into deep sockets, reached into her soul, searching for the fidelity of her statement. An almost imperceptible nod of his head told Ekundayo that he had found it.

The white men were coming. It was true.

\*

Rothwell Spurt led his men through the tangle of jungle. They were heavily armed with muskets, machetes, swords,

---

1        Trouble.

cutlasses, knives and axes. They followed the river, and Rothwell wondered why they hadn't thought to make some sort of barge or raft, to make use of the river. *It'd be better than busting a gut hacking through the wretched jungle,* he thought. *I'll get that ugly bastard carpenter of Dunsmoore's to build us somethin'.*

The band of pirates crept up on the outskirts of the village. Another half hour, and the jungle would come to life. Shifts would change. The men were in a half circle, and with the element of surprise, they intended to capture the inhabitants whilst they slept, with the minimum of fuss.

Rothwell signalled his men forwards and gave the order. A musket was fired into the air. Now there would be a flurry of activity. They would stumble out of the huts into captivity. All Rothwell had to do was hold a pistol to a child's head and maybe beat a few helpless souls. He supposed their fierce communal spirit and their will to live made them compliant.

As the report of the musket subsided, Rothwell became uneasy. He instructed two of his men to look in one of the huts. They kicked the frail bamboo door open and burst into the dark space. It was empty.

There was a yell. One of Rothwell's men staggered forwards with a spear between his shoulder blades; he collapsed to his knees and then fell to the ground, smashing his face into the earth. A painted black man disappeared back into the jungle.

"Fuck me, this is all we need." Rothwell spat the words to no one in particular. "Fuckin' savages." He ordered his men to form a large circle around the village. They all pointed their muskets at an invisible enemy.

A wizened, old man walked out of the jungle holding a stick, the nub of which had been carved into an animal's head. He posed no threat.

Rothwell shouted the order not to shoot. He pushed past his men and met the old man. "You killed one of my men, old man."

The old man gave his customary nod.

"You know why we're 'ere?" Rothwell snarled.

There came the same response. Then the old man raised his stick, just a few inches.

A tribesman walked from the jungle unarmed, his arms spread in a submissive gesture. He spoke to Rothwell. "Dis is Chief Abioye. He know dey comin' to take uz. He wetin' fo' dey. He vex. He wan' make deal wid dey."

Rothwell Spurt had thought he had actually seen it all. Nothing could surprise him. But this bag of skin and bones brandishing a stick and negotiating with him in the middle of the fucking godforsaken jungle just about took the biscuit. "Go on then, old man, make my fuckin' day, why don't ya?"

"We gon do dey job for dey. Dey makes it *wahala*. We gone do de job simple. Get dem ready wetin' when dey gets 'ere. Dey bring da nice stuff we gone give dey 'eathens from up dat river. Dey be 'ere wetin'."

Rothwell dissected the information the best he could. If he'd interpreted the savage correctly, they would capture the "heathens" upriver and imprison them here in the village. In return they wanted "nice stuff" from the unknown world. His days of hacking through the poxy jungle could be over. Whatever the case, it seemed like a decent solution to the current predicament.

"Tell Chief Abiho, or whatever his fuckin' name is, that we've got a deal," Spurt confirmed.

"Dey no need tell. Dey already know," the tribesman responded.

"I bet he does, the old fucker."

\*

The village was a hive of industry during the following days. Trees were lopped and two large rafts were constructed. Rothwell's men and the tribe seemed to work in relative harmony. There had been the odd kerfuffle, especially when the womenfolk returned to the fold. They were bare breasted, and some were completely naked. Rothwell had to threaten his men with severe punishment if they interfered with them. They were strictly out of bounds – for now, at least. He did not want any unnecessary aggravation.

The rafts were basically flat platforms. There were no handrails. Four men with long poles pushed them along; they were simple but effective. It was much better than hacking through thick vegetation. The elder tribesman who had stood beside the chief during the negotiation sat with Rothwell, who was ripping meat from the hind leg of a yellow mongoose, not that he knew what it was. *Good rabbit, that*, he said to himself.

"He ever say anythin', the old man?" Rothwell picked at piece of meat wedged between his front teeth as he spoke.

"Nutin' anyone dey 'ear," the tribesman replied.

"If it's you I'm gonna be dealin' with, I'd better know your moniker."

The man cocked his head to one side, a look of confusion on his face.

"What's ya name?"

"Bukar."

"Okay, Bucker. Me an' you an' the old man are gonna be partners." Rothwell stuck out his hand.

Bukar just stared at it.

"It's what we gentlemen do in the civilised world. It's called a handshake. It means you can trust me, and I can trust you."

Bukar stuck out his hand. Rothwell clasped it firmly and shook it vigorously. Bukar felt the strange, white skin – which was clammy to the touch – and his long slender fingers being scrunched together; this was not how he would declare a bond of trust.

*

Rothwell remained at the village. Thirty men had joined the foray upriver, ten of which were Rothwell's men. Rudd was in charge. He had Darricot and a party of men constructing a jetty at the riverbank. Another group of men were building a compound to hold the captured indigenous people.

Rothwell was happy with the progress. If Abioye's men proved reliable, then this should prove a most satisfactory arrangement. He thought about what he could bring them in exchange for their cooperation. One thing he would bring was some of that shitty, old broad cloth. Perhaps he could persuade them to make some clothes. There were only so many droopy tits and saggy bollocks he could bear to look at.

His thoughts turned to Dunsmoore. It struck him that he would have been the sort of man to go down fighting rather than be bossed around on his own ship. *He's a clever bastard. Perhaps I will have to kill him or maybe he'll fall into line. It's the woman: Marrick's widow. All the while he thinks she's safe, he'll behave himself. I'll have to satisfy myself with the daughter, perhaps. If that bastard Paz is agreeable.*

He shook his head; there was no need to worry about any of that now.

# Chapter Twenty

Progress towards the river was painfully slow. The African tribespeople, however, were adept at forging their way through the thick vegetation. Now supplied with machetes found in one of the carts, they sliced the burgeoning growth, carving a path of sorts amidst the shrubbery. Essentially, they had formed a slow-moving queue.

They had taken what they needed from the carts and left them on the track. They'd unhitched the mules and loaded them with the supplies. Ostensibly, the headstrong beasts were happy enough with the pace.

Before darkness fell the men spent time clearing extra space so they weren't stretched out in a long line as they camped out for the night. Several fires were lit the smoke from which lingered in the still air, emitting unknown aromas from unknown genera, providing comfort and a measure of asylum.

Ezra sat with his back to a tree, somewhat aware that a monstrous snake might join him at any moment. He hadn't had much chance to dwell on the encounter. Staring into its black eye for those few seconds, he'd not known if it would strike or just open its huge mouth and swallow him up. What he did know, however, was that he had shared a moment with the creature, and he would never forget it. Ezra was a guest in this world, and the snake had chosen to let him stay.

He was jolted from his reverie by a low voice.

"Dey mind if I sit?"

Ezra looked up, slightly taken aback. A girl, who was maybe around his own age, stood at his feet.

"Sure," he said, "it's a big tree." He shuffled along, and she plonked herself down next to him.

"Dey call me Afia," she stated.

Ezra stammered over his name. He didn't know where to look. The girl was naked apart from a narrow strip of cloth around her waist. He made a determined effort to look her in the eye, although that proved no great hardship. *She is beautiful,* he thought, *and strangely familiar.*

"I wan' tank dey for wat dey done for uz. Dey men dey kill, dey's evil. Dey do bad tings to uz. Dey da man, mistah, wat save uz." Her dark eyes filled with tears as she spoke. "Dey take my famlee. My daddy, my mammy, my sistah. Dey man take my sistah; I no' know wat dey do to her. I nevah gon see dem agen, dat I know."

Ezra wanted to comfort the girl. He couldn't touch her. She didn't have any clothes on. "Don't move, Afia; I'll be right back."

He went to where the mules were tethered and grabbed a tarpaulin that had been stowed over the rump of one of the animals. He returned to Afia and after giving the sheet a good shake and a brush off with his hand he stooped down and carefully wrapped it around her shoulders. He pulled it together at the front momentarily grazing her breast with the side of his hand. He let go immediately. The tarpaulin fell away exposing her.

"It can get a bit nippy later in the night," he said. He could feel his face colouring, burning with embarrassment. *Shit,* he thought.

Afia pulled the shabby material around her, and a smile diverted the tears momentarily. "Tanks."

Ezra sat down next to her. "My mother and father are in England. They don't know where I am. They probably think I'm dead. I miss them very much." Unwittingly he had mimicked her short sentences.

For a short time they sat in silence.

"Dey a coupla tings I no' *sabi,*[2] Ez," Afia continued before Ezra could respond. "Wat is Engeland?"

Ezra thought for a moment. "England's the country where I was born. It's many thousands of miles away, maybe forty-five days away by ship, across the great ocean." Before Ezra had realised, he started telling Afia about England: where he lived; how he worked with his father, who had taught him how to make bows and arrows, and shoot with them; how the houses were made of stone; and how it got cold in the winter. He tried to explain snow to her.

She couldn't grasp the concept of white rain. *Perhaps that's why they have white skin,* she thought.

Ezra studied her face. He sensed she was processing the information.

Then she said, "Wat is nippy, Ez?"

---

2     Know.

Ezra had spent quite a lot of the past few minutes deciphering different words and their meanings. He hadn't realised he'd used a word she was unlikely to understand. "Nippy," he explained, with a broad grin, "means cold."

"I nevah know cold all da nights I bin in dis land, Ez."

Hiding his embarrassment with the help of the fading light, he declared, "Well, Afia, you can't be too careful; the weather could turn at any moment."

\*

Late in the afternoon of the fourth day, they reached the river. The day after Ezra had warned Afia about the weather, so the rain had begun, and it showed little sign of abating. When it started, it had felt refreshing and never cold, but now it was irritating. The joy of wandering around naked or sparsely clad had dawned on Ezra. He'd discarded his shirt for now, though he hadn't plucked up the courage to ditch his breeches – not yet.

Horace Clunk and Potts had noticed how much time Ezra and Afia spent together. They both formed the opinion that it was nice to see two youngsters with a smile on their faces. God only knew, there was little to be cheerful about. Horace had spoken with Potts about the likeness Afia bore to Tomilola. He decided he would ask Afia about it. If they were sisters, he could tell her that her sister was still alive, a week or so ago at least. He would pick his moment.

They made the decision to make camp. The next morning, Ezra and Taylor would make their way along the riverbank in search of the Tupi tribe.

A short while later, after the tasks to set up the camp

were complete, Ezra sat cross-legged by the fire. He snapped little bits of twig and threw them idly into the flames. The rain had finally quit. The atmosphere was humid, and everything was damp. The fires had been troublesome to light. He was thinking about Joanna, and how she was with him. It confused him. He was sure she liked him, but why was she so snotty with him at times? He couldn't work it out. With Afia, it was much simpler. She never made him feel awkward, and there was no pretence. *God,* he thought, *I can't imagine Joanna showing me her titties.* All he could tell himself for sure was that the more he saw Afia, the more he wanted to see her.

\*

Ezra and Potts set off at sunrise in search of the Tupi village. At times, they were able to follow the riverbank without too much difficulty. Periodically, they were forced inland. What they'd give for Agu's canoe. Even though hiking through the rainforest was becoming a routine occurrence, it was arduous toil. A rotting trunk, now horizontal after centuries of rooted existence, invited them to sit.

Potts spoke first. "You like her; Afia, I mean." His tone was matter of fact.

Ezra cocked an eyebrow at Potts. "I like you too. I like Horace Clunk…"

"Okay, okay! You know what I'm on about." Potts seemed a little flustered. "It's just… well… you know… she's a girl, ain't she?"

"You've been paying attention then."

"I'm just sayin', that's all."

Ezra got up, walked over to a spikey-leaved plant and cut down a strange looking fruit. It was a yellowy-green colour with strange leaves growing out of the top. The fruit was encased in a gnarly skin, which Ezra began peeling with his knife. He passed a slice to Potts. "Afia showed me this. What d'ya think?"

Potts munched on the succulent fruit; rich syrup dripped off his chin. "Got any more?"

Ezra sliced off a chunk and passed it to his friend.

"These last few days with Afi, Taylor." Ezra paused. "I can't remember when the time passed so quickly. When I'm with her, I don't think about our situation, the captain, Cordelia and Joanna. Or Tod Harris. Is that bad, Taylor?"

"No, lad, it's not." A purposeful silence lingered. "Give us another lump of that. Woss it called anyway?"

Ezra cut another slice. "I think Afi called it *anass*[3] or somethin'. Good, innit?"

Potts smiled. "I'll try not to let the name put me off."

\*

When they arrived at the Tupi village, the two men were greeted like long-lost relatives. The hubbub spread through the village. Agu hugged Ezra like a brother he'd not seen for a thousand sunsets.

Jonas Carp scanned them both with a quizzical frown. "Our Lord God Almighty has seen fit to show our friends the way home. Praise be to our Lord who sacrificed His only child to show us the way and—"

---

3      *Ananas* – that is, pineapple.

"Bloody hell, Jonas," Potts interrupted, "'scuse me, Padre; we've only bin gone five minutes an' we found our own way."

"No, no, Taylor, God shows us the way; He lights our path."

"Okay, okay, you win." Potts stuck out his hand. "It's good to see you, Jonas Carp."

Carp took the offered hand. "It's good to see you, Taylor Potts." He turned to Ezra. "It's good to see you too, young man, and with no ill effects, by the look of you. Although a good wash and brush up wouldn't do either of you any great harm."

Ezra smiled. "Thanks to you and Agu's people, I'm fine. A week trekking through the forest, though, can have its drawbacks."

"Indeed, it can. Let us sit and take some refreshment. I see through God's eyes that you have troubles to impart."

They followed Jonas to the place where the refreshments were to be offered. They sat cross-legged on the floor with the tribal elders, of whom there were four, all male. Agu, Idogbe, Ilamyo and a bunch of youngsters all stood nearby, gibbering excitedly; they hadn't been invited to sit and were soon shooed away.

Potts, with a little help from Ezra here and there, explained the events that had happened since they had departed the village. The elders were impatient for Jonas to translate. It was a painful process.

When the explanations were over, the elders huddled together and spoke in earnest with each other. The other three left the elders to their deliberations.

"They make their decisions based on the facts," Jonas

said. "Emotions are discarded when they have to make a decision that could have an impact on their way of life, or their survival even. I suppose that makes the decision easier to reach. What I can tell you is that, whatever it is, there will be no argument and no more debate. We shall have to wait for their declaration and abide by their ruling."

Potts and Ezra nodded in agreement.

The elders called them back.

Jonas began the translation: "The African people cannot come into the village. The generations whose spirits live in the trees now, the Tupis' fathers and their fathers, knew of their suffering. They were enslaved by the people who had similar skin to us white people. I think they must mean the Portuguese or Spanish. The Tupi people were infected with disease by these accursed tribes. They had no immunity to European ailments." Jonas elaborated periodically to make the point. "As slaves, they became less and less desirable until they gave up on them altogether. Now they bring ugly black people from another land – who, like us white people, can't help being ugly – to serve them. It seems that we proper white-skinned people have no effect on the Tupi. They know this because I have lived amongst them for many sunsets, and your visit is a blessing from the spirits." Jonas smiled. "I'm not sure how they came to that conclusion."

He continued translating, "They have no quarrel with these people who have been stolen from their homes. They can make a village of their own along the riverbank. They can be neighbours. The great forest provides plenty. They can learn the humble ways of the Tupi tribe. We can show them." Jonas pointed at the three of them. "Tonight, we will feast in honour of our new neighbours, and when they have lived under the protection of the mighty tree for many sunsets, the forest will enshrine us and guard us from the spirit of evildoers."

*

That night, a tapir was butchered and roasted. Its large carcass hung on a spit over bright-red embers. Fat fell from the beast periodically, causing flames to leap up and scorch the hide. Neither Ezra nor Potts had ever seen such a strange animal; nevertheless, the aroma of roasting meat was intoxicating.

Everyone in the village had a taste of the tapir meat. It was good. There was much excitement that reverberated around the Tupi encampment. Their demeanour was infectious, and Ezra wished Afia was there to share it with him.

Jonas Carp climbed into the canoe with Potts and Ezra, who dug the paddles into the opposing current. A foray from the village was a rare thing for Jonas, and he enjoyed chatting in his native tongue to his new-found friends. Potts had warned him, though, that God was off the agenda today; unless they found themselves in a situation where a prayer may come in useful.

Jonas had been given the responsibility of selecting the site for the Africans' village. They had been paddling for an hour or so when he pointed to the opposite bank. There was a natural clearing with a carpet of lush grass. They paddled further upriver before crossing, to where the current eased them to the opposite bank with minimal effort.

The three of them got out of the canoe and wandered around the clearing. It must have been a hundred paces along the riverbank and fifty deep. It would make an excellent start. Pleased with their find, they returned to the canoe and continued the journey upriver.

After a few minutes paddling, the river began to curve and, isolated from the main flow, a lake had formed. It was a beautiful sight; viridescent plants floated on the surface, and the foliage of the overhanging branches skimmed the surface, creating ripples on the placid water. Brightly coloured birds flew across the lake, snatching insects from the air.

"God's creations," Jonas declared, "may they never cease to rouse our spirits."

"Amen to that, Padre," Potts muttered.

# Chapter Twenty-One

Horace Clunk sat with Afia. She asked him about Ezra. He had told her how they had plucked him from the sea, how Captain Dunsmoore had cared for him, and how Cordelia Marrick had taught him to read and pronounce his words properly. She was a proper lady, and Ezra was a fine young man. Then, he asked about her sister. Afia told Horace they were born together. Tomilola first and Afia second. They did everything together. She saw the men take her sister away. She saw her kicking and screaming. She saw the men beat her and touch her, laughing. They clawed at her, all of them wanting to touch her. Then she never saw her sister again. They could have taken her, she told Horace. The pain of her loss was etched in her beautiful face, as it had been in Tomilola's, he remembered.

Horace told Afia that her sister was still alive. He explained how they had rescued her from the island, omitting the gory details; how they then sailed straight into the clutches of Garcia Paz; and how he decided to keep Tomilola as a servant at the fortress. He told her how Cordelia and Joanna had cared for Tomilola, and now they too were being held at the fortress by Paz.

Afia flung her arms around the big man and clung on fiercely. She whispered in his ear. "Tank you wid all my 'eart."

Only a few minutes later, the three men in the canoe arrived at the spot where the Africans had been waiting. They heaved the primitive craft onto the riverbank, and there to meet them was the biggest man Jonas Carp had ever seen in his entire life.

Potts introduced them. "Jonas Carp meet Horace Clunk."

Jonas extended a hand and found it engulfed in a huge mitt. The pressure was considerable. "I'm very pleased to make your acquaintance, Mister Clunk."

Horace stared down at Jonas, his question obvious: *Where the bloody 'ell 'ave you come from?*

Jonas answered before it was asked. "Our Creator brought me to this magical land, Mister Clunk, on a mission to spread the Word of God, and Taylor Potts and young Ezra have brought me here so that, together, we can take these homeless souls to the garden of Eden, where they will flourish and give praise to our Lord Jesus Christ who gave His life so we may live…"

"Ah, fair enough." Horace looked at Potts and Ezra, who were trying desperately not to laugh. Potts had a handful of his bottom lip and Ezra was hiding behind Potts, his head buried between Potts's shoulder blades.

*

The following morning they began the hike to the "garden of Eden". Ezra was at the rear of the procession, leading the mules. Afia walked at his side.

"I miss you dese last days, Ez," Afia declared.

"I missed you too, Afi," reciprocated Ezra.

"Dat nice."

"You're nice." He gave her a playful shove with his shoulder.

She smiled at him. Her face lit up. Her eyes sparkled. "Tomi, my sistah, she alive, Ez. Dat big man, 'e tell me she at dat fortress. Dey save 'er from da men. I tell big Horiss we born da same time. We da same, Ez; we da same."

Then it hit him – not in the way Taylor Potts had that day he walked into the storeroom, not physically – but the shock felt the same. The girl on the island, the girl in the blue dress at the fortress, the same girl was Afia's twin sister.

Then he saw Joanna, aboard *Rebecca-Ann*, standing at the bow with her parents, wearing the same blue dress.

"You okay, Ez?" Afia asked.

"Yeah, sorry. I was thinking, Afi. I saw her: Tomilola. She was wearing a blue dress. Joanna must have given it to her. Now I can see her face, Afi; now I recognise her," he confirmed.

"She alive, Ez; she alive."

"She is, Afi; she is." And then he thought, *As Jonas Carp's God is my witness, I am going to fetch them away from that place – or die trying.*

*

Eventually, they reached the spot where they would cross the river. To get there, Jonas had taken the canoe, packed with four of the African men. They waved at their comrades across the river.

*How we could do with a dozen such canoes,* Jonas thought.

It had been a long day. Ezra and Afia stood with the mules. They were on the wrong side of the river. There had been much discussion about how the mules would cross the river. Ezra didn't know if they could swim. The two Africans who had ferried people across the river all day returned to collect the last two passengers. Ezra led one of the animals down to the river's edge. The beast snorted, stamped and shook its head. Ezra went behind the confused animal and leant into its rump with his shoulder. Nothing. The other mules observed this with bewildered expressions, cocking their heads from side to side and trying to walk backwards.

The dark creature lurched from the water with incredible speed. Huge jaws clamped around the mule's neck and dragged the helpless beast into the fearsome reptile's domain. Ezra fell flat on his front and stared in dismay at the thrashing tangle of mule and monster, which formed a swirling vortex of horror.

Ezra climbed into the canoe, still shocked at the vicious attack. The two Africans paddled across the river; the only evidence of the mule's existence was now a floating patch of red, which was diluting gradually. The other five mules grazed idly, the demise of their companion a momentary glitch in their routine.

Potts had witnessed the scene from the opposite bank. "Jesus Christ Almighty, Jonas, what in God's name…?"

"That, Taylor, was a black caiman," Jonas explained. "The Tupi people have learnt to live with these creatures. They rarely bother the tribe, but they have been known to steal a small child occasionally, so a degree of caution is advisable."

Potts muttered, "No shit."

"We are all God's creatures, Taylor, including the black caiman." If Jonas had taken offence at Potts's blasphemous remarks, he'd hid it well.

*

The fires crackled, releasing crimson specks into the night air. They were the first fires of many that would signify the end to their nomadic existence of the previous months.

Oluwafunmilayo sat with his back straight, his legs crossed and his palms upturned on his knees. He stared, unblinking, into the fire. He saw Zoella (his wife), he saw Chi (his twelve-year-old son) and he saw his two youngest: his daughter Lumusi, who was just five, and his other son Ebrima, who was now seven. Their faces were clear to him. He implored the spirits to send him their forgiveness for not protecting them. He, Oluwafunmilayo, should have kept them safe. His punishment was a heart snapped in two, which is impossible to mend. A tear plopped into his lap, then another. But no more. They were tears of self-pity; he knew that. He would not cry those tears. When he had earned the right to cry tears of sadness, then he would cry. Until then, he would be strong, so his family would be strong. They would take their strength from him, Oluwafunmilayo.

A short distance away, Ezra etched a line on a length of hardwood that he'd beaten into the ground with a log destined for the fire. He was marking off the days. The one he'd just made was the twenty-third. He thought about *Rebecca-Ann* and her captain – her *real* captain.

A familiar voice severed his thought process: "Wat you gon do wen dat mark reach eighty, Ez?"

Ezra looked at the beautiful girl next to him. He knew that she knew the answer. "I'm going to Belém, Afi, with Taylor and Horace. And that's all I know. That's all I can tell you, Afi."

"Dat a very importan' lump of tree, dat is." Afia kept her emotions in check.

Ezra smiled. "It is, Afi; it is."

*

The African people were an industrious bunch. Their desire to make the best of the situation was inspirational. According to Jonas Carp at least. He believed his sermons were having an impact on their lives, and in some cases on their spiritual beliefs. He wanted to stay. He felt the Word of God was infiltrating their souls, and perhaps they would even build a church of sorts one day. It was a fanciful notion, maybe, but faith in the Lord could bestow rewards beyond expectation and even defy the mysterious dreams that occasionally clouded his judgement. He decided that, in a few days, he would return to the Tupi tribe and tell them of the progress. There would be much to tell, for much had been achieved.

Jonas spoke with Potts, and they decided to leave the day after tomorrow. Several canoes had now been made, including a slightly larger model to accommodate Horace Clunk. It had been noted during the initial crossing that the Tupi canoe sat dangerously low in the water with Horace aboard. In the oversized craft, Horace and Olu would follow Ezra, Potts and Jonas to the Tupi village, which would allow them to return the borrowed canoe.

*

The next morning after Ezra had marked the stick, he grabbed his bow and a handful of the arrows he had made over the last few days, and along with Afia, set out from the camp. He told Afia that he wanted to find the lake they had spotted from the canoe. She clutched his hand, and they set off into the forest.

They had been hiking through the brush for the better part of an hour, and Ezra was beginning to think he had somehow miscalculated. The perspective from the river had misled him, and he had wandered inland, perhaps too far.

Then they heard the sound of water, gurgling and splashing. Intrigued, they followed the sound. Suddenly, they were in the open and confronted by a plume of clear water cascading from a towering cliff. It was a magnificent sight. The sunlight refracted off the shimmering deluge, creating rainbows that danced amidst the falling water, like shattered fragments of coloured glass. A misty spray rose from the lake, engulfing the spill as it pummelled the placid surface.

They stood in silence, admiring the spectacle. Ezra desperately wanted to plunge into the water and swim beneath the cascading deluge. He was, however, in no mood to encounter a black caiman. He was curious whether they inhabited the lake. Perhaps Agu would know; after all, they had swum in the same river, albeit at a fair distance from here. For now, he would remain on land. Just in case.

Afia broke away from Ezra and knelt down by the riverbank.

"Careful, Afi." He knelt down next to her, his eyes fixed on the water.

"Iss okay, Ez." She scooped a handful of water from the lake and took a sip. She could feel it's slightly gritty texture scratching at her throat. "No black monstahs, Ez; dey don't like dat water. Try dis." She scooped up some more water and held it to his lips.

He looked at her. His expression told her he didn't want to taste it.

"Dis not kill, Ez. Try."

He sipped the water from her hands. "That's strange stuff, Afi." He screwed up his face and spat out the gritty liquid.

Afia had reshaped the scraggy piece of tarpaulin so she could pull it over her head. She yanked it off, exposing her breasts. She untied the narrow piece of cloth from around her waist and let it fall. She stood in front of him naked. She smiled at him, completely unabashed, with no inhibitions; her nudity was perfectly natural.

"Com' on, Ez." Afia walked into the water. She felt the soft bed of the lake squidge between her toes, and she watched as millions of little particles swirled around in the disturbed current, the unwitting guardians of their new-found pool.

He admired her shapely bottom. When the water reached her waist, she turned to face him. Ezra pulled off his shirt. She waited for a moment, watching.

He was struggling to control himself. *Shit,* he thought. He pulled off his breeches and began walking towards her.

She admired his physique, totally unashamedly. "Dey very beaut'ful for a whitey."

He smiled. "You're very beautiful."

He put his arms around her and lifted her to him. She responded, wrapping her legs around his waist. His feet sank into the silt of the lakebed. Her body pressed hard against his, and together they fell under the water. They broke the surface unable to resist each other for another second. They kissed. Softly, gently, their wet lips pressed together, freeing a deluge of emotion to stream through their young bodies. He felt her hand around him, guiding and probing. They groaned in unison, trembled and shuddered at the intensity of the repressed desire. There were fleeting moments of absolute bliss, then release – his release – pulsating through them. They remained wrapped around each other, in a fierce embrace; still coupled. Slowly, he relented, and they parted.

"Swim with me, Afi," he suggested.

Ezra guided her under the misty water. They resurfaced behind the waterfall. The noise consumed their world. Their view was a distortion created by a curtain of tumbling water. It was a magical place, reserved solely for them.

They swam back to the bank and lay there together, allowing the sun to warm them. As they dried, their skin felt smooth and somehow replenished. They kissed, they touched, they explored and they made love; together they reached that serendipitous moment – the apogee of the act. With their bodies entwined and completely relaxed, they slept, more contented than they could have ever imagined.

# Chapter Twenty-Two

Garcia Paz was not happy. They should be back by now. They were a motley crew, and he would exercise some much needed discipline on their return. He called for Captain Marinho, who did not take long to join him.

"Marinho, those men should be here by now and with a cart load of silver," Paz said in his native Portuguese. "Dispatch your sergeant and a detail to the mine."

Paz had made the captain stand to attention for the duration of the meeting. He saluted and turned to leave.

"Make sure they know it's not a punishment detail, Captain; if those bastards have turned, they need to be alert. I don't want excuses. I want my silver," Paz demanded.

Tiago Marinho left the presence of his superior feeling somewhat irked. Not only was he a vicious tyrant but he also could be a condescending prick at times. *Like it's my fault those filthy travellers aren't back yet,* he thought.

*

Sergeant Otavio Sousa was a product of the Fuzileiros, the Portuguese marines. The posting to Belém was a chance for him to see out his service in relative ease and serve under a captain who, although a little weak at times, was – in the scheme of foppish officers he had served under – a decent enough *caudillo*.[4]

This was a shit detail. A trek through the godforsaken jungle searching for a band of low-life scum. Not what he had signed up for. The military doctrine that was ingrained in his character, however, enabled him to accept the mission without rancour – towards the captain at least. The men in his detail would likely suffer. That's how it works: top to bottom. At least he wasn't the poor bastard at the end of the line.

The persistent rain began discovering a route through the dense canopy, slowing the deluge to a constant drip.

Private Luis Fernandes was at the rear of the line. "Poxy rain. Poxy mission." He spoke to the back of Fernao Lopes.

"Stop moaning and groaning, Fernandes, you miserable bastard. If you want to speak to me, say something to make me forget about this shithole." Lopes tried to sound upbeat, but he knew they had weeks of misery in front of them. There would probably be no fire tonight or the next, and he'd be eating fucking cornbread, with water dripping out of the crack of his arse. But still he didn't want to hear it from that whining bastard Fernandes. He knew one thing for sure: if they didn't keep their powder dry, Sousa would be on their case and that would only compound the misery.

---

4     Military leader.

At sunrise on the third morning, they awoke to intermittent drips. The rain had stopped. They struck the camp, made of tepee style tents, crude, but practical enough under the circumstances. They began their march. Fernandes began his wearisome drivel.

"Dear Mary Mother of God, Jesus, Joseph, the donkey, the Holy fucking Ghost, my back is killing me," groaned Fernandes.

"You blasphemous dog, Fernandes. We've only been walking for ten minutes. I swear if I have to listen to you for another second, I'm going to stick this musket up your arse and blow your fucking brains out," Lopes stated.

"Humph, you'd have to shoot me in the head to do that, you idiot."

"Think what you want, Fernandes, but in my humble opinion, your arsehole would be the most straightforward route."

Before Fernandes could respond, Sousa halted the short column. They'd found the carts, which were abandoned on the track. They were empty. To the side of the track, Sousa could see where a path had been forged into the vegetation. He barked the order to unsling their muskets and to stay alert. He silenced their mutterings and led them along the pathway of sliced shrubbery, downtrodden shoots and squashed fungi. It was not difficult to follow; this, Sousa knew, was not a track forged by a handful of men. His instinct told him that they were hunting a pack of black savages, although how they had managed to escape, he had no idea.

They continued along the makeshift pathway until they reached the abandoned campsite of the fleeing slaves, where they remained for the night.

Sometime tomorrow, they would reach the river, where Sousa believed he would find more clues as to their whereabouts. Perhaps the brainless savages had made a permanent camp at the river. So far, they had made no attempt to hide their tracks, although Sousa conceded it would have been difficult, if not impossible, to conceal so many footsteps. They should have hidden the carts and disguised the pathway into the vegetation. That's what he'd have done. Still, he wasn't complaining; they had made it easy for him. Dim-witted barbarians. One thing he was sure of was that, when he caught up with them, he would mete out some stiff lessons.

*

Potts sat in the bow of the giant canoe. Horace sat in the centre; ballast, Jonas Carp had called him. He'd not taken offence. Olu and Ezra were paddling. It was hard work, but much easier than hiking overland.

Jonas had reported the good progress of the African people. They were hard workers, survivors, and – in Carp's decorous opinion – disposed to extend their worship to God Almighty, notwithstanding some more gentle preaching from his good self. And with that belief, his unwavering faith in the good Lord and his copy of the Bible, he made the decision to spend the next few months with the African people.

They were paddling on the Tupi side of the river. Ezra had been keen to see if the mules were still about, as he had grown fond of them during their journey. He still felt the guilt of trying to force the poor beast into the river. The fearsome power of the black caiman sent a shiver down his spine.

Abruptly, Potts turned and signalled Ezra and Olu to stop paddling. He put a finger to his lips. He pointed to the bank. "Soldiers," he whispered, "from the fortress."

They secured the canoe and scrambled soundlessly onto the riverbank.

*

Sousa and his men had arrived at the river's edge and began following the trail downriver. The sound of a mule braying alerted them. The sergeant ordered his men to spread out, and with muskets raised, they stalked through the forest, allowing the screeching to guide them.

They soon found the beasts. Sousa scratched his head. Five mules, skinny and wandering aimlessly in the forest. It was strange. *Why abandon them?* he wondered. The only solution to his musing was that the slaves had crossed the river. That would cause him a problem. Goddamn savages.

With their muskets raised, they continued stalking in a scattered formation, each man having to seek his own passage through the vegetation.

Potts leapt out from the cover of a liana vine, which clung vigorously to a Brazilian logwood, and launched his machete. It span through the air: blade over handle, blade over handle, blade. It had found its mark. The soldier grunted and collapsed to his knees, clutching the weapon with both hands, his eyes wide in disbelief. He slumped forwards, resting his forehead neatly on the handle, his campaign at an end.

Potts disappeared into the forest.

The soldier nearest the fallen man fired his musket. The shot ripped through shrubbery, tearing apart waxy leaves until a hardwood trunk halted its progress. He stopped to reload. As he poured the black powder down the barrel, an arrow pierced his heart. He took an involuntary step sideways and fell backwards into a large shrub. The musket lay at his feet, and his arms were spread in an "okay, you got me" expression; the broad leaves embraced him in a salutation to his eternal resting place.

Fernandes looked across at his dead comrade. His heart was pounding; all he could hear was his blood pumping, and the sound filled his ears. A layer of sweat formed on his forehead and began to trickle slowly into his eyes, past his cheeks, through his coarse stubble and off his chin, plopping onto his white knuckles. He gripped the musket as he had gripped his favourite toy when his elder brother had tried to take it from him. He wanted to turn and run. Any courage that may have existed in him had been diluted to fear. It stopped him running. He could hear Sousa's voice, but he couldn't decipher the instruction. It was too late now.

The arrow entered just below his right ear and exited just below his left one. A plume of blood sprayed into the humid air. An instinctive reflex made his finger pull back on the trigger. Somewhere in the distance, far away, he heard a dull clunk. Damp powder. Fernandes fell to the ground; he lay motionless whilst his heart continued the task of pumping warm blood into the earth.

Sousa knew the mission had failed. They were fighting an invisible enemy. Self-preservation now lay at the forefront of his mind. He had attempted to regroup his men. The stupid bastards had ignored him. Sousa got down on his belly and crawled towards the riverbank. A scream echoed through the forest: another dead soldier.

Sousa spotted a white man clutching a Bible and mumbling words to the sky. A savage stood nearby, staring into the forest. He was hopping from one foot to the other. The sergeant saw the canoe tethered to the bank. It was his route out of this *shithole*. He checked behind him. He saw no one. He got to his feet and rushed towards the two men. Olu was no match for Sousa. He smacked the stock of his musket into Olu's face, knocking him unconscious, then pointed it directly at Jonas Carp.

"In the boat," Sousa commanded.

Jonas stared at the sergeant and shrugged his shoulders. "*No comprendo,*[5] senor."

"Get in the boat or I'll blow your fucking head off."

In any language that was clear enough. "Ah, *comprendo*; you want me to get in the boat."

Sousa didn't have time for this. He didn't want to fire his weapon because it would give away his position, and he wanted this putrid little Bible-basher as protection. He would hold a pistol to his head, in case he came under attack from the riverbank. He backhanded Carp, knocking him sideways. Before he could regain his balance, Sousa hit him again, and Jonas fell into the canoe, blood streaming from his nose and mouth. Sousa shoved the craft from bank and leapt in. The current began to take them downriver. Sousa ordered Carp to help paddle.

---

5        Understand.

*Christ, this is an ungainly vessel for two men,* he thought.

He looked over his shoulder. He saw the savage getting himself to his knees. Then the huge *mestizo*[6] came crashing through the vegetation. He knelt by the dazed Olu and helped him to his feet. He stared at Sousa, who was drifting further away by the second and had a pistol pointed at the head of Jonas Carp.

\*

Lopes stood bolt upright against the massive kapok tree, his musket pointed upright. He was breathing heavily, but trying not to. Ezra was no more than twenty paces from him. Lopes had no idea who his enemy were or where they were. Ezra stepped into the open, drew back the bow string and fired. There had been no clear shot to the heart, as the musket and the soldier's arms were obstructing Ezra's preferred target.

Lopes saw his attacker. The few seconds it had taken him to register his predicament were a liberty he could ill afford. The arrow sank into his groin; ripped through muscle, arteries and tendon; and exhausted its energy in the trunk of the kapok. Lopes screamed in agony; nevertheless, he attempted to level the musket at his attacker, but the man was gone. He tried to free himself from the tree. The pain was unbelievable. He yanked on the shaft of the arrow, shrieking in pain. His musket pointed to the ground.

Ezra stepped into the open again. He put the poor man out of his misery. The second arrow once again pinned Lopes to the mighty tree, after penetrating his heart.

---

6      Mixed-race person.

*

Sousa put the pistol down. He felt reasonably safe. The bumbling idiot in the canoe with him was no threat. The Africans had heard the musket shots. They gathered at the bank and watched the soldier and the preacher in the oversized canoe that was hogging the far bank. They must have been a hundred yards or more away. Sousa raised the pistol again, and told Carp to raise his hand as a signal for them not to give chase.

*

Ezra and Potts hurried downriver as fast as the terrain would allow. Horace followed on, supporting Olu, who was still struggling with the effects of concussion. When they reached the riverbank opposite the African village, they tried to shout instructions, but their voices were carried away in the light breeze. They must have looked ridiculous waving their hands and pointing.

Afia had seen the white preacher in the canoe. When she saw Ezra, an audible sigh escaped her lips. "Tank you, white-man God." She had whispered the words. "Dey need a boat. Quick, quick."

She ushered the men into a canoe, and they set off across the river. Another pair followed.

Ezra waved to Afia as he and Potts struck out in pursuit of Jonas Carp and the Portuguese soldier. Potts had instructed the African men to wait for Horace and Olu.

*

Jonas knew they would be passing the Tupi village very soon. He wondered if an opportunity to escape would present itself. He felt sure that would be his last chance. *Perhaps it may be advantageous to be nearer the bank,* he thought.

Jonas began dipping his paddle a couple of extra times on the left side, hoping his captor wouldn't notice. He was mistaken. He had inadvertently aroused Sousa's suspicions.

Jonas had his back to Sousa, whose voice suddenly sent a shiver up his spine.

"Don't fuck with me, preacher. Dip your paddle to starboard, or I'll blow you straight to heaven," Sousa threatened.

Jonas was learning Portuguese fast.

When they passed the village, they were in midstream. Sousa scanned the shore. More fucking savages.

Agu, Idogbe and Ilamyo were at their favourite pastime: diving for mussels and searching for pearls. They were huddled together, prising open their latest cache when Ilamyo spotted the canoe. The boys studied the occupants from their distant perch. They saw Jonas Carp's bloodied face and a mean-looking foreigner sitting behind him. They knew instantly that he needed help. In unison, they dived into the water and disappeared into its shadowy depths.

Agu watched as the hull passed over him. He broke the surface and lightly grabbed the transom. Ilamyo and Idogbe came up alongside the bow, one each side.

Sousa shouted at them and pointed the pistol at each of them in turn. He put the paddle down and leant to one side. He would shoot one of the little fuckers.

Jonas shouted a warning to the boys, telling them to go: *"The man will shoot you. Quick – go! He is the devil and he will kill you. Go, go!"*

Agu swung his leg over the gunwale and hauled himself into the boat. Sousa felt the slight movement and turned. Agu flung himself at the burly sergeant. His crude knife stuck into Sousa's gut. The pistol went off.

Sousa looked at the stubby, wooden knife sticking out of his belly. *Fucking savages*, he thought.

Jonas hit him with the paddle, using all the force he could muster. It was a huge swipe to the side of his head, and Sousa toppled over the side into the river. Idogbe and Ilamyo clambered into the boat, and they watched Sousa's body sink lower and lower, a spiral of blood now the only clue to his whereabouts, and his remains a month's supply of food for a black caiman.

Agu lay slumped in the gunwales with blood oozing from a hole in his shoulder. The shot had been at such close range that the skin around the wound was burnt. The good news was that it had exited through his back, passing in and out in less than a second, with a lifetime of damage and storytelling in its wake.

*

A short while later, Agu lay on the same rush mat that Ezra had lain on not so many weeks ago. Ezra sat with his friend, willing him to mend. He and Potts had found them struggling with the cumbersome canoe. Agu had lost consciousness and was deteriorating fast. The villagers had never seen a gunshot wound, but their tried-and-tested remedies had stabilised the young man, and his spirit would do the rest.

Potts had returned to the African village to report the news. Ezra would stay until Agu was on his feet.

Jonas had prayed continuously for the boy's recovery. The preacher had lost his Bible in the melee with Sousa, and although he consoled himself that it was a small price to pay, he missed the comfort of its words, bound in leather and inscribed by his parents.

The young lad had hurled himself at a trained soldier, a ruthless killer, with no thought for his own safety. The other two had presented themselves as a target – a human distraction. Jonas felt unworthy of their actions. Yet those thoughts would only serve to diminish their bravery. Jonas thought to himself, *After all these years of preaching the Word of God to them, they still offer up their prayers and their chants to spirits who dwell in the canopy of the great forest. I am something to them. They don't need to pray to my God, but they accept me, Jonas Carp. They saved me. I am a part of them.* The realisation that he had not wasted years of his life on a mission of self-glorification gave him great comfort. He was with his family.

Agu would live. And he would tell the story to his children and his children's children. He would show them the twisted skin where the lead ball went through his body, and they would cheer and dance and chant to the spirits who dwell in the canopy of the great forest.

# Chapter Twenty-Three

The ships were loaded with human cargo. It was a sight that would haunt him. He vowed he would not contemplate another such expedition. The barbaric treatment of these people was intolerable. Whatever happened, he would not make this voyage again.

Isaac rubbed at the livid welts the irons had inflicted on his own skin. He could only imagine the horror these people were enduring. *No*, he thought to himself, *I will not be any part of this, whatever the consequences.* However, he knew they would be severe, and not only for him.

Rothwell had been pleased with the expedition. One man had been lost, which was a small price to pay for the current arrangement. He reckoned he would only need to make this trip himself a few more times. Once a routine had been established, Rudd could take command of *Gemini*. A suitable cadet for *Angerona* would emerge over time, he felt sure. The lure of a big house and a comfortable bed, shared with any amount of fresh skin – nubile or otherwise, and any colour, it didn't matter to him – all these things were beginning to overwhelm his thoughts.

*Be patient, Rothwell,* he told himself, *you have earned these luxuries; they will be yours.*

The slaves had been counted into the holds. Three hundred and nine in *Gemini's* and two hundred and eleven in *Angerona's*. Five hundred and twenty wretched souls ripped from their homes for profit.

It did not take long for the sound of retching to filter on deck. Children, men and women – the motion of the ship served to upset them all, bar a few who were spared the contrary ailment. They were not, however, spared the stench of vomit and the overflowing buckets of putrid sick. The seasickness only compounded the stinking conditions. The consolation, albeit under the circumstances a meagre one, was that the swaying sickness would abate. The vile stench of human waste, the foetid air, the screams and sobs of children unable to cling to their mother, and the aura of impending doom hovering over them would remain, however.

The task of getting the slaves on deck once a day to allow them some fresh air to breath and to stretch out their limbs into a natural position was a logistical conundrum. Rothwell was tempted not to bother, but he knew he would lose too many to illness if they weren't given this privilege. He had them brought up in batches and allowed them fifteen minutes each. The stench that followed them was horrendous, and he generally ensconced himself in his quarters at that particular time of the day.

A bang on the cabin door caused him to swear. "God's breath, is there no peace to be had?"

"We need you on deck, sir; a bit of a kerfuffle needs sortin'," came the explanation.

Rothwell made his way past the throng of stinking

savages, doing his utmost to ignore the pungent fug. At the head of the line, he was confronted by a bony African who somehow managed to wrap his chains around the neck of a crew member and was threatening all sorts, none of which made any sense, least of all to an irritable Rothwell Spurt. Life for the crew member, however, was becoming more and more uncomfortable.

Rothwell snatched a young girl from the line. Perhaps she was twelve, though she could have been younger; it was difficult to tell. He dragged her to the front so the deranged savage had a good view. He drew his knife, an ugly blade that was probably eight inches long and razor sharp, and held it beneath the child's quivering chin. An eerie silence ensued.

Rothwell commanded, "Release that man."

The enslaved African was terrified. He'd acted on impulse. He had thought for one second that he could make a difference. He would threaten to strangle one of the crew, and demand better treatment for himself – for his people. He had made an error of judgement that would stay with him for as long as he survived these abominable conditions. He released the pressure slowly, allowing the sailor to duck free of the chains. He believed he had understood. Let the man go and everything would be okay. A few lashes perhaps. He hadn't grasped the situation at all.

Rothwell tilted the girls head backwards and ran the blade across her throat. He wiped the bloodied blade on the freed sailor's shirt sleeve and slid it back into its sheath, whilst supporting the limp frame of the pitiful girl. Then he launched her over the rail into the ocean. He turned to the sailor, who was rubbing his neck, and Rothwell punched him in the face, breaking his nose.

"You cost me one and a half slaves. Someone fetch me an axe. Now. Not next fucking week," Rothwell bellowed.

Broken-nose gawped at his captain. He had no idea what was coming next.

"Get those chains off that piece of shit." Rothwell spat out his orders.

He had the bewildered slave held with his wrist on the handrail. Rothwell swung the axe and severed the man's hand. It plopped into the Atlantic.

Rothwell barked his orders. The slaves were stunned; they were shocked into screams of terror and sorrow. The man with one hand was dragged screaming to the galley, where his stump was thrust into the hot oven. The wound was cauterised. If he were unlucky, he would live.

Isaac had never felt so wretched or so helpless. He vowed to himself that he would kill Rothwell Spurt. He would find a way. It would cost him his own life; he knew that much. And the lives of Cordelia and Joanna.

As much as he willed it, the image of that helpless girl, no more than a piece of trash to Spurt, would not leave his thoughts. She hadn't spoken; she hadn't screamed. She had been selected for maximum impact. Spurt had achieved his objective. As the days passed, he stopped trying to block out the image; he allowed it to flood his thoughts, and he would never forget her. That was all he could do for her now.

*

Rothwell had explained to Rudd that, providing the return voyage was progressing without problems, he was going to raise all the sail available. He wanted to know if *Gemini* was all she should be. It was an itch he needed to scratch.

Ten days into the voyage, Rothwell gave the order. The ship came alive. They had been stuttering along, keeping *Angerona* in sight, but now they would see what all the fuss was about.

The power of the wind billowing the sails keeled her to port, pushing her through the steely grey ocean at seventeen knots, creating a foamy wake for Rudd and his crew to envy. At this rate, they would reach Belém three or four days ahead of *Angerona*. Rothwell Spurt was a happy man.

Now Rothwell Spurt knew what all the fuss was about.

Isaac was on slops detail. A length of frayed cloth, tied at the nape of his neck, covered his mouth. The fact that he had to wear it embarrassed him. The hold was a living hell. There were no other words to describe it, not that Isaac could think of. He thought of the girl. *Perhaps she was better off. No. She didn't deserve to die. Not like that.* He shook the thought away. Emptying their waste was the least he could do for them.

He pulled the mask from his mouth and gritted his teeth. He would bear it as they were.

Isaac filled two buckets with fresh water. They were the same buckets that had contained human waste. Isaac had rinsed them with salt water until they were as clean as he could make them. He knew they were normally just given a cursory rinse. He sat them on the deck and stretched his back. As he grasped the handles, he gazed into the pails, watching the water sway gently. He caught sight of himself. His hair was the colour of straw and it hung loose to his shoulders. His eyes were dull, sunken into their ports. A full set of whiskers grew carelessly around his face. He scarcely recognised himself. He looked down and surveyed his clothes. They were filthy and torn. He was a mess.

He carried the buckets into the hold, still without wearing his mask. He settled the buckets down and made his way to the stern. The light was dingy, and the air almost unbreathable. The rattle of chains, the constant groans and sobs created an atmosphere that would trap you in a nightmare for the rest of your days. It was a dream that would afford you no peace. He checked behind him. No one had seen him, except three hundred and ten pairs of eyes. Isaac knew the ship inside out. He knew *her* as well as the men that built *her*.

To the rear of the hold, a person could access the steering mechanism. Spurt's men had built shelving across the access wall. Idiots. Isaac felt the eyes watching him, curious. The bottom shelf was about eighteen inches off the floor. He laid on his back and shuffled underneath. He waited, allowing his eyesight to adjust. He could see the void. He pushed himself along using the heels of his hands until he reached the corner. There, he knew he would be able to gain entry to the hidden space. He shuffled out and returned to his duties.

*

The days collided into each other as *Gemini* consumed the miles of empty ocean. Isaac had counted the days. Some passed easier than others. Some people fared better than others. Three slaves – two dead and one still breathing, but only just – were thrown overboard. More would follow before the journey's end.

There was two or maybe three days left, he reckoned. It was time. Isaac carried his buckets into the hold. He had managed to make eye contact with some of the captives. They would exchange cursory nods. They knew he was one of the good ones. He rinsed their buckets. He cared, and it meant something. He checked none of the other crew were about; not even his own men knew what he was doing. It was better that way.

Isaac crawled under the shelf and into the dark space. He could hear the Atlantic Ocean crashing against the hull; the whirring of cable through pulleys; the creak of seasoned oak, engineered to respond to the helmsman's requests; and the piteous sobs and groans of the unfortunate wretches, chained and trapped. He pulled his knees up to his chin, covered his face with his hands and tried desperately to block it all out. All he could see was the small girl, her frail body pirouetting into the ocean and her life's blood, still warm, gushing from the lethal wound.

*

Rothwell was relaxing in his cabin. He'd considered having one of the black savages cleaned up and brought to him. He thought better of it. He knew it would piss off his men. Not that it really mattered, but he couldn't be arsed with any more aggravation. He sat at Isaac Dunsmoore's desk, which was now his desk. He tugged at the long, narrow drawer just below the desktop. It moved a fraction and then came up against the locking mechanism. He felt around. The key dangled from a hook. It was probably there for safekeeping as much as anything.

Rothwell opened the drawer. Inside were charts and a journal; he flicked through the pages and flung it one side. There were also two letters. He broke the seals and began to read.

*Dear Edward,*

*I have not the first clue when you will get to read this letter. I will only dispatch it if I should consider it necessary and, of course, if I am able. I fully expect to hand it to you personally on our safe return. Here follows a summary of events that I felt compelled to record.*

*Not yet a full day from Milford Port, a figure was spotted clinging to a square of driftwood. To spare you the tiresome details, we soon had the unfortunate wretch aboard ship, with I might say, little time lost. The figure was a boy of seventeen years of age, who – as we discovered when he had regained his wits – was swept away whilst swimming off Milford beach. The rip tide, as we well know, is uncompromising at this time of year. I now come to the difficult part of my discourse, and I can think of no other way to say what I know will be a great shock to you. Edward, the boy is your son. The fact is undeniable. I apologise for my impoliteness and trust that you know I have your best interests at heart. The boy's name is Ezra Quicklock, and he was raised by Fred and Mary Quicklock on the outskirts of Old Milford. He is a fine young man and is the image of his father. I pledge to treat the boy as your son, and I will do everything in my power to ensure that he returns safely to his home.*

*Your humble servant,*
*Captain Isaac Dunsmoore*

Rothwell skimmed through the second letter. It proved of little interest, being merely a note to distraught parents telling them their son was still alive.

Rothwell opened the cabin door and yelled for someone to bring Dunsmoore to him. He waited.

"For fuck's sake, if you want somethin' doin' round 'ere…" he chuntered.

He opened the cabin door and was confronted by a nervous-looking crew member with his hand raised, his knuckles about to rap the door. Rothwell glared at him.

"Sir, we can't find 'im; Dunsmoore, I mean," confessed the man.

"Who the fuck else would you be on about, you dozy prick. What d'ya mean you can't find 'im?" demanded Spurt.

"We're still 'untin' for 'im, sir."

"Just find 'im an' get 'is sorry arse down 'ere." Rothwell sighed. "Fuck me. Can't find 'im." He shook his head and slammed the door, still muttering. "Can't find 'im. Fuck me."

And they couldn't. Rothwell had his men scouring the ship. Isaac Dunsmoore had disappeared.

# Chapter Twenty-Four

Cordelia and Joanna had been kept in the same room for no more than a few hours. They hadn't seen each other since. Their only connection came through Tomilola.

Joanna sat up in bed, with the cover at her waist. Her nightdress dipped to a vee revealing the soft, white skin of her cleavage. The familiar sound of the key grating in the lock was a sound she had become accustomed to and one she contemplated with a sense of restless apprehension, perhaps anticipation.

She was shocked to see Garcia Paz step into her room. She grabbed the cover and pulled it up under her chin.

"How sweet." Paz's voice had a patronising tenor. "There's no need for modesty on my account. Expecting someone else?" He cocked his head to one side and raised his manicured eyebrows in a quizzical gesture.

Paz took the few paces required and perched himself on the edge of the bed.

Joanna felt her insides turning to liquid. Defying her emotions, she said, "You call yourself a gentleman, and yet you'd burst into a lady's boudoir without so much as tap on the door?" She applied her haughtiest tone to the remark.

Paz smiled. Its effect was sufficient to send a chill through Joanna. She felt her body shudder.

"Allow me to correct you on one or two discrepancies that have arisen in your discourse. Firstly, this is not your boudoir as you so eloquently stated. It is a room that belongs to me and in which I have chosen to incarcerate you. Therefore, I see no reason why I should not come and go as I please, regardless of your sensitivities," Paz continued in his obsequious manner. "And as to me being a gentleman, I'm not sure I qualify. You see, my lovely, you should not confuse me with someone who gives a goddamn shit." The last few words were delivered with a snarl.

Paz snatched the cover from Joanna's grasp, ripping the front of her nightdress at the same time.

Her arms instinctively covered her exposed breasts. She trembled. *God in heaven, no,* she thought.

There was a knock on the door. Paz's icy stare dissolved, and he went for the door. "What the devil do you want?"

Tomilola stood there with a jug of water and a fresh cloth over her arm. "Oh," she said in a shocked tone when she saw Paz. "Beggin' dey pardon, sir. I no' know dey here." Tomilola stood her ground.

Paz composed himself. He was tempted to stay and watch the black girl wash the white girl. Perhaps another day. He pushed past Tomilola and disappeared. Tomilola let her breath go and stepped into the room. She locked the door. She had her own key, which she shared with Conny and Enny, another slave girl.

Joanna allowed the tears to escape. Tomilola sat where Paz had sat. She took Joanna in her arms and held her. She felt her sobs, her trembling body.

"Thank you, Tomi," said Joanna.

Tomilola had been to Joanna's room already that morning. She had noticed Paz unlocking the door and knew his motives would not be good. She could only hope that her presence would be enough to distract him.

The girls broke from their embrace. Tomilola brushed Joanna's tears away with a delicate touch. It felt the most natural thing in the whole world. Their lips touched. The merest of contact. It happened again, as neither could resist. Another light touch. The sensation magical. And then a long, lingering kiss with their lips together, unbridled and greedy. Then the exploration with hands feeling each other's bodies, shuddering as they each found pleasure in the caress of inquisitive fingers and tongues. They admired each other enquiringly, totally beguiled. It was the most natural thing in the whole mad world.

The girls lay naked on the bed, entwined in each other. They were taking a huge risk.

"Dat man nevah gon leave you 'lone." Tomi kissed Joanna on the forehead and untangled herself. "I be missed."

"Tomi, I have a plan," Joanna declared.

The girls dressed quickly whilst Joanna outlined her idea. "I know it's a bit sketchy, but if we don't try…" she allowed the words to trail off.

"Okay, Jo, I wid you." Tomi kissed her and left. She would take her opportunities as they arose.

Joanna sat on the bed. She was flushed with excitement and trepidation. Those precious moments shared with

Tomilola had reinvigorated her and frightened her in equal measure. *My God*, she thought, *what would my mother say?*

Her thoughts strayed to Ezra. She had wanted him. She had found him attractive and desirable. Now her desires were overwhelmingly for Tomi. She knew that now. Maybe that's what had prevented her from progressing things with Ezra or why she had treated him so badly for no good reason. If they ever got themselves out of this mess, she would explain and apologise for her behaviour.

\*

Paz poured himself a generous port. He felt flustered, which was an unusual emotion for him. He'd wanted her to give in to him. He could satisfy his longings with any number of black women. Indeed, Conny had proved most accommodating, but he'd had to force her to be submissive. That didn't bother him particularly; it was the indifference she exhibited that took the edge off his pleasure. He wanted something different this time. After all, he was a fine-looking man and powerful; what woman wouldn't want him? He knew he had frightened Joanna, although he admired the way she had met his stare and the way she confronted him. The thought made him smile. Feisty mare. The interruption had been fortunate; he had lost his poise momentarily. He would probably have forced himself on her.

However, he wanted her to desire him and covet him; mutual lust would be his reward. Persuading her to surrender her virtue willingly would be a challenge, and Garcia Paz loved a challenge.

# Chapter Twenty-Five

It had taken many weeks for Fred Quicklock to recover from the beating meted out by the cowardly Persius Milford. Ma Fish had stayed with Mary and helped nurse Fred back to good health. The harmony of his agreeable face, however, would never be the same.

There were multiple scars scattered about his features; above his left eye was a permanent swelling that caused his eyelid to flicker involuntarily; his nose – once long, straight and elegant – was now twisted and flat; and his mouth drooped slightly in one corner, enough to attract a second glance. His features were now a collection of distorted symmetry.

Fred had taken himself back to work, although much of his business had been lost. Walking into his workshop for the first time for months tugged at his emotions. Ezra's bow and his leather wrist guard were still waiting for their owner to return. His consolation was the time spent with Mary.

Fred had spoken for many hours with Mary. He discussed why he had decided to return to the house that day. Plus he unburdened himself of all those memories of his father and his brothers, the misery, underlying guilt and subliminal recriminations – all those things that destroy relationships, and erode the love and the trust and the companionship, which are accumulated through years of steadfast commitment.

He had been heading home to tell her he would not let that happen.

\*

Henry Dunsmoore was pacing. He knew he was; he couldn't stop himself. He paused momentarily to look out of the window overlooking the harbour. Winter was closing in. The sky was low and oppressive, which didn't help his mood.

*Rebecca-Ann*'s arrival was overdue by nearly a month in Henry's reckoning. Edward Buckingham had contacted Henry whom he told that he himself had been summoned to a meeting with Baron Milford to discuss the ramifications for Edward's business. Henry knew those would be severe if *Rebecca-Ann* was lost. His overriding concern was the safety of his treasured son and the crew.

\*

Edward took his carriage to Baron Milford's stately home. His mood was sombre. He had tried hard these past weeks to convince Rebecca that the ship would return. They had probably put into port somewhere for supplies or to make repairs. Henry had made enquiries to incoming vessels along the coast. There had been no word of shipwrecks, or not in the Bay of Biscay, at least. There were no reports of hideous storms. Bad weather, yes, but nothing that should upset a good, seaworthy vessel. Edward knew he hadn't convinced his daughter and he certainly hadn't convinced himself.

On Edward's arrival, Baron Rufus Milford welcomed him into his study. It was a sumptuous room; a space Edward was no stranger to. He wondered why men with wealth aspired to similar trappings. His own study was not dissimilar. Perhaps these things would prove more tenuous than he realised. He dismissed the thought and accepted the glass of brandy.

"So, Edward, I take it there is no news of the ship?" enquired the baron.

"None." Edward took a gulp of brandy. "Henry has made enquiries along the coast. There is no hint of her whereabouts nor any good reason to be had for her late return, although any number of disasters could have befallen her."

Rufus nodded his agreement. "My brother, Lionel, has heard nothing. He has spoken with his agent in White Bay, and no correspondence has been received from Belém to confirm their arrival or otherwise. There's nothing from that scrimshank Blink in London either. Bloody swill-bellies the lot of 'em."

"If I were a man prone to wagering, I would bet skulduggery of one sort or another will be the root of the problem. Damn it all to hell, Rufus!" Edward's calm demeanour dissolved. "I stand to lose everything." He swigged the remainder of his drink.

Rufus Milford knew that Buckingham would struggle to bear the financial burden of losing *Rebecca-Ann*. He had wanted to invest a sixteenth, maybe more, but he had been unable to sway the successful merchant. There had been no shortage of willing investors, who were keen for a decent return. The decision to rebuff the offers would haunt Buckingham for years, perhaps forever.

"If I had invested, Edward, I would now be sharing some of your pain. However, I have a proposal that may alleviate the encumbrance and enable you to at least continue your lifestyle, without the woes of business to hamper your well-being." Rufus sat back in his captain's chair and allowed his visitor to absorb the prospect.

Edward Buckingham knew that, in the world of Rufus Milford, nothing was for nothing. "You have my attention, Rufus."

"It is no secret that my eldest son, Persius, has been a little... What shall we say? High-spirited over the years. His mother and I are of the opinion that the time has come for him to take a bride and start producing heirs; after all, Edward, none of us are getting any younger. I believe a union between our families would create the ideal solution for both our needs. And I'm sure you'd agree that they would make a fine couple." Rufus continued before Buckingham could interrupt,. "I see Persius taking command of the business, bringing with him an injection of funds. I'm sure you and Dunsmoore would pass on the benefit of your experience to the boy and give him some initial guidance. He's a bright lad, Edward, and with a beautiful new wife at his side, I'm positive it would prove a most satisfactory arrangement."

Rufus poured some more brandy. "What say you, Edward, eh?"

It was a rare occasion that Edward Buckingham was stuck for words. What little he knew of Persius Milford, he disliked. Surly and disrespectful was how he would describe him, not high-spirited. Still, he was young and had been afforded life's luxuries since he'd been old enough not to know any different. Was he the man for Rebecca? Could he make a success of the business? He seriously doubted it.

"Think about it, Edward." Rufus could see he'd taken him aback. "Persius will become Baron Milford, and his wife will be Baroness Milford. He will inherit the estate, and their son will inherit the estate. The legacy starts here, Edward, and I foresee a long and fruitful dynasty for generations to follow. Our families united in the face of adversity. Furthermore, Edward, if *Rebecca-Ann* should sail into port this very afternoon, I see no reason for the liaison not to proceed."

It was certainly a compelling argument. As always with Rufus Milford, however, his dialogue rarely involved polite requests; they were underpinned with factual stipulations and requirements to be met. Edward was uncertain if his situation had just improved or taken a nasty turn for the worse. What he knew for absolute certain was that he would have the devil's own task convincing Rebecca.

"I shall inform Persius of the arrangements the day after tomorrow. That will give you a couple of days to mull it over and put your young filly in the picture." Rufus stood, extending his hand to Buckingham; the meeting was over. "To the future, Edward, and our families united."

*

Edward trudged up the wooden steps to Henry's office. They exchanged a handshake. Happier moments had been shared here. Both men stood at the window, gazing across the picturesque harbour and looking as far out to sea as their ageing vision would allow, willing *Rebecca-Ann* to appear on the horizon.

Edward furnished Henry with the details of his meeting with Rufus Milford.

"May God refute me, Edward. The boy's an arseworm. I can think of no politer phrase," declared Henry.

"Careful with your words, Henry. The arseworm is my future son-in-law," Edward chided.

"So you have agreed to this preposterous foxtrot?"

"I see no way forward, Henry. My reckless decision to fund the procurement of *Rebecca-Ann* without investors will leave me bankrupt if she is lost. Rebecca may not thank me now; indeed, I'll be surprised if she ever speaks to me again, but her future will be secure. She will become Baroness Milford, and as such will warrant the esteem afforded her by the eminent title."

"Fine words, my friend, but my oversized gut tells me they are spoken in haste," Henry continued, "This is a difficult moment, Edward, for both of us, but I feel sure we can persevere. The other ships turn a profit, so let us batten down the hatches and tighten our belts; we can get through this turmoil, so let us not give up hope, Edward. *Rebecca-Ann* is a fine ship, and her crew a resourceful bunch. I need to believe it; my right-mindedness is dependent on providence – the sliver of hope they will return – and I will cling to that sliver until the evidence tells me otherwise."

"I cannot run the business, or bargain my daughter's future, on a sliver of hope, Henry, as harsh as that may sound to you. I have prayed for Isaac's safe return, which is something I swore I would never do again since the death of Rebecca. My mind is set, Henry. And even if it wasn't, Rufus Milford has his mind set on the liaison, and I don't have the wherewithal to argue."

Henry placed his hands on the windowsill and flexed his spine; he tilted his head back to ease the cricks. "So, Edward, the manifestation of the mulish wraith has – not for the first time – emerged victorious. I will not waste my words any further. I cannot be a part of this, Edward; my conscience will not allow it. I shall put myself out to seed; it will save any awkwardness that may arise."

Edward Buckingham stared at his lifelong friend and companion. "Henry, please—"

"I shall return in a few days to collect my things. Goodbye, Edward."

Henry Dunsmoore left the office, eased his creaking frame down the wooden steps, took his heavy coat from the peg and stepped onto the quay. He pulled his collar up against the biting wind, and with an overwhelming sadness blighting his demeanour, he trudged a weary path towards home and the solace of his dear wife. Together they would espy the horizon. One day, maybe, they would be rewarded. Meanwhile, hope would be the essence of their existence. Unwavering faith in their son's fortitude and their love for each other would prevail.

Edward stood in the office and watched his friend pull up his collar and walk away, his shoulders slightly hunched. He never looked back. And then the sad figure was lost to the throng. The thread of their friendship, thirty years in the making, had been snapped in a moment. *Now who's being stubborn*, he thought.

*

Rebecca Buckingham had enjoyed her summer. She had spent many hours riding Bobbin. The dappled grey mare was twelve years old now, nearly thirteen, and Rebecca couldn't remember a day when she hadn't at least been to the stable to say hello, stroke her ears and feed her an apple. There was always a warm welcome for Rebecca, apple or no apple.

Today, even the outing with Bobbin refused to appease her troubled mind or her troubled heart. The wind was blowing from the east, bringing with it a harshness that chilled and reddened her exposed features.

Inexplicably, her muddled thoughts took her back to a time when she had not seen Bobbin for a whole week. She must have been eleven, or was she still ten? It didn't matter. A moment ago, she couldn't think of a day when they'd been apart. Rebecca had been ill. The doctor couldn't come so, beside himself with worry, her father had sent for the old lady who helped bring babies into the world throughout the town of Old Milford. Rebecca remembered the woman's soothing voice telling her she would be okay. Telling her – as she bathed her burning forehead with a cold, damp cloth – that the fever would pass, she was a beautiful child, and she would grow up to be a beautiful young lady and marry a handsome young man. The old lady had made Rebecca feel like a princess. Her face was a mystery, but her voice sounded clearer to her now than it ever had. Strange that it should come to her now.

She gave up on the ride and returned to the stables. She handed Bobbin to the groom, stroked the horse's ears and headed for the house. Having discarded her riding boots, she padded across the spacious hallway in stockinged feet, heading for the staircase. She heard her father's voice calling her. He stood at the door of his study.

"I'm just going to change from my rid—" she told him.

Edward interrupted her. "That can wait. Please, come." He beckoned her in and closed the door behind her once she had entered the room.

"What is it, Papa, that can't wait until I've changed my clothes?" Rebecca's face was still flushed from the cold, and her skin stung with the change of temperature. "Do you have news of the ship?"

"No news, I'm afraid. Come, sit." Edward showed her to a chair by the fire.

They sat opposite each other, with the flames a momentary distraction.

"Winter descends upon us without a care," he stated.

Rebecca looked at her father, and she sensed she wasn't there to discuss the seasons. "What is it, Papa?"

"It is time to face reality, Rebecca. In all probability, *Rebecca-Ann* and her crew are lost."

Rebecca stopped him. "It's only a month late. You surely don't believe they are lost? What does Uncle Henry have to say?"

"I'm afraid Henry and I have come to an unfortunate disagreement over the issue. He walked out of the office yesterday, and I don't expect him to return. I believe his grief for Isaac has overpowered his senses, and after all these years, we find ourselves at loggerheads with no clear path to a solution."

Rebecca flinched at her father's reasoning as to why Henry had walked out. "You of all people, Papa, should know how grief can wither a person, to the extent their behaviour becomes irrational. Perhaps it is difficult to understand for someone who has still to encounter its debilitating capabilities and yet is feeling it evermore as the days pass. To underestimate your friend's feelings at this time would be an error on—"

"Enough, Rebecca." Edward snapped at his daughter. "I do not require a discourse from you regarding my friend's feelings, or my own for that matter. The situation is more complicated than you realise, so allow me to continue without interruption if I may?"

Edward's stern response had quietened Rebecca. A sense of foreboding began to overwhelm her. Then all she could hear were a jumble of words that made no sense: "Baron Milford", "Persius Milford", "marriage", "heirs", "security", "baroness", "bankrupt", "saviour" and "future". This was not what the old lady had meant. Persius Milford was not the handsome young man she was to marry. There had been a terrible mistake.

"So that is why Uncle Henry walked out on you. Not because his grief had overwhelmed him." Rebecca's voice was remarkably calm. Eerily so. "I will not marry Persius Milford."

"That's not an unexpected response; nevertheless, you will do as I say." Edward's tone was stark. The atmosphere felt cold, despite the roaring fire.

Rebecca's mind was racing. The man had tried to rape her on her seventeenth birthday. She had wanted to tell her father of the incident the next day, instead she had decided to lock the episode away. She had gone to the stables early the next morning and searched for the brooch. Distraught that she had lost one of her late mother's favourite pieces of jewellery, Rebecca chose to remain silent about the whole affair. She took the decision to explain the missing brooch only if the need should arise. She had no idea how, but she would think of something.

"Does me having a title mean that much to you, Father, that you would condemn me to a lifetime of misery, shackled to an obnoxious bully? Surely you must know that I could never love such a man, not for a hundred titles." Rebecca tried to relax so as to remove the edge from her voice.

"Rebecca, please, it is not all about the title – although you will learn that the status of baroness will endear you to people of great note and privilege. It is about your security, your future and the future of your children. If you were my son, things would be different, but you are my daughter, Rebecca, and although I would not change that, it is because of this that you must do as I bid and marry Persius. Your union with him will preserve the legacy of our families for generations to come."

Edward leant forwards and tried to take his daughter's hand. She pulled it back. He looked into her eyes; their verdant green reflecting the glow of the fire. He thought of her mother and how they had fought to be together. He knew that, despite his spiel, he was denying his daughter the chance to marry a man of her choosing and someone she loved, as he had loved.

Rebecca rose from the chair. She stared at her father with a look of utter dejection. "Just my luck, eh?" She turned to leave.

"What do you mean, Rebecca, 'Just my luck'?"

"*Femina natus est.*" She uttered the words over her shoulder as she left the room.

Edward slumped in his chair. *God in heaven*, he thought, *she has her mother's intellect as well as her beauty*. He searched his memory for the meaning of the Latin phrase: born a woman.

# Chapter Twenty-Six

E zra made another notch in the wood: the seventieth. It was nearly time to leave.

*

Horace Clunk and Taylor Potts had guided the oversized canoe down the now familiar stretch of river, heading for the Tupi village to collect Ezra. They arrived as expected and disembarked.

Horace was, as ever, a great source of amusement to the Tupi people. They made no attempt to conceal their fascination with the giant; his skin was the colour of their much favoured tapir, although they had no desire to eat him. He pretended to chase a young boy who dared to run up and poke a finger at him, imitating the roar of a wild beast at the same time. The child ran and hid behind his mother. All the other children laughed, and Horace gave another loud roar banging his chest for extra effect.

Ezra was with the much recovered Agu and Jonas Carp. The commotion drew them from Agu's hut.

Horace walked up to Jonas, dwarfing him and providing him with shade at the same time. "I b'lieve this is yours, Mister Preacher." Horace took the leather-bound book from inside his shirt and handed it to Jonas. It was a little muddy, but not really any the worse for being abandoned in the Amazon Rainforest.

Jonas took the Bible and held it with all the reverence he could muster. He looked up into the face of the giant man standing before him. He tried to speak. The words refused to be expelled. He altered his gaze to examine his most precious possession, opening the cover as if to check it was definitely his. A tear plopped onto the inside page, smudging the word "loving", the penultimate decree of his parent's inscription.

"Thank you, Mister Clunk, from the bottom of my heart." Jonas stepped forwards, and so far as he could, he wrapped his arms around the startled Horace, uttering godly phrases, assuring the giant a place in our Father's heaven. "I will never again refer to you as ballast, Horace, I promise."

Ezra stood with Agu and the two boys: Idogbe and Ilamyo. He thanked them again for their bravery. Without realising, Ezra touched the pearl at his throat. He asked Jonas to tell the boys they were leaving, and that he wasn't sure when he would see them again, but they would be in his heart forever. He would never forget their kindness and their brave actions.

Jonas translated Ezra's sentiments.

Agu responded, staring at Ezra as he spoke, his deep-brown eyes engaging his friend, relaying a simple message hidden in a jumble of strange words.

Jonas pointed to the knife at his ankle. "Take out your knife, Ezra."

Ezra looked puzzled but he pulled the captain's knife from its sheath.

"Agu has seen white man's blood. He had always believed that it would be different to his. He says that you are his brother, and that you should share the same blood so that, wherever you are, you will always be together. Brothers."

Ezra handed Agu the knife. "Tell him it is very sharp, Jonas."

"I think he knows."

Agu took Ezra's right hand and turned it palm up. He ran the knife across the inside of Ezra's forearm, with just enough pressure to split the skin. The blood ran free. He did the same with his own arm and then held it outstretched, an invitation. Ezra accepted and they clasped each other's arms, their blood mingling, uniting them, wherever and whatever.

*

The three men paddled the cumbersome vessel against the current. Jonas said he was staying with the Tupi tribe, but he would visit the Africans regularly. His vision of a church and prayers on the Sabbath had diminished since the humbling experience with Agu. He had been sad to see his friends leave, but he had given them his blessing during an emotional farewell. Before they left, he smeared a weird concoction on Ezra's cut: a purply paste that would heal the cut and keep it clean.

Taylor Potts turned his attention to their next move. "It'll soon be time to head for the fortress. I s'pose some sort of plan would be in order." He wiped the sweat from his brow with his forearm. It hadn't rained for a couple of days. "We must be due some rain," he said, almost to himself.

"Must be," confirmed Ezra.

"You could bet on it," Horace agreed.

A long moment of silence ensued. Not a few seconds – a few minutes.

"That it with the plan then?" Potts asked.

"I reckon," Ezra replied.

"Sleep on it, shall we?" Horace suggested.

"Probly best," Ezra and Potts replied in unison.

They continued in silence, dipping their paddles and absorbing the extraordinary sounds of the rainforest.

Ezra resumed the scintillating discussion, disrupting the aura of obmutescence. "Did you ever get to fire your bow, Horace?"

The question disrupted Horace's rhythm momentarily. He held the paddle in abeyance whilst he pondered the question or the answer, or maybe both. In fact, he was trying to recall its whereabouts. "I never did, no. I'm tryin' to remember where I left it. I think I mighta left it in the gig. I 'ope it ain't lost. The first present I ever 'ad, that is."

"Maybe it's just as well you never did fire it," Potts said, "Christ only knows where the bloody arrow would have ended up. Not where you were aimin' it, that's for sure."

"Ah, don't be like that, Tay; I reckon he was getting the hang of it." Ezra retorted.

"Woss that? Before or after he put a hole in the captain's handrail?" Potts said with a grin.

Ezra laughed.

Horace ignored him, but then he explained, "I wus practisin'. It coulda 'appened to anyone, that."

They continued on their journey for a while, with a comfortable silence between them.

"Why did you want to know where the bow was?" Potts asked Ezra.

"I was just wondering that's all. Depending on how far and how accurately, of course, Horace could send one of them missiles, we could perhaps create some sort of diversion? I dunno; I was just thinking, that's all."

*

The trio arrived at the now thriving African village. Afia launched herself into Ezra's arms, flung her legs around his waist and clung to him with all her strength.

Horace and Potts looked on in amazement.

"Well, that friendship's moved on a step." Potts scratched his head in wonder.

Horace clapped Potts on the back. "Lucky boy." He shouted, "*Hi!*" to Afia and added, "Be careful with 'im now; 'e's a delicit soul."

Ezra felt a little embarrassed and self-conscious. He and Afia kissed, and those emotions were replaced with others that were dissimilar in most respects.

"You miss me then?" he asked.

"Nah." Afia smiled, her face alight with joy. "Wat give dey dat impresshun?"

They kissed again.

*

The days prior to Ezra marking the seventieth notch had passed quickly. Every chance they had, Afia and Ezra would disappear to the waterfall. They spent their time swimming, making love and just revelling in the joy of being naked together, enjoying each other. It was a time neither of them wanted to end. Ezra taught Afia about holding her breath underwater, how Agu had showed him how to relax, and how to breathe. They counted and counted. Ezra could now stay under for a count of three hundred and forty-one. Afia was on one hundred and twenty. It proved a strange process in many ways, because whilst the count tended to rise, some days it refused to go any higher and sometimes it even fell.

It didn't matter. It was exhilarating and they wallowed in their freedom and their desire. Ezra pictured Jonas Carp's heaven to be like this. *If it is*, he thought, *then it's little wonder he goes on and on about it.*

\*

Now, though, there was work to be done.

Horace and Potts set about the task of organising the weapons at their disposal. They had a heap of muskets, which they had purloined from the travellers and the soldiers. The problem was that the powder was mostly spoilt due to its exposure to moisture, rendering them unreliable at best and useless at worst. Maybe they would be useful as a threat? There were a couple of hefty axes, machetes, and a selection of swords, cutlasses and knives. It was not a bad cache.

Ezra made himself a good stock of arrows, and Afia fashioned a quiver to store and carry his large stock. She had made him stand upright and still whilst she assessed the measurements, insisting it had to fit comfortably over his shoulder. It proved to be worth the few moments of inconvenience.

Ezra asked Olu to help him find a suitable tree from which he could make a bow. They cut and stripped several branches before deciding which one to use. Ezra could tell it was a hardwood, and he liked the way the outer layers peeled off leaving the heartwood. He remembered making Horace's bow aboard ship. The big man had yet to fire it. Perhaps he never would.

Olu looked at Ezra slightly puzzled when he saw the size of the bow.

"It's made for a certain person to fire," Ezra explained.

Olu nodded his head. "It 'as come to me now."

"Olu," Ezra asked, "do you know what we can use for a bow string?"

Olu nodded his head; it seemed to be his default position.

They returned to the village, and Olu took Ezra to where a large and now unrecognisable animal lay on a mat of broad leaves. An African man had butchered the beast expertly, and a pile of pink and reddish-grey organs were heaped into a grotesque pile. Olu spoke to the man, who was engulfed with insects, and he then plunged his hands into the mash of slimy innards. He held up a bundle of sinewy strands. The animals intestines.

Ezra tried not to baulk at the sight, but the smell was beginning to overpower him. "What next?" he asked, and he turned away from the makeshift abattoir. The insects were happy to stay. Ezra, though, gulped the clean air.

Olu dumped the gut into a container of water and spent some time removing the fat and washing away the residue. He had Ezra fetch clean water continually. He then stretched the intestines out and laid them flat. He compared the length of the bow to the strands and realised he would have to join them to make them long enough. Olu splayed the end of one length and using Ezra's knife, made a slit roughly the length of his thumbnail and about the same distance from the end. He repeated the process with another strand. He then threaded the ends through the slit and spliced them together. Ezra watched Olu work, fascinated. Olu, knowing the bowstring would be under considerable tension, made six long lengths, and then, after securing them at one end to a stake that he had hammered into the earth, he dextrously braided them together. He then dampened them with water, tensioned the gut between the first stake and another he'd fixed in the ground, and left them to dry.

"Olu, I have another question for you," Ezra stated.

Olu nodded.

"Do you know of a substance that will burn? I mean some sort of oil or anything like that."

This question was not greeted with a nod. Ezra took that as a bad sign.

Olu asked Ezra what he had in mind. Ezra explained what he hoped to achieve, and then Olu nodded. The two of them disappeared into the forest.

Olu was looking for a particular shrub. He stopped when he noticed a flowering plant with yellow petals. He held one of the flowers in a cupped hand and examined the stamen sheltering in the whorl of the delicate petals. He pulled the stamen free and squeezed it between his fingers. A clingy substance oozed out. Olu nodded his head.

They had to pick a lot of stamens to get a small amount of the substance stored within them.

Ezra was keen to see if his idea would work, so they headed back to the village with their gooey substance almost set hard in the bottom of the stone cup. Ezra collected his bow, and after selecting an arrow from his new quiver, he dipped the point into the resin. He twirled the arrow around and watched as the substance built up, layer by layer. Ezra went over to a dying fire and plunged the tip of the arrow into the embers. The resin ignited and he held the arrow at arm's length, watching the flames burning hungrily, desperate to consume the matter that fed them. Ezra nocked the arrow and positioned himself at the riverbank. He aimed high and released the blazing missile. The flames continued to burn even against the rushing wind, only quenched when the arrow pierced the surface of the water.

"Perfect." Ezra turned to Olu. "Thank you, my ingenious friend."

Olu nodded.

*

And so the preparations continued. The next day, Ezra strung Horace Clunk's new bow. He'd made a handful of arrows, which he reckoned would be the correct length. They were formidable-looking weapons, which if he could get Horace to discharge in the general direction of their target, should prove most effective.

Horace stood at the riverbank, facing downriver. Ezra stood next to him, plying him with hints and tips, though he was basically wasting his breath. Horace was determined that he had learnt enough from his previous experience and needed no tuition.

Potts, Afia and Olu watched the big man pull back on the bowstring, Ezra had insisted that he at least accustomed himself to the tension. The strength required was unfathomable. They watched the huge muscles in his shoulders and his biceps expand, his veins became gorged, awaken from their latency.

Ezra passed him an arrow. Horace sat the nock over the string and retracted the braided gut, inch by inch, until he felt the feather brush his cheek. He breathed out and released the arrow. Instead of veering off on a tangent, as Potts had predicted, the arrow departed with a twang and a whoosh, rocketing into the air as if propelled by some magical potion. It was still on its upward trajectory when it disappeared from sight.

The onlookers fell silent.

A short while later, Ezra sat with his friends. He had made the seventy-third notch. Tomorrow they would leave. He outlined his plan – such as it was, being full of holes – to Horace and Taylor. For want of a better one, they agreed to it, knowing that improvisation and a fair degree of good fortune would be key to any success.

*

Ezra and Afia spent the night together. She begged him to take her with them. She was afraid she would never see him again. Ezra removed Agu's special gift from around his neck and put it on hers.

"See, Afi." He fiddled her hair back into place. "I'll have to come back for my pearl."

*

The next morning, they loaded the oversized canoe (which was now tied to a pontoon built by the Africans) with supplies and the weaponry, all carefully selected.

It was an emotional moment. Not one that either Ezra or Afi wanted to prolong.

The three men set off in the canoe and soon disappeared out of sight, taken by the current and guided by the paddles dipping and trawling; it was easy enough. The pulsating African farewells were soon overtaken by the sounds of the forest, which were now very familiar.

# Chapter Twenty-Seven

*Gemini* was ploughing her way through a choppy sea. The waves were nothing serious, but they were serious enough if you happened to be human cargo or hidden away in a cramped, dark space in the bowels of the ship.

Rothwell Spurt had ordered the *ugly bastard carpenter* to report to his cabin.

Aubrey Darricot swallowed his top lip and tugged at the unsightly hair protruding from his turgid growth. He was not a man generally given to nerves, but as he tapped the cabin door, a sense of foreboding crept over him.

Rothwell eyed the combination of Darricot's features with disdain. *God save us,* he thought, *he's an ugly fucker.* Rothwell came straight to the point. "Do you know what 'appened to Dunsmoore?"

Aubrey was equally blunt. "Nope."

"Don't lie to me, carpenter man. If you know, just tell me, and that'll be the end of the matter." Rothwell had no intention of sacrificing Darricot. He had seen his carpentry skills at the African village, and even if his fizzog was highly offensive, his ability to fashion lumber was an asset that would always prove beneficial.

Aubrey released his top lip. "I ain't one to be strung up for no good reason, Mister Spurt. If I knew where he was, I'd tell 'ee and no mistake. I reckon he couldn't take it anymore – you know the thought of 'ee takin' over 'is ship an' all – an' I reckon he popped hisself overboard, in search of ol' Davy Jones's locker."

Rothwell looked directly into Darricot's odd-coloured eyes, confident he was telling the truth. "If you 'ear a whisper as to 'is whereabouts, I'll be the first to know, right?"

"Rest assured you will, Mister Spurt."

Rothwell changed the subject. Darricot had confirmed his own belief that Dunsmoore had decided the only way out for him was a watery grave. "What d'you know of the boy who was rescued from the sea?"

Aubrey was initially taken aback at the question. He wondered how Spurt had known of the incident. "Young Quicklock, he was a good lad; willin' an' keen t' learn. I dunno where he is neither."

"So you don't know anythin' about 'im?"

"No, nothin', 'cept that the cap'n took a shine to the boy; he took him under 'is wing a bit, an' got the lady t' teach him 'is letters an' stuff. Good lad he was. Devil of a shot wi' that bow of his too."

"Very informative, carpenter man." Rothwell raised his eyebrows to emphasise the sarcasm, which was completely lost on Aubrey Darricot. "Okay, fuck off, but don't forget, if you 'ear anything…"

\*

Isaac could sense the ship slowing. He couldn't gauge accurately how long he had suffered his self-isolation, concealed in the claustrophobic void. His stomach was aching for food, but the thought of relieving that ache made him retch. His throat burnt, his head thumped, he needed fresh air and he needed water.

\*

*Gemini* nestled at the quayside. She was tethered fore and aft to pawn-shaped lumps of iron embedded in the ground. At the extremity of the quay, a compound had been constructed. The beleaguered Africans were ushered from the hold and herded into the compound. They were a pitiful sight. The process of shifting hundreds of confused, weak people who were all shackled together was frustrating work, and this cargo's legacy was a cavern of stinking waste, festering in the heat, waiting for the cleaning detail to purify as best they could. In truth, the process would entail buckets of salt water being sloshed around allowing the waste to run into the bilges where, although diluted, it would maturate and spawn disease. The reluctant gift of human cargo.

Garcia Paz strode along the quay, and Captain Marinho walked alongside him, matching his stride. Two privates followed, and behind them, a dejected figure trudged in silence. The waterfront was thronging with people. Tomorrow, after Paz had taken his pick, the slaves would be auctioned, bringing merchants and their entourage to the town. The ale houses and bordellos relished the surge in clients. Enslaving Africans was certainly good for business, and the recent shipload would be no exception.

Sabina da Costa stepped from the entrance of her inn. A painted sign swinging from a bracket above the door read "*A Taverna des Chaves Cruzadas*"[7]. Enclosed in parentheses beneath the main title, the smaller text read "(*Cidade Pecaminosa*)"[8]. She stepped out in front of Paz and Marinho. "Will you gentleman be gracing us with your fine presence this evening, Senor Paz?"

"Oh, I think you will have more than enough custom tonight, Sabina, without our patronage. Although I can't really speak for Tiago here." Paz admired Sabina's ample breasts, which were straining to be released from their confinement. *She still looks good,* he thought, *even though the years are beginning to betray her.*

"We haven't seen you here for many a night, Captain. I trust my girls have not deterred you in any way?" she enquired.

"You may rest assured, Sabina, I have not been deterred, in your establishment or any other," the captain confirmed.

Sabina bade them goodbye, and they continued their walk along the quay.

"It will be a raucous night, I fancy. Perhaps it would be beneficial to have a presence, perhaps half a dozen men patrolling. Talking of which, "Paz continued, "we've heard nothing of Sousa and his patrol."

"I think we can afford to wait another week before the alarm bell is rung," Marinho responded.

"Well, I'm glad you think so, Captain, but then again, it's not your silver at stake, is it? Although I imagine you'll

---

[7]     The Cross Keys Tavern

[8]     Sinful City

be quick enough to bleat if your stipend is not forthcoming on the appropriate day."

Marinho baulked at Paz's condescending tone. "I didn't mean—"

"No, no, of course you didn't. Let us wait a day or two, and see what the wind blows our way. If Sousa is as good a sergeant as you say, then I'm sure he'll have the situation well in hand."

Tiago Marinho kept his silence; once again he had suffered Paz's patronising suppression, which was a constant reminder of his status.

*

Rothwell and Paz greeted each other with a vigorous handshake.

Paz was delighted with the number of slaves. "Good work, Senor Roth. And what of *Angerona*?"

"She'll be along in a day or two," Rothwell confirmed.

"I take it you gave the ship her head?" Paz nodded towards *Gemini*. "Was she all you hoped for, Senor Roth?"

"She was indeed, Senor Paz." *With fucking knobs on,* he thought, but never said.

Rothwell went on to explain the details of the deal with the African tribe, which impressed Paz. The loss of Dunsmoore, however, rankled to the extent that he practically accused Rothwell of losing his temper and killing Dunsmoore in a fit of rage.

"You can take it from me, Senor Paz, for what it may be worth, if I had killed Dunsmoore in a fit of rage or just for pleasure, I would not pretend otherwise, either to you or anyone else," Spurt declared.

"My apologies, Senor Roth. I just never had Dunsmoore down for someone who would end his own life. Still, I suppose each of us has our limit, and it seems the good captain had reached his."

"So it would seem, Senor Paz; so it would seem."

Paz continued, "I see no reason why Marrick's widow should not become available, Senor Roth, now Dunsmoore is no longer a consideration; a bonus for your strenuous efforts these past weeks."

"I rather thought I would start with the slutty daughter. It strikes me that a good length wouldn't do 'er any 'arm." Spurt covered his privates with a splayed hand and gave them a tug. "I'm about ready."

"I'm sorry to disappoint you my friend, but I have plans of my own for the daughter. She will remain out of bounds, Senor Spurt, until I say otherwise."

*Fuckin' prick*, Rothwell thought. He managed to constrain himself. "As you wish, Senor Paz; as you wish. I shall satisfy myself with the widow; she will know the extent of 'er 'usband's debt when I have finished with 'er."

During this conversation, Captain Marinho had stood in the partial shade of the buildings with his men. Paz and Spurt together were more than he could stand.

A barefoot African man – who was maybe thirty years old, though it was difficult to tell – was beckoned into the compound by Paz. The African knew the routine, and although he had learnt the task at hand, the sight of his fellow Africans – bedraggled, frightened and bewildered – turned his stomach inside out. Or that's what it felt like. He could not afford to expose his emotions to Paz, so he kept his head slightly bowed. He would avoid eye contact at all costs; it enabled him to obey orders, although in terms of physical pain, this was not a moment to fear. Physical pain would become an emotional distraction, like the moment the mark becomes permanent. That hurt. If the African man were to pull his short sleeve back a few inches. the letters "GP" would reveal themselves, etched into his flesh with a hot branding iron. If they proved themselves worthwhile, this would be their reward.

He followed Paz along the lines of shackled people. At a signal from Paz, the African would dip two fingers into the dark, mud-coloured substance he had carried with him from the fortress. He stepped forwards and smeared the dye on the chosen forehead. He tried not to put too much on, knowing it would take many months to fade. His fingers were a testament to that. They were now permanently stained.

The dye was made from the crushed bark of the Brazilian logwood tree, and it was becoming more and more popular, and therefore more and more valuable as a commodity. There were worse thing to trade in, but for Paz, silver and sugar remained his priority. Of course, the slaves were a natural progression. You couldn't have one without the other.

Garcia Paz only chose his slaves through what he saw. Keeping families together meant nothing to him. He had grown accustomed to the pitiful sobs and the screams, immune to the devastation he created and left in his wake. Rothwell had joined him in the selection process.

"What misdemeanour has befallen this wretch, Senor Roth?" questioned Paz.

The man with one hand stood with his head bowed, trembling, his forehead glistening with globules of sweat, and his cauterised stump a coagulum of scab and pus.

"Sometimes they benefit from a harsh lesson." Rothwell never mentioned the young girl he had thrown overboard with her throat slashed.

"Indeed they do, Senor Roth; indeed they do. But perhaps you should consider something a little less disabling? Perhaps the testicles would suffice; I fancy that the outcome would be just as effective, if not more so. Bollock-less he would be of more use, do you not think?"

"I suspect someone'll be glad of 'im, and'll pay a few pennies for the piece of shit. If not, I'll chop off 'is other hand and toss 'im in the 'arbour. 'E can practise 'is swimmin'." Rothwell could feel himself becoming agitated with the pompous Paz.

"Very droll, Senor Roth. My point is that a two-handed slave is a worthwhile commodity. A slave with a festering stump is no more than a mouth to feed – a liability. And if I may say, the wound doesn't give any indication that the healing process is overcoming its confrontation; in fact, I would estimate a couple of days would see the putrefaction process completed." Paz put his right hand over his heart and added, "Not that I'm any sort of medical expert, you understand."

Rothwell Spurt took the hint. He called a couple of his men over. The trembling slave lifted his head. His eyes relayed a message – one of terror – plain enough. The men unshackled him and dragged him to the edge of the quay. It was over in a moment. The knife opened his throat, and the kick sent him into the water.

Paz and Spurt continued their inspection. The African man followed dutifully, daubing foreheads as requested. After all, he had little choice.

Captain Marinho watched the man's fate unfold. He was sickened by the brutal treatment of the enslaved people. The killing of his fellow man was reserved for the battlefield. That was his code of conduct. Killing in the defence of the Crown. What he was witnessing under Paz's command was criminal at best and genocide at worst. Marinho was a good soldier. He didn't know how much more of this he could stomach; at the same time, he could see no easy way out. Perhaps his soldiering abilities would be called upon elsewhere. Soon, he hoped. Maybe a visit to Sabina's would ease his conscience, for a few hours at least.

*

Isaac had listened to the clatter of chain and the clanging of iron. They were unloading the Africans. He was unable to track the hours; his mind would not allow it. He would close his eyes, not because he wanted to but because they refused to remain open for any prolonged period. When they did unlock, he could discern only foggy shapes with incongruous outlines. They were confusing. He had to get out of his cell – whatever the consequences.

Isaac eased his stiff joints into a prone position and hauled himself along beneath the bottom shelf. The hold was in darkness, but the hatches were open. The stench had yet to dissipate. He rolled out and tried to stand. He soon realised that would take longer than he'd anticipated. He used the shelves for support, and his limbs gradually responded until he stood unaided. His back was painful. He rested his hands on the edge of a shelf, and with one eye to the hatchway, he stretched his reluctant body. He felt the knots protesting, but they unravelled somewhat, allowing him to walk (albeit unsteadily) across the hold to the steps. He crept cautiously up and peered over the top.

It was a warm night, but the air tasted good. He took a deep breath and his head swam. He felt himself falling and he grabbed at the sides of the steps, trying to regain his balance; his sense of time and space had deserted him. It returned when his fragile body thumped against the slimy floor. He took a few moments to assess the damage, testing different parts of himself gently. Satisfied that he was no worse off than he had been a few minutes ago, aside from the bruising that would inevitably follow, he climbed back to the top. There had been nobody to hear him tumbling down the steps.

He checked around one more time. He decided there was no other way. He would walk down the gang plank and bluff it out. The state he was in made him practically unrecognisable, although he was pretty sure that if someone spotted him walking off the ship, they would confront him and realise who he was.

He traipsed off the ship onto the quay and disappeared down a side street. Nobody saw him or if they did, they paid him no heed.

Isaac kept to the shadows of the buildings. Further along the quay, he could hear the unmistakeable noise of sailors exchanging weeks of toil for a few hours of unadulterated pleasure. He saw the Africans had been herded into a compound, shackled, but able to breath refined air. As the merchants and the second ship arrived, he knew the town would become a cauldron of bawdy affray.

Isaac twisted the narrow, gold band on the little finger of his left hand. *If I get any skinnier,* he thought, *it will fall off.*

He kept walking, his head bowed and turned slightly to one side, until he arrived at a square. In the centre, he could make out a statue mounted on a plinth. It was a lady, the Virgin Mary perhaps, though it was of little consequence. The small taverna occupying the far corner caught his attention. He ambled casually across the square, and without hesitation, he entered the premises and selected an empty table at the opposite side of the dingy parlour. He sat with his back to a dark, wood-panelled wall, from where he could survey the room. He felt dreadful.

A young female came to the table carrying a jug and a terracotta cup, which she filled with warm ale. Isaac stared at the brown liquid as it settled, leaving a patchy film of grey froth. The smell turned his stomach. He managed to keep his revulsion under control. He knew it was caused through lack of food and water, not necessarily the ale. On another day, he would have welcomed a *goodly slurp*.

The girl spoke to him.

He struggled to understand, although his command of Spanish helped, it having some similarities with Portuguese. He spoke to her in English. "May I speak with the patron?"

Without response, she turned and walked away. She must have understood, because he was interrupted from his trance by a buxom woman, who was attractive, even with her dark hair scraped back in the harshest of fashions. *Her complexion is a little ruddy,* Isaac thought, *but her eyes are captivating; they shine out from beneath the most beautiful brows, which define her expression.* Isaac stared into the deep amber of the glistening jewels, searching for a glimmer of compassion.

"Madam," he said, his voice raspy and barely audible, "my pockets are empty, but I am wanting. I find myself needing food, water and a place to rest – a sanctuary for a few nights. Until my strength is regained." Isaac twisted the gold band from his finger. "I can give you this for payment. It is all I have."

Isaac felt nothing as his head thumped onto the hardwood of the table, spilling the ale.

# Chapter Twenty-Eight

They moored the canoe a safe distance from the fortress. They would attempt the journey to the far side of the port under the cover of darkness.

Ezra sliced the rough skin from one of the yellow fruits and passed the juicy chunks to his friends.

Horace asked Potts about the quay. It was, Potts explained, like most others they had encountered. It was maybe a quarter of a mile in length and dominated by the fortress at this end, with a section of forest and a craggy outcrop of rock defining the far end. Beyond that lay a sandy cove: their destination.

The generous craft hugged the riverbank. In the distance, the fortress – visible only as a shadowy blur nestled into the landscape – sat in silence. Its presence provoked thoughts of Cordelia, Joanna and Tomilola for all three men, each in their own way.

They continued paddling as if heading for home. When they could no longer discern the shoreline, they turned south and began the arduous journey across the bay. Even from their position, they could hear sounds: meaningless words drifting across the untroubled waters. They altered their course for the last time and paddled towards the sandy beach, where they would camp until they were ready to strike.

*

*Angerona* sailed into port late in the afternoon. *Gemini* had been shifted along the quay to allow *Angerona* to take the berth. She was three days behind.

Rudd was in a foul mood; he hated being second, although he would demonstrate no such behaviour in front of Spurt. He wanted the stinking cargo off the ship, he wanted the hold rinsed of shit and piss and vomit, and he wanted to get in the ale house. Then his mood would lift. A few hours in bed with a decent whore would set him straight and ease the tension.

The process followed the same pattern as with *Gemini*. In the compound, there were around fifty Africans, all of whom were accounted for but not yet collected by their new owners. As the latest contingent were herded in, anxious eyes searched for family and loved ones separated by the abhorrent actions of avaricious man. The selling and distribution procedure would begin again tomorrow.

*

Rothwell had all Dunsmoore's crew aboard the *Gemini*. He had given them permission to use the tavernas, but only the ones along the front. They were to bunk on board and were not to leave the quay under any circumstances. Rothwell was still unsure which of them he could trust, if any. He was sure they would fall into line, especially since the demise of their captain. They had served Dunsmoore dutifully and now he expected them to do the same for him. They were like the slaves to him: a valuable commodity that was essential to operating both ships. The thought occurred to him that maybe he could train up the odd black person although that was dipping into the profits. Still it was something to consider.

Rothwell had pondered Paz's invitation to stay at the fortress for these past few nights. However, the lure of Sinful City – with its cheap ale, bawdy atmosphere and willing whores – proved too much for Spurt. He was no different to any other sailor or the majority, at least; there were basic requirements after a long voyage, especially a successful one, and Sabina's establishment met them in full. The widow would keep. She wasn't going anywhere in a hurry.

\*

Tomilola knew what she was about to do would define not only her own future but the future of the woman she had fallen in love with. She was about to gamble on Garcia Paz's lurid sexual appetite. It was maybe his only fallibility. If he didn't recognise it as such, then she would have a chance; *they* would have a chance. She knew there was something coursing through a man with the power to skew his senses and stop him thinking with his brain. If she could make that happen…

Conny had merely raised her eyebrows when Tomilola had asked to attend to Paz's toilet. Now, Tomilola tapped his door and waited. Her free hand remained balled in a fist to ease the trembling.

"Come in, come in." His voice sounded irritable.

If Paz was surprised to see Tomilola, he kept the emotion to himself. She had deliberately left her hair loose, and the black waves fell to her shoulders. There were four buttons on the bodice of her blue dress. She had left the top two undone, revealing the swell of her breasts.

Paz was naked from the waist up and Tomilola made a point of eyeing his lean torso and then coyly averting her gaze. Paz was pleased with himself momentarily, a little flattered even. She was playing a dangerous game, but it had begun and the thought eased her nerves.

Tomilola could feel Paz's gaze on her. It was strange because she knew he could just take her at any time. She sensed that he wanted to play the game; he wanted to be the irresistible one: the one who could have any woman without beating her into submission. She leant over, perhaps a little too far, and filled his bowl with his washing water, exposing more of her breasts.

"Forgive me, mastah, fo' speakin' outta turn, buh de mistriss as'd I give dey a messidge."

The words distracted Paz from the stirring at his crotch. "Tell me."

"She say she sorry fo' de udder day." Tomilola hesitated. "Iss a bi' delicat mattah, mastah. Dey see, de udder day she in 'er momen' – she blids. Dat why she in no mood fo' shananagans. Dey see wat I mean."

Paz dried his face and stared at the black woman in disbelief. "She confided this in you?"

Tomilola pressed on; there was no backing out now.

"See, de ting iss, mastah, we got very close, if dey see wat I mean. Dey mistriss wan' know if p'raps de tree of us… dey know. She be okay in coupla days." Tomilola braced herself for the reaction.

Paz tried desperately to process the information with his brain, the interference from another part of his anatomy, however, was making it difficult. A romp with two willing, beautiful women – one white, most likely a virgin, and one black – massaged his overblown ego. *How close have they become?* he asked himself. He would find out soon enough.

Paz composed himself. "You tell your mistress that it will be my pleasure, and hers and yours." Paz went up behind Tomilola and took her breasts roughly in his hands, pushing himself hard up against her. "But you tell your mistress that I will not be dallied with. I will have no more excuses. She will give herself to me, as will you, without rancour or fuss. You may have noticed the half-eaten body dangling from the gibbet. It makes no difference to me who hangs there: man or woman, black or white. The eagles love them all. You tell me when she is finished. I can feel myself preparing for the moment as we speak." Paz pushed her away. "Now be gone. I have business to attend to."

\*

They marched along the quay at a lively pace, Marinho observed. They were in the same formation – Paz and him; two privates; and an enslaved African with his head slightly bowed and his fingers stained, carrying his pot of dye – and all were scurrying to keep up. Paz certainly had a spring in his step today. Things were obviously going well for him, so much so that he never mentioned Sousa and his men, even though a few days had passed. Marinho took the small blessings as they came his way.

As they passed Sinful City, Paz turned to Marinho. "So Tiago, did you partake of the delectable Sabina's offer the other day?

"No, sir." Marinho had loitered at the door for a second or two, but then thought better of it. It was gradually filling with drunken heathens, and he could live without their company.

"You should give it a go one of these nights, Tiago, and get some of the starch out your collar; it'll do you good."

Even when he was in a good mood, Paz knew how to press his buttons. *Condescending prick*, Marinho thought, and not for the first time. All he said was, "Maybe, one of these nights."

It had been a busy day. Slaves had been auctioned, marked and made ready for the journey to their new homes. Money had been counted and recounted, with the goods sold on again not an hour since belonging to another. All in the name of profit. It was a busy day for the merchants, and for the owners of plantations and mines, which were dependant on African labour to generate their revenue. And when all this was done, and the slaves were safely shackled, marked with their new owner's stamp and locked in the compound, the Merchants could go and celebrate in the local tavernas where their money was as good as anyone's. Here, they could boast of their good deals and their fine ability to barter in human flesh. They could toast their good fortune. It was a prosperous future for all. Depending on the colour of your skin; of course.

The crews had worked hard. The sun beat down on the port of Belém from a clear sky, generating yet another reason for the men to gripe. The foetid air rose from the open holds, clinging to the still air. All they had to do was get through the day as best they could, and the night would be theirs. They had earned it.

*

Isaac opened his eyes. For the first time in many days, he felt comfortable. His head hurt, though it was not thumping, just a dull ache at most. He could feel his body was bruised, but they were bruises that were healing; the sharpness had receded. He could touch them now without wincing.

"Good day to you, senor." The words were said in English with a strong Portuguese accent. "My name is Maria da Sylva. You are lying in my bed."

Isaac remembered her deep-amber eyes. He hauled himself into a sitting position. He felt himself blushing, as he was naked. The bed linen was clean and felt good against his skin.

She poured him a cup of cool water. "Sip gently, senor."

"Thank you, Madam da Sylva. My name is Isaac Dunsmoore," he replied.

"Please, Senor Isaac, call me Maria."

"Thank you, Maria. How long have I been in your… have I been here?"

"Three nights, senor." Maria refilled the cup. She smiled at his reluctance to admit he was in her bed. She couldn't recall when she'd last had a true gentleman in her bed.

Probably never. It hadn't stopped her recognising one when she saw one.

Isaac went to get up from the bed. "Three nights!" he exclaimed. He got as far as swinging his legs out before remembering his predicament.

"Don't mind me, Senor Isaac; get up if you wish." Maria raised her beautiful eyebrows and smiled. "If it is the two grey ships that concern you, do not worry; they are still at the quayside. Today, the second lot of black people is being sold. The town is very busy. Please drink some more water, Isaac. I will bring your clothes."

Isaac slumped back onto the soft pillows, unsure if he had ever lain in such a comfortable bed. *What drew me to this place?* he wondered. He had witnessed all that savagery and barbaric behaviour over the past weeks, and yet this woman – a complete stranger – had taken him in and nursed him back to health. The thought gave him much needed succour. He would make one last attempt to regain command of his ship or die trying. He would not suffer another voyage with Rothwell Spurt. Cordelia and Joanna would, in all probability, lose their lives, but he knew in his heart that, whatever his actions, they would suffer terribly at the hand of Garcia Paz and Rothwell Spurt. A small part of him, however, would never give up hope for their safe release.

Maria came back with a neat pile of laundered clothes and placed them on the end of the bed. She topped up his water.

Isaac recollected the night he stumbled into Maria's tavern. What had drawn him there, he couldn't fathom. "Maria, please tell me why you never had me thrown onto the street that night."

Maria perched on the edge of the bed. She took Isaac's hand. "I have seen every kind of man that walks the earth come through my doors, Isaac, and I have learnt they can be very different creatures. Some I know from bitter experience are very violent, dangerous, cruel men, with their filthy talk, and the belief they can treat women however they choose. I know these men, Isaac. Since my husband passed… Sometimes He takes the good ones, perhaps by mistake…" Maria looked to the heavens, crossing herself as she spoke the words. "I have had to deal with them the best I can, to defend my girls and try to keep them safe. I look to our Mother Mary; she presides over us from the square, giving us guidance. Alas, she also makes mistakes. But not this time, Isaac; she sent you to me, and you have her to thank for my kindness."

"Nonetheless, Maria you are a good woman, and I thank you again." Isaac raised her hand to his mouth and kissed it gently.

It was Maria's turn to blush, something she hadn't done for many years. "Get yourself dressed, Isaac; I shall prepare you some food." With that, she left the room.

Not wasting any time, Isaac got out of bed and dressed himself. The clothes felt good. The rips had been darned, and there was no hint of the stench that had been following him around; his boots were gleaming. He hadn't felt this respectable for a long time. He sloshed water on his face from a stone bowl sitting atop a small dresser. A mirror was fixed to the whitewashed wall. He remembered the reflection that had haunted him from the pail of water. His hair seemed blonder – *It's bleached by the sun*, he thought – and hung to his shoulders. He would ask Maria if she had something with which to tie it back. He ran his hands through the full set of whiskers that were gradually overtaking his visage. He remembered his father. That was an involuntary habit of Henry's. He also thought of his mother, and he wondered how they were both coping. He felt for the gold band; it was no longer on his finger. He remembered he had offered it as payment for help. *Forgive me, Mother, but it was a good trade,* he reasoned to himself.

Following the sounds and smells of cooking, Isaac made his way to the kitchen. He sat at the table, positioning himself behind a plate of food he had not witnessed before. It smelt good. Eggs. He hadn't eaten one for a very long time. His mother used to cook him an egg; it was one of Henry's favourites. He had never seen them made like this, though.

Maria saw him staring at it. "The Spanish call it an 'omelette', Isaac. It tastes very good, considering it is a Spanish recipe. Eat it slowly; your belly is empty."

Maria was right: it was very tasty. When he was halfway through the omelette, she brought him out a pork chop and put on his plate. It smelt as good as the eggs. He forced himself to eat slowly, as he knew his gut was being bombarded. Despite himself, he managed to chew the delicious food, savouring the flavours and washing down each mouthful with a sip of water, as per Maria's instruction.

After lunch, Maria walked to the quay. She strolled casually amongst the throng of people. *In a few more hours,* she thought, *business will be done and the drinking and the whoring will begin.* She took notice of the rough-looking sailors: the enemy Isaac would have to confront if he wanted his ship back.

Maria described the scene for Isaac on her return. She was at a loss to see what could be done. He told her that his own men were there, in amongst the chaos, and he was hoping he still had their loyalty. He told her about Potts and Ezra being out there somewhere, although he admitted that he had little idea if they were still alive. Isaac knew from Maria's information that Spurt's men would be hitting it hard in the tavernas tonight. His best chance – probably his only chance – was to catch them unawares, and the best time to do that was just before sunrise.

"Will you put up with me for a few more hours, Maria?" Isaac asked.

"Oh, I think so; just about," she replied.

*

The pair of them lay on Maria's bed, fully clothed, staring at the wooden boards that separated them from the attic space. Isaac could see strange faces in the knots and the grain of the orangey-coloured wood. She had asked if he had a special woman in his life. He found himself telling her of Rebecca and how he believed they could never be together. She had coaxed the information out of him, and he felt guilty suddenly, as if he had betrayed her in some way. He spoke of his fondness for Cordelia and how much he enjoyed her company.

"I don't know, Maria," he said, "I think sometimes that I want Rebecca because I can't have her. Perhaps that sounds a little stupid; I'm not overly experienced in these matters of romance and the like. I've never actually, you know… with a woman." Isaac covered his face with his hands. "I can't believe I've just told you that."

"You know, Isaac, that sometimes you have to grab the opportunities when they come your way, regardless of the outcome. It is a tragedy to live your life not knowing. So my advice to you is that if you ever get back to England, tell Rebecca your feelings and see where it takes you both. It doesn't have to be any more complicated than that. And if I were a woman prone to wagering, I would say she feels exactly the same about you – unless, of course, she is a little simple."

Isaac smiled. "I don't think she is simple, although I could hope her vision suffers some impairment, perhaps that would help my cause."

Maria rolled onto her side to face him. "You are a fine-looking man, Isaac Dunsmoore; a little skinny at the moment, but nothing a few good meals wouldn't fix." She patted his flat stomach. "Any right-minded woman wouldn't not want you, and I should know, as I have seen you in all your glory."

Isaac laughed. "I wondered how I ended up in that state. Fancy taking advantage of a helpless stranger; honestly, is no one to be trusted around here?"

"See how easy it is when you are relaxed and in the right company."

Isaac looked confused. "How easy what is?"

"Flirting, Isaac; flirting. You are really rather good at it."

Isaac blushed, and not for the first time that day. He turned to face her. "You are a remarkable woman, Maria." He kissed her gently on the mouth.

"See, you're improving all the time."

They kissed again.

"It would be terrible if something happens to you tonight," declared Maria. "My heart tells me that I cannot stop you leaving, nor would I try. Make love to me, and I will go to our maker contented, knowing you have tasted the love of a woman – however briefly – and, equally, I will pray for your safe return into Rebecca's warm embrace."

*

A little while later, as they lay naked and entwined with each other, Isaac considered the time he had wasted when it came to women. He now knew what he'd been missing. Not just the act of sex but the closeness, the feeling of wanting someone and the ultimate expression of feelings towards another, and he had discovered it in the most unlikely of circumstances.

*

Isaac awoke an hour before sunrise. He found his newly darned and laundered clothes strewn across the floor. He gathered them up and dressed quickly. The bed was empty. Feeling sleepy, he splashed water on his face with cupped hands, rubbing the rheum from his eyes. Once he had completed his ablutions, he left the bedroom in search of his hostess. He found Maria in the parlour. She handed him a cup of water and a slab of flat bread. They sat for a few moments whilst he ate the simple breakfast, engulfed in a comfortable silence.

"I must go, Maria," stated Isaac.

"I have a couple of things for you." She took a length of crimson silk from her pocket. "Turn around and stoop a little; I can't reach all the way up there." Maria pulled his hair back and tied it in place with the silk. "There," she said, and she stood back to admire her handywork.

"Maria, I—"

She held up her index finger in a gesture to silence him. She disappeared into the back room and reappeared seconds later carrying an elegant sword in a black, leather scabbard.

"Take this, Isaac, it may help to keep you safe. It belonged to Pedro... my husband. God rest his soul." She held it flat with outstretched arms.

Isaac took the sword from her with gratitude and fixed the belt about his waist. Then he stood at the door ready to leave. The sword sat comfortably at his hip.

"I cannot express in words my gratitude for your kindness, Maria. Last night..." He paused. "I had thoughts of betrayal, but you have washed them away in a blur of euphoria, which will stay with me whatever happens. Thank you." He kissed her gently on the lips.

Maria fought back the tears. "Lovely words, but you have no need to thank me." Maria smiled as she wiped her beautiful eyes with the back of her hand. "The pleasure was nearly all mine. And besides..." she struggled on, keeping her tone light, "the last thing a young bride needs on her wedding night is to share her bed with a monk."

Isaac smiled. "I don't qualify for that title anymore." He kissed her again.

"Oh," she said, "I have one more thing for you." Maria slid the thin, gold band over his little finger. "Take care, my dearest Isaac."

Isaac stepped into the darkness; he never looked back.

Maria stood at the door and watched him disappear. She walked to the statue and knelt, praying silently for a man that had appeared in her life for moments, but whose memory she would cherish until she took her last breath on God's illusory earth.

# Chapter Twenty-Nine

Paz had word from Tomilola that all was now well with Joanna, as if she had fully recovered from some awful disease. He had been looking forward to this. It had been a hectic few days. Conny was curious as to his intentions; it was not often he took a full bath of an evening. She supposed he'd had a busy day and needed to rid himself of any lingering odour that may have clung to him. She knew the smell well enough. *Mercifully*, she thought, *he has no interest in me tonight*. She handed him a glass of white port and left the room.

Paz wallowed in the warm water, sipping his drink. It had been a prosperous few days – chaotic but profitable. Rothwell Spurt's crude behaviour still rankled with him, but there was no denying that he had done a fine job. The ignorant pirate's crusades to the African continent were reaping great rewards. At least he had chosen to stay at Sabina's these past few nights. No doubt he would be back here soon enough to vent his anger on Marrick's widow and guzzle his port. He almost felt sorry for the woman. Still, he'd promised Spurt that he could do as he wished with her; after all, he was about to take the real prize. The only thing blighting his outlook was the patrol he'd sent out in search of those filthy travellers. He would address that issue with Marinho tomorrow. Tonight, he had other things on his mind – things that would obscure any thoughts of the miserable vagabonds who may think they could steal his silver and live to enjoy it.

Paz stepped out of his bath and dried himself. He stood there naked, admiring his body. He took his flaccid penis and rested it in his hand. "Well, my naughty friend, we have important business tonight; I trust you are up for it, so to speak." He smiled to himself and gave it a wiggle.

When dressed once more – in a loose-fitting, white, cotton shirt; tan breeches; and his black, leather boots – Paz grabbed the decanter of port and a couple of glasses, and then headed up the tower to Joanna's room. At the top of the stone stairway, Paz stopped for a brief moment to admire the bust of Mark Antony, one of his heroes from the Roman dynasty. He tutted to himself having spotted a spider's web clinging from Mark Antony's left ear and the stone wall of the recess, which had been home for the bust since Paz had acquired it. He made a mental note to have Conny clean it up. *Damn servants,* he thought, *they can't do anything right.* Paz tapped a finger on Mark Antony's nose. "Worry not, my hero, I will soon have you looking pristine; for now, though, I have other business to attend to, of which I'm sure you would approve."

When he reached his much anticipated destination, Paz tapped on the door once and entered the room before locking the door behind him. The two women were lying on the bed together. Joanna had found a white, linen nightdress for Tomilola, which was edged at the bust with a strip of intricate lace. The colour enhanced the richness of her skin, and the deep vee accentuated the swell of her breasts. Joanna wore one of her father's shirts with the sleeves rolled back. A band of red satin material tied around her slim waist cinched the material tight and then allowed it to fall to her thighs.

Paz admired both women, making no attempt to hide his lustful intentions.

For Joanna and Tomi, it was a moment they had conjured, and now they had to play the role. They were committed. Joanna knew that, whatever happened, Paz would have taken her; his intentions had been clear enough. This way they had a chance; however slim, it was a chance.

Paz poured himself a drink. He had believed he may have to loosen the girls up with a drop of his fine port, but it looked like he was mistaken.

Joanna and Tomi began touching each other, caressing their bodies gently. They kissed. It was long and lingering. Joanna eased Tomi's nightdress off her shoulders and let it fall to her waist. She fondled and kissed Tomi's breasts.

Paz couldn't contain himself a moment longer. He yanked his shirt over his head; pulled off his boots, nearly falling over in his haste; and removed his breeches. He stood at the foot of the bed, a proud and extremely excited man.

"I think there's room for one more, ladies," he declared.

He lay down between them, and they began touching him and themselves, trying desperately to keep it real. They made eye contact with each other, and Tomi leant over Paz, smothering his face with her breasts. Joanna slid down the bed kissing his belly and running her hand tantalisingly over his hard penis. She fumbled under the mattress and felt her hand tighten around the handle of the kitchen knife Tomi had smuggled into the room. She allowed her spare hand to massage Paz's erection keeping him distracted. As she eased the knife from its secret home, Paz took Tomilola's head and pushed it the direction of his throbbing sex. There was little doubt what he wanted now.

\*

Tiago Marinho walked along the quay towards the fortress. The evening was going as he had expected. The tavernas were packed with hard-drinking sailors and greedy merchants, none of whom he cared to share an evening with. Something wedged half in the water and half on the bottom step of the stairs that led down to the water caught his eye. He trod carefully down the slimy steps to take a closer look.

"Jesus Christ," he blasphemed. The bloated and chewed remains of Sousa would haunt his dreams for many nights.

The last thing he needed tonight was a confrontation with Paz. He knew that he couldn't keep this from him. He would have his men retrieve the sergeant, and then he would find Paz and give him the news. Tomorrow, they would give Sousa a decent burial.

\*

Marinho tapped the door of Paz's private quarters. There was no answer. He tapped again and waited. He turned and headed for the kitchen, thinking that perhaps one of the staff would know where he was.

Marinho stopped outside the laundry room. He discerned voices, but not two people engaged in conversation; it was more like guttural moans. He opened the door and was confronted by one of his men, his breeches at his ankles and Conny the servant girl gripping him firmly at the waist, her ankles locked for maximum effect.

"Jesus Christ, Henriques." Marinho had blasphemed twice in the space of ten minutes. "What the devil do you think you're doing?"

"Sorry, sir, I was just—" spluttered the soldier.

"Yes, yes, I can see very well what you're doing. What I meant was… Oh never mind. Have either of you seen Senor Paz?" Marinho queried.

Conny peered over Henriques's shoulder. "I see 'im earlier; dey 'eadin' fo' upstairs in de tower, I tink."

"Thank you, miss. Henriques, when I have left the room uncouple yourself from this poor creature and round up a couple of men. You will find the remains of Sergeant Sousa at the foot of the steps opposite the fortress. See to it that he is put in a suitable place. Tomorrow, we shall bury him properly, and you, Henriques, for your indiscretions, can dig his grave."

Marinho left the pair, walked to the tower and climbed the stone stairway. He always found the air a little dank in the tower. There were candles perched on protruding stones, flickering gently and offering subdued light. Marinho's heart beat a little faster. He was unsure if the climb was the cause or, as was more likely, it was the reception he was about to receive from Paz. Marinho's instinct told him that he would find Paz in Joanna Marrick's room.

Tiago Marinho took a breath and raised a knuckled hand to tap on the door.

*

The glint of silver saved Garcia Paz from serious injury, maybe even death.

Joanna pulled the knife from its hiding place and went to thrust the shiny blade into Paz's gut. If the blade had been dull, it would have escaped his notice.

Joanna's movements were a little awkward because of the situation, and the seconds it took for her to adjust her position cost her the opportunity to inflict serious damage.

Paz reacted lightning quick, despite his predicament. The flash of the blade had alerted him to the danger. He smashed Tomilola's head against Joanna's. A sickening crunch echoed around the room. Paz let out a yell, as Joanna had managed to stick the knife into the flesh just above his hip. Although the wound bled profusely and hurt like hell, it was fairly superficial.

Paz flung Tomilola from the bed. She landed in a crumpled heap, blood running from a wound above her eye; her head flopped to one side, unmoving.

Joanna had let out a scream and tumbled backwards off the end of the bed. She was still conscious. She tried desperately to arrange her thoughts; she needed a weapon. She couldn't work out what to do, her mind was spinning and there was something in her head, smashing against the inside of her skull. She couldn't make it go away.

Paz swung his legs off the bed, groaning. He pulled the

knife from his hip releasing a gasp as the blade slid free. He grabbed the bed sheet and held it against the wound to staunch the flow of blood. He looked at Tomilola; she still hadn't moved. "Black fucking bitch," he muttered.

Using the knife, he tore off a strip of sheet and tied it tightly around his waist. He stood up, taking a moment to steady himself. Paz grabbed Joanna by the hair and lifted her up. She screamed. He struck her backhanded across the cheek. He bent her over the end of the bed and exposed her rear. He put a hand around her neck and pushed her face into the mattress.

"You fucking little whore. You have no idea what's about to happen to you. And when I'm finished, the eagles will tear you apart, bit by fucking bit."

Marinho could hear muffled sounds. Then he heard Paz. It sounded like he had yelped in pain. Then came the scream; it was unmistakeable. He tried the door. It was locked. He took a step back and charged the door with his shoulder. Nothing happened. He thought for a moment, and then ran to the top of the stairs and lifted the bust from its home. It must have weighed eighty pounds, and he grunted as he felt its full weight. He staggered back to the room and hefted the statuette into a comfortable position. He swung it back once, twice, and on the third swing, he smashed it into the door with all his might.

The door swung open and crashed against the wall. At the same time, a muffled but terrifying scream filled the room. Marinho's momentum carried him into the room, still clutching the bust. The sight of Garcia Paz stood over the defenceless girl sickened Marinho beyond belief. Paz turned to the intruder, shocked but totally unabashed.

"Get out, man. What the devil do you think you're doing? God's blood, you idiot, can't you see I'm busy?"

In those few seconds, Tiago Marinho's experiences at the hand of this pitiless barbarian flashed through his mind. *No more*, he thought. He raised the bust above his head and smashed it onto the skull of his tormentor. Paz staggered sideways and collapsed to the floor. He lay on his back, his eyes wide open, registering a display of total disbelief, and the side of his skull caved in. Marinho stood over him, hoping that Paz could still see him. Mark Antony was getting heavier and heavier. Marinho released his grip.

Garcia Paz's hero smashed his face to pulp.

# Chapter Thirty

The night air had begun to lift; the dark mask was gradually diminishing, exposing the moody allure of dawn. Horace, Ezra and Potts stood on the rocky outcrop. They had brought with them the makings of a small fire. Potts fiddled with the twigs and dried grass, and he soon had the beginnings of a sturdy little blaze. Enough for their purpose.

Horace nocked one of the huge arrows, and with Ezra's guidance, he aimed it across the bay.

"Christ, Ezra, that must be five hundred yards."

"I reckon it must be, Tay, at least." Ezra turned to Clunk. "If you use your arm for a guide, Horace, like this…" Ezra held his arm out, with it pointing upwards, his bicep just below his ear. "That is the sort of elevation you need."

Horace raised the bow. "I got ya. Don't worry, I'll git the 'ang of it right enough. You two git goin'. I'll be with ya as soon as I've fired these arras."

"Good shootin', Horace," Potts said.

"Remember your arm position, by your ear," Ezra reminded him.

"Go on, git, and don't go gittin' yersens killed or summat stupid like that," chided Horace.

"We'll try not to," Ezra and Potts replied in unison, and they left Horace practising his elevations.

Ezra and Potts made their way along the rock until they reached the patch of forest. As they looked back, the huge outline of Horace Clunk was just discernible, his arms aloft, pointing the tip of an arrow towards the grey sky. Their trust was with the big man. If his aim was true, then they had a chance.

*

In due course, they reached the quay. It would have been completely silent if not for the faint chink of chains and the haunting reverberation of the sleeping Africans.

They ran, their knees bent to lower their profile, until they reached the first side street. The corner of the building would be their only cover. They stood with their backs pressed to the wall. Ezra knelt and peered round the corner of the building. *Angerona* was maybe fifty yards away. He could see that *Rebecca-Ann* was further along the quay, and out of harm's way, he hoped. Ezra stood up and resumed his position.

"What d'ya reckon, Ezra?" Potts whispered.

"I reckon if the captain were here, we'd have a better plan," Ezra confirmed.

A soft, familiar voice took them by surprise. "I wouldn't be so sure."

The shocked pair turned to see their captain stepping out from the cover of a doorway opposite.

"Good to see you two are up to no good again," Isaac declared.

Before any of them could say another word, the sky lit up, with a blazing trail of flame illuminating the grey dawn. The arrow dropped into the sea just short of *Angerona*.

"What the devil…?" Isaac never finished his utterance.

Another flaming missile flew through the air. It thudded into the deck near the ship's bow. A few seconds later, another tore through the furled sail at the main mast and embedded itself into a spar, igniting everything in its path. The flaming missiles kept raining down on the ship.

"It shouldn't be long now," Potts observed.

Ezra stepped out into the street, with an arrow loaded and ready to fire.

Isaac drew Pedro da Sylva's sword and joined Ezra on the quay. Potts had a machete in his belt and an axe in his hand.

"Dare I ask who is firing the ordnance?" enquired Isaac.

"Horace Clunk, sir," Ezra said.

"The last time I saw him he was in irons heading for the silver mines."

"It's a long story, sir."

"I shall look forward to its telling when this nonsense is done with."

"Here we go," stated Potts.

Two of Spurt's men ran from the burning vessel onto the quay. The second man stared as his mate grunted and fell to the cobbles. Before he could register his predicament, an arrow punctured his jugular, and he joined his comrade in a bloody heap.

Suddenly, the ship was alive with men running and shouting. Some tried to get buckets of water to try and combat the fire, but their efforts were futile. They clamoured at the gangway, desperate to escape the roaring flames. A few jumped overboard into the harbour.

*

Horace dipped his last arrow into the pot of resin and touched it to the embers of the transient fire. It ignited, just the same as the others. Horace raised the bow as Ezra had shown him and released the arrow.

*

Treadwell had staggered from his bunk onto the deck, cursing and bemoaning the chaos around him. "God..." That was his last word. The flaming arrow hit him square in the chest and pinned him to the door he had just exited. The resin continued to burn.

*

Ezra waited momentarily before unleashing another arrow. He needed to ensure that he wasn't shooting his own men. So far, he hadn't seen any of his mates. Now, though, the men were flooding down the gangway, jumping their fallen comrades and scrabbling for protection from the lethal arrows. There were bodies writhing and groaning; some just lay where they had fallen, their warm blood coursing through the shallow troughs between the cobbles.

A couple of Spurt's men hid behind a cart abandoned on the quay. It rested on its shafts at a jaunty angle, waiting to be hitched to a faithful mule.

Isaac knew the initial advantage had begun to ebb. The three men stood in the open, surveying the enemy. There was no clear shot for Ezra.

The cart began to trundle towards them, with a group of men now crouching behind it for cover. There was still no clear shot for Ezra. He laid the bow down and took off his quiver. Potts passed him the machete.

\*

On board *Gemini*, Elwyn Sakkit was the first to stir. He made his way quickly onto the deck. The sight of *Angerona* lighting up the grey dawn stunned him; his features distorted into a gawp of disbelief. "Holy shit," he muttered. He noticed a group of Spurt's men pushing the cart along the quay towards three men. Sakkit squinted his eyes. "*Holy shit! Fucking shit. Shit.*" He ran down the companion way to where the crew were quartered; he was shouting and hollering, and tipping men out of their hammocks.

\*

Rudd rolled out of the warm bed, naked. He walked across the room and positioned himself above the chamber pot. He felt flecks of warm urine splash his legs. The explosion made him jump, causing him to piss over the floor.

"For fuck's sake! What the hell…?" he declared.

The woman in the bed woke for a second or two, turned

herself over, pulled the cover over her head and went back to sleep. Rudd yanked his breeches on and grabbed his cutlass as he ran from the room. He met Rothwell Spurt on the landing in a similar state to himself. They careered down the two flights of creaky, wooden stairs, through the bar and onto the quay.

"Fuckin' arseholes." These were the only words that came to Rothwell Spurt's mind.

*

*Angerona* was a sorry sight. The fire had reached the store of gunpowder, and the ensuing explosion had ripped a hole in her hull. The gaping void invited the sea to invade her bowels, and she had begun listing precariously to port.

Notwithstanding the occasional sleepy whore, the dockside was awash with chaotic action. The acrid smoke from the burning ship created an ominous cloud that was randomly punctuated with crimson sparks, shrouding the port in an ethereal haze. Seasoned timber and pitch was always an effective combination for a good fire.

Isaac, Ezra and Potts braced themselves for the onslaught. It was about to get up close and very personal. The rest of Spurt's men were now charging along the quay, screaming and cursing like a band of demented savages, unaware of Dunsmoore's men now closing in behind them.

Isaac, Ezra and Potts had now engaged with the group pushing the cart. Ezra hadn't the first clue how skilled his captain was with a sword. It was no surprise to Potts, however, who had witnessed his craft on the odd occasion over the years. Isaac had dispensed with three men in quick succession.

Ezra, armed with the machete, dodged a scything swipe from a cutlass and sliced the blade across his attacker's chest. The man fell to the ground dropping his cutlass. Ezra stooped to grab it and was immediately confronted by a snarling pirate, whose sword was arcing towards him. The axe punctured the man's chest, splitting it open and sending him cartwheeling backwards into the next opponent. Ezra grabbed the fallen sword and glanced over his shoulder. Horace Clunk was charging towards them. He had launched the axe when he realised he couldn't reach Ezra in time. His aim had been perfect.

Horace hurled himself into the affray. He'd pulled the axe from the dead sailor and was swinging it in savage arcs, dismembering limbs and carving chunks of flesh from anyone brave enough, or stupid enough, to get in his way.

Suddenly, Dunsmoore's crew were on top of them, evening out the numbers.

It was a brutal, bloody confrontation, and a battle in which Isaac and his crew were beginning to get the upper hand.

*

Rudd and Spurt watched as Dunsmoore's crew swamped his men from the rear. Rudd went to run towards the action, but Spurt put a hand on his arm to restrain him.

"Too fuckin' late now, Rudd, unless you want to get yourself butchered. Quick, let's collect our shit and get to the fortress," Spurt suggested.

*

The explosion had aroused the sleepy occupants of the fortress. It was well past midnight when Marinho had dealt with the carnage left in the wake of Garcia Paz, including the disposal of his corpse. He had slept for a couple of hours, amidst the confusion of his next problem: Rothwell Spurt.

Marinho shouted to his corporal to have all the men ready for action. He wanted them in a column two abreast and ready for action at the double.

He ran up the stairs of the tower to Cordelia's room. He noticed Mark Antony had been cleaned and reappointed. He tapped the door lightly and pushed it ajar, just enough to poke his head into the room. Cordelia came to the door, and joined him in the hallway.

"My apologies for the intrusion, madam, but I wanted to check on the girls' condition and to inform you that I am leading my men from the fortress with the intention of apprehending Rothwell Spurt and his crew. There is mischief afoot, and the sun has barely risen. Please keep the door locked. I shall post one of my men at the door and give him orders to shoot Spurt or anyone he doesn't recognise," Marinho explained.

"I cannot thank you enough, Captain, for everything; I don't have the words…" Cordelia pressed Marinho's hand between her own and gently squeezed, seeking reassurance within herself that he would restore certainty to her uncertain existence. "The girls will be fine, I'm sure; although the memory of last night will beset them for many a night, of that I have no doubt."

Marinho acquiesced with a nod. "I must leave now; please, madam, remain in your room. With any luck, I shall be back in time for breakfast." He deliberately kept his tone light.

*

The wharf at Belém had become a battleground – a scene of grizzly carnage.

The survivors from Spurt's crew began laying down their weapons, with some pleading for mercy and others adopting a neutral approach to their predicament: just drop your weapon, raise your hands and hope for the best; no pleading required. Hopefully, the giant with the axe won't split you apart.

Isaac had cleaned de Sylva's sword and slid it back into the scabbard. Sweat trickled down his face; his newly laundered clothes were splattered with blood. A cut on his left shoulder made him wince, but after a cursory inspection, he deemed it reasonably superficial. During the affray, he had been searching for Rothwell Spurt. There had been no sign of him.

Amongst the five dead crew, Isaac noticed Ed Monk, with the sword that had killed him still protruding from his chest. His resolve to find Spurt flared inside him.

"*Mister Clunk,*" Isaac shouted over the groans of dying men, "*let us have these survivors clapped in irons. We still have much work to do before we are spared.*"

A handful of men went into the compound and began freeing the Africans, using the irons to shackle the prisoners. Once a few had been freed, the slaves began unshackling their comrades, reuniting themselves with family where possible. Horace pointed the way to the beach beyond the patch of forest and suggested they would be safer there for now.

Isaac was proud of his crew – not one had defected to Spurt – and to a man, they had fought like Old Scratch himself. He now led them along the quay to face thirty or forty trained soldiers; they were outnumbered nearly three to one. He weighed the odds in his head: Horace was equal to three, maybe four men; Potts at least two; Ezra the same; and perhaps, modesty notwithstanding, he could count two men for himself. Outnumbered two to one. Isaac preferred that statistic, albeit somewhat contrived and mathematically bogus. Nevertheless, it instilled in him a much needed degree of solace; he wasn't leading his men into a certain massacre.

*

Captain Marinho led his men along the quay. Acrid smoke still hung in the air, although there was little evidence of its source. He saw Spurt and Rudd heading directly for them unaware of the change in circumstance.

"Ah, Marinho, about fuckin' time. These bastards 'ave sunk my—" Rothwell was rendered speechless as he stared down the barrel of Marinho's pistol.

Suddenly, there were a dozen muskets aimed at the pair of them.

"Rothwell Spurt, you and Rudd are under arrest." The words felt good to Marinho.

"What the devil are you talkin' about, you fuckin' jumped-up excuse for a soldier? What's the charge?" Spurt was livid; as he ranted, he spat on the floor at Marinho's feet.

"Where's Paz? Get 'im out 'ere to sort this mess. 'E'll 'ave you strung up for this outrage, you docile piece of stupid shit."

"Piracy is the charge." Marinho glanced up at the gibbet. "Hanging the cure. And I shouldn't worry too much about your mate Paz; he's in no position to help, I can assure you."

*

Isaac watched the scene unfold before him as he led his men along the quay. The dynamics had altered dramatically, and he felt his mood lighten. Marinho was pointing his pistol at Spurt's head – and that was a sight he wasn't expecting.

"*Captain Dunsmoore, it's good to see you.*" Marinho shouted the greeting.

The words sent a cold shiver through Rothwell Spurt the like of which he'd not experienced for a very long time.

"Dunsmoore," Rothwell spluttered the word. He and Rudd turned to see Isaac Dunsmoore, as large as life, leading his men. "I should 'ave fuckin' known."

A pause ensued, which appeared to stretch endlessly, with questions not yet asked and the answers, therefore, untold.

Isaac asked first, "Captain Marinho, may I enquire after the ladies well-being?"

"They are safe, Captain," Marinho confirmed.

"And Paz?"

"Shall we say he is no longer a threat." Marinho looked at Horace Clunk. "The last time I saw the giant, he was heading for the silver mines. May I ask how you escaped, and what of my men who were dispatched to search for the travellers? Although, judging by the remains of my sergeant, I can only imagine they will not be reporting for duty any time soon."

Ezra and Potts exchanged glances.

Isaac noted the exchange. "Perhaps now is not the time for recriminations. I think now is the time to conclude this distasteful business. What do you say, Captain?"

"I couldn't agree more. Corporal, have the noose slung over the gibbet."

"You can't do this," Rudd protested. "All we've done is fetch these black bastards back 'ere to do an 'onest day's work, and you wanna 'ang us."

In a flash, Horace Clunk lunged forwards and wrapped a huge hand around Rudd's neck. He lifted him a foot off the ground. Rudd kicked his legs, uttering unintelligible grunts.

"*Mister Clunk,*" Isaac shouted, "*release that man.*"

Horace waited for a second and opened his hand. Rudd collapsed to the cobbles, grasping his throat and gasping for air.

"Thank you, Mister Clunk." Isaac turned to Spurt. "Your man here thinks it's okay to treat these people no better than a man would treat common vermin. Indeed, you yourself think it is acceptable to slit the throat of a young girl and discard her into the ocean like a piece of trash. And, moreover, you thought you could steal my ship and use her for your own ends. Well, Spurt take a good, long look at *her* whilst you dangle from the rope; and may your soul rot in hell."

Rothwell looked at Isaac, unmoved. He pointed at Ezra. "I suppose that's the bastard son of Edward Buckingham.

I wondered when 'e was gonna crawl out of the fuckin' woodwork."

It took Ezra a few seconds to load an arrow and aim it at Spurt's pockmarked face. "I ain't no bastard son of anyone." The sound of Persius Milford taunting him and his father flooded Ezra's senses. "Tell him, Captain."

"Ah, I see you've not bothered to enlighten the boy, Dunsmoore; very remiss of you, I must say." Rothwell could see he'd stirred up a hornets' nest, his parting shot before he dangled from a rope.

"Put the bow down, lad," Isaac said gently.

"Tell me what he's on about. Tell me he's lying," demanded Ezra.

"I will tell you, Ezra," Isaac agreed, "but first put the bow down, and let us hang this filthy vagabond so the whole of Belém can see that justice has been served."

Rothwell smiled at Ezra. "Makes you wonder, though, boy, don't it? You know, whether 'e was ever gonna tell ya?"

"Ezra, no." Isaac sensed that Spurt had pushed him too far.

Ezra was standing no more than five paces from Rothwell Spurt. The arrow smashed its way through Spurt's mouth and exited at the base of his neck. It tore through tissue, sinew, muscle, vertebrae and bone on its relentless journey. Rothwell collapsed face up on the cobbles, with the arrow protruding from his mouth as if he had tried to eat it.

"Jesus Christ, Ezra." Isaac took the bow from him.

The quayside fell silent.

After the silence, Marinho spoke. "Ah well, Captain Dunsmoore, it's one fewer to hang."

Rudd groaned. Marinho's men hoisted him from his prone position, slipped the noose around his neck and secured his hands behind his back.

"Mister Clunk, perhaps you would do the honours." Marinho extended his arm, completing the invitation.

The corporal handed the rope to Horace, who took up the slack and, with a mighty yank, lifted Rudd off his feet. A couple of half hitches around an iron cleat bolted to the outer wall secured the end of the hangman's noose.

Rudd dangled by the neck, kicking at empty space, his feet tantalisingly close to the ground. As the minutes passed, so his eyes distended. His natural pallor was progressively supplanted with a purple hue, and his tongue drooping from the corner of his mouth accentuated the grotesque image.

# Chapter Thirty-One

The last thing Roly Smith saw before jumping overboard was Treadwell's burning corpse pinned to the door of the companionway. He swam like an overweight bulldog. Amidst the haphazard strokes, his head continually disappeared beneath the water as he spluttered his way to the stone stairs, where just a few hours earlier a bloated corpse had occupied the bottom step.

Roly Smith slunk up the stairs and peered over the top step. Rudd was hanging by the neck, as dead as hanging could make a person. He had been hoisted high for everyone to see. The soldiers had dispersed, and Dunsmoore's crew were heading for their ship. He decided that he would try to lose himself in the town and keep his head down until the chance to join another ship presented itself. He was pleased that Spurt and Rudd had met their end, even though it left him in a predicament. He did, however, have a secret that gave him a certain confidence when it came to saving his own neck from being stretched.

Roly brushed himself down, ran his fingers through his

hair, and with as much nonchalance as he could muster, sauntered along the quay in search of sanctuary, at least until things settled.

*

Isaac promised Ezra that he would talk to him, but he needed to check on Cordelia and Joanna first. He was also angry that Ezra had directly disobeyed him. Whatever the circumstances, an order is an order, and without fear or heed for the consequences, he had killed Spurt. Isaac understood why, God knows he'd wished it had been him who had put the arrow in Spurt. Captain Marinho, however, could have taken a different view on the situation, and Ezra could have found himself on a charge of murder. After all they'd been through, it could have been young Ezra hanging from the gibbet.

After talking with Marinho, Isaac had told his men to head for Sabina's and have a hearty breakfast with just enough ale to wash it down. Also, they should get Seddon to check out any injuries they had. "Assure the good lady if you will, Mister Clunk, that I shall be along to settle the tab."

*

Potts and Ezra sat at a table by a window. Ezra stared blankly; he could see *Rebecca-Ann*, and her dowdy, grey livery failed to inspire him. "Did you know, Tay?"

"All I knew was that the captain saw you as someone…" Potts struggled for the words. "Christ, Ez, I've met your father; there ain't no mistakin' who you are."

"How'd that bastard Spurt know about me?"

Potts shrugged. "Beats me, but know this, Ez: from the moment we plucked you from the channel, the captain has had your best interests at heart. You done wrong, shootin' Spurt like that; although the bastard deserved it, I'll give you that. He'll explain it all, Ez, just give him a chance."

Before Potts could say any more, Ezra jumped up and ran onto the quay. He'd seen a vaguely familiar shadow walk by the window.

"Hey," Ezra called.

Instinctively, Roly Smith turned.

A few seconds passed as the two strangers assessed one another.

They spoke in unison. "You."

Potts followed Ezra out, machete in hand. "Who's this?" He pointed the machete at Smith, who held his hands up, palms out in a submissive gesture.

Ezra stared into Roly Smith's deep-blue eyes, and not for the first time, he now knew. He saw something, maybe a reflection of himself. "It's fine, Taylor; I believe he's a friend."

Roly caught on quick. "Smith's the name, Roly Smith." He offered his hand.

"Ezra Quicklock and Taylor Potts; it's good to see you again, Roly," Ezra said, and they shook hands. God knows there had been enough killing.

# Chapter Thirty-Two

Tomilola sat up in Cordelia's bed; she had been badly concussed, but insisted she felt no ill effects from the clash of heads. The purple bruises around her eye told another story.

Joanna sat on the edge of the bed; she could scarcely believe that they were still alive. *There's no time like the present,* she thought, and she told Cordelia of her relationship with Tomi, with no apologies and no hesitation, just the truth, how she felt and what she wanted.

Cordelia had been pacing the room, hoping desperately that Captain Marinho would deal with Rothwell Spurt and his men successfully. The alternative was unimaginable. Joanna's confession had stopped her in her tracks. Now she had something else to ponder. Something she never expected. Her daughter, however, never failed to surprise her. Cordelia knew in that moment that she would be unable to return to her home in England. Two women together would be a difficult, probably impossible situation to contemplate; two women together, one black and one white, would be insurmountable.

*

Marinho thought he would never pass Mark Antony without a wry smile.

"Is that an ancient Roman leader of some description?" Isaac enquired.

"Mark Antony, apparently," Marinho said. "I have made a point to read about his exploits, should I happen across such a tome. At ease, soldier. There's been no disturbance, I take it?"

"No, sir," the man confirmed.

Marinho dismissed the private and tapped on the door.

*

Cordelia's heart felt like it had missed a beat and then restarted too quickly. She relaxed when the captain's voice filtered into the room.

"Madam, I have someone who wishes to see you. May we come in?" he asked.

Cordelia unlocked the door. Marinho had stepped to one side. When she saw Isaac framing the doorway, her heart decided her next move; any control she may have had over her actions were thus superseded, and she flung her arms around him. "Thank God," she whispered.

*

A short time later, the three of them sat in Paz's opulent quarters. Marinho had unearthed the bogus paperwork appertaining to the plantation.

"I see no reason why we shouldn't find these people and reimburse them," Marinho said. "I shall write and inform them of the change in circumstances, although I'm afraid it is too late for the poor souls who perished at Paz's hand."

"Rosario Bay. It has a certain resonance, don't you think?" Cordelia enquired.

"It sounds rather grand," Isaac answered. "I understand the place is a little neglected, though?"

"That was Paz's ploy," Marinho explained. "He always told potential buyers that the place needed a little work, but this was reflected in the price. There was never any shortage of people who believed they were getting a bargain, which I may say, madam, you most certainly are, albeit that you have suffered immensely in the process."

"So tomorrow, Cordelia, if the young ladies are sufficiently recovered, we shall go and investigate Rosario Bay, see if our return cargo is ready for dispatch and make sure your new home is all you could wish for." Isaac then excused himself. "I have matters that require my earnest attention. It's so good to see you, Cordelia; I had wondered at times if... and thank you once again, Captain Marinho, without your brave intervention—"

"Please, Captain," Marinho interrupted, "my conscience tells me that I should have taken action against the man before now."

"It is not an easy thing to act against a commanding officer, Captain; you know that as well as anyone." Isaac extended his hand to Marinho. "Captain, Cordelia."

With that, Isaac left the fortress and headed for *Rebecca-Ann*. There was much to be done.

\*

Roly Smith joined Horace, Ezra and Potts in the gig. They had already stopped at the Tupi village and explained the events to Jonas, who in turn related the story to an overexcited group of young men. Agu had pointed to Ezra's neck. He explained to Agu that he had left the pearl with Afi for safekeeping. That was okay then.

They continued their journey to the African camp, telling Roly of their exploits as they rowed against the current. Roly, in turn, told of Rothwell Spurt's deeds since he had been pressed into his service, from which he had been waiting for an opportunity to safely retire. He had never imagined it would have been under such circumstances.

"There is another thing, Ezra…" he began.

"What's that then, Roly?" asked Ezra.

"I was part of a detail that dug a deep hole on the island; you know, where we were when you cut the ship free."

"A hole for what?" Potts asked.

"Spurty's loot," confirmed Roly.

"And I thought it was just a tall tale that all pirates had buried treasure!" Potts said. "I reckon, with the captain's permission, I see no good reason why we shouldn't retrieve said loot. What do you say, Horace?"

"If I think o' one I'll let ya know," Horace replied.

\*

Afia had been feeling a little queasy, so she lay in her hut. She could hear a commotion, but chose to ignore it. She had convinced herself that she would never see Ezra again, and the pain of it was beginning to overwhelm her.

Ezra eased the crude, wicker door to one side and poked his head into the gloomy space. "Has anyone seen a beautiful young lady? She is guarding my pearl, and I have come to claim it."

Afia leapt from her bed and flung herself at Ezra. She wrapped her legs around his waist, her usual greeting, and clung to the man she had fallen helplessly in love with.

The party were soon back aboard the gig and heading downriver. Their numbers had swollen by two. Afia and Olu sat in the bow and insisted that the story be retold once more. Afia was desperately excited at the thought of seeing her sister, and Olu believed that there was a chance his wife Zoella and his son Chi were at the plantation or the fortress. The notion of being reunited with them had kept his spirit extant.

*

Aboard *Rebecca-Ann*, Isaac had instructed his men to remove the shelving that had been installed previously for the transportation of the Africans. The bilges were to be sloshed until the last remnant of waste had disappeared. Her livery would have to keep; the dull-grey would feature for a while.

The quayside had begun to fill with disgruntled merchants, some with bullish overseers who were becoming impatient, threatening even. The sight of the empty compound, where their merchandise should have been shackled awaiting transportation to their new homes, and the heaps of dead bodies littering the cobbles was something they had not expected.

Isaac was pleased to see Marinho's corporal leading a dozen men towards the band of resentful merchants. Marcos Ferreira, who had his eye on another stripe due to Sousa's demise, was armed with a purse of silver and the enthusiasm of someone seeking to enhance their rank. He had orders from his captain to have the buyers assemble on the beach with the Africans. Ferreira's instructions were that, under no circumstances, were families to be separated or any of them shackled. The merchants were to be reimbursed where necessary.

*It is a small step,* Tiago Marinho thought, *towards treating these wretched souls with a modicum of civility.* He sat at the polished, teak desk. He had to admit that it was a fine piece of furniture, but he reasoned with himself that he could write a letter just as well sitting behind something far less grand. The trappings of wealth, he supposed.

His note was addressed to the governor general, Raphael Mendoza. That was as far as he'd got. Marinho had considered inventing an elaborate tale of how Garcia Paz met with a tragic accident. He decided otherwise. He knew the governor was an ambitious man, but his instinct told him that he was a man who dealt in the truth; although Mendoza was strict, Marinho had always considered him reasonable and fair. His future now depended on that assumption. Whatever the outcome, he would not spin a web of lies.

On completing it, Marinho sealed the letter and dispatched it to Sao Luis. He would know Mendoza's reaction soon enough.

# Chapter Thirty-Three

The track snaked along the coast for nearly ten miles before it revealed its secret: Rosario Bay.

The happy party stopped to admire the vista. The bay itself was maybe eight or nine hundred paces wide. The buff-coloured sand darkened at the shoreline where the turquoise ocean lapped onto the beach. The sea turned to darker shades of green and blue as the water deepened. The exquisite arc of the cove was formed at each end with outcrops of cliff face, which framed the bay perfectly. Maybe fifty paces from the shoreline and slightly off centre, a craggy rock grew from the seabed, separated from the land by the unrelenting roll of the Atlantic and the passage of time. It was a stunning sight that silenced its onlookers.

The four ladies rode in Paz's open carriage. They had chattered the journey away. Now they were silenced by the serenity of Rosario Bay.

Tomilola and Afia had been reunited at the fortress. They had embraced each other with a fervour that reduced Cordelia and Joanna to tears. Neither of them had imagined they would see each other again. In that precious moment, they believed nothing would part them.

Joanna and Ezra had a few moments to talk, soon realising that explanations were not required. It was a moment that not one of them could have dared to contemplate during the past weeks.

The chief overseer at the plantation stood on the portico of what he took to be his home, eyeing the small procession as it came to a halt. Oscar Joubert was a white South African and a brute of a man who had been enjoying the trappings of Rosario Bay since Garcia Paz had put him in charge. He saw before him a threat to that status, one he determined he would not surrender easily. Joubert hooked his suspenders over his bare shoulders and picked up his whip, which sat on a round occasional table in the shade of the colonnade.

"*This is private property. I'll ask you to leave,*" Joubert bellowed, his accent still thick with the South African cadence.

Cordelia had hopped down from the carriage, and before anyone could intervene, she was marching across the manicured lawn towards the misinformed overseer. "I am afraid, sir, it is you who is on private property."

"And who the fuck are you, lady?" Joubert sneered.

Cordelia was surprised to hear a voice behind her answer the question.

"Dis lady is Cordelia Marrick, an' she gonna be da boss now." The voice belonged to Horace Clunk. He eased Cordelia to one side and stood facing Joubert.

"Don't you fuckin' talk to me until I tell you, you fuckin' overgrown fuckin' cocoa bean."

Horace punched Joubert in the face, breaking his nose and knocking out a handful of brown teeth. The overseer crashed backwards through the closed door and landed flat on his back in the hallway, with his feet on the porch.

"Sorry 'bout the door, missis." Horace looked apologetically at Cordelia.

"That's okay, Horace; it was worth it," she declared.

Horace stepped onto the porch, took the whip, broke it over his knee and threw it on the prone body of Oscar Joubert. One more vile weapon that wouldn't be used to mark another enslaved African.

Notwithstanding the unconscious South African lying in the hallway, the house welcomed Cordelia. *Strange,* she thought, *having a feeling of acceptance from a house.* She and the girls could be happy here. And she vowed to make changes. There would be no more slave labour. These people would be paid for their efforts. Not abused and beaten for them.

Ezra and Afia went with Olu in search of his wife and son. They headed into the sugarcane fields, where men women and children were toiling beneath the harsh sun. Some had fashioned themselves hats from the dried leaves of the cane; their clothes were little more than rags.

Afia approached a lady and enquired about Zoella and Chi. The lady looked confused and nervous. She stared at Ezra, and an expression of fear and hatred swamped her troubled face. The sound of hooves refocused her efforts.

"It's okay, miss, you can talk to us. The plantation has a new owner." Ezra tried to reassure her.

She continued with her labour, refusing to engage with him.

"She frightened, Ez," Afia said in a soft voice.

The man on the horse wore a wide-brimmed hat and held a whip in his right hand. The horse scuffed the ground with a hoof and jerked its head up and down, indicative of its skittish disposition.

"Who are you?" he demanded, pointing the whip at Ezra. "Why're you two blacks not workin'?"

"I ain't no slave," Afia declared.

"The hell you ain't, bitch."

The leather thong of the whip lashed Afia face; she screamed in pain. The horse reared, throwing the rider to the ground; its front legs flailed – thrashing at the air and clawing at an illusory foe – until, finally, they struck.

Olu grabbed the reins and used all his strength to calm the beast. Ezra pulled the man to his feet and delivered a wicked punch to the man's throat. The second one hit him on the temple, and the bewildered overseer fell sideways into the sugarcane.

Ezra turned and saw Afia sprawled on the ground. He knelt by her side. Her hands clutched her belly, and blood trickled from her ear. He put his hands under her and lifted her beautiful face towards him.

She was desperately trying to speak. Afia's eyes pointed to her hands. "Dey our babies, Ez," she whispered.

# Chapter Thirty-Four

They buried Afia in the rear garden of Cordelia's house. The simple grave overlooked Rosario Bay. Ezra knew she would like that. He sat cross-legged at her feet talking to her; it was the only thing that eased his grief, and he knew he had to leave her.

To help combat the pain of his loss, Olu had found his wife and son. There had been much excitement, tempered with sadness; the loss of Afia would resonate around Rosario Bay for many years to come.

The sugar was ready for dispatch, and Isaac needed to return to the port. Transportation had been organised, and *Rebecca-Ann* would be loaded and ready to sail for England the day after tomorrow.

Joanna had been searching for Ezra, but no one had seen him. Tomilola stood at her sister's grave and stared out into the bay. Joanna joined her. Tomi pointed to the craggy rock in the bay that cast its shadow over the sea. The figure was barefoot and bare-chested. He clambered over the precipice and balanced himself on the summit. They stared in silence as the familiar shape hurled himself into space and plummeted into the blue-green ocean, creating the merest splash.

\*

Ezra swam near the seabed, heading towards the horizon. He was counting: two hundred, three hundred, three hundred and fifty, sixty, seventy…

He saw Afia. The last time an image, unknown to Ezra, had saved him; she had somehow forced him to the surface. But now all he could see were his dead babies and their beautiful mother. Three hundred and eighty, ninety…

His lungs began to burn. He remembered the feeling. Her voice penetrated his soul. Three hundred and ninety five…

He felt himself being pulled to the surface. He gasped at four hundred and took a deep breath. His vision was blurred, but he remembered Agu's instructions.

As his head cleared, he looked around him, searching for his rescuer. There was no one.

\*

Joanna and Tomilola scrutinised the ocean for a sign of the mystery figure.

"That was Ezra, Tomi," Joanna confirmed.

"How you know dat, Jo? He too far 'way."

"It was him, Tomi, I know. No one can stay under the water that long; it's just not possible." Joanna put her head in her hands. *Please God,* she thought, *not Ezra too.*

Tomilola nudged Joanna. "Look, Jo."

Joanna saw a speck in the ocean swimming towards the shore. She shook her head in disbelief. "How's that possible?"

\*

Isaac sat with Cordelia. He was ready to leave.

"Cordelia," he began, "there is something I need to tell you before I leave."

"There is no need to say anything, Isaac, because if you're going to tell me what I think you're going to tell me, I already know," she stated.

Isaac took a moment to digest the information. "Well, I'm not sure—"

Cordelia interrupted him. "You were going to tell me about Rebecca. I saw you when we left Milford Port. I knew then."

"Sorry, Cordelia. You know I have a fondness for you and that I truly believe if it wasn't for…" Isaac stumbled over his words. "My feelings for Rebecca…"

"I know, I know. Please, there is no cause for explanation. You have a special place in my heart, Isaac Dunsmoore, and I shall treasure our friendship for the rest of my days. And, besides, Tiago – Captain Marinho – has intimated his feelings towards me, and I think a girl could do a lot worse."

"Indeed she could." Isaac took Cordelia in his arms and embraced her tightly. "You are a special woman." Isaac kissed her gently on the lips. "I shall look forward with great anticipation to our next meeting. Take care."

\*

Ezra was still dripping as he said his farewells. Cordelia gave him a package; she had made him some more clothes during her incarceration. It had helped with her sanity, she said. Ezra hugged the girls. He had no idea that they had watched him dive from the rock.

He went to Afia. He thought about the pearl at her slender throat. It would provide comfort on her ultimate journey. Agu would understand. "Sleep peacefully, my beautiful Afi," he whispered.

Now he had to leave.

# Chapter Thirty-Five

Isaac sat in his cabin. He tried to erase the thought of Rothwell Spurt's presence. His private letters were strewn across his bureau. He refolded them and returned them to the drawer. There was no choice; he would have to tell Ezra of his sister. *God Almighty,* he contemplated, *the lad has been through the mill.*

Stacked to one side were four wooden crates with the lids nailed down. The bottom box was made of some exotic hardwood, he noted, and was not so deep as the others. He supposed they contained Rothwell's loot. Isaac shuddered at the thought of it. A part of him wanted to launch it overboard, but there were people who would benefit from it, one of whom he needed to see before they departed.

Isaac had summoned Potts to his quarters. He arrived with a crowbar and levered the lid from the topmost box. It was full of gold coins. The two men stared in disbelief.

"There you see it, Mister Potts," Isaac said, "the plunder of a murderous bastard."

"Aye, sir. Enough is never enough for a man like Spurt." Potts shook his head as he spoke. It was an astute observation.

Isaac nodded in agreement. "We'd best keep it quiet for now. We'll investigate the rest during the voyage. Talking of which, Mister Potts, how are the preparations proceeding?"

"Within the hour, sir, she will be ready to sail."

"Very well, Mister Potts; in the meantime, I have an errand that requires my attention. I shall not be long."

\*

Isaac entered the small taverna in the square. Maria greeted him with a cool demeanour. She beckoned him into the back room.

"You don't seem surprised to see me in one piece, Maria?" Isaac said.

"Oh, I knew you were alive and well. I made it my business to know." Maria cocked her head to one side. "I was just a little curious whether you were going to say goodbye, that's all."

"Well, I wouldn't be here to say goodbye if it were not for you and your husband's fine sword." Isaac offered the weapon to Maria, laying it flat across his hands as a sacred gift.

"Please keep it, Isaac. Pedro would be pleased to know it was in such fine hands."

Isaac refastened the sword to his waist and took off the ring his mother had given him. Maria tried to protest as he slid the gold band on the little finger of her left hand. There were no more words.

Maria told him, "Do not say goodbye. It sounds too final. A hug would be perfect."

Isaac squeezed her; she felt good. "Maria," he said, "may I trouble you for a cup of your refreshing ale before I go?"

Maria nodded, went to the bar and soon returned with the drink. "One last taste of the finest ale in the port of Belém, eh?" she said.

Isaac had slipped the bulky purse from the back of his waistband and placed it on the mantle above the grate. He knew she would protest if he tried to give it her directly, and he didn't want to offend her. He knew, however, that the gold coins would keep her financially secure for many years.

Isaac lifted the cup. "Your very good health, Maria da Sylva."

\*

Captain Marinho was on the quay when Isaac returned to the ship.

"I took the liberty of placing a gift in your quarters, Isaac. It's a shallow box," Marinho continued, "but the sentiment is well meant. Hopefully, it will go some way to alleviate the burden of your horrific treatment at the hands of Garcia Paz."

"Thank you, Tiago; that's most thoughtful, although completely unnecessary," Isaac stated.

"That is why I took the liberty earlier, whilst you were absent. I knew you would protest."

Isaac realised he had just done the same thing to Maria. "Well, my friend, I shall accept your gift with all the good grace with which it was given. Thank you again, Tiago. Oh, I have something for you. I have no idea if will help, but I have written a full account of the atrocities during these past weeks. It is signed, dated and witnessed by Taylor Potts. I trust that the governor will see it as the truth and exonerate you from any wrongdoing." Isaac handed Marinho the letter.

"Thank you. A most valuable document. I am indebted to you." Marinho tapped the letter against his other hand and slipped it safely into the pocket of his tunic. "Would you mind if I were to enquire as to your opinion on a somewhat more sensitive issue?"

"Would it by any chance have anything to do with a certain proprietress of a sugar plantation, a mere handful of leagues from where we stand? Because, Captain Marinho, if it is, then my advice is to ask her at your soonest convenience." Isaac knew that if he had been asked such a thing a few weeks earlier, he would have floundered for a response; indeed, he would have required the question to have been asked in full.

The men shook hands.

"Godspeed, Captain," wished Marinho.

Isaac nodded his acceptance and strode onto the ship. She was ready. Weather permitting, they would be home for Christmas.

# Chapter Thirty-Six

The Atlantic Ocean had thus far provided excellent sailing conditions, and *Rebecca-Ann* responded with exuberance. Her sails billowed from the three masts, pushing her sleek hull through the chop at unchartered speeds. They were a little shorthanded, but Roly Smith was proving a worthwhile addition to the crew. If the weather held, they would celebrate Christmas in their homes.

Isaac had opened the boxes stowed in his cabin. He was stunned by the contents, but it wasn't until he opened the box from Captain Marinho that the true extent of the wealth dawned on him. The box contained silver ingots. Isaac could only guess at their value. He sighed as he examined the fraudulent yield. How many lives had been lost? How many lives ripped apart? Countless. The thought plagued him. The crew would have a Christmas to remember, at least, if a few gold coins had anything to do with it.

Isaac had spoken to Potts about Ezra, and about what happened when they were separated from him and the crew. He had listened intently to the story, prompting Potts when he tried to skip the detail. It had been an incredible adventure, and one that Taylor Potts could scarcely believe himself as he revealed their exploits to the captain.

"To go through all that and lose Afi…" Potts could feel himself losing control. "Shall I fetch him, sir?"

"If you would; thank you, Taylor." Isaac stood and offered his hand, "You're as good a friend and colleague as a person could wish for."

Potts wiped the back of his hand across his eyes. "Aye, sir." He shook his captain's hand, and he went to find his friend.

\*

Isaac and Ezra sat on Rothwell Spurt's plunder with their feet on Marinho's silver.

"Taylor Potts has told me of your exploits over these past weeks. Without your endeavours…" Isaac paused. "Well, the consequences hardly bear contemplating."

Ezra said quietly, "It wasn't just me."

"I know…" Isaac never got to finish his words.

"Why didn't you tell me about… what Spurt said?" Ezra's tone was accusatory.

"You were never meant to hear it from anyone. I wrote a letter, which I locked away in the drawer of my bureau, to document what I believe to be indisputable fact. I also had addressed one to your parents, Fred and Mary Quicklock, only to inform them that we had rescued you from the channel and that you were alive and well, nothing more. You see, Ezra," Isaac continued, "I didn't think it was my place to tell you… though perhaps I was mistaken… perhaps if the voyage had been straightforward, I would have talked to you; I don't know. If I hadn't become so fond of the piteous wretch floating on a plank in the channel…" Isaac felt his voice wavering. He took a breath.

"I wasn't swimming from the beach," Ezra said.

Isaac looked surprised; he wasn't sure what he meant.

"I told you that I'd been swimming and the tide swept me out to sea. The being swept out to sea part is true enough, but I wasn't swimming from the beach. There was a special place I used to visit whenever I had free time. It's where I learnt to swim and dive. I always felt something tugging at me, though I never really knew what it was. I thought it was the ocean. Every day I spent there, I would stare at this huge rock – it's like the one at Rosario Bay – and wonder what it would be like to dive from the top of it. Anyway, not long after my birthday, I climbed this rock, and I cut my arm…" Ezra ran his finger over the scar on his forearm, which Seddon had stitched for him. "And then I dived into the sea. The feeling was incredible, but when I tried to swim for the shore I couldn't. I believed I was going to drown, as the tide was so powerful. In the end, I had to let it take me; I had no choice. If it wasn't for that little piece of driftwood… And then you found me."

The silence stretched on.

Isaac said eventually, "There is something else I need to tell you."

Ezra raised his head, but said nothing.

"There are certain things my father told me; Henry, that's his name. Edward… your father and Henry have known each other for, oh, countless years. They sailed together, and Henry captained *Rosetta-Ann*, one of Edward Buckingham's ships, until his creaky joints overwhelmed his enthusiasm for the sea. Edward then insisted that he retire to the office where he could oversee the business."

Isaac paused. "It was Henry who taught me the skills of fencing. Whenever he returned from a voyage, he would spend hours in our back garden showing me the techniques and insisting I repeat the actions, over and over. He told me that one day it would come in handy. 'It will probably save your skin,' he said; it had his."

"I noticed in the battle with Spurt's crew. I suppose I was a little surprised, you know, how skilful you were with the sword. Henry was right about it comin' in handy." Ezra's mood had lifted slightly.

Isaac smiled. "Sorry, Ezra, what I was trying to say was… This is difficult. The day you were born… your mother, Rebecca, died giving birth."

Ezra tried to interrupt, but Isaac insisted he hear the whole story as he understood it.

"She gave birth to a daughter – Rebecca, named for her mother – and she has grown into a fine young woman. What happened that day has been shrouded in secrecy and inuendo, so I don't have the facts. There are probably only one or two people who are aware of the truth, one of them being Edward Buckingham. Based on rumours circulating at the time, there was a second child born that day. Some people say the child died, but some said… Well, they were just rumours, gossip, and never spoken about in the presence of Edward Buckingham. So, Ezra, that's how it was until I set eyes on you – bedraggled, skinny and barely alive, but without question, the son of Edward Buckingham. I was stunned and shocked; I stared at you in disbelief. I still do sometimes, as the likeness to your father is uncanny."

A silence prevailed between them.

Ezra covered his face with his hands digesting the information. "I have a twin sister, is that what you're saying?"

"Rebecca, yes," Isaac confirmed.

Tears escaped through Ezra's fingers; he had tried to force them to stay in, but he couldn't. "Afi's last words to me… She told me… there were babies… growing inside her…"

When Isaac Dunsmoore had set sail from Milford, as captain of a new ship, he had considered himself a successful, practical, fair-minded and logical person, one who was capable of making difficult decisions under pressure and of meting out punishment where necessary; he believed that was a reasonable summation of his attributes. However, he never believed he had the capacity to put his arms around another man to offer comfort. He could think of nothing else to do when Ezra told him about Afia. These past months had taught him much.

Isaac broke the silence, as Ezra wiped the salty tears away with his hands. "I have something else to tell you, Ezra, something I never imagined I would be telling you." He hesitated for a moment. "At the soonest opportunity, I intend to ask Rebecca – your sister – if she will do me the honour of becoming my wife. If I've learnt anything from this adventure… Well, I'm going to ask her, regardless of who disapproves, because I am in love with her."

Ezra looked at his captain. "Does that mean we'll be brothers?"

Isaac pondered for a moment. "I reckon it will… the brother I never had."

# Chapter Thirty-Seven

The wedding was set for Christmas Day. The ceremony was to be held at Milford Priory, and the reception for sixty guests would be at the Milford's grand manor.

Edward and Rebecca had been invited to dinner at the manor. She had protested vigorously; the arguments were protracted and vicious. Eventually, Rebecca succumbed; she couldn't see a way out that didn't involve killing herself. She had spent hours – mainly during the long, dark nights when sleep evaded her – contemplating suicide.

The dinner had been even more hideous than she'd imagined. She sat opposite Persius, listening to his inane drivel regarding the peasants who laboured for pennies, thus providing the bountiful profits that enabled the gentry to indulge in the fruits of their good fortune – or at least that's how Rebecca had interpreted his waffle. Persius had said they should be grateful for the baron's benevolence, as he put food on their tables and a roof over their heads. As the evening passed, she realised she could not spend another evening with this dreadful excuse for a man, never mind the rest of her life. She would be better off dead.

After dinner, the three men retired to Baron Milford's study whilst the baroness invited Rebecca into the sitting room. The feeling between them created a stiffness to the atmosphere, intensified by the protracted silence.

"You disapprove of the arrangement?" The baroness's tone was formal.

Rebecca locked eyes with her foe; she could think of her in no other way. "With all my heart."

"Still, there is little to be done, as the arrangements are settled upon; however, you and I may regard their propriety. I have something for you." Baroness Milford handed Rebecca a small object wrapped in a sliver of velvet material. "I thought you may like it back. I know it belonged to your mother."

Rebecca was shocked to see her mother's brooch with the diamond-studded pin. "How...? Where...? You must know."

"I know nothing except that my son lost his eye the night of your party, and I found this in his room the following day. Perhaps you would care to explain?"

"Why don't you ask your precious son? I'm sure he would give a commentary on the events."

"He has given me his version of the events, and I believe he has concocted his story to save you any embarrassment, but to what end I am at a loss to understand."

"You will receive no validation from me on the events of that night, but I thank you for the return of the brooch."

"I had hoped we could have become better acquainted; after all, you will be an inhabitant of our residence, such as it is." The baroness swept her arm slowly before her, as if mocking her surroundings. "I know Persius can be a little… What can I say? Overzealous, or impetuous perhaps, but he's not a bad person. I'm sure you will grow to love him and produce the heirs of which Baron Milford is so desirous."

Rebecca could feel herself sinking into a bottomless pit. There would be no happy ending. She would be there for Persius Milford to take his pleasure with when it suited him, to produce sons. The thought sickened her.

\*

On the journey home, Edward had asked Rebecca how she and Baroness Milford had got along, adding that Persius had been most respectful and was looking forward to the wedding. Rebecca turned her head away from her father and remained quiet.

\*

For weeks up until Christmas, Rebecca had endured strange people in the house taking her measurements, and asking her stupid questions about dresses, flowers, materials and so on, and she'd had as much as she could bear.

On Christmas Eve, Rebecca and Edward dined together in silence. Rebecca asked him one more time to relent. To see reason. He lost his temper with her, and she went to her room.

Rebecca waited until the house fell silent. She wrapped herself in the warmest clothes she could find and crept noiselessly down the staircase, using the handrail to guide her. She pulled on her riding boots and let herself out of the back door into a blanket of darkness. The night air was cold; there would be a frost soon if the cloud continued to blow over. Perhaps the moon would make a welcome appearance.

Rebecca saddled Bobbin quickly and walked her to the gates. The iron hinges gave a familiar squeal as she pushed them apart. She mounted the horse and together they made their way along a familiar track, slowly, deliberately, step by careful step, leaving their home behind.

\*

Despite not getting his statutory seven hours' sleep, Henry Dunsmoore woke early on Christmas morning, which was no different to any other morning. Once dressed, he pulled his warm coat on and walked to the end of his back garden. The house was situated on the cliff top, and the view extended across the picturesque harbour of Milford Port. Every morning since his disagreement with Edward Buckingham, he would look out to the horizon as far as his ageing eyes would permit in the hope he would see *Rebecca-Ann* cruising into her home port, bringing with her his beloved son. He had come to believe that his actions were more in hope than expectation; nevertheless, he could not change his routine. It would be like giving up. He wouldn't do that.

Henry blew on his hands. The air was cold, and the clouds had blown over. The frost twinkled as the winter sun threatened to melt the fragile crystals. Henry squinted. He needed to get himself a looker. They had made much progress with them, he had heard tell.

*Damn shrubbery wants cutting back,* he thought. He pulled a few branches apart and gained himself another yard of vision. Henry tried to keep the branches from twanging against his ear. Every time he moved one another would ping loose and shower him with flakes of melting frost. He stepped back. "God's breath," he muttered, rubbing his ear.

He could see the dull-grey outline of a ship. This was not unheard of on Christmas Day, but it was unusual. He decided to walk down to the quay. They may have news; the chances were slim, but he would make his customary enquiries.

*

There was a buzz on board *Rebecca-Ann* as she sliced through the cold, glassy water. The small, uninhabited islands peppering the harbour were a welcome sight. Christmas Day had brought with it a calm atmosphere, and tranquillity engulfed the harbour. The population were relishing a rare holiday.

Ezra was excited. The prospect of seeing his parents distracted him and gave him respite from his sombre mood. He had invited Taylor Potts to come home with him, as there would be no way of him travelling to Lowestoft today. Taylor had protested, but Ezra insisted. He would not have his friend spend the night on board ship, although some of the crew would.

Isaac held the looker to his eye. The house he grew up in filled the lens. He saw movement in the overgrown garden. The smile lit up his face. There he was, his father, wrestling with the bushes and trying to get a better view of the horizon. *He needs the looker*, Isaac thought. The glimpse of Henry, alive and well, elated Isaac; this would surely be a Christmas to remember!

\*

*Rebecca-Ann* bumped gently against the deserted quayside. To a permanent land dweller, the manoeuvre would have appeared straightforward enough, but to the bewhiskered gentleman huddled in his winter coat, it was an exercise in coordination between the captain and his crew, combined with an intuitive knowledge of the elements – a skill honed through years of seafaring.

Henry was confused; he imagined he recognised the ship, but it had dull-grey livery and the name *Gemini*. None of it made any sense. He was overwhelmed with nervous anticipation. He stood in the shadows, maybe thirty or forty paces from the ship, trying desperately to recognise a face. Had the ship been procured by undesirables? If it had, why would they return to Milford? *Damn it all*, Henry thought, and he marched towards the ship.

Isaac hurried down the gangway and met Henry. They took the briefest of moments to register each other's presence. Isaac ignored Henry's outstretched hand and embraced his father. It had been many years since Henry had felt his son's body next to his. They clung to each other in silence. There were questions to ask and stories to tell, but all in good time.

Isaac had given each of his crew three gold pieces, which was more than double their wage for the voyage. To a man, they bit on their reward, checking the authenticity. Half a dozen men would be staying on board. Tomorrow, the ale houses would be open.

Isaac took Henry to one side. "Father, there's someone I need you to meet."

"Who might that be then, son?" Henry could not disguise the joy of seeing Isaac again, and his smile refused to wane.

"Give me a moment; I'll be right back."

He soon returned, announcing, "Father, I'd like you to meet Ezra Quicklock. Ezra, this is my father, Henry Dunsmoore."

Henry's cranky knees nearly betrayed him. Isaac put his arm out to steady him. Henry grasped Ezra's outstretched hand, and between them, they kept him on his feet.

"Good Lord above." Henry could think of nothing else to say, which was an unusual event in itself.

"Good to meet you, sir," Ezra said.

Henry still gripped the youngster's hand, his eyes transfixed on Ezra's familiar face. The rumours, the accusations and the denials all those years ago flooded into the present, into that moment.

"Sorry, Father, perhaps I should have warned you. I suppose a part of me needed confirmation. It's okay; I have explained to Ezra, well, as much I knew. He knows who Edward is… and he knows he has a twin sister, Rebecca."

Ezra looked down at their clasped hands in a silent request to disengage.

"Sorry, lad." Henry shook his head. "I fancy this will be a Christmas tale worth the telling."

Isaac instructed the crew to meet on board ship before midday the day after tomorrow. He headed home with

Henry and Horace Clunk, who had greeted his old captain as though it had been a mere day or two since they last met. The invitation to share Christmas with the Dunsmoore family, however, now cemented the sense of kinship that had eluded the big man for much of his life.

*

"How far is it you say?" Potts enquired.

"I'm not sure really, perhaps a mile or two, or three; I dunno," Ezra replied.

"I suppose that if we're not gettin' shot at or likely to get eaten by some wild animal, then I shouldn't complain."

Ezra smiled at his mate. "My pa's workshop is not far. I'll show you. It's where I learnt to shoot arrows, in the back yard."

It was only a few minutes more before they arrived. The old place looked different to Ezra – a little forlorn, neglected even. Ezra put his hand inside the wooden gate and slid the bolt back.

"Top security, I see," Potts said with a smile.

They walked through the yard in which offcuts of timber were stacked in random piles.

Ezra lifted a bleached seashell that sat inconspicuously on the stone step. He smiled; it was still there. Top security indeed! He took the key and unlocked the wicket door. Ezra went inside and immersed himself in the familiar surroundings, the smell of cut timber pervaded the air. He unbolted the rear door. It was just how he'd remembered it; nothing had been altered and nothing moved.

Potts watched him with interest.

Ezra took the leather wrist guard from its hook and laced it in place. "My pa made me this. C'mon, Taylor, let's go see 'em."

The two men continued along the well-trodden path towards the small, stone cottage. They heard the pounding of hooves and stepped off the track. The three horses were galloping along it, devouring yards at a blistering pace.

"Someone's in a hurry," Potts commented, "and get the one with the eye patch in his fancy slops."

Ezra recognised the motifs on the tabards of the other two. He felt his blood run cold.

*

Edward Buckingham had initially gone into a rage when he discovered his daughter was missing. When he was told that Bobbin was not in the stable, he allowed himself to believe she had gone for an early morning ride, which enabled him to bring his temper under control.

The dawn hours of Christmas Day passed sluggishly. The words "I will not marry that man" – he was sure that's what she had said – reverberated inside his head. He thought he could impose his will on her and manipulate her. He should have known better. He knew she had fled. He would find her and tell her it was a terrible mistake. He loved her. Suddenly, Henry's words hit him. *Once again, the mulish wraith emerges victorious.*

"God Almighty, Rebecca, what have I done?" he whispered to himself.

He'd uttered the words before, many years ago.

*

Persius Milford snatched the note from his father's hand. He read it himself whilst his father lapsed into a rant.

"That bastard Buckingham! Who the devil does he think he is? If he thinks he can withdraw from our arrangement, then he's sadly misguided. Christ, can't he keep the wench under control? What is he a man or bloody housemaid? Damn the man to hell!" thundered the baron.

The baroness tried in vain to quell her husband's vociferous rhetoric. "Perhaps it's for the best, dear." She regretted the words the second they were delivered.

"For the best? Are you demented, woman? All this fussing around. Piss and pomp and bloody ceremony. All those damn people waiting to see my son…" Rufus corrected himself, "our son get wed. All that money. The bloody embarrassment. He'll pay for this. They both bloody well will, you mark my words. I'll break that man; I'll see him begging in the streets – and his stuck-up bitch of a daughter."

Persius crumpled the note and threw it to the floor in disgust.

"Bitch," he snarled. "Go to the priory. I'll meet you there," he told his parents.

"What are…? Where are you…?" His mother never finished the question.

*

The horses' hooves showered loose gravel into the air as they skidded to a halt at the main entrance to Buckingham's house. Persius leapt from his mount and marched through the unlocked door; his guards followed him in, a few paces behind.

A timid servant tried to protest at the invasion. Persius struck her backhanded across her cheek. She screamed in pain, staggered sideways and collapsed onto the unforgiving tiles.

"*Buckingham!*" Persius yelled his name. He put his hand to his throat, as shouting still gave him pain. *That bastard, Quicklock.*

"What the devil...?" Edward burst from his study, shocked at the scene before him.

"Where is she?" demanded Persius.

"I told you in the note." Edward was shaken, but he'd quickly regained his composure. "Rebecca's not here. She left; during the night, I assume."

"Don't lie to me, old man." Persius nodded to his men.

They went to go upstairs, but Edward stepped across them. "I would ask you to leave now. There will be no wedding today, Milford."

The guard on the left stuck Edward on the jaw. He fell back, smashed his head on the brass ball sitting atop the newel post and slumped to the floor.

The three of them searched the house, kicking down doors and threatening staff.

She wasn't there.

*

Isaac was surprised to see a horse nibbling at the grass in the front garden. "Does Mother know there's a four-legged beast devouring her sacred veld?" Isaac looked at his father in surprise. "Isn't that Bobbin, Rebecca's horse?"

Henry had always suspected that there was something

between his son and his employer's daughter. He couldn't decide how Edward would react if such a liaison were to materialise. He supposed it was irrelevant now. Still, a part of him would have relished his approval; he knew Edward held Isaac in high esteem. Whether that high esteem would have been sufficient to allow his daughter to embark on such an alliance, he couldn't fathom. Nonetheless, it was obvious that she would not marry the obnoxious Persius Milford. She had made that plain enough to her Uncle Henry and Aunt Emily in the small hours of Christmas Day.

\*

Ezra took a breath. He ran his hands through his hair. Like it made a difference.

"Just knock on the door, Ezra." Potts said. "You look fine."

\*

"There's someone at the door, Fred." Mary declared. She was busy chopping turnips.

"Who's that, then, on Christmas Day?" grumbled Fred.

"You say some daft things, Fred Quicklock," Mary chided him.

"Whadaya mean, I say some daft things?"

"Well, 'ow am I s'posed to know who's at the door 'til it's opened?" Mary shook her head.

Fred could see she was smiling.

"Don't worry yerself, Fred, I'll go." Ma Fish brushed the front of her apron and went to the door. She was looking at her son-in-law as she opened the door. "If you want somethin doin', Mary, you might as well do it…"

"Hello Gran." The voice penetrated the house.

Ezra wrapped his arms around his grandmother and squeezed her. Fred and Mary stared at each other in total bewilderment.

"Ma, Pa." Ezra released his gran in time to catch Mary in his arms.

"I knew it, I knew it, I knew it! Didn't I tell you, Fred Quicklock? Oh my, oh my." Mary smothered her son in kisses.

Fred hovered, waiting his moment. "C'mon, woman, let the dog see the rabbit."

Ezra embraced his pa. The excitement was infectious. Ezra introduced Taylor Potts to the family. They were all of a dither. Pa Fish greeted his grandson as though he'd never been missing and continued supping his cider.

Ezra spent the next hour explaining what had occurred the day he went missing. Taylor helped out with some of the story after that.

Mary couldn't leave Ezra alone, she needed to be next to him, to feel his physical presence. Her son returned from the dead.

When everyone had settled, Ezra could not wait a moment longer. He needed to know what had happened all those years ago. Mary explained how her ma had arrived with a newborn child. How his real father had discarded him. She begged her son's forgiveness for not telling him the truth. Ezra hugged her and told her it didn't matter. She was his mother, and Fred was his father. They always would be.

"So, Gran, my mother – Rebecca Buckingham – was still alive when my sister was born?" Ezra asked.

"Yes. Ya were trapped inside 'er. Me an' the doc managed to get ya out, just in the nick o' time as well. Yer fath— Master Buckin'am, well, 'e blamed ya; stupid man, 'e said it were your fault and said 'e didn't want ya in the 'ouse, so I wrapped ya up, an' me an' Pa brought ya 'ere to our Mary's. She an' Fred brought ya up like their own; ya couldna wished fer betta parents neither."

"No, Gran, I couldn't." Ezra smiled and squeezed his grandmother's hand. "Isaac, Captain Dunsmoore, told me of my sister Rebecca. I should like to meet her."

"Oh, she moves in diff'rent circles, young Ezra. I 'erd tell she was gettin' wed today. Reck'n she needs 'er bumps read, marryin' that piece o' work, 'specially after what 'e done t' yer father."

Mary shot her mother a look. It was too late now.

"What piece of work? Who you talking about, Gran?" Ezra had noticed his pa's face. He knew something had happened, what with the scars flecking his complexion, a swelling over his left eye, his nose being flat and slightly twisted, and one corner of his mouth turned down. Although shocked initially, he had been waiting for the right moment to ask. "Has someone done this to you, Pa?" Ezra pointed to Fred's face.

"The Milford boy, 'e's weddin' ya sister, an' 'e done that t' ya pa." Ma Fish answered for Fred, curling her lip as she spoke. "'Eaven 'elp the poor lass, tha's what I say."

"It's water passed under the bridge now, son." Fred knew his boy well.

*Christ Almighty,* Potts thought, *here we go again.*

Ezra stood up. "You fit, Taylor?" he asked his friend.

"Aye, lad." Potts also knew him well. It would be pointless to argue.

"Ezra," Mary's voice quivered, "where ya goin'? Please don't leave."

Ezra hugged his mother. "Don't fret, Ma, I'll be back for Christmas dinner." He poked a finger at the fat goose cooking gently in the grate. "I wouldn't miss a share of that for anything. What about you, Taylor?"

"Not for a pile of gold coins, ma'am," Potts said.

They set off in Pa Fish's creaky tumbril. Ezra reckoned Persius must have been heading for Rebecca's home, not that he knew where it was. Fred had the reins and was cajoling the old mule along at a fast walk. When Ezra told him that he had seen Persius and his two thugs riding this way, they made the assumption that the wedding was being held at Edward Buckingham's stately house. Ma Fish had no details; after all, she never received an invitation, so how would she know? She gave Fred directions, although he knew roughly where to find it.

Fred quizzed his son about his intentions, reminding him of Persius Milford's status. Ezra told him he would give Persius a chance to explain himself, but unless he was too late, he would put a stop to the marriage, somehow.

He told Fred that Persius Milford's status meant nothing to him. And it would mean nothing to his parents after today.

*

"Aye, lad, that's Bobbin," confirmed Henry.

"Is she here? Rebecca?" Isaac felt his insides churning.

"She rolled up in the early hours. Fair put the wind up your mother and me."

"Why? What's happened?"

"Let's get indoors, son, and see your mother; she'll be beside herself with joy, you see. I'll tell you all about Rebecca after."

\*

Emily Dunsmoore had almost fainted when she saw her beautiful son. If Rebecca had not been at her side, she probably would have fallen to the floor in shock, not that Rebecca was much steadier; together, they managed to support each other.

Isaac was desperate to discover why Rebecca was there, but relating the story of the voyage to his mother would not keep. He resigned himself to its telling. Again.

When the furore of Isaac's return had settled – although Emily found it difficult to stop touching her boy, patting him and checking he was all in one piece – Rebecca told Isaac of her father's intention to have her wed the despicable Persius Milford. She told him the reasons behind the decision: how it would secure her future and what a fortuitous union it would be for the two families. She told him about the night of her birthday: how he had tried to rape her and how she had stuck the pin in his face. She had told no one of the incident, and it felt good to unburden herself, as if it justified her refusal to marry him and to go against her father's wishes. She poured it all out. And then she told him how much she had missed him.

Isaac invited her to take a stroll in the garden, which she agreed to. They walked to the boundary, guarded with overgrown shrubs, and looked out over the bay. They stood close to each other, deep in conversation.

*

"What do you think they're talking about?" asked Emily.

She and Henry were looking at the couple from the kitchen window.

"I suspect we'll know soon enough." Henry turned to his wife. "Happy Christmas, my lovely," he said.

*

Pa's mule had slowed a little, but the game beast stuck to its task. Fred eased the tumbril onto the grassy verge. The three riders never slackened the pace. They rode past without pause and without a sideways glance. These people they were passing were nothing – garbage on the road and low-life peasants. It had been just as well for them they had given way.

Ezra saw the patch. He wished it had been him who'd poked his eye out. His retribution, it seemed, would have to wait for another day.

"Somethin's amiss," Potts remarked. "That's the same lot goin' the other way. Somethin's up; it's gotta be."

"That's Milford," Ezra stated, "the one with the eyepatch.

"You do that to 'im?" Potts asked.

"No, but I wish I had."

*

Isaac had proposed to Rebecca without hesitation. She had accepted without hesitation. He desperately wanted to embrace her and to feel her body next to his. They resisted the temptation, as eyes were upon them. Isaac had insisted that they go straight to see Edward; there was no other way.

Isaac clung to Rebecca. Bobbin was trotting along steadily, coping well with the extra burden. The three horses thundered towards them, with no respect for any traveller sharing the byway. Rebecca recognised Persius; his head was low over his horse's neck, speed his only concern. She warned Isaac, and then dug her heels into Bobbin and the faithful mount responded.

The brief moment it took Persius to realise that his fiancée had just passed him cost him the chance to block her path. The delay gave Isaac and Rebecca the opportunity to gain the precious yards they needed.

*

Fred told Ezra that he would sit on the cart and wait whilst he went in the house. Potts considered that was a good idea, and he also stayed put. Ezra felt nervous suddenly. *I'd be better off going to find Milford*, he thought.

The front door was hanging open. He stepped tentatively into the grand hallway. A servant girl, he assumed, was kneeling over a man lying still on the floor. He could hear her sobs.

Ezra walked up to her, trying not to startle her; he failed miserably.

"What's happened, miss?" he almost whispered the words.

She looked up surprised. She kept looking. Staring. She turned back to the man on the floor, then back to the man standing over her.

Then he saw why she was so confused and distraught. He was looking at his father. Now he could see what Isaac had seen. Ezra knelt down beside the girl. He looked into Edward Buckingham's eyes; they were wide open, seeing nothing. He saw his reflection in the deep-blue pools. He rested his hand on Edward's cold face and pulled his eyelids down gently, encapsulating his son's reflection for eternity.

"Who is responsible?" Ezra queried softly.

The distraught girl told him what had happened. Gently, Ezra examined the purple swelling below her eye. "Milford's handywork?"

She nodded.

\*

Bobbin hurtled into the grounds, spraying gravel from her hooves. The mare was lathered with sweat and breathing hard. Isaac could barely contain his joy at seeing Taylor Potts sitting with a battered-looking man on a battered-looking cart, hitched to a battered-looking mule.

Taylor hopped off the cart in time to watch the three riders gallop into the drive. Rebecca had to steady Bobbin, as the mare was unsettled suddenly.

Persius reined in his horse, pulling hard at the bit and causing obvious distress to the exhausted beast. He took a moment to survey the situation. A look of complete surprise enveloped his face when he noticed Fred sitting on the cart.

"Quicklock. What the devil are you doing here?" Persius snarled.

Ezra came out of the house and stood on the porch, staring out at the scene before him. He knew all of them except one. She distracted him. He needed to deal with Milford and his thugs, but he couldn't stop looking at her. All these years they'd been apart, neither of them knowing of the other's existence. The man responsible now lay dead not ten paces from where they stood. He didn't know how he felt about that. His chance to explain had died with him. Perhaps Ezra could forgive him. In that moment, he swore to himself that he would try.

The voice of Persius Milford focused his attention. The three of them had dismounted. The two guards stood a pace back, watching intently.

"You stupid little bitch. Did you honestly believe…?" Persius began.

Isaac stepped forwards, trying to put himself between Persius and Rebecca. Persius pulled a pistol from his belt and pointed it at Isaac's head. He gave Isaac a sly grin, but said nothing. He turned to Rebecca.

"Get on the horse, and let's get going or I'm going to blow this stupid bastard's head off." He kept the pistol steadfastly pointed at Isaac. "Hey Pissquick, I thought you had drowned. you dozy prick."

Fred launched himself from the cart. He smashed into Persius, knocking him to the ground. The pistol discharged. Taylor Potts smacked his elbow into the face of the nearest guard, and he heard the crunch of cartilage from a shattered nose. The guard furthest away hesitated for a moment too long. The indecision cost him any advantage that may have been his. Potts swivelled and kicked him between the legs, and as the guard bent forwards, Potts brought his knee up under the man's chin, snapping his neck backwards with a sickening jerk. The first guard, spitting blood and overwhelmed with mindless anger, launched himself at his attacker. Potts neatly sidestepped, then punched him hard and straight in the throat. It was a clinical blow.

Ezra jumped from the porch step to where his father lay across the prone form of Persius. He helped Fred to his feet.

Isaac had swept Rebecca from danger, ready to intervene should Taylor Potts have required any assistance. Perhaps if there had been three or four of them, a little help would not have gone amiss.

Ezra embraced Fred, then he looked down at Milford. The ball had entered under his chin and exited through the top of his head.

# Chapter Thirty-Eight

The intimate chapel overlooking Milford Port could not accommodate more than twenty people. The vicar, Morris Hermitage, had come to accept that its pews would only ever be full at weddings or funerals. However, the sight of gold coins spilling out of the collection box gave him hope. The old chapel had a future after all.

The handsome young couple were chatting and smiling as the two-seater carriage, pulled by Bobbin, came to a halt. Ezra held out his hand. Rebecca accepted and stepped elegantly from the trap. They walked towards the chapel between two lines of cheering men: the crew of *Rebecca-Ann*.

Taylor Potts shook his captain's hand and took his seat.

Isaac turned to see Ezra walking his beautiful sister up the narrow aisle. It was a sight he would never forget.

As they walked, their arms linked, Rebecca saw the lady. She was sat nearest the aisle in the second row of pews, dabbing her eyes with the freshly laundered hem of her tabard. They were tears of happiness, Rebecca knew, because her lined face was aglow with a beaming smile which had spread to her misty eyes. Rebecca knelt before her and took her time-worn hand.

"You told me I would marry a handsome young man." She whispered.

Ezra handed his sister to Isaac, his captain, his good friend, and, when Morris Hermitage completed the ministrations, his brother.

# Acknowledgements

I f you have managed to get this far I would like to thank you for your perseverance. Unless, of course, you started from the end!

I need to confess to my limited knowledge regarding much of the subject matter scattering the pages you have just turned, (or clicked on). I have done my utmost to try and ensure, where appropriate, the details are factual, but please remember this is a concoction of events set in an era where we can only determine the facts from people's recordings through the centuries. I in turn have used these events for the purpose of creating a work of fiction, which in its telling, has been manipulated to suit the story. So, any historical, or otherwise, cock ups are all mine, for which I apologise.

I would like to say thank you to some people for their invaluable support.

Firstly to my wife Christina, for putting up with me, and looking after me through thick and thin. My two beautiful daughters, (I know, all daughters are beautiful), Dani and Sophie, and to my two inherited sons, Kev and Nick.

To my mum, Jean, probably my biggest fan. To my sister, Jayne, for constantly pestering me for more chapters. To my brothers Barry and Andrew, always there when I need them.

To the people peppered around the Cantal and Aveyron, there when you need a helping hand. You know who you are.

To the people at the Book Guild who took the leap of faith.

Thank you all.